Music in the Vedas
Its Magico-Religious Significance

Music in the Vedas
Its Magico-Religious Significance

G.U. THITE

SHARADA
Sharada Publishing House
Delhi - 110035
1997

First Published 1997

ISBN: 81-85616-42-6

Published by B.L. Bansal
SHARADA PUBLISHING HOUSE
(Publishers on India's Past and Present)
40, Anand Nagar, Inder Lok, New Delhi - 110035
Phones: 5117390, 5116763
Typeset by Neographics
1811, Gyani Bazar, Kotla, New Delhi - 110003
Printed at Santosh Offset, Delhi - 110035

Contents

Acknowledgement

I sincerely thank Dr. R.N. Dandekar for the encouragement and help which I received while carrying out this work. When this project was done he was the Director of the Centre of Advanced Study in Sanskrit (University of Poona), and I was a Senior Research Fellow.

I gratefully remember Late Prof. A.J. Karandikar, in whose company, I read almost all the works in German and French mentioned in this book.

Prof. Pūja and Prof. Maitreyi helped me in reading the proofs. I thank them.

I am also thankful to Shri B.L. Bansal of Sharada Publishing House, Delhi for taking keen interest in the publication of this work.

I dedicate this work to the memory of my father, Umakant Keshav Thite, who used to sing Sāmavedic Mantras. He was very much interested in my research-work. I also remember with gratitude Prof. G.H. Ranade, Professor of Physics and musicologist who encouraged me to do research-work in music, but died before I actually started this work.

5th October, 1995. G.U. THITE

Department of Sanskrit and
Prakrit Languages
University of Poona
Pune-411007

CHAPTER I
Introduction

Primitive music

In this book we are dealing with the ideas on music of the vedic people who may be described as primitives. Now it must be noted at the very beginning that, when we are studying the music of a primitive society, we have to understand the word music in a very broad sense. Music of the primitive peoples is not necessarily an art of combining sounds with a view to beauty of form and expression of emotion etc. In fact it has no such aim of any formal beauty or taste. For the primitives every sound is music. It has according to their point of view some good or bad significance for their life. The primitive people therefore, produce or aviod a sound according to the significance they have attached to it. Even a din or cry also can be a musical phenomenon to the primitives. "Pour nous crier n'est pas chanter; pour certains primitifs c'était peut etre la meme chose"[1] Inaudible or silent recitation also can be sometimes significant. While studying the various aspects of vedic music we may at a few times be tempted to see semi-aesthetic ideas about musical beauty. But they are also, it must be remembered, not significant from the point of view of artistic pleasure, but from the point of view of the magicoreligious efficacity of music.

Nature of vedic music

The vedic music is an essential part of the vedic sacrifice. We get the information of vedic music mainly in the context of the vedic ritual. As regards whether in the vedic period there was any non-sacrificial music or not we have to confess our ignorance. But the music we notice in the Vedas is by one or the other way connected with some magicoreligious ritual, or some kind of sacrifice etc. In the sacrificial performance there are numerous recitations of verses etc; singing of sāmans (melodies) etc. There are numerous hymns. They seem *mostly* to be not prepared for the sake of being read or pleasing a reader by their aesthetic beauty if at all one may find any therein. In all possibility they were originally not *written but recited vocally* by the poetsingers. In the ṚV many expressions used in order to indicate a hymn e.g. *gir* (song), *vacas, vāc, vāṇī* (speech), *stoma, stotra* (sung praise), *uktha, ukthya, ucatha* (praise-song) etc. directly reveal their *vocal* character. It is, however, very difficult to point out exactly the difference between one expression and the other. It is also difficult to translate those words adequately in any language familiar to us. Speaking in general for the purpose in this book, we may group all such expressions under a common title "elements of vedic music". The formulas from the Yajurveda or the Atharvaveda and from other vedic sources also can be, for the sake of studying the magicoreligious significances of vedic music, treated as elements of vedic vocal music. The Sāmaveda consists mostly of the verses taken from the Ṛgveda. Those verses serve as the "texts" for the "melodies (*sāman-*)" which are sung in the course of the vedic sacrifice. They are also the most important part of the vedic music. Besides, there are various numerous utterances like the *hiṁkāra, vaṣaṭ-kāra* etc. All these constitute the Vedic vocal music. We also get a few references to the vedic instrumental music and to dance also.

Music from the magicoreligious point of view

It is intended here to take into account the Vedic music from the magicoreligious point of view. In the Vedic texts we find quite often magic and religion mixed,[2] with each other in a very complex manner. In magic one takes for granted some fundamental laws of the happenings in the world. One believes then that one can control a phenomenon if one knows and operates according to the laws of that phenomenon. But in religion one seeks to propitiate or please some superior beings who govern a particular phenomenon. A magician therefore, uses some power-substances and controls a phenomenon. A religious person prays, requests a god or the gods to grant his desires. In the vedic literature both these attitudes are found in a mixed manner in many cases including music. Sometimes music is considered to be a power-substance and the musicians use it with confidence in its efficacy for bringing out the desired result. Sometimes however the musicians use their music for the sake of propitiation of gods and it is the gods who are supposed to ultimately fulfil the desires of men. So music is supposed to be working magicoreligiously. It propitiates as well as controls the gods. In this work I intend to study the magicoreligious significances of the vedic music.

Sources of this study

This study of the Vedic music is obviously based on the Vedic texts. Here and there sometimes a few references to the post-vedic literature also will be found. At times for the sake of comparison and contrast references to the literature dealing with the music of parts of the world other than the vedic are also given. Still the main emphasis is given on the vedic literature only. As in the case of vedic sacrifice, in the case of vedic music also I am of the opinion that in order to have a correct or at least a less incorrect notion about its significances we have to take recourse to the vedic literature itself and particularly to the Brāhmaṇa-texts. The nature of Brāhmaṇa-texts is rather very unique. The Brāhmaṇa texts, do not merely describe but explain the vedic sacrifices. They represent, broadly speaking, the science of sacrifice. But this science is a pre-scientific science[3] or pseudo-science.[4] Their ways of argumentation are strange. They have their own pre-logical logic. They are full of mystical symbolizations, identifications, cause-and-effect-relationships, fanciful etymologies, henoistic[5] praises, ontological stories etc. All this material if studied seriously is of very much importance for understanding the views of the Vedic people on many points. Therefore while studying the magicoreligious significances of the Vedic music I have used the Brāhmaṇa-texts as the predominant source.

Main contents of this work

The study in this work begins with discussion on the problem of the position of music and musicians in the Vedic and allied literature. Music and musicians receive a double treatment. Sometimes they are honoured and sometimes deplored. Starting with an exposition of the social position of music and musicians I have tried to maintain that music is supposed to be double-natured. It is supposed to be double-natured for it is believed to be a power-substance. So in the following chapter I have given details of music as a power-substance. But the power of music does not work merely magically. It works both magically and religiously; it is a magicoreligious force. In order to illustrate this, the connections of music with gods and sacrifice are dealt with in the next chapters. In order to illustrate the double-nature of the music and musicians and the magicoreligious significances of the music, I have further studied some musical elements like the use of particular words, of some utterances (viz. *vaṣaṭkāra, hiṁkāra*), musical instruments, metres and the divine musicians viz. Gandharvas and Apsarases. Then follows a detailed study of some of the magicoreligious significances of music: thus how music is supposed to be helpful (or non-helpful) to obtain rain, cattle, diseaselessness, long life, victory in the wars, victory over or destruction of enemy through sorcery, progeny or removal of the evil spirits etc. Then follows a study of the doctrine of the Vedic music: its nature, the ways of performing it, directives of its performance, its cosmic nature, and its connection with knowledge. In the final chapter the conclusions are given.

REFERENCES

1. Combarieu, *La musique et la magie,* p. 250.
2. For the mixture of magic and religion see Frazer, *Golden Bough,* p. 52.
3. Rf. Oldenberg, *Die Weltanschauung der Brāhmaṇa-texte.*
4. Rf. Winternitz, *HIL,* I, p. 165.
5. Cf. My Paper "Henoritualism of the Brāhmaṇa texts", *JUPHS,* 33, 1970, p. 23.

CHAPTER II

Dvisvabhāva (Double-natured) Music

The importance of music can be observed in all the parts of the world and in all the periods. Music plays prominent role in all the events of social as well as individual interest. Primitive men used to consider and use to consider music as the most important of all the arts.[1] They ascribe a great magico-religious significance to music. Among the Egyptians,[2] Sumerians,[3] Chinese people,[4] Greeks,[5] Romans,[6] Biblical peoples,[7] and Mohamadans[8] music was used at various social and individual occasions and its importance for them is well-known.

Indians were not an exception to the general rule. They also attached great importance to it. Some people are mentioned in ṚV II.23.16 who knew nothing higher than sāman[9] (melody). Music was amply used in the sacrifices (This topic has been dealt with by me elsewhere). In the later periods music used to be an essential part of many festivals (*utsava* -) and religious observances (*vrata* -) (see e.g. Mbh XIII. app. I.15.3454; cf. also Vṛddhahārītasmṛti VIII. 354; 365; 488; 498; 515; 519; Caturvargacintāmaṇi, Vratakhaṇḍa, Calcutta, 1879, p. 375). "Les Hindous ont eu de tout temps une prédiléction marquée pour la musique...... Le grand nombre d'ouvrages qu'ils ont écrits sur le sujet, les nombreux systémes musicaux qui se sont successivement developpés dans l'inde, les légends merveilleuses, les allusions fréquentes, les renseignements positifs méme dont toute leur litterature est pleine, depuis les temps védiques jusqu'á notre époques, le montrent clairment."[10]

The Sāmaveda (which is traditionally regarded as the origin of the music in general - cf. Saṅgītaratnākara, I.1.25) the sāmans, and the singers are many times highly praised. The Sāmaveda is identical with glory (*yaśaḥ*) according to the ŚB XII.3.4.9. After the aspersion in the Sautrāmaṇī— sacrifice, Saṁśānasāman is to be sung. This sāman is said to be identical with the kingly power (*Kṣatraṁ vai sāma* ŚB XII. 8.3.23). Therefore by singing this sāman one gets that power. This sāman is also identical with empire (*sāmrājyaṁ vai sāma* ŚB XII.8.3.23). Therefore one also gets empire. The chief Sāmaveda priest viz. Udgātṛ is said to be identical with Prajāpati (*Prajāpatir vā udgātā* e.g. JB III. 203). ṚV IV. 17.19, the singer is said to be dear to Indra. The sun is said to be the celestial Gandharva (a semidivine singer genus) (ŚB VI.3.1.19). The Hotṛ-priest who recites the Vaiśvadevaśastra is said to be belonging to all the deities (*sarvadevatyo vā eṣa hotā yo vaiśvadevaṁ śaṁsati* AB III. 31).

Honour is sometimes given to the sāmansingers, to those who know the power of sāmans as well as to the musicians in general. Thus once Prajāpati desired to get himself honoured by others. Then he thought, "The Udumbara-tree is the vigour (*ūrj* -); food is vigour; the sāman is food. Let me, therefore, honour the sāman-singers" (ṢaḍB IV.3.6). Brahmadatta Caikitāneya was a knower of powers of sāmans. Therefore, when he went to the king Abhipratārin Kakṣaseni, he received a honey-potion (*madhuparka* -) as a token of honour from the king. He drank the honey-potion without addressing the king's Purohita, named Śaunaka. Then Śaunaka asked Brahmadatta angrily, "As knowing what O Dalbhya, dost thou drink the honey-potion without addressing me ?" Then Brahmadatta replied that he knew that what belongs to the power of Sāman (JUB I.18.4.1 ff). To give daughter to a singer of Sāmans (*Chandoga*-) was considered to be auspicious (Mbh. XIII. 96.44; cp. 95.75 f).

In other parts of the world also musicians are known to be sometimes honoured very much by the society. Among many primitive races musicians are considered to be important. No girl wants to marry a man unless he can play on the hunter's bow and a girl feels proud of her man if he has been victorious in a singing contest. That singer is mostly esteemed who can sing a proverb or saying at the right moment. The arrival of a musician often turns the whole village upside down and his departure is often accompanied by scenes of lamentations, especially among the women.[11] In Combodia and Malaya, female as well as male dancers are respected.[12] Among the Egyptian people under the old and middle kingdoms, the court musicians were considered as "near relatives" of the king. Under the new kingdom their significance was weighty.[13] Among the Sumerians, also musicians were persons of great importance.[14] Among the Romans the musicians had a place of honour. In the list of trade guilds into which the people of Rome were traditionally divided by Numa, Pipers came first.[15]

In the antiquities of India, music was supposed to be representing perfection. Thus when Prajāpati spread the earth, the earth (f.) thinking herself quite perfect sang. According to some other thinkers it was Agni (m.) who thinking himself quite perfect remained singing. Having narrated this, the ŚB VI.1.2.15 remarks "And hence whosoever thinks himself quite perfect, either sings or delights in song (*tasmādu haitadyaḥ sarvaḥ kṛtsno manyate gāyati vā gīte vā ramate*)". The vocal and instrumental music along with the arts like drama and painting has been very much praised and elevated when it is said to be equivalent to the Vedic sentences. (*vādyaṁ nāṭyaṁ tathā geyaṁ citraṁ vāditameva ca / vedamantrārthavacanaiḥ samaṁ hyetad bhaviṣyati // Nāṭyaśāstra* of Bharata, 36.21).

Music is also elevated when divine[16] origin is ascribed to it. Thus we can understand how much important music must have been considered by the people of various places and various times when we observe that they suppose it to be obtained from some divine or superhuman genii. "In Manipur the deity long ago distributed songs among the tribes. The Marrings caught them in a wide meshed basket, but they escaped; hence they have no songs....... The Navaho gods Hasjelti and Hostjoghon are the great song-makers of the world and myth tells how they communicate the sacred songs and dances to men. With the Zulus the *amatongo* or spirits, cause men to compose songs when they are about to become diviners. Among the Maoris, as among the folk of Europe, Songs have been learned from fairies. The Maidu Indians believe that the original sacred rattle as well as the dance was given to them by two old diviners ...... Similarly the Menomini Indians think that the Good Mysteries gave the drums ..... In the Torres strait Islands the old culture-heroes are thought to have taught the sacred dances and cults with sacred songs. The Asaba people think that music and dancing were first learned from a hunter who heard the songs from a party of forest spirits."[17] Socretes has already said, "Gymnastic and music are given by a god."[18]

Coming to the ancient Indian context one may note that the Sāmaveda the supposed starting point of all the music, is said to be born out of a manifestation of the Sun-god viz. Āditya (AB V. 32; cf. ŚB XI. 5.8.3 ff and JB I.357 which mention another manifestation viz. Sūrya). Mārkaṇḍeyapurāṇa 45.31 ff. We read how Brahmadeva created, among other things various kinds of sāmans, vedas, stomas and metres. Thus facing towards the east, he created the Gāyatrīmetre, Ṛgveda, Trivṛt-stoma and Rathantara-sāman; facing towards the South, he created the Yajurveda, Triṣṭubh-metre, Pañcadaśa-stoma and Bṛhat-sāman; facing towards the West, he created the Sāmaveda, Jagatī-metre, Saptadaśa-stoma, and Vairūpa-sāman; finally facing towards the North he created the Atharvaveda, Ekaviṁśa-stoma, Anuṣṭubh-metre and Vairāja-sāman. The science of music was gathered together from the Sāmaveda by the god Brahmā according to the Saṅgītaratnākara I.1.25 (*sāmavedādidaṁ śāstraṁ saṁjahāra pitāmahaḥ*).

ŚB III. 4.2.16, giving the origin of the Tānūnaptra-rite, describes indirectly the origin of sāman in general. Thus at the time when the gods performed the primordial Tānūnaptra, "What favourite forms and desirable powers (of them) they laid together, all that was brought together and became the sāman; wherefore they say: The sāman is truth; sāman is of gods (*atha yās taddevāḥ juṣṭāstanūḥ priyāṇi dhāmāni sārdhaṁ samavadadire tat sārdhaṁ saṁjaghne tat sāmābhavat tasmādāhuḥ satyaṁ sāma devajaṁ sāmeti)*". It was the gods who created the speech-goddess (ṚV VIII.100.11). The poet-singers are asked, ṚV VIII.32.27, to sing the powerful hymn in praise of Indra, given by god (*devatta*). The god Soma is also described as the creator of songs (ṚV IX. 95.1; 96.6). In ṚV VIII. 59.6 Indra and Varuṇa are addressed, "You O Indra and Varuṇa, have given, in the beginning, the thinking power, the thinking of speech, unto the seers."

In the Brāhmaṇa-texts many sāmans are said to be "seen" by the gods in general or by individual gods (this topic has been dealt with by me elsewhere).

From all this information illustrating the divine origin of music, we know again the importance of music.

For the sake of understanding the importance of music, it will be also useful to go into the details of the association of music and Viṣṇu, who as is well known, occupies very much prominance in the mythology of the classical Hinduism. The Sāmaveda is considered as one of the manifestation of Viṣṇu-Kṛṣṇa (*vedānāṁ sāmavedosmi* Mbh. VI.32.22). In the Viṣṇu-purāṇa I. 9.21, the Lord Viṣṇu is said to be identical with the sāman and the goddess Lakṣmī with udgīti which forms a part of the sāman (*sāmasvarūpī bhagavān udgītiḥ kamalālayā*). Among the thousand names of the Lord Viṣṇu, following are to be noticed here. Trisāmā (with three sāmans); Sāmagaḥ (singer of sāman, cp. Sāmagāyanaḥ XII.135.119) and Sāman (Mbh. XIII.135.75). Viṣṇudharmottarapurāṇa III.350.1, he is described as the singer of the *Jyeṣṭhasāman* (*Jyeṣṭhasāmagaḥ*, also Mbh. XII.325.96), and elsewhere as the sound of sāmans (*sāmadhvani* Skandapurāṇa, Vaiṣṇvakhaṇḍa, Veṅkaṭa. I. 20) and as "attractive like the sound of sāmans (*sāma-svanamanoramaḥ* - I. 90). If idols of different vedas are to be prepared, the idol of the Sāmaveda should be nothing but that of Viṣṇu (Viṣṇudharmottarapuraṇa III.73.13). At the time of Bore-incarnation of Viṣṇu, the sound of sāmans was his voice (Viṣṇusmṛti I. 4). Among the sāmans, the Bṛhat-sāman is Viṣṇu-Kṛṣṇa's manifestation (*bṛhatsāma tathā sāmnām* Mbh. VI. 32.35). All the poems and all the songs constitute the body of Viṣṇu who has word as his form (*kāvyālāpaśca ye kecid gītakānyakhilāni ca / śabdamūrtidharasyaitad vapur viṣṇor mahātmanaḥ* // Viṣṇu-purāṇa I.22.84).

In worshipping Viṣṇu, one should use vocal and instrumental music as well as dance (Viṣṇudharmottarap. III. 341.19 ff : *śvayaṁ gītena sampūjya tasya cānucaro bhavet / vādyaṁ dattvā tathā viprā (ḥ) śakralokamavāpunyāt //19// svayaṁ vādyena sampūjya tasyaivānucaro bhavet / vādyānāmapi devasya tantrīvādyaṁ sadā priyam //20// tena saṁpūjya varadaṁ gāpatyamavāpnuyāt / nṛtyaṁ dattvā tathāpnoti rudralokamasaṁśayam //21// svayaṁ nṛtyena saṁpūjya tasyaivānucaro bhavat /..... //22//*). Viṣṇu becomes pleased when music is performed in his honour *nṛtyatām gāyatāṁ caiva nānāvādyaṁ prakurvatām / yathā santuṣyate devo na dhyānādyairiti śrutam //* Jaiminīyāśvamedha XII. 22). The Gandharvas and Apsarases also please Viṣṇu by means of music (cp. Skandap. Māhe. Kedāra. XI. 78: *evaṁ vādyaprakāraiśca Viṣṇuṁ sarvātmanā harim / atoṣayan sugītajñā gandharvāpsarasāṁ gaṇāḥ //*; cp. Viṣṇupurāṇa III.11.16: *stuvanti taṁ vai munayo gandharvair gīyate puraḥ / nṛtyantyapsaraso yānti tasya cānu niśācaraiḥ //* When once gods were defeated by the Asuras, they sang (*jaguḥ*) praise of Viṣṇu for pleasing him so that he would help them (Viṣṇupurāṇa III. 17.10 ff).

Music and Viṣṇu are connected in the sphere of sacrifice also. The music that is used in the sacrifice is henoistically mentioned to be ultimately connected with Viṣṇu. Thus Kṛṣṇa says, "The priest Udgātṛ also sings for me with sounds of songs in a great sacrifice (*udgātā cāpi māṁ stauti gītaghoṣairmahādhvare* Mbh XIV. 53.10). Similarly XIII.143.15 it is said, "To him the reciters praise; him the sāman-singers praise-sing in the Rathantara (-sāman) .... (*tamadhvare śaṁsitāraḥ stuvanti rathantare sāmagāś ca stuvanti ....*) Elsewhere Viṣṇu is described methaphorically as the sacrifice and then the Udgātṛ priest has been identified with his entrails (Viṣṇu-smṛti I.6). When Bali was sacrificing, Viṣṇu in the form of a small boy performed the activities of the Udgātṛ-priest in his sacrifice (*udgāpayan sāma yato hi sākṣāt cakāra devo baṭurūpaveṣaḥ / udgīyamāno bhagavān sa īśvaro vedāntavedyo hari-rīśvaraḥ prabhuḥ* / Skandapurāṇa. Māhe. Kedāra. XVIII.166).

The importance of music can be revealed from the close connection of music with seers also. Thus while the river Mahānadī is being described, it is said in the Mbh. that near it, the seers like Marīci, Pulaha, Bhṛgu and Aṅgiras, having auspicious tone use to sing sāmans (*atra sāma sma gāyanti sāmagāḥ puṇyaniḥsvanāḥ / 11 / marīciḥ pulahaścaiva bhṛguścaivāṅirāstathā* / 12 / III. app. 1.16.11 f). The seers used to take delight in music and the Gandharvas, it is said, used to make them happy in the Mayasabhā (royal palace of the King Yudhiṣṭhira) (Mbh II.4.30 ff; 33: *gāyanti divyatānaiste yathānyāyaṁ manasvinaḥ / pāṇḍuputrān ṛṣīṁścaiva ramayanta upāsate /*). The hermitage of the sage named Upamanyu, was full of the sounds of currents of rivers, and birds, elephants, songs of the Kinnaras and tunes of the Sāman-singers (Mbh. XIII. 14.35: *dhārāninādairvihagapraṇadaiḥ śubhaistathā bṛṁhitaiḥ kuñjarāṇām / gānaistathā kinnarāṇāmudāraiḥ śubhaiḥ svanaiḥ sāmagānāṁ ca vīra //*). Singing of sāmans as well as music in general is helpful for reaching to the highest principle viz. brahman and obtaining salvation. Thus according to the Yājñavalkyasmṛti III.112 ff, if one chants verses from the Sāmaveda, according to the rules and attentively, one would reach, by this practice, the high brahman. The songs like Aparāntaka, Ullopya, Madraka, Prakarī, Auveṇaka, Sarobindu, Uttara, Ṛggāthā, Paṇikā, Dakṣavihitā and Brahmagītaka are called "*mokṣa* (salvation)" because the study of these is a means of salvation. Further it is said that he who is well versed in the principles of playing on lyre, who understands the *śrutis* and *jātis* in music or is versed in *tālas,* will easily obtain the road of salvation (*yathāvidhānena paṭhan sāmagāyamavicyutam / sāvadhānastadabhyāsāt param brahmādhigachhati // 12 // aparāntakamullopyaṁ madrakaṁ prakarīṁ tathā / auveṇakaṁ sarobindumuttaraṁ gītakāni ca // 13 // ṛggāthā paṇikā dakṣavihitā brahmagītikā / geyametattadabhyāsakaraṇānmokṣasaṁjñitam // 14 // vīṇāvādanatattvajñaḥ śrutijātiviśāradaḥ / tālajñāścāprayāsena mokṣamārgaṁ niyachhati // 15 //*.

Music is supposed to be useful in obtaining various kinds of results e.g. obtainment of heaven, rain, cattle, food etc. as well as freedom from diseases, from the evil spirits etc.[19] It is in a henoistic way[20] said that by the use of some musical elements one gets all[19]. These suppositions also prove the importance of music.

We saw above how musicians and music are considered to be important and how they have been glorified. But the musicians and music have also another, exactly opposite side. They are also very often abused and looked down. There is a constant antipathy towards the musicians and music. In the ṚV Agni is requested to destroy a wicked magician singer (*rebha-*) (X. 87.12). Elsewhere the singers of the praise-song are described as robers of the life (of sacrificial victims)[21] and are said to be wandering, while being covered with fog and talking twaddle (ṚV X.82.7). ṚV III.41.6 Indra is requested not to make the singer blameworthy (cf. also VI.45.27) and the likelihood of singers, being blameworthy is hereby suggested. ṚV II. 23.16 the sāman-singers get the worst treatment. There is the following imploration to Bṛhaspati: "Do not give us to the robers who depending upon the traces of falsehood, the cheaters and greedy for food. They contemplate upon the weaknesses of the gods and deny those (weaknesses) of their own hearts; O Bṛhaspati, they knew nothing more than the sāman (*mā naḥ stenebhyo ye abhi druhaspade nirāmiṇo ripavonneṣu jāgṛdhuḥ / ā devānām ohate vi vrayo hṛdi bṛhaspate na paraḥ sāmno viduḥ*" //)

In the classical Hinduism, the musicians were considered as declined Brāhmaṇas.[22] In the Bṛhaspati-smṛti the profession of musician along with some other professions is treated to be of lower social standard, and a person belonging to any of those professions is said to be equal to niṣāda (*gāndharvo lohakāraśca sainikastantuvāyakaḥ / cakropajīvī rajakaḥ kitavastaskarastathā* // 11 // *sainiko varṇikaścaiva niṣādena samāḥ smṛtāḥ* // 12 // Bṛhaspatismṛti[23], Prāyaścittakhaṇḍa, 11 f). Further it is told that if a Brāhmaṇa lives by any of these professions, he will have to take an expiation (14). It is then added that a Brāhmaṇa, practising music etc. is to be considered as a Brāhmaṇa-cāṇḍāla or even as a killer of Brāhmaṇa

(14). This passage can throw sufficient light on the social position of musicians. According to Auśanasmṛti, 19, a person, born out of the secret intercourse of a Śūdra man and queen becomes a 'dyer' and the son of a dyer and a Vaiśya woman becomes dancer and singer (*nṛpāyāṁ śūdrataścauryājjāto rañjaka ucyate /vaiśyāyāṁ rañjakājjāto nartako gāyako bhavet //*). Thus a dancer or a singer is considered to be an illegal progeny of persons of low standard (cp. Vaikhānasagṛhyasūtra X. 13 f: *viprācchūdrāyāṁ pāraśavaḥ bhadrakālāpūjana-citrakarmāṅgavidyātūryaghoṣaṇamardanavṛttiḥ* / 13 / *cauravṛttāt (nṛpāyām) velavaḥ jambhakartanagānakṛtyaḥ* / 14 /. All the craftsmen (*śilpin-*) (among whom musicians can be included because *śilpa* comprehends dance, and vocal instrumental music according to KB XXIX. 5 and physicians etc. go to hell according to the Padmapurāṇa II. 67.86 (*śilpinaḥ kāravo vaidyās tathā devalakā narāḥ / bhṛtakā dūtyakarmāṇaḥ sarve niraya-gāminaḥ //*). Kathāsaritsāgara I.6.51 ff, we read a story in which people make fun of an ignorant and naive sāman-singer (*chandoga-*). Thus a sāman-singer who has obtained eight māṣas (beans : a measurement) of gold was advised by a Viṭa to learn the worldly wisdom at the cost of that money. The sāman-singer went to the house of Caturikā, a courtisan, gave her money and requested her to teach the worldly practices. This foolish man then observing that others were laughing at him, began to sing a sāman in a very loud voice, having made his hands like the ears of a cow. All this caused still more laughter. The people around him said, "Let a half-moon (*ardhacandra*: the hand bent in a semi-circular shape for seizing somebody at the neck for the sake of removing him away) be given to him." The poor sāman-singer, ignorant of the phrase, thinking of an arrow of semi-circular shape, and fearing that his head would be cut, runs away from that place and cries, "I have learnt worldly wisdom". No comments are required to explain the pitiable position of the sāman-singer described here.

In other parts of the world also, musicians are sometimes looked down. They are sometimes kept away from the major part of the society. In many primitive societies musicians are often feared for the mysterious power of their songs. The effect of the song, it is believed, cannot be checked even after the singer is punished or banished for a satirical song.[24] In the Sachel and the Western Sudan, society is divided into five castes: aristocrats, bondsmen, smiths, bards and musicians.[25] The musicians, receive there an inferior position. In Malaya, the dancers of Ma'yong are somewhat excluded from the society.[26] Musicians are regarded there as sacred and therefore kept away from the society, which is considered to be profane.[27] In China, chorists were inferior to warriors and civil even though they did not form a separate class.[28] In Rome, even though the musicians used to obtain majestic titles and high rates of pay, they stood much lower in the social scale than doctors or teachers of grammar and rhetoric.[29]

Music is sometimes regarded as a part of bad behaviour. Thus the two young sons of a merchant named Hemakuṇḍala, are described to be of bad character. They were proud of their wealth, addicted to bad habits, neglecting religious duties, adulterous etc. They were also fond of vocal and instrumental music; they themselves also used to sing (*atha tasya sutau rājan mahāmānasamanvitau / taruṇau rūpasampannau dhanagarveṇa garvitau // 17 // duḥśilau vyasanāsaktau dharmakarmādyadarśakau / na vākyaṁ cāgatau mātuḥ vṛddhānāṁ vacanaṁ tathā // 18 // Kumārgagau durātmānau pitṛmātṛniṣedhakau / adharmaniratau duṣṭau paradārābnigāminau // 19 // gītavāditraniratau vīṇāveṇuvinodinau / vārastrīśatasaṁyuktau gāyantau ceratustadā // 20 //* Padmapurāṇa I. 20.17 ff). Similarly a badly behaving king named Sauvarṇa, being surrounded by vocal and instrumental music, who is said to have wasted all the money which he had obtained by unjust way and to have never performed any sacrifice or given gifts, is mentioned by Padmapurāṇa (Śrīveṅkaṭeśvara Press) VII.10.41 : *anyāyopārjitaṁ vittaṁ gītavādyādibhir vṛtaḥ / samastaṁ nāśayāmāsa yajñadānavivarjitaḥ //* In the Abhidharmakośavyākhyā[30] IV. 260 music is mentioned as a part of bad behaviour due to a bad characteristic named insolence of mind (*auddhatyaṁ nāma cetaso' vyupaśamaḥ iti / nṛtyagītādiśṛṅgāraveṣālaṅkārādyauddhatyasaniśrayadāna-karmakaḥ cetasiko dharmaḥ*).

In other parts of the world also music is connected with bad behaviour. Thus, according to Homer[31] bad music and the lascivious chants pervert the manners. Didorus Siculus writes that in Egypt Music was considered as not only useless but also as morally injurious. Moreover, in Egypt the root '*sem* to sing', came to mean something unrighteous (to be perverse, to corrupt - see *JA* Mars - Avril, 1908, p. 263, 260).[32] Mohammedan writers also supposed that music led to immorality.[33]

Many other expressions are also used to express the low status of music. In Kaṭhopaniṣad we read that Yama offers to Naciketas many worldly pleasures among which dance and vocal music are mentioned (I.26). But Naciketas is desirous of getting the highest knowledge and he therefore rejects all that is merely worldly pleasure (II.1 ff). In Mbh. XIV. 31.13; dance along with the vocal and instrumental music is considered as *rājasa* and thus has received a lower position (*nṛttavāditragītāni prasaṅgā ye ca kecana / sarva ete guṇā viprā rājasāḥ parikīrtitāḥ //*). In the Mārkaṇḍeya-purāṇa, music receives still lower position. There, the Sāmaveda is considered to be the lowest of all the vedas. Thus the ṛcs are, according to it *rājasa*, the yajus-formulas *sāttvika* and the sāmans are *tāmasā*.[34] The Atharvan-mantras have both the *sattva* and *tamas* type of qualities (*ṛco rajoguṇāḥ sattvaṁ yajuṣāṁ ca guṇo mune / tamoguṇāni sāmāni tamaḥsattvamatharvasu* // 99.7). Music is also considered to be "vain (*mogha*)" elsewhere. Thus in order to obtain Soma, which was under the guardianship of Gandharvas, the gods sent the speech (Vāc-fem.) to the Gandharvas who were notorious for their lust for women. After the obtainment of soma, in order to regain the speech, the gods began to sing and play on the lute. Because women like a singer the speech came back to gods (ŚB III. 2.4.1 ff). In this context, ŚBK IV. 2.4.4 comments, "And hence it is to him who is given to the *vain things*, who dances and sings, that women are the most attached (*tasmād ya eva mogha saṁhito yo nṛtyati yo gāyati tatraiva yoṣā nimiślatamāḥ* cp. ŚB III. 2.4.6).

It is quite in keeping with this antipathetic attitude towards music, that we find numerous texts mentioning severe rules prohibiting music and musicians. They might have mostly originated out of a the Puritan mentality, but in the ultimate analysis we have to judge that they are due to the double nature of music itself. Let us first see the rules.

A student of the Veda (*brahmacārī*) has to keep himself away from singing, dancing etc. Thus GB I. 2.7 says that a *brahmacārī* should not be either a singer or a dancer (*na gāyanaḥ syān na nartanaḥ*). It is further said at the same place, "If he were to be a singer, (in that case) they will have to cleanse out weepings. If he were a dancer, (in that case) they will have to remove dead bodies (*yad gāyano bhavatyabhīṣṇaśaḥ ākrandān dhāvante yan nartano bhavatyabhīṣṇaśaḥ pretānnirharante* GB I. 2.7).

According to the Vārahagṛhagasūtra VI.33f he should neither attend the music concerts nor should perform music (*na nṛtyagīte gacchet / 33 / na caine kuryāt / 34 /*). Manusmṛti, while giving the rules of the behaviour of the vedic student adds other avoidable things, playing upon musical instruments to the singing and dancing (II.178 : *abhyaṅgamañjanaṁ cākṣṇorupānacchatradhāraṇam / kāmaṁ krodhaṁ ca lobhaṁ ca nartanaṁ gītavādanaṁ //* cp. Gautama-dharmasūtra I. 2.19: *varjayen madhumāṁsagandhamālyadivāsvapnāñjanābhyañjana-yānopānacchatrakāmakrodhalobhamoha-vādanasnānadanta-dhāvanaharṣanṛtya-gītaparivādabhayāni;* cp. Baudhāyana-dharmasūtra I.3.25: *nṛtyagītavāditragandhamālyopānacchatra-dhāraṇāñjanābhyañjanavarjī;* Āpastambadharmasūtra I.3.11 mentions dance alone: *anṛttadarśī;* Hiraṇyakeśidharmasūtra I.8.83f mentions singing and dance : *na gāyenna rodet / 83 / anṛttadarśī /84 /* cp. Saṅkhasmṛti III. 13 *madhumāṁsāñjanaṁ śrāddhaṁ gītanṛtyaṁ ca varjayet / hiṁsāṁ parāpavādaṁ ca strīlīlāṁ ca viśeṣataḥ //* Devalasmṛti, quoted by Smṛticandrikā (Bombay, 1918), p. 63, prohibits the Gāndharva (art belonging to Gandharvas = muṣic) to a student. *Viṣṇusmṛti* 28.11. : *śrā-ddhakṛtalavaṇaśuktaparyuaṣitanṛtyagītastrīmadhumāṁsāñjano-cchiṣṭaprāṇihiṁsāślīlavarjanam / Laghuviṣṇu-smṛti* IV.8: *nṛtyaṁ gānaṁ sabhāsevāṁ parivādāṁśca varjayet:* Hārītasaṁhitā III.8:

nṛtyagītamathālāpaṁ maithunaṁ ca vivarjayet; Agnipurāṇa 153.14: *sāyaṁ prātaśca juhuyān nāmedhyaṁ vyastahastakaṁ / madhumāṁsaṁ janaiḥ sārdhaṁ gītaṁ nṛtyaṁ ca vai tyajet //;* Viṣṇudharmottarapurāṇa II. 86.9: *madhumāṁsāñjanaṁ śrāddhaṁ gītaṁ nṛtyaṁ ca varjayet* and III.228.5: *madhu-māṁsāñjanaṁ śrāddhaṁ nṛtyaṁ gītaṁ ca sāhasam / hiṁsāṁ parāpavādaṁ ca maṇḍanaṁ ca vivarjayet //* ; Padmapurāṇa I. 53.16 ff : *Prayuñjīta sadā vācaṁ madhurāṁ hitakāriṇīm / gandhamālyaṁ rasaṁ kalpaṁ śuktiṁ prāṇivihiṁsanam //* 16 // *abhyañjanāñjane pānaṁ chatradhāraṇameva ca / kāmaṁ krodhaṁ bhayaṁ nidrāṁ gītaṁ vāditravartanam //* 17 // *ghṛtaṁ ca lavaṇaṁ sarvaṁ varjyaṁ paryuṣitaṁ ca yat / anṛtyadarśī satataṁ bhaved gitādiniḥspṛhaḥ //* 20 // and I. 55.63 : *na nṛtyed athavā gāyen na vāditrāṇi vādayet / na saṁhatābhyāṁ pāṇibhyāṁ kaṇḍuyedātmanaḥ śiraḥ //* ; Vedavyāsasmṛti I. 29 : *tauryatrikānṛtonmādaparīvādānalaṁkriyām /.* Manusmṛti IX. 59 ff a list of minor sins (*upapātaka*) is given and among them to acquire false sciences (*asacchāstrā-dhigamanam*) is mentioned in 65. According to the Kulllūkabhaṭṭa's commentary on it, the word means "to enjoy dance and vocal instrumental music (*nṛtyagītavāditropasevanam*). If a veda student takes pleasure in dance, singing and playing on instruments, he has to perform three Kṛcchras as an expiation (Saṁskāraprakāśa, p. 563).

Sāmaveda and music are considered to be impure and the students are advised to stop their study of other sacred vedas whenever they come to hear the noise of these. Thus Manusmṛti says: nobody should study the ṛc or yajus after hearing the noise of any sāman (*sāmadhvanāvṛgyajūṁṣi nādhiyīta kadācana* ...... Manusmṛti IV. 123 cp. Viṣṇusmṛti 30.26 *na sāmadhvanau ṛgyajuṣī (adhīyīta);* Gautamadharmasūtra II. 7.21 *ṛgyajuṣaṁ ca sāmaśabdo yāvat.* Yajnavalkyasmṛti has mentioned the sound of sāman, along with the noise of dogs, foxes, asses etc. and advised not to study after having listened to any of these: *śvakrostugardabholukasāmabāṇārtaniḥsvane / amedhya-śavaśūdrāntyaśmaśānapatitāntike* (I. 148). cp. Āpastamba-dharmasūtra I. 10. 19 f: *śvagardabhanādāḥ sālāvṛkyeka-sṛkolūkaśabdāḥ sarve vāditaśabdāḥ rodanagītasāmaśabdāśca (anadhyāyahetavaḥ)// 19 // śākhāntare ca sāmnāmanadhyāyaḥ /* (cp. Satyāśs XXVI. 3.4); Garuḍapurāṇa I.96. 51: *śvakroṣṭugardabholūkasāmabāṇārtaniḥsvane.*[35] The reason why the Sāmaveda is considered to be impure is as follows—Gods are the deity of the ṚV. Men are the deity of the YV and Fathers are the deity of the Sāmaveda; therefore its sound is impure (*ṛgvedo devadevatyo yajurvedastumānuṣaḥ / sāmavedaḥ smṛtaḥ pitryaḥ tasmāt tasyāśucir dhvaniḥ* Manusmṛti IV.124). In Viṣṇusmṛti, 30,13, a Vedic student is advised not to study when he hears any sound of musical instruments (*vāditaśabde.* cp. Baudhāyanadharmasūtra I.1.21: *vāte pūtigandhe nīhāre nṛttagītavāditraruditasāmaśabdeṣu tāvantaṁ kālam*; Gautamadharmasūtra II. 7.7: *bāṇabherīmṛdaṅgaśabdeṣu*; also Padmapurāṇa I. 53. 74: *nīhāre vāṇaśabde ca sandhyayorubhayorapi / amāvāsyācaturdaśyoḥ paurṇamāsyaṣṭamīṣu ca //* ; Viṣṇudharmottarapurāṇa III.233.172: *sāyaṁ niśīthe nādhyayanaṁ vāditre na ca vādyati /).*[36]

On the other hand, the teaching of music is praised. Thus according to the one who teaches Veda, Śastra, dance and singing, goes to the heaven [*veda śāstraṁ nṛtyagītaṁ yodhyāpayati sa nākabhāk* (Agnipurāṇa 211.54)].

Although JUB I.6.3.2 gives a rule that a student should not accompany the Udgātṛ-priest in singing at a sacrifice (*tasmādu nopagāyet*), Further, JUB I.6.3.3 allows him to accompany the Udgātṛ in singing at a sacrificial performance, if the student is directed to do so by his own teacher.

There are restrictions in connection with music, not only on him who is a veda-student but also on him who has finished his study and taken the bath (*snātaka*-) indicating the end of his career as a veda-student. Thus a *snātaka* should not sing, dance, or play on the musical instruments according to Manusmṛti IV. 64: *na nṛtyennaiva gāyecca na vāditraṇi vādayet /* cp. Mānavagṛhyasūtra I.2.19: *pratiṣiddhamaparayā dvārā niṣkramaṇaṁ malavadvāsasā saha saṁsravaṇam rajaḥ suvāsinyā saha śayyā gurorduruktamavacanamasthāne śayanaṁ smayanaṁ saraṇaṁ yānaṁ gānaṁ tasya cekṣaṇam /*. The Pāraskaragṛhyasūtra gives the same rule but afterwards quotes an unknown vedic sentence and on the authority of it allows to sing as well as to enjoy a song (II. 7.3 f: *nṛtyagītavāditrāṇi na kuryānna ca gacchet / 3 / kāmaṁ tu gīte gāyati caiva gīte vā ramate iti sruter hyaparam / 4 /*. In the commentary of Devapāla, on the Laugākṣigṛhyasūtra III.19 ff, where this rule is mentioned, it is said that singing etc. is prohibited only at the improper occasion or place. But when one is in the company of one's friends, one can perform music. Similarly, at the time of festivals, and rituals like Mahāvrata, music is allowed. (Laugākṣigṛhyasūtra III. 19 ff - *gāyanam / 19 / nartanam / 20 / tasya cekṣaṇam (pratiṣiddhaṁ snātakasya) / 21 /* Devapāla says: *evaṁ gāyanaṁ gītaṁ nartanaṁ cāsthāne pratiṣiddhaṁ na tūtsavādau samānaśīamadhyagatasya guptasthāne / tathā mahavrate gıtavādyanartanakartavyatāvacanaṁ tamudgātā vāduyilvā prastotre prayacchati prastotādhvaryave adhvaryur-anyasmai brāhmaṇāya iti vīṇāvādavacanaṁ śrūyate* / cp. Also Kāṭhakagṛhyasūtra III.17 *asthāne smayanaṁ saraṇaṁ gāyanaṁ nartanaṁ tasya cekṣaṇam*; cp. the commentary of Devapāla on it also).

A snātaka is also asked to avoid the food given by a singer (Manusmṛti IV. 210: *stenagāyanayoścānnaṁ takṣno vārdhuṣikasya ca / dīkṣitasya kadaryasya baddhasya nigaḍasya ca //*).

A *gṛhastha* (householder) has also to abstain from singing and dancing as Viṣṇusmṛti 71.70 says (*na nṛtyagīte (kuryāt)*; cp. Dakṣasmṛti III. 14: *Gītanṛtye kṛṣiḥ sevā vāṇijye lavaṇakriyā /* ; Manusmṛti IV. 64: *na nṛtyedathavā gāyenna vāditrāṇi vādayet /* see Viṣṇudharmottarapurāṇa III.233.161 ; Padmapurāṇa I. 55.63 etc. Nobody should make friendship with dancer etc. (Kṛtyakalpataru, Baroda, 1944, p. 299). When the husband is on journey, the wife should avoid adorning herself, attending the performances of dance and singing, gatherings, festivals, and enjoyment of meat and wine (Bṛhaspatismṛti 25.13 - *prasādhanaṁ nṛtyagītasamājotsvadarśanam / māṁsa-madyābhiyogaṁ ca na kuryāt proṣite prabhau //*). One who has renounced the world, should also avoid any conversation etc. with women and dancing, singing and censure etc.

(Laghuviṣṇusmṛti-8: *saṁbhāṣaṇaṁ saha strībhir ālambhaprekṣaṇe tathā / nṛtyaṁ gānaṁ sabhāsevāṁ parivādāṁśca varjayet //*).

A householder should not accept food from some kind of persons among whom musicians, dancers etc. are mentioned (Padmapurāṇa I. 56.4 f: *naṭānāṁ nartakānāṁ ca caṇḍāla-carmakāriṇām / gaṇānnaṁ gaṇikānnāṁ ca ṣaḍannaṁ ca vivarjayet // 4 // cakropajīvirajakataskaradhvajinām tathā / gāndharva-lohakārānnaṁ mṛtakānnaṁ vivarjayet // 5 //* cf. Garuḍapurāṇa I. 122.9: *rajakānāṁ śailūṣaveṇucarmopajīvinām / etadannaṁ ca yo bhuṅkte dvijaścāndrāyaṇaṁ caret //* cp. I. 96.61; Agnipurāṇa 168.3 ; Viṣṇudharmottara. II.73.8). If one eats food given by singers etc. one has to live only on milk as a way of expiation (Viṣṇusmṛti 51.7 : *gaṇagaṇikāstenagāyanānnāni bhuktvā sapta-rātraṁ payasā varteta* ; cp. Atrismṛti VII. 2). JUB I. 18.2.1 gives following story : "That Gāyatrī cleansed itself with the *gāthā*, the Triṣṭubh with the *Narāśaṁsī*, the Jagatī with the *Raibhī* : 'Lo, they have struck away fearful (*bhīma*-) defilement (*mala*). Therefore, these devices are terrible (*bhīmala*-). 'Verily these devices have struck away defilement and therefore they are terrible'. And therefore one should not eat (anything) from those singers for they live on defilement (*tasmādu gāyatāṁ nāśnīyāt, malena hyete jīvanti*).

Even though a gṛhastha should not practise music sometimes there seems to be no harm to him in hearing it. In Mbh. XII.184.16, in a description of the life of the gṛhasthas, enjoyment of music is mentioned[37] (contrast however, Padmapurāṇa IV. 9.58 below).

Those who are consecrated for a sacrificial session should avoid dance and vocal as well as instrumental music (Āśs XII. 8). Among the rules of behaviour of a brāhmaṇa, there is one rule that he should not be addicted to the instrumental music (Padmapurāṇa IV. 9.58 : *tauryatrikapriyo na syāt*). According to GB I. 2.21 a brāhmaṇa should not either sing or dance (*tasmād brāhmaṇo naiva gāyen na nṛtyet*). A brāhmaṇa who sings in order to get his livelihood, is compared to a monkey (*mūlyaiścikitsāṁ kurute kathāṁ citrāṁ karoti yaḥ / gītaṁ gāyati vṛttyarthaṁ naraḥ sa plavago mataḥ //* Prajāpatismṛti 51).

Among the deeds, having which performed a brāhmaṇa gets devalued, and becomes a śūdra, dancing is mentioned and such a dancer-brāhmaṇa must be avoided in any sacred work (*śūdro rājan bhavati brahmabandhuḥ duścāritro yaśca dharmād apetaḥ / vṛṣalīpatiḥ piśuno nartakaśca grāmapraiṣyo yaśca bhaved vikarmā // 4 // japan vedān ajapaṁśāpi rājan samaḥ śūdrair dāsavaccāpi bhojyaḥ / ete sarve śūdrasamā bhavanti rājannetān varjayeddevakṛtye* // 5 // Mbh. XII. 63.4 f). Padmapurāṇa (VII. 21.12 ff: Śrīveṅkaṭeśvara Press) gives a list of persons to whom no obeisance (*namaskāra*) should be paid. Among them a brāhmaṇa singing sāmans is mentioned (*Puṣpahastaṁ paryāhastaṁ devahastaṁ ca jaimine / na named brāhmaṇaṁ prājñas tailābhyaṅgitavigraham* // 12 // *jalasthaṁ devavaṁśasthaṁ dhyānamajjitacetasam / devapūjāṁ prakurvantaṁ na named brāhmaṇaṁ budhaḥ* // 13 // *bahiṣkriyāṁ prakurvantaṁ bhuñjānaṁ ca dvijottama / tathā sāmāni gayantaṁ na named brāhamaṇaṁ budhaḥ* // 14 // *brāhmaṇā yatra tiṣṭhanti bahavo dvijasattama / pratyekaṁ tu namaskārs tatra kāryo na dhīmatā* // 15 //).

Giving anything to a singer is, according to the rules, interdicted. In the process of the fire-building i.e. building of the great sacred altar and places of fire, human head is to be put down like a brick as it were. At that time, verses (*gāthā*-) belonging to Yama, are to be recited. Having prescribed this, the vedic texts remark, "Of all those that were comrades of death, Yama holds the lordship; One sings the verses of Yama; verily from Yama, one redeems it (the human head)". Then further it is said, "Therefore one should not give (anything) to a person who sings; for the gāthās appropriate it (*tasmād gāyate na deyaṁ gatha hyeva tad vṛṅkte* TS V.1.8.1 f; cp. KS XX.8; Kpks XXXI.10). Whatever one gives to a singer is merely for the sake of name and fame and this act of giving can by no means be called a religious, true "gift" or *dāna*. Moreover, one should rather never give for the sake of mere name and fame. This point can be illustrated from the Mbh. III.*1383 and Viṣṇudharmottarapurāṇa III.316.2. Thus Yakṣa asks the following question to Yudhiṣṭhira—"For what reason one should give gifts to a Brāhmaṇa ? for what to an actor or dancer ? (*Kimartham brāhmaṇe dadyāt kimartham naṭanartake/*). The answers given by Yudhiṣṭhira were following — "One should give to a brāhmaṇa for the sake of religion, to an actor or dancer for the sake of fame (*dharmārtham brāhmaṇe deyam yaśo'rthe naṭanartake* Mbh. III.*1383). But elsewhere it is said that one should not offer any gifts to the musicians, nor for the sake of obtaining fame (Mbh. XII.37.29: *na dadyād yaśase dānam na bhayānnopakāriṇe / na nṛttagītaśīlāya hāsakeṣu ca dhārmikaḥ//* cp. Viṣṇudharmottarapurāṇa, III.316.2: *na dānam yaśase dadyānna dadyānnopakāriṇe / na nṛtyagītaśīlebhayaḥ nāstikebhyaś ca dhārmikaḥ //* cp. Viṣṇusmṛti 93.14; Viṣṇudharmottarapurāṇa III. 233.149).

Similarly, one should not accept anything from a singer. Thus we read, "One who obtains (his livelihood) by means of (singing) gāthās and nārāśaṁsīs, nothing should be accepted from him; he (the singer of them) obtains by means falsehood (*yo gāthānārāśaṁsībhyām sanoti na tasya pratigṛhyam anṛtena hi sa sanoti* MS I.11.5; KS XIV.5). KS XIV.5 adds, "Gāthā is falsehood; nārāśaṁsī is falsehood (*anṛtam hi gāthā anṛtam hi nārāśaṁsī*). TB. I.3.2.6 f, following story is given: Gods removed the impurity of hymn and food. What was the impurity of hymn, that became the gāthā nārāśaṁsī; and what of food that (became) liquor. Therefore one should not accept anything from a singer and from one who is intoxicated; if one were to accept, one would accept impurity (*tasmād gāyataśca mattasya ca na pratigṛhyam; yat pratigṛhṇīyāt śamalam pratigṛhṇīyāt*).

One should not receive anything which comes as a result of singing. In the Buddhist literature we often observe such a rule. Thus in the Kasibhāradvājasutta (No. 4 of the Suttanipāta), we find that the Buddha visits, on his round for alms, the farm of a brāhmaṇa named Bhāradvāja, who is farmer by his profession. The brāhmaṇa refuses to give any alms to the Buddha and asks him why he does not practise farming. The Buddha tells him that he is also a farmer but his farming is not in the material field but in the moral and mental field. This answer of Buddha was in sung-verses (*gāthā* -). Being convinced by the Buddha's speech, the Brāhmaṇa offers him alms. But now the Buddha rejects to accept the same, saying,

"*gāthābhigītaṁ me abhojaneyyaṁ sampassataṁ brāhmaṇa esa dhammo /*
gāthābhigītaṁ paṇudanti buddhā dhamme sati brāhmaṇa vuttiresā/[38]

I cannot accept the alms which comes as a result of singing verses. This O Brāhmaṇa is the rule of the seers. The Buddhas reject what is obtained as the result of singing verses; and this O brāhmaṇa is the procedure followed as long as the Dhamma (Sacred Law) exists" (Suttanipāta p. 14; cp. p. 84; and also Sāñyuttanikāya I, p. 166;167;173: Pali text Society editions). The rule seems to be connected with the general view which condemns musicians who are many times no more than bards and obtain their livelihood by means of praise-songs. We have already referred to JUB I.18.2.1 where singers are said to be living by means of dirt. Even though the Buddha seems to have learnt music (see e.g. Lalitavistara (ed. J. Lefman, Halle, 1902, p. 178), he must have been aware of the social beliefs, and therefore avoided to obtain alms by means of singing.

A king has to avoid ten bad habits which are a product of desire (*kāmaja* -). Among them instrumental music is one. (Manusmṛti VII.47: *mṛgayākṣā divāsvapnaḥ parivādaḥ striyo madaḥ / tauryatrikaṁ vṛthāṭyā ca kāmajo daśako gaṇaḥ //*). In the usual time-table of the king, however, he is expected to enjoy the sound of instrumental music after dinner and then he should go to sleep (Manusmṛti VIII. 225: *tatra bhuktvā punaḥ kiñcit tūryaghoṣaiḥ praharṣitaḥ / saṁviśet tu yathākālam uttiṣṭhec ca gataklamaḥ //*). According to Āpastambadharmasūtra II. 24.14 and Satyāṣāḍhaśrautasūtra XXVII.5.194 (*āyudhagrahaṇaṁ nṛttagītavāditrāṇi iti rājādhīnebhyo'nyatra na vidyeran*), the weapons, dance, singing and play on the musical instruments should be limited to the persons in the service of the king only. In the late antiquity, among the Greeks and Romans, a musical emperor was considered to be a disgrace.[39]

According to the Buddhist ten commandments (*dasa sikkhāpadāni*) a monk has to refrain from being a spectator at shows, at fairs with nautch, dance, singing and instrumental music (*bhikkhū naccagītavāditavisūkadassanā paṭivirato hoti,* Dīghanikāya P.T.S), I. 64; for similar rules cp. p. 146, 250; Majjhimanikāya I.63; 235 ff). A Jaina monk was also not expected to go there where sounds of musical instruments viz. Mṛdaṅga, Nandimṛdaṅga, Jhallarī, Vīṇā, Veṇu etc. are heard (Āyāraṅgasutta, II.11.1 ff).[40]

In other societies also there were some rules against music. Thus Egyptians wanted to avoid its practice because they considered that it made men effeminate and as such was undesirable.[41] They allowed only that music which was approved by the priests and no deviation was permitted from the established forms of art and music.[42] In Greece, it was duty to ban the music which was pernicious to virtue.[43] In Greece and Rome, no reputable woman would play an instrument and no gentleman would dance in late antiquity and "unheard music is better than heard" was a proverb.[44] In Rome, the nobles rejected ecstasy in dance as utterly unseemly and unworthy of a nobleman's sense of honour. Most of the other Romans also considered dancing and music as unseemly.[45] Among the Romans, there was severe punishment for enchanting crop.[46] In the post biblical Judaism any instrumental music was probihited in the Synagogue.[47] Worldly music was considered by the Church-fathers to be a work of devil and therefore it was to be kept away from the divine worship.[48] The early christians banished the elements of joy from their chants.[49] A composer, according to Gretty, who worked for the church should not be a mixer of compositions which belonged to the theatre.[50] The Parsis did not allow music at the time of sacrifice.[51] Among the Muslims, a rule was laid down that a faithful Muslim must not listen to any music at all, if he found that it stirs up in him thoughts contrary to the moral precepts of the Qura'an. Ecstasy caused by music was also prohibited for a Muslim by Al-Ghazli.[52]

The various reasons why music was sometimes abused or why there are restrictions on music, and rules prohibiting it etc. can be given as follows.

One of the reasons of keeping music and musicians away seemed to be come out of somewhat puritanistic outlook. Music was a means of enjoyment, a part of luxury. The puritans asked people to avoid music because of this.

Music has many magico-religious significances and it was also used for the sake of them. But it was also a means of enjoyment. Thus the Gandharvas used to please the Brāhmaṇas at the time of intervals of the sacrificial activities, by means of songs (Mbh. XIV. 90.39). Music was often considered to be a source of joy and pleasure. One used music for pleasing gods (the vedic details will be given elsewhere). Nāradīyaśikṣā I.1.15 f describes what note pleases what genii of beings. Thus the Ṣaḍja pleases the gods; the Ṛṣabha the seers; the Gāndhāra the Fathers; the Madhyama the Gandharvas; the Pañcama the gods, fathers and the seers; the Niṣāda pleases the Yakṣas and the Dhaivata the beings called Bhūtas. In the so called paradise, the dancers and singers constitute the highest delights.[53] In the Bible the employment of music in connection with the religion is a later development. Earlier, it was used on occasions of rejoicings.[54] (See e.g. Ex. 15.1 f; Jg. 5.1 ff; Ex. 15.20 f; 2CḤ.20.28; Mt. 11.17 etc.) In Egypt all music whether in temple, palace or the street, was called hy which primarily meant "joy", "gladness", etc.[55] Shamans sometimes beat drums and sang music for their own pleasure.[56]

In many Indian festivals music is used as a means of enjoyment. Thus the evil Asuras named Sunda and Upasunda in their pride of valour and victory, asked their subjects to perform the "Moon-light-festival" even in the absence of real moon-light. And then in every house, different kinds of noises were heard. "Eat, enjoy, take pleasure, sing, drink, and give" (Mbh. I.201.30). Thus music has been included here in the activities of enjoyment.

It is exactly on account of this pleasing nature of the music, that it came to be condemned. Thus Plato criticised the poets, who being ignorant of the laws of music produce whatever pleases the listener. The poets according to him deceive themselves into thinking that there is no right or wrong way of music—that it is to be judged good or bad by the pleasure it gives.[57] Nicet says, "We must chant as if we were in presence of god and not for pleasing the men".[58] In Rome, a number of anti-luxury laws were passed to restrict ostentatious performances and banquets in which music had a great role.[59] The early christians banished elements of profane joy from their chants.[60] There was also a rule that a composer who works for the church should not be a mixer of compositions which belong to the theatre.[61] According to the Padmapurāṇa VII.21.81 f., "A king who remains under the control of fools and women, one who always enjoys vocal and instrumental music, and one who is devoid of horses and chariots, is forcibly led to calamities. (...........*mūrkhastrīvijito rājā gītavādyarataḥ sadā // 81 // turaṅgavāhanair hīnaḥ sahasā vipadaṁ vrajet* // 82 //).

It seems thus that music becomes objectionable on account of its being a means of enjoyment. The attitude of renunciation or puritanism was possibly behind such a condemnation of music.

Another reason for music being prohibited was because of its sensuality[62] and its aphrodisiacal quality. The Gandharvas and Apsarases are notorious for their sexy behaviour (more deatils will be given elsewhere). A Gandharva uses the power of music for obtaining an Apsaras. Thus Ūrṇāyu Gandharva was desirous of Apsarases. He then saw the Aurṇāyava-sāman. He used to sing that sāman and obtain every Apsaras he liked (JB III.76). Similarly an old seer named Cyavana desired to be young and to get a young maiden as his wife. He saw then Cyāvana-Sāman, sang it and then his desire was fulfilled (JB III.120-128). The Kāmasūtra II.10.1.7, prescribes vocal and instrumental music with or without dance in the beginning of intercourse. It also prescribes among others, music after the intercourse (II.10.1.25). Even though, Pāṇḍu was avoiding intercourse (for he was cursed by a seer that he would die at the time of intercourse), one day there was erotic atmosphere and he was attracted towards his younger wife Mādrī. At that time among other aphrodisiacal elements there was sweet music in the form of the humming of the bees and crying of the cuckoo, being sung by the Gandharvas (*mattabhramara-saṁgītaṁ kokilasvaramiśritam / gāyamānaistu gandharvaiḥ purā nāgapure yathā //* Mbh.I.*1254). Devayānī was attracted towards Kaca because he used to please her by means of singing, dancing and instrumental music (Mbh. I.71.22). Mbh. I. *698 in this context comments: "Women love the man who is a singer, one of white complexion, a giver, sweet-tongued, of good appearance and wearing garlands (*gāyantaṁ caiva śuklaṁ ca dātāraṁ priyavādinam / nāryo naraṁ kāmayante rūpiṇaṁ sragviṇaṁ tathā*" //). Among the gāthās (verses) which are sung at the time of marriage (see Laugākṣisūtra, commentary of Devapāla on 25.19), the twentieth gāthā is uttered by Sarasvatī (goddess of speech), "I turn myself to gods. (We) (women) love the singers; for women like a singer and not one who recites vedic hymns (*abhyāvarte'haṁ devān gāyataḥ kāmayāmahe / gāyantaṁ striyaḥ kāmayante na tathā brahma-vādinam//*). This verse has its origin, probably, in a story from the Brāhmaṇa texts. Thus for obtaining Soma which was under the protection of Gandharvas, gods sent speech (*vāc*-fem.) in the form of a woman. "For the Gandharvas desire women". But after obtaining Soma, the speech went away from the Gandharvas. Then both the Gandharvas and gods tried to win her. The Gandharvas recited vedic hymns and the gods sang songs. The speech then went to gods and not to the Gandharvas. In this respect, the following comment is made, "Therefore a woman loves one who is singing and not one who is reciting a vedic hymn (*tasmād gāyantaṁ strī kāmayate na brahma vadantam* KS XIV. 1. KPKS XXXVII. 2., cp. MS III. 7.3; TS VI. 1.6.5; ŚB II. 2.4.6). Thus women like music and musicians. This liking, however, leads them sometimes to danger.[63] Sumitra Kautsa attracted Dīrghajihvī Āsurī by means of Saumitra sāman which was discovered by him and then Indra could kill her (TMB XIII. 6.9; JB I. 161 f). Women use music for seducing. RV VIII. 11.7, a *gir* (fem. song) is considered to be a woman and it is hoped that she will seduce and bring Agni towards the singer named Vatsa. An Apasaras named Varcasā wanted to seduce a Brāhmaṇa. She, then, along with her friends sang songs (Skandapur. Māhe. Kaumā. I. 36). Flute has always been considered in many parts of the world as a sexual instrument. At the temples of Serapis at Canobus, there used to be recitals of flute and reed-pipe accompanied by dancing and extreme licentiousness.[64] Among Jews, the flute named *ugab* signified passion-exciting effect and it was banned in the god-worship.[65]

The ancient vedic texts connected with the Sāmaveda and music sometimes teach the philosophy of sexuality. Thus JB III.352 says, "To nobody women are non-desirable (*na hi kasyacana striyo'priyāḥ*)". Similarly Chāndogyopaniṣad II.13.2 says, "Let him avoid no woman; that is a vow (*na kāñcana pariharet tad vratam*").

It is likely that those who preached renunciation or were puritan, they might have condemned music, taking into account the above mentioned aphrodisiacal character of music.

Another likely reason for the condemnation of music may be sought in its connection with women and in the belief that music effeminates[66] a man. Women perform music in the Mahāvrata-ceremony which is a part of the vedic sacrificial session. Thus when in that ceremony, the Udgātṛ sings the Rājana-Sāman, the wives of the sacrificers accompany that chant by playing on Apaghāṭilās (a musical instrument) (TMB V. 6.8; Cp. Lāṭyāśs IV. 2.5-7; Drāhyāśs XI. 2.6-8; Satyāśs XVI. 6.21; Māśs VII. 2.7.8). AV VIII.6.11, the evil beings who destroy embryos are described as "dancing like eunuchs (*klībā iva pranṛtyantaḥ*)". It is well-known that Arjuna lived in the house of the king Virāṭa in the disguise of a eunuch and taught vocal and instrumental music as well as dance to the ladies there (cp. Mbh. IV. 2.24: *gītaṁ nṛttaṁ vicitraṁ ca vāditraṁ vividhaṁ tathā / śikṣayiṣyāmyahaṁ rājan virāṭabhavane striyaḥ //*). It is remarkable that the god Śiva (Rudra) who is closely connected with music is sometimes regarded as hermaphrodite (*ardhanārīnaṭeśvara*). According to Didorus Egyptians did not like to practise music because they considered that it effeminates a man.[67]

A further reason explaining why music and musicians are criticised and looked down is perhaps that the musicians are at many times supposed to be no more than bards who praise the great deeds (either real or imaginary) of their lords. Thus they are no more than beggars or parasites. They praise their lords and obtain their livelihood thereby. Very often these poet-singers express their poverty and desire for getting wealth. Thus ṚV VII. 32.18, a poet-singer says to Indra, "If, O Indra, I were to be the possessor of so much as you possess, I would have given it to a praise-singer". Similar expressions are found elsewhere also. Thus ṚV VIII.19.25 f a poet-singer says, "If O Agni, I were you ...... then my praise-singer would not be poor and suffering;" or ṚV VIII.44.23 we read, "If I were you, O Agni, and you I, your aspirations would have been effective."

The poet-singers often request the gods to help them. Thus ṚV VIII.44.22, Agni is requested to favour the singer. Elsewhere Indra is addressed in the following manner, "The Gotamas have cried by means of their song (*gir*-) so that you may give them an impatiently expected gift (ṚV IV. 32.9). ṚV I.116.26, the poet-singer after having sung the wonderful activities of Aśvins, makes numerous demands as follows: "I have described your masterpieces; and now I shall be a lord with good cattle and heroic progeny. Seeing and winning long life may I become old" (cp. I.117.25). The praise-hymns (stoma -) are also described as "begging (*vanīvānāḥ*)" (ṚV X. 47.7). Those who win Indra's favour by means of praise - songs are said to be "great (*bṛhataḥ*)" (ṚV II. 11.16). Indra has proved himself to be effective for the reciters and singers. (ṚV VIII.62.12). He makes good luck for the praise - singers (ṚV

VIII.14.11). ṚV X. 112.1, the poet-singers say to Indra, "We shall sing loudly your activities of valour by means of praise-songs". Indra's greatness (ṚV VIII.46.3) or valour (VIII. 54.1) is praise-sung by the poet singers through songs. ṚV VIII. 32.1, the poet-singers are requested to sing the deeds of Indra by means of sung verses (*gāthā-*). It is under the care of Indra that the "praise-song-singers (*ukthaśāsaḥ*)" sing the praise-songs (ṚV VII. 19.9).

Thus there seems to be a relation like that of a king and protégé between the god and his devotee-singer. The singers sometimes sing the noble and valorous deeds of human kings also. Thus in the Aśvamedha-sacrifice, after the horse has been let loose for a year, everyday two singers sing in the morning and in the evening. Out of them one is a Brāhmaṇa and he sings, "Thus he (the king) sacrificed; thus he gave". The other singer who belongs to the warrior class, praises the king by singing, "Thus he fought, thus he won that battle" (ŚB XIII. 1.5.6; Māśs IX. 2.2.7). After the sacrifice is over gifts are given to these bards (Māśs IX. 2.2.12). In this way the singers had to sing the praises of the kings etc. in order to get their livelihood and were parasites as it were. "As all beings live having taken support of the mother, similarly all the beings live, being supported by the house-holders (Mbh. XIII. app. I. 15.836; see further for details). In the list of various kinds of persons who are said to be depending on the householders for the sake of their livelihood, among many others, the persons belonging to the theatre (*raṅgopajīvinaḥ*) and knowers of all crafts (*sarvaśilpajñāḥ*) are mentioned and the musicians may be supposed to be included in the two (for the word *śilpa* meaning music see KB XXIX. 5: Śilpa, verily is three-fold viz. dance, singing and instrumental music—*trivṛd vai śilpaṁ nṛtyaṁ gītaṁ vāditram iti*)". According to Mbh. XIII. app. I. 15.2007 ff, the men who are very egoistic and selfish, they become, in their next birth, parasite-like and depend upon others for their livelihood. Among such parasite-like persons actors and singers are mentioned (*ye purā manujā devi stabdhā mānayutā bhṛśaṁ* /2007/ *darpāhaṅkārasaṁyuktāḥ kevalātmaparāyaṇāḥ* / 8/ *tādṛśā manujā devi punarjanmani śobhane* / 9 / *kāravo naṭagandharvāḥ sambhavanti yathā tathā* / 10 / *nāpitā bandinaścaiva tathā vaitālikāḥ priye* / 11 / *evaṁbhūtāstvadhovṛttiṁ jīvantyāśritya mānavāḥ* / 12 / *paraprasādanakarāste paraiḥ kṛtavetanāḥ* / 13 / *parāvamānasya phalaṁ bhuñjate paurvadehikam* / 2014 /). The professional bard (*māgadha*-) is said to be born in the ladle while the sāman-singers were singing in the sacrifice being performed by the king Pṛthu. Afterwards the Sūta and Māgadha praised the king Pṛthu (Vāyupurāṇa 62.137 ff).

From this we are able to know what was the position of the musicians in the society. They were considered as dependents, parasites, beggars etc. Devayānī felt very much insulted when Śarmiṣṭhā, daughter of the Daitya King named Vṛṣaparvan described Devayānī's father, Śukrācārya as a singer (*gāyana* -) of praises of Daityas. Devayānī narrated this incident before her father. She further reported the very insulting words uttered by Śarmiṣṭhā. Thus Śarmiṣṭhā had said to Devayānī, "You are the daughter of a praiser, beggar and receiver; while I am the daughter of one who is being praised, who is a giver, and not a receiver". (Mbh. I. 73.30 ff:) Devayānī says to Śukra—*śarmiṣṭhayā yaduktāsmi duhitrā vṛṣaparvaṇaḥ* / *satyaṁ kilaitat sā prāha daityānāmasi gāyanaḥ* // 30 // *evaṁ hi me kathayati śarmiṣṭhā vārṣaparvaṇī* / *vacanaṁ tīkṣṇaparuṣaṁ krodharaktekṣaṇā bhṛśam* // 31 // *stuvato duhitā hi tvaṁ yācataḥ pratigṛhṇataḥ* / *sutāhaṁ stūyamānasya dadato'pratigṛhṇataḥ* // 32 // The society of early days condemned the profession of musicians. This tendency is found in countries other than India also. Thus in Rome society was shocked not by Nero's appearance as a musician but by his pose of being a professional artist.[68]

We have detailed a few reasons explaining why music and musicians were condemned or looked down upon. But we have earlier seen that music and musicians are sometimes valued and honoured also. Therefore, the above given reasons do not and cannot fully explain the social position of music and musicians. We have now to seek the very cause of the social position of music and musicians. The antipathy towards the music, thus cannot be explained by saying that it was due to the supposition that music was a part of enjoyment, or that the musicians behaved liecenciously or immorally or that they were like parasites or that music effeminates etc.

We can explain their social position when we take into account that music and musicians are of double nature (*dvisvabhāva*-). Because they are double-natured they receive the double treatment. Music is sometimes considered to be pure and auspicious, and sometimes as impure and inauspicious. Sometimes it is considered to be an offensive arm and sometimes to be a defensive one.[69] "Telle autre musique nous oppresse telle autre nous fortifie".[70] It sometimes attracts the dead, sometimes removes them.[71] "La musique est capable poster l'homme aux pires actions comme aux meilleures".[72] According to Plotin, music leads sometimes to good and sometimes to bad.[73] Music is connected with fertility as well as sterility. It is connected with procreation as well as with death. Thus the Ājyadoha-sāmans are connected with death and procreation. Prajāpati devoured the creatures by means of the Ājyadoha-sāman with ī as finale. He then caused them to procreate by means of the Ājyadoha-sāman with triple finale. "Through these sāmans, death here (on the earth) devours the creatures and makes them procreate" (TMB XXI.2.1). The Udgātṛ (sāman-singer-priest) is both beneficent and maleficent. "Whoso (sacrificer) by sacrificial gifts conciliates the Udgātṛ, unto him, the stream (in the form of speech) runs and whoso does not conciliate him, he drives it (stream) away". (JUB I.18.3.5). The metre Anuṣṭubh is said to be identical with truth and untruth (*satyānṛte vā anuṣṭubh* TB I. 7.10.7). The calling of *śrauṣaṭ* can give good or bad results according to the modes of its utterance (ŚB XI. 4.2.5 ff). Thus the music and musicians sometimes lead to profit and sometimes to loss. Thus they seem to be double-natured. Therefore, naturally they receive double treatment. Sometimes they are honoured and sometimes condemned.

Let us delve into some more details of the double nature of music.

Music is sometimes considered to be a pure and sometimes to be an impure substance. Thus ṚV VIII. 95.7, the poet singer says, "Let us praise Indra, the pure (*śuddha* -) with the pure (*śuddhena*) sāman; him who grows powerful by means of pure praise-songs (*uktha* -)". Elsewhere, a poet offers a purified (*pūta* -) praise-hymn (*stoma* -) to Indra. The poet-singers are sometimes very alert in making their songs pure. Thus, ṚV IX. 2.7, Soma is informed, " The songs (*gir* -) are being purified (*marmṛjyante*) by means of your power. In the Caraṇavyūha IV, Sāmaveda is described to be a man with clean garments as it were (*sucivasāḥ*). Mbh. V.44.21, the sāmans are mentioned to be stainless (*amala* -).

The music is supposed to be a means of purification also.[74] Thus ṚV IX. 29.2, it is said, "The poets purify (*mṛjanti*) the horse (i.e. Soma) by means of a song (*gir*-)". Music is, further, often used for purification from any sin or guilt. Thus ṚV I. 185.8, the poet-singer says, "May this visionic poem (*dhī* -) be an apology for whatever sin (*abhva* -) we have committed against the gods, friend or houselord". For the sake of removing the sin of all sorts, one gets help of music along with that of plants etc. Thus we read in AV X.1.12 f, "From the sin against the fathers, from name taking, that is designed, that is devised against (any one), let the plants, free thee by their valour, with the powerful formula (*brahman*-) with the milk of the seers (12). As the wind sets in motion the dust from the earth and the cloud from the atmosphere, so from me may everything of evil nature go away, pushed by the powerful formula (*brahman*-). (13)". Once gods after having killed the Asuras felt impure and unworthy of sacrifice as it were. They desired to be pure and worthy of sacrifice. Then they saw the Saumedha-sāman praised with it and got their desire fulfilled. The Saumedha-sāman is thus helpful for purification (JB I. 227). On another occasion, gods, after having killed the

Asuras, felt impure as it were. They desired to be pure and discovered the Sauhaviṣa-sāman. They became pure after having sung this sāman (JB. III. 196). Similarly, at another time, Indra felt impure as it were after having killed the Asuras. Then Indra desired, "May they (the seers) praise-sing me, the pure (as it were) with a pure sāman". He then asked the seers to praise-sing him in the desired way. The seers discovered the Śuddhāśuddhīya sāman and praise-sang him. Then Indra became pure (JB. III. 288). Indra, according to another story, gave the Yatis over to the hyenas. An inauspicious voice reproached him and he deemed himself impure. He saw the Śuddhāśuddhīya-sāmans and purified himself. (TMB XIX.4.7 f; cp. XIV. 11.29). Similarly, Indra, after having killed the son of Tvaṣṭṛ purified himself by means of the stomas that are used in the Agniṣṭut-sacrifice (TMB XVII. 5.1 ff).

Sāmavidhānabrāhmaṇa (V. 1 ff) prescribes various formulas from the Sāmaveda to be used in expiations to be performed for removing various sins.

Sāmans are often prescribed by the Dharmasūtras and Smṛti-texts in the expiation-rites for being purified from sins. Thus Baudhāyanadharmasūtra III.10.9 f, among various means of removing sins, the following sāmans are mentioned: Rājana, Rauhiṇa, Bṛhat, Rathantara, Mahāvairāja, Mahādivākīrtya and Jyeṣṭha-sāman. Similarly, recitations of the Vedic texts in general and of the Puruṣasūkta (ṚV X. 90), Bahiṣpavamāna-chant, Kūṣmāṇḍī-verses, Pāvamānī-verses and Sāvitrī-verses, in particular are prescribed (*tasya pāpasya) niṣkrayaṇāni japastapo homo upavāso dānam* / 9 / *upaniṣado vedādayo vedāntaḥ sarvachandaḥsu saṁhitā madhūnyaghamarṣaṇamatharvaśiro rudrāḥ puruṣasūktaṁ rājanarauhiṇe sāmānī bṛhadrathantare puruṣagatir mahānāmnyo mahāvairājaṁ mahādivākirtyaṁ jyeṣṭhasāmnām anyatamaṁ bahiṣpavamānaṁ kūṣmāṇḍyaḥ pāvamānyaḥ sāvitrī ceti pāvanāni* / 10 / cp. Gautamadharmasūtra III. 1.12—*upaniṣado vedāntaḥ saṁhitā madhūnyaghamarṣaṇamatharvaśiro rudrāḥ puruṣasūktaṁ rājanarauhiṇau sāmānī bṛhadrathantare puruṣagatir mahānāmnyo mahāvairājyaṁ mahādivākīrtyaṁ jyeṣṭhasāmnāmanyatamad bahiṣpavamānaṁ kūṣmāṇḍāni pāvamānyaḥ sāvitrī ceti pāvamānāni* cp. also Śaṅkhasmṛti XI. 1 ff—*aghamārṣaṇaṁ devakṛtaṁ śuddhavatyas taratsamāḥ / kūṣmāṇḍyaḥ pāvamānyaśca sāvitryaśca tathaiva ca* // 1 // *tryabhiṣṭvaṁ drupadā caiva stomāni vyāhṛtīstathā / bhāruṇḍāni ca sāmāni gāyatrī cauśanaṁ tathā* // 2 // *puruṣavrataṁ ca bhāṣaṁ ca tathā somavratāni ca / abliṅgaṁ bārhaspatyaṁ ca vāksūktamamṛtaṁ tathā* // 3 // *śatarudrīyamatharvaśirastrisuparṇaṁ mahāvratam / gosūktamaśvasūktaṁ ca indrasūktaṁ ca sāmānī* // 4 // *trīṇyājyadohāni rathantaraṁ ca agnivrataṁ vāmadevavrataṁ ca / etāni gītāni punanti jantūñ jātismaratvaṁ labhate yaddīcchet* // 5 // cp. also Vasiṣṭhasmṛti XXVIII. 10 ff: *sarvavedapavitrāṇi vakṣyāmyahamataḥparam / yeṣāṁ japaiśca homaiśca pūyante nātra saṁśayaḥ* // 10 // *aghamarṣaṇaṁ devakṛtaṁ śuddhavatyastaratsamāḥ / kūṣmāṇḍāni pāvamānyo durgāḥ sāvitrireva ca* // 11 // *abhīṣaṅgāḥ padastomā sāmāni vyāhṛtīstathā / bhāruṇḍāni ca sāmāni gāyatraṁ raivataṁ tathā* // 12 // *puruṣavrataṁ nyāsaṁ ca tathā devavratāni ca / abliṅgaṁ bārhaspatyaṁ ca vāksūktaṁ madhvṛcastathā* // 13 // *śatarudrīyamatharvaśirastrisuparṇaṁ mahāvratam / goṣūktaṁ cāśvasūktaṁ ca śuddhaḥ śuddheti sāmanī* // 14 // *trīṇyājyadohāni rathantaraṁ ca agnervrataṁ vāmadevyaṁ bṛhacca / etāni japtāni punanti jantūñ jātismaratvaṁ labhate yadīcchet* // 15 // for the last verse see also Viṣṇusmṛti 56.27).

Sometimes the Cāndrāyaṇavrata is prescribed as an expiation of sins. In this Vrata, one eats fourteen morsels on the first day of the black fortnight of a month and reduces one morsel every day. In the following bright fortnight, one increases one morsel every day. In this Cāndrāyaṇavrata singing of sāmans and uttering of vyāhṛtis (sacred utterances viz. *bhūḥ, bhuvaḥ svaḥ*) occupy some place. This is a general expiation for any sin (Vasiṣṭhasmṛti XXIII. 39 ff:—*atha cāndrāyaṇavidhiḥ* //39// *māsasya kṛṣṇapakṣādau grāsānadyāccaturdaśa / grāsāpacayabhojī syāt pakṣaśeṣaṁ samāpayet* // 40 // *evaṁ hi śuklapakṣādau grāsamekaṁ tu bhakṣayet / grāsopacayabhojī syat pakṣaśeṣaṁ samāpayet* // 41 // *atraiva gāyet sāmāni api vā vyāhṛtīr japet / eṣa cāndrāyaṇo māsaḥ pavitramṛṣisaṁstutaḥ // 42 // anādiṣṭeṣu sarveṣu prāyaścittaṁ vidhīyate vidhīyate iti // 43 //*). Śātātapasmṛti II.16 prescribes the recital of the sāmans as an expiation for one who has become leprous. According to Manusmṛti XI. 262, one becomes free from all the sins by reciting the Ṛgveda or Yajurveda or Sāmaveda. The recital of the individual sāmans like Vāmadevya or Bṛhat is to be done for the same reason (Saṁvartasmṛti 228). Thus sāmans are connected with purification from sins.

Bad fame is supposed to be like dirt attached to the body. So one has to remove that dirt and be purified. In order to be purified from the bad fame, the morning recital in the course of the Agniṣṭoma - sacrifice, is useful. Thus "if the sacrificer who is being called 'not a brāhmaṇa' (due to his wrong behaviour) or is ill spoken of and being seized with defilement, performs a sacrifice, the hotṛ should recite eight hundred verses in the morning recital of the Agniṣṭoma sacrifice. For the Gāyatrī has eight syllables; by means of the Gāyatrī, the gods smote away the evil, the defilement; verily thus by the Gāyatrī, he smites away the evil, the defilement" (AB II. 17).

Singers are sometimes described to be pure. Thus ṚV VIII. 3.3 we read, "the bright, pure (*śuci* -), knowing priests have sung the praise-hymns together". Elsewhere, it is said, "(O Indra), when the praise-singer dedicates the praise-song (*uktha* -) at the proper time, he is called clear, pure (*śuci*-), wonderful" (ṚV VIII.13.19).

One sings songs and purifies soma (ṚV IX. 96.15). According to ṚV IX. 29.2, "The poet-singers purify the horse (= soma) by means of the songs".

Sometimes, however, music is supposed to be impure. According to JUB I.18.2.2, Ṛc assuming that Sāman is impure, asked it to purify itself. According to Mārkaṇḍeyapurāṇa " Brahmā, at the time of creating the world, consists of Ṛcs; Viṣṇu, at the time of its preservation, consists of Yajus; and Rudra at its end consists of Sāmans; Therefore, its sound is impure (*visṛṣṭau ṛṅmayo brahmā sthitau viṣṇur yajurmayaḥ /*

rudraḥ sāmamayo'nte ca tasmāt tasyāśucir dhvaniḥ 99.19). The sound of music is impure also because manes are the deity of the Sāmaveda (Manusmṛti IV.124). The metres are said to be dirty (*malātmaka* -) and born out of the sweat of Prajāpati (*svedācchando malātmakam* Mbh. XIII. 85.19). The gāthās (sung verses) are also considered as something impure. Gods, in order to deceive the Asuras mixed the vedic lore with the gāthās. And thus when the vedas had become impure, the Asuras left them. The gods then took the vedas and made them pure again (JB. III. 41). TB I.3.2.6 describes the gāthānārāśaṁsīs as the impure part of the vedas. Thus when the gods removed the impure part of the vedas, that became the gāthānārāśaṁsī.

It is, however, interesting to note that sometimes *gāthā* becomes the means of purification. Thus JUB I. 17.1.9 the Ṛc is said to have purified itself by means of *gāthā* (cp. I. 18.2.1).

Music is sometimes considered to be auspicious and sometimes inauspicious.

In the Aśvamedha sacrifice after the horse is let loose for one year, everyday lute-players play upon the lute and praisesing the heroic and generous activities of the sacrificing king. In this context, the following remark is made: "The lute verily, is a form of glory ... when a man obtains glory, lute is played on for him (*śriyā vā etad rūpaṁ yad vīṇā ... yadā khalu vai puruṣaḥ śriyamaśnute vīṇāsmai vādyate*" TB III.9.14.1). The most auspicious goddess Lakṣmī says to the Earth - goddess "I live in the sound of musical instruments" (Viṣṇusmṛti 99.15). The noise of sāman-singers is described as auspicious (*śubha*-) by Mbh. XIII.14.35.

Music is considered to be a good omen at the time of going out. Thus at the time of going if there are sounds of vocal music that must be regarded as helpful for the success of the intended work (*śubhā gītādiśabdāḥ syur īdṛśaṁ syāddhi siddhaye*/ Agnipurāṇa 294.37). Viṣṇusmṛti mentions among other good omens, lute also (*Vīṇācandanāyudhārdragomayaphala-puṣpārdraśākagorocanādūrvāprarohāṁśca* 63.31, cp. 39: *vīṇā-candanārdraśākoṣṇīṣālaṅkaraṇakumārīstu prasthānakāle 'bhinandayediti*). Sounds of other musical instruments like bell, conchshell, flute, drum etc. are also mentioned to be auspicious by the Mārkaṇḍeyasmṛti (*ghaṇṭāśabdaḥ śaṅkhaśabdaḥ veṇuvīṇādisusvaraḥ / tūryaśabdo gītaśabdaḥ tālasvastika-vaiṇavāḥ / bherīmṛdaṅgapaḍahadhakkaḍiṇḍimasaṁbhavāḥ*).

Mbh. V.40.9 f, we get a list of auspicious things which should be kept in the house and may be used in paying honour to the gods and brāhmaṇas or to guests. Among them lute and conchshell are mentioned (*ajokṣā candanaṁ vīṇā ādarśo madhusarpiṣī / viṣamaudumbaraṁ śaṅkhaḥ svarṇaṁ nābhiśca rocanā // 9 // gṛhe sthāpayitavyāni dhanyāni manurabravīt / devabrāhmaṇapūjārtham atithīnāṁ ca bhārata //* 10 //).

Music is considered to be inauspicious also.

One can appease the bad omen particularly that of the noise of an inauspicious bird by muttering a verse (ṚV II. 43.2) in which the bird is described to be singing a sāman like Udgātṛ as it were (Satyāśs XIX. 5.19). From this it seems that sometimes the noise of the singers of sāmans was considered to be inauspicious.

As regards the social order, harmony etc. also music is supposed to have two fold function. Thus it is supposed to be bringing about quarrels or to be harmful to social order and morality. But it is also used for appeasing quarrels, and bringing social harmony, order etc. We have detailed earlier how musicians are supposed to be like bards, protégés and parasites. Closely associated with this is the idea of rivalry among musicians. Hesiode[75] describes Greece of the eighth century B.C. that it was a land "where beggar bears spite to beggar and bard to bard". In the Veda also we find that the poet-singers compete with each other in order to win the favour of gods. Thus a poet-singer says to Indra, "May our praise-hymn (*stoma* -) be the best carrier (of gods), be the nearest to you" (ṚV VI.45.30). ṚV VII. 25.2, another poet-singer requests Indra, "Keep aside the song (*śaṁsa* -) of one who blames us". Similarly, ṚV VIII. 1.3, one says, "Even though these people from different sides, invoke you for favour, still, may *this* our powerful hymn (*brahman*-) be strengthening one to you, Indra, for all the days". Another poet-singer is so confident about his power of songs that he says, "So many seers have praised you and others have not praised you; grow powerful only when being praised by me (ṚV. VII. 6.12, cp. 18). In the war of the ten kings priests of both the parties used the power of musical praise-songs and tried to win the favour of gods to the side of their patrons. Thus we read at ṚV. VII. 83.4, "The priesthood of Tṛtsus proved to be effective" (cp. VII. 83.6; 85.2). The morning - pressing in a soma - sacrifice is said to be gāyatra i.e. belonging to the Gāyatrī-metre. But it is a fact that other metres also are used at the time of this pressing. So fear of quarrel is expressed in the following way: "They make a quarrel as it were for the metres; for all the metres are sung in the morning pressing which really speaking, belongs to Gāyatrī. Then the offsprings will be of quarreling nature". (JB I.103). The quarrel between the catholic masses and protestant masses was increased by the cantics.[76]

Thus we know that music can create quarrels and is connected with rivalry.[77]

Music can, however, also be useful in bringing harmony among the people who have quarreled with each other. Thus the ṚV X.191 is traditionally known as *saṁjñāna-sūkta* (a hymn that effectuates mutual understanding and concord of mind). A priest can use this hymn and create harmony among quarrelsome people. Music is useful for social order. Among the Chinese people, there was a belief that music, if rightly employed, is conductive to good government.[78] Ancient Chinese kings knew the power of music and while prescribing the rules about it, they wanted to make their people just.[79] The Pythagorians considered that the man instructed since his childhood, the sacred rules of music, will approve the good, disapprove the bad, will not stain himself ever with any dishonest action, will show himself always useful to his country, will not injure the social harmony either by his actions or through his speech.[80] The following proclamation of Celine indicates the power of music in social order and laws: "Donnez moi le privilege d'écrir les chanson d'un peuple, et je serai bien au-dessus de celui qui fait les lois".[81] Milton says that music has a great power over disposition and manners to smoothen and make them gentle from rustic harshness and distempered passions.[82] In the mediaeval period, music was supposed to build a step on the way to reach the good.[83] One was not only expected to think in accordance with the song; but also behave in accordance with it. Thus Ivo Comotens says, "What you sing with mouth, believe in it with the heart; and what you believe in with your heart, prove it through your work". (*Decret* IV. 9).[84]

Thus we find that music is supposed to lead to social disorder as well as order; to the worst as well as best actions.[85] Thus it was supposed to be doublenatured.

Music is closely connected with Vrātyas, Rudra and Varuṇa and they are of double nature. A study of their connection with music illustrate the double nature of music.

The Vrātyas who are at times glorified (see e.g. AV XV) and sometimes looked down (cf. e.g. Manusmṛti 2.39) are connected with music. They used to be accompanied by persons who performed their ceremonies along with songs and dance.[86] AV XV. 3 and 4, Vrātya is described as a mythical priest-singer. The first Vrātyastoma-sacrifice is for those Vrātyas who are connected with music (cf. Kātyāśs XXII. 4.2: *Vrātyagaṇasya ye sampādayeyus te prathamena yajeran.* The commentary of Karka on this is as follows: *Sampādanaṁ ca gāyananartakādīnām*). Kauṣītaka Sāmaśravasa was a Vrātya and he occupied the post of the household (*gṛhapati*-) at the time of a performance of the fourth Vrātyastoma-sacrifice (TMB XVII. 4.3). The sāmans, it is said, move according to the movements of Vrātya (AV XV.2). Thus when he went eastwards, Bṛhat and Rathantara followed him (2); southwards, Yajñāyajñiya and Vāmadeva (10); westwards Vairūpa and Vairāja (16); and northwards, Śyeta and Naudhasa-sāmans followed him.

The Vrātyas are often associated with Māgadha,[87] (a person belonging to Magadha-country) (cp. e.g. AV XV.2.5; 13; 19 etc.). The dakṣiṇās (gifts) of the Vrātyastoma-sacrifice which are nothing but the various characteristic possessions of the Vrātyas (*Vrātyadhana*) are to be given to a māgadhadeśīya i.e. according to the Commentary (1) either not a very good singer (2) or one belonging to the Magadha-country (cf. Lāṭyāśs VIII. 6.28 Commentary). According to the Vāyupurāṇa 62.137 f, a māgadha sūta (bard) was born in the sacrificial ladle while singers of sāmans were singing in the course of a sacrifice being performed by Pṛthu.

Music is often connected with Rudra. Now, Rudra in Vedic, epic and classical periods, is well-known for his double-nature. He brings diseases - he is himself disease - and he cures diseases.[88] He is the best physician among the physicians. He presides over death; he presides over generation of beings and fertility in general. His very names Rudra (which denotes the terrible aspect) and Śiva (which denotes the auspicious aspect) quite indicate his double nature. So the connection of music with double-natured Rudra is very significant in explaining the double-natured music.

This Lord loves music (cf. Skandapur. Māhe. Kaumā. 11.10). He knows the principles of vocal and instrumental music, and vocal and instrumental music is dear to him (*gītavāditratattvajño gītavādanakapriyaḥ* Mbh. XII. app. I. 28.279). One of his thousand names is *nṛtyapriya* (to whom dance is dear; Mbh. XIII.17.49). Because he likes the vocal and instrumental music, it is to be performed in his worship. (*tasmāttataṁ ca vitataṁ ghanaṁ suṣirameva ca cāmarāṇi mahārhāṇi mañcakāḥ śayanāni ca* //103// *gāthāśca itihāsaśca gāyanaṁ ca yathāvidhi/ bahurūpādikaṁ śaṁbhoḥ priyāṇyetāni kalpayet* // 104 // Skandapur. Māhe. Kedāra. 5.103 f). Among his thousand names there are some which indicate that he possesses numerous musical instruments (cp. *vaiṇavī paṇavī tali* Mbh. XIII. 17.56; *sarvatūryaninādī ca sarvavādyaparigrahaḥ* 59; further, in 96 he is named as Tumbavīṇī and in 97 his following names are mentioned—*vaṁśakaraḥ, vaṁśaḥ, vaṁśanādaḥ*). Some other names indicate that he is a dancer (*nityanarta, nartaka, sarvalāsaka,* Mbh. XIII.17.49; *mahānarta* 114). Elsewhere, he is mentioned to be a singer, instrument-player and dancer (*hasate gāyate caiva nṛtyate sumanoharam* / 56 / *vādayatyapi vādyāni vicitrāṇi gaṇairvṛtaḥ* / 57 / .... *vādako gāyanaścaiva sahasraśatalocanaḥ* / 74 / Mbh. XIII. app. I. 4.56 f. and 74; cp. Vāyupurāṇa 24.142 f: .... *namo'stu nṛtyaśīlāya vādyanṛtyapriyāya ca* // 142 // *manyave gītaśīlāya sugītaṁ gāyate namaḥ* / .... // 143 //). The family of Śiva according to Nārada who is describing him before the mountain Himālaya is nothing but the "sound (*nāda*-); he is established on the sound and the sound is established on him (*asya gotraṁ kulaṁ caiva nāda eva paraṁ gire / nāde pratiṣṭhitaḥ śambhur nādo hyasmin pratiṣṭhitaḥ* // Skandapur. Māhe. Kedāra. 25.72). The speech (*vāc*-) is connected with Rudra. She says, "I stretch the bow for Rudra (*ahaṁ rudrāya dhanurātanomi*" (ṚV X.125.6).

Because he loves music, he is always surrounded by the divine musicians viz. Gandharvas and Apsarases and praised by them (see e.g. Mbh. XIII. 15.25: *gandharvāpsarasaścaiva gītavāditrakovidāḥ / divyatānena gāyantaḥ stuvanti bhavamadbhutam* //). His other associates who are equal to him in valour and surround him are also singers and dancers (Mbh.XIII.14.118: *gāyadbhir nṛtyamānaiś ca utpadadbhiritastataḥ / vṛtaṁ pāriṣadair divyairātmatulyaparākramaiḥ* //). Those who sing praises in honour of him or dance for him, their evils go away (Skandapur. Māhe. Aruṇā. II. 45) and they get salvation (Padmapur. I.34.22).

The Sāmaveda as a whole and the individual sāmans are said to be connected with Rudra. Thus according to the Caraṇavyūha IV, the deity of the Sāmaveda is Rudra. Elsewhere it is said that at the time of creating the world Brahmā consists of Ṛcs; while maintaining it, Viṣṇu consists of Yajus and at the end of it Rudra consists of Sāmans; therefore the sound of sāmans is inauspicious (Viṣṇupur. II.11.13; Mārkaṇḍeyapur. 99.19). Upamanyu praises Rudra by saying, "Among the vedas you are the Sāmaveda (Mbh. XIII. 15.159). Mbh. XIII. 77.88, Rudra is described as Sāmāsya (one, whose mouth is sāmans). He likes sāmans very much and is, therefore, called Sāmapriya (Skandapur. Māhe. Aruṇā. 9.7). Other gods praise him with sāmans. Thus according to the Mbh.

XIII. 14.147, Brahmā praised him with Rathantarasāman and Nārāyaṇa with Jyeṣṭha-sāman. Elsewhere gods like Indra, Viṣṇu, Sūrya and Brahmā are said to be singing Rathantara-sāman in honour of Rudra (Mbh. XIII. 15.16). In the marriage of Śiva and Pārvatī, Hāhā, Hūhū, Tumbaru and Nārada sang sāmans (Skandapur. Māhe. Kaumārikā. 26.54).

In the vedic ritual Rudra had a very little place and whatever little he had was rather left-handed one. But still, in the epical, henoistic style Rudra tells to his wife, "In any sacrifice, it is to me that all that reciters praise; to me the sāman-singers praise-sing with Rathantara-sāman (Mbh. XII. app. I. 28.61 f; Vāyupur. 30.112). Similarly, the sacrifice of Dakṣa was ruined because he had not invited Rudra. Dakṣa pacified Rudra by praising him. In that praise it is mentioned that the sacrificial singers sing for Rudra and Rudra himself is a singer, dancer and player on instruments (Mbh. XII. app- I. 28.168 ff—*gāyanti tvā gāyatriṇo arcantyarkamarkiṇaḥ* / 168 / ..... *namo nartanaśīlāya mukhavāditravādine* / 198 / *nādyopahāralubdhāya gītavāditraśāline* / 199 / ..... *hāyihāyi huvāhāyi hāvu hāyi tathāsakṛt* / 263 / *gāyanti tvāṁ suraśreṣṭhā sāmagā brahmavādinaḥ* / 264 / cp. also Vāyupur. 30.184; 198 f; 229 f; 248). Not only the sāman-singing but the recitations of Ṛcs and Yajus are also mystically supposed to be in honour of him (*ṛgbhir yamanuśaṁsanti tantre karmaṇi bahvṛcāḥ / yajurbhir yaṁ tridhā vedyāṁ juhvatyadhvaryavo' dhvare // 48 // sāmabhir yaṁ ca gāyanti sāmagāḥ śuddhabuddhayaḥ / yajñasya paramā yoniḥ patiścāyaṁ paraḥ smṛtaḥ // 49 //* Mbh. XIII. 16.48 f).

Thus even though in epics and purāṇas, all the sāmans are henoistically attributed to Rudra only, it is a curious fact that in the Vedic ritual itself, there is no sāman in praise of Rudra.[89] In the ṚV, however, sometimes we get the reference to the praise-songs in honour of Rudra. ṚV I. 43.1, the poet-singers are asking of themselves, "What shall we speak about Rudra that will be the most pleasant to his heart"? ṚV I. 114.11, it is hoped, "May Rudra listen to our call". Elsewhere a poet-singer declares, "I praise you (O Rudra) giver of many things" (ṚV II. 33.12). He is requested to show favour unto the singer after having been praised (ṚV II. 33.11). One asks some other person to praise Rudra (ṚV V. 42.11) to sing for him (ṚV X. 92.9), to make him grow powerful by means of songs (ṚV VI. 49.10, or bring a song for him (ṚV VII. 46.1). ṚV II. 11.3, the praise - songs (*uktha*-) and praisehymns (*stoma*-) are said to be "Rudrīya—(belonging to Rudra)". We also get references to him as singing a sāman. Thus the Jarābohīya-sāman is described as belonging to Rudra. By means of it, he became the lord of cattle. But because it has thus some connection with Rudra, who is regarded to be terrible, this sāman is also described to be cruel and unpacified (*krūra-aśānta*-) But this sāman is actually in praise of Aśvins. Now the sāman which praises Aśvins, is according to the Brāhmaṇa-texts identical with the whole speech; the brahman. "Therefore, one pacifies it thus with the whole speech, the brahman which is belonging to Aśvins (JB. III.11). Antipathy to Rudra at the time of sāman-singing is observed elsewhere. Thus the Vāmadevya-sāman is asked to be sung in an " unexpressed (*anirukta* -)" manner. This is explained by the following story—When gods divided the cattle among themselves, they excluded Rudra. He, became angry and planned to kill the cattle, fixed his eyes on the cattle during the Vāmadevyasāman; for Vāmadevya is identical with cattle (TMB IV. 8.15). Therefore it is to be sung unexpressedly. If it were sung expressedly the cattle would be delivered to Rudra. Rudra would then slay the cattle during the same year (TMB VII. 9.16).

Thus we see that music and Rudra are connected with each other in two ways. Sometimes in favour of each other and sometimes in opposition to each other. The duality of the nature of Rudra also must have contributed to the double nature of music. Since Rudra is sometimes honoured, and sometimes avoided, music which is closely connected with him, is also sometimes honoured and sometimes avoided.

Like Rudra, Varuṇa also is well known as a double-natured god who is also connected with disease and its cure,[90] with fertility, generation and destruction, with anger and forgiveness. It is interesting to note that he is also connected with music and this connection contributes very much to our knowledge of double-nature of music.

Varuṇa is supposed to be at the origin of music. Thus he gave formidable spells (*vacas*-) to a magician-singer and the magician-singer refers to this incident while reciting formulas for pacifying the poison of serpent (AV V.13.1). According to Vāyupurāṇa, Brahmā was performing a sacrifice in the form of Varuṇa. From his semen various seers and vedas etc. were born. Among them Sāmaveda, rich in metres, was born along with the Gandharvas like Viśvāvasu (*sāmavedaś ca vṛttāḍhyaḥ sarvageyapuraḥsaraḥ / viśvāvasvādibhiḥ sārdhaṁ gandharvaiḥ saṁbhṛto 'bhavat* // 65.26 //). Elsewhere, Varuṇa, is told to have seen a sāman which is named as Varuṇa-sāman. Thus he wanted to be the king and then practised brahman-fare near Prajāpati. Then a sāman approached him and asked him to go to the gods. Then he went to them and they made him the king (JB III. 152; cp. TMB XIII. 9.23). Metres also are connected with Varuṇa. The nooses of Varuṇa are said to be identical with metres (*chandāṁsi varuṇapāśāḥ* KS XII. 6).

Songs are sung in honour of Varuṇa. Thus in ṚV. VIII. 41.1, a poet-singer is asked to sing nicely for Varuṇa. Varuṇa becomes powerful by means of obeisance, good hymns (*sūkta* -) praise songs (*uktha*-) and speeches (*vacas*) (ṚV X. 61.26) ṚV V. 42.1, the poet-singer hopes, "May the song reach to Varuṇa".

Sometimes, however, music is dissociated from Varuṇa. Thus in the Varuṇapraghāsa-offering, at the time of the Avabhṛtha-bath, no sāman is to be sung (ŚBII. 5.2.46). Otherwise, in the Avabhṛtha-bath connected with other sacrifices, there is a sāman to be sung. ChāUp,II. 22.1, ascribes the parts of a sāman uttered in various tones to various deities. The part, roaring like animal, belongs to Agni; the indistinctly hearable part to Prajāpati; the distinct one to Soma; the soft and smooth to Vāyu; the smooth and strong to Indra; the heron-like to Bṛhaspati; and the ill-sounding (*apadhvāntam*) to Varuṇa. One is advised to practise all the kinds except that belonging to Varuṇa. Here it is significant to note that the ill-sounding part is ascribed to Varuṇa and then prohibited for singing. This illustrates the dissociation of good sāmans, of good music and Varuṇa to some extent.

We have thus given above the details of the double nature of music and musicians. But why are they double natured ?

The double nature of the music & musicians and thereby their double treatment by society can be explained when we take into account that music is supposed to be a power-substance. The musicians, further are the possessors of some invisible power. Music and musicians are thus sacred. Now, the power like electricity is by itself indifferent. It can be useful as well as harmful, creative as well as destructive and can be used with good or bad purpose.[91] The persons who possess this power are also then considered to be double natured. Everything or everybody that possesses some extraordinary power is conceived as sacred[92] & the sacred is experienced in two ways: fearful, destructive etc. and attractive, life-furthering[93] etc. There cannot be any strict distinction among the primitive medicine-men[94], priests, musicians and the magicians.[95] So it is natural that all these persons receive a double treatment: honour and reception as well as condemnation and avoidance. When a particular kind of music or one who practises it is supposed to be useful and good, it or he is honoured; in the opposite case, rejected. According to Plato melodies which express virtues are good those which express vice are the reverse.[96] Mbh XII.225* gives a very practical advice to a king in this respect. "These persons do help to the state; they are also antagonistic to the state. Either bold or humble, they all must be won by means of efforts". Here along with the cāṇḍālas, mlecchas, heretic people etc. singers and dancers are mentioned. (*rāṣṭrakarmakarā hyete raṣṭrasya ca virodhinaḥ / durvinīta vinītāśca sarve sādhyāḥ prayatnataḥ / cāṇḍālā mlecchajātyāśca pāṣaṇḍāśca vikarmiṇaḥ / balinaścāśramāścaiva tathā gāyakanartakāḥ /*) In this way the double social position of the musicians is obvious and this position has to be explained on the basis of their double-nature. Their double-nature, again must be explained on the basis of the supposition that they are powerful, sacred etc.

REFERENCES

1. M. Schneider in E. Wellesz, *AOM* = *Ancient and Oriental Music*, p. 60
2. H.G. Farmer, in E. Wellesz, *AOM*, p. 260 f.
3. Virolleaud, in A. Lavignac, *EnM* = *Encyclopedie de la musique*, I, p. 38.
4. M. Courant, in Lavignac, *EnM*, I. p. 142.
5. I. Nenderson, in Wellesz, *AOM*, p. 378.
6. J.E. Scott, in Wellesz, *AOM*, p. 413.
7. C.H. Kraeling, L. Mowry, in Wellesz, *AOM*, p. 290 f.
8. H.G. Farmer, in Wellesz, *AOM*, p. 434.
9. cf. A. Bergaigne, *La religion védique d'après les hymnes du Rigveda*, I, p. 297
10. J. Grosset in Lavignac, *EnM*, I, p. 259.
11. Schneider, in Wellesz, *AOM*, p. 40.
12. J. Cuisinier, *La Danse Sacrée*, p. 28.
13. H.G. Farmer, in Wellesz, *AOM*, p. 260.
14. Virolleaud, in Lavignac, *EnM*, I, p. 38.
15. J. E. Scott in Wellesz, *AOM*, p. 411.
16. For the divine origin of music cf. J. Combarieu, *La Musique et la Magie*, p. 122.
17. Quoted from J. Hastings (ed.) *ERE* = *Encyclopaedia of Religion and Ethics*, IX, p. 6(b).
18. cf. E. Belvianes, *Sociologie de la musique*, Paris, 1951, p. 66.
19. The details of these subjects will be given elsewhere.
20. For this expression see my paper "Henoritualism of the Brāhmaṇa-texts", *JUPHS*, 33, 1970, p. 23.
21. Cf. L. Renou, *Études Védiques et Pāṇinéenes*, 1966, XV, p. 171.
22. Grosset, in Lavignac, *EnM*, I. p. 265; For the lower position of singers etc. cf. A. Hillebrandt, *Rituallitteratur, Vedische Opfer und Zauber*, p. 101; He confesses that it is not clear why the sāman-singers are not important. cf. also M. Winternitz, *Geschichte der Indischen Literatur*, (reprint), p. 146 f.
23. ed. by K.V. Rangaswami Aiyangar, Baroda, 1941.
24. Schneider, in Wellesz, *AOM*, p. 40.

25. Schneider, in Wellesz, *AOM*, p. 41.
26. Cuisinier, *La danse Sacrée*, p. 27.
27. Cuisinier, *La danse Sacrée*, p. 29.
28. M. Courant, in Lavignac, *EnM*, I, p. 142.
29. I. Henderson in Wllesz, *AOM*, p. 401.
30. U. Wogihara, Th. Stccherbatsky, Leningrad, 1931, p. 55.
31. Cf. Belvianes, *Sociologie de la musique*, p. 63.
32. Quoted by H. G. Farmer, in Wellesz, *AOM*, p. 265.
33. Cf. Grosset, in Lavignac, *EnM*, I, p. 66; see also Hastings, *ERE*, IX, p. 55 (b)
34. Sound is sometimes regarded as the substance of the powers of darkness (the word *tamas* means darkness) and dwelling place of them; cf. Schneider, in Wellesz, *AOM*, p. 51. Contrast, however, the section "Music and light in the Veda", in this book.
35. Cf. M. Bloomfield, *WZKM*, 17, 1903, p. 162.
36. Contrast, Belvianes, *Sociologie de la musique*, p. 209.
37. *api cātra mālyābharaṇavastrābhyaṅgagandhopabhoganṛttagītavāditraśrutisukhanayanābhirāmasandarśanānāṁ prāptirbhakṣyabhojyapeyalehyacoṣyāṇāmabhyavahāryāṇāṁ vividhānāmupabhogaḥ svadāravihārasantoṣaḥ kāmasukhāvāptiriti* Mbh. XII.184.16.
38. P. V. Bapat ("Vedic sources of some Buddhist beliefs" in the *Journal of the Asian Research Society*, 14 = *H. Goswami Commemmoration Vol.*, Gauhati, 1960) incompletely quotes and wrongly compares KS XIV.5 with this Pali passage. KS XIV.5, following rule is given: "One should not accept anything from one who obtains by means of singing the Gāthānārāśaṁsīs" and NOT "one should not take anything which comes as a result of singing the Gāthānārāśaṁsīs". The latter rule is found in the Pali text, but not the former, which the KS contains. See the KS XIV.5 *in the original* and compare also MS I. 11.5 and TB I. 3.2.6 f.
39. I. Henderson, in Wellesz, *AOM*, p. 401.
40. Cf. S. Lévi, *Le théatre indien*, p. 324; cp. Grosset, in Lavignac, *EnM*, I. p. 266.
41. Cf. Hastings, *ERE*, IX. p. 33 (b).
42. H. G. Farmer, in Wellesz, *AOM*, p. 265.
43. Belvianes, *Sociologie de la musique*, p. 202.
44. I. Henderson, in Wellesz, *AOM*, p. 401.
45. Max Weber, *Sociology of the Religion*, London, 1965, p. 180.

46. Combarieu, *La Musique et la magie*, p. 26.
47. E. Werner, in Wellesz, *AOM*, p. 314.
48. H. Abert, *Die Musikauschauung des Mittelalters und ihre Grundlagen*, p. 2.
49. Belvianes, *Sociologie de la musique*, p. 88.
50. Belvianes, *Sociologie de la musique*, p. 92, n.1
51. F. Pelagaud, in Lavignac, *EnM*, I. p. 47 f.
52. Hastings, *ERE, IX*, p. 55 (b).
53. Belvianes, *Sociologie de la musique*, p. 102.
54. Hastings, *ERE, IX*, p. 39 (b).
55. H. G. Farmer, in E. Wellesz, *AOM*, p. 262.
56. E. Rhode, *Psyche, The cult of souls and belief in immortality among Greeks*, London, 1925, p. 180.
57. Plato referred to by I. Henderson, in Wellesz, *AOM.*, p. 395.
58. Referred to by Combarieu, *La Musique et la magie*, p. 9.
59. J. E. Scott, in Wellesz, *AOM*, p. 404.
60. Belvianes, *Sociologie de la musique*, p. 88.
61. Belvianes, *Sociologie de la musique*, p. 92, n. 1
62. *Porphyrius* rejects music on account of its sensual charm: cf. Abert, *Musikanschauung*, p. 52. Musicians were discredited because of their free temperament in connection with women according to Grosset in Lavignac *EnM*, I. p. 265.
63. In Greek and Roman mythology Sirens are described as attracting the navigators by the sweetness and loveliness of their songs and this led obviously to destruction of ships and death of the navigators; cf. Belvianes, *Sociologie de la musique*, p. 49; on p. 124, music is mentioned as used by hunters and fishers to attract animals and fishes and the result of this was, of course, death of these.
64. Cf. H. G. Farmer in Wellesz, *AOM*, p. 262.
65. F. Behn, *Musikleben im Altertum und frühren Mittelater*, p. 60.
66. For the supposition that music makes a man effeminate, see Belvianes, *Sociolgie de la musique*, p. 65; cp. p. 69, where Homer's opinion is mentioned.
67. Hastings, *ERE*, IX. p. 33 (b).
68. J. E. Scott, in Wellesz, *AOM*, p. 417.
69. Combarieu, *La Musique et la magie*, p. 66, cp. Belvianes, *Sociologie de la musique*, p. 42.
70. Belvianes, *Sociologie de la musique*, p. 134.
71. Belvianes, *Sociologie de la musique*, p. 108.

72. Belvianes, *Sociologie de la musique,* p. 53.
73. Abert, *Musikanschauung,* p. 49 f.
74. For the music as a means of purification see Abert, *Musikanschauung,* p. 23, cp. p.20 etc.
75. Referred to by I. Henderson, Wellesz, *AOM,* p. 376.
76. Belvianes, *Sociologie de la musique,* p. 185.
77. Belvianes, *Sociologie de la musique,* p. 184.
    Quarrelsome significance of music in the *abhicāra*-rites, saṁsava etc. will be detailed elsewhere.
78. Hastings, *ERE,* IX, 17 (a).
79. Combarieu, *La musique et la magie,* p. 346 f.
80. Referred to by Belvianes, *Sociologie de la musique,* p. 63
81. Belvianes, *Sociologie de la musique,* p. 182.
82. Referred to by C. A. Patrids, *Milton and the Christian tradition,* p. 41 f.
83. Abert, *Musikanschauung,* p. 46.
84. Referred to by Abert, *Musikanschauung,* p. 91.
85. Belvianes, *Sociologie de la musique,* p. 53.
86. J. W. Hauer, *Der Vrātya,* Stuttgart, 1927, p. 148.
87. Hauer, *Vrātya,* p. 147; For the Vrātya and Sāmaveda connection see also p. 117; 250; 306, 335 etc.
88. Cf. My paper "Cāturmāsya-sacrifices Researched", *JUPHS,* 31, 1969, p. 69 f.
89. Hillebrandt, *Vedische Mythologie,* Hildesheim, 1965 (reprint), II. p. 433.
90. Cf. My paper "Cāturmāsya - sacrifices ... " *JUPHS,* 31, 61 ff.
91. S. Mowinkel, *Religion and Kultus,* Göttingen, 1953, p. 25; cf. also H. Webster, *Magic,* p. 5; 11; 12 ff; 25 etc.
92. Musicians who are regarded to be sacred are kept away from the society which is profane: Cuisinier, *La danse sacrée,* p. 29.
93. Mowinkel, *Religion and Kultus,* p. 36; cp. p. 45.
    cp. G. J. Frazer, *The Golden bough* (abridged edition), p. 607.
94. For the double position of medicine-men etc. because they possess magical powers cf. L.V. Schröder, *Mysterium und Mimus in Rigveda,* Leipzig, 1908, p. 458.
95. The King Gudea of Lagash in Babilonia says in his inscriptions that he has driven all the magicians and witches out of his land - cf. Mowinkel, *Religion und Kultus,* p. 26.
96. *Laws,* II. 433.

CHAPTER III
Music : A Power-Substance

The sound of music is regarded in many parts of the world and by many peoples as a power-substance;[1] The primitive people consider the voice of the enchanters as *ordenda*[2] or mana.[3] One supposes, "Ou je suis entendu, je commende" and the blower of the counch, trumpet etc. dilates the spaces and announces its power to the four quarters of the sky.[4] The Vedic people also believed that the sound of music is powerful[5] and gives power to others. Thus ŚB V. 3.5.9 we find that sound (*ghoṣa*) and noise (*śloka* -) are identified with valour (*vīrya* -). Offerings are offered to Sound and Noise after the consecration ceremony in the Rājasūya-sacrifice for the sake of obtaining valour. Similarly at the Mahāvrata ceremony Vāṇa (a musical instrument) is played upon. This play is supposed to give valour to the sacrificer (JB II.404).

The poet-singers of the Vedas know the power of music very well. Sometimes they describe that their prayers, songs etc. are powerful. ṚV I.143.1, the poet-singer says, "I carry forth a (still) more powerful and newer visionic poem (*dhīti*-) a well-thought speech for Agni, the son of power".[6] The praise-songs (*uktha* -) which went towards Indra and delighted him are described to be full of manly valour (*pauṁsyāni*) (ṚV IX.113.3). The poem sung for Indra by Bṛhaduktha was strong (*śūṣam*) (ṚV X.54.5). The power of a praise-hymn addressed to the god Pūṣan is emphasised by means of a negative expression, "It does not become lame (*na tandate* ṚV I.138.1). An Atharvavedic poet-singer gives expression to his confidence in the power of his song. "By means of the valourous hymn we shall destroy the Gandharva" (AV IV. 37.11). Viśvāmitra is also aware of the power of his hymns when he declares, "This powerful hymn (*brahman* -) of Viśvāmitra protects the people of Bharata's family".

The sāmans are supposed to possess power, valour[7] etc. and also helpful for the sake of obtainment of power etc. Even the gods become strengthened by means of the power of sāmans. Thus "Indra killed Vṛtra. He became devoid of power and valour. He saw this (Śrāyantīya) sāman and "joined" himself (by the loss of valour; he was "broken into pieces" as it were). One who gets himself consecrated by the Rājasūya, becomes devoid of power and valour. He can join himself by means of this (sāman)" (MS IV. 4.9; cp. TMB XVII. 11.1). According to another story, the Śrāyantīya-sāman is the one-third part of the sense-power and valour of Varuṇa, Thus, "When he was being consecrated, his sense-power and valour departed. It fell assunder in three parts; one third became the seer Bhṛgu; one third the Śrāyantīya-(sāman); one third entered the river Sarasvatī. That (in the Daśapeya-rite of the Rājasūya) the Hotṛ-priest belongs to the clan of Bhṛgu, that the Śrāyantīya is used as the chant of Brahman, that the waters of Sarasvatī are used, he (the sacrificer gets that sense-power and valour back (MS IV.3.9; cp. TMB XVIII.9.1; JB II.202). According to still another story, Prajāpati felt to be milked out, emptied out after creating the beings. He saw the Śrāyantīya-sāman and braced himself by means of it fully by progeny, cattle and valour. In a soma-sacrifice, when one's trough bursts one is milked out, emptied out as it were and when the Śrāyantīya-sāman is used as a brahman's chant, for the sake of expiation, then one braces oneself again fully with progeny, cattle and valour (TMB IX.6.7 f).

Similarly, the Vāravantīya-sāman is also helpful in obtaining valour. "One becomes devoid of sense-power and valour who is consecrated by means of Rājasūya. The Vāravantīya-sāman is verily, identical with sense-power and valour" (MS IV. 4.9; cp. TMB XVIII.11.1). If the soma-trough is broken, in order to expiate the sin accruing out of it the Vāravatīya-sāman is to be used as an Agniṣṭoma-sāman. This is also to obtain of sense-power and valour (JB I.352). The same expiative use of the Vāravantīya-sāman is prescribed by the TMB IX. 5.9, if the soma is robbed. The sāman then helps to obtain sense-power and valour. The use of this sāman in the

Vājapeya-sacrifice also serves the same purpose. (TMB XVII. 6.16).

The Traikakubha-sāman is similarly identified with the sense-power and valour. "Of triple valour and triple sense-power, verily, is this sāman. For to Indra are addressed the verses, to Indra is addressed the sāman and (the word) *Indra* is its finale. One who sings this sāman at the midday-pressing of the Agniṣṭoma-sacrifice gets firm support in valour and sense-power" (TMB VIII.1.7). The singing of this sāman on the ninth day of the Daśarātra of the Dvādaśāha, is useful for the sake of being established firmly in power and valour; for it is identical with power and valour (*ojo vīryaṁ traikakubham*) (TMB XV. 6.5). Similarly if the introductory (*Prāyaṇīya*-) day of the Gavāmayana-sacrifice is performed as an ukthya-day, the Traikakabha and Udvaṁśīya-sāmans are to be fixed at the end. These are identical with valour and the performers then become established in the valour thereby (TMB IV.2.10; cp. JB II.378).

There are many other sāmans supposed to be full of power and let us mention a few of them. Thus Prajāpati filled the worlds with sap (*rasa*-) by means of the Ākṣāra-sāman. Therefore, he who having been formerly successful, afterwards fares worse should take the Akṣāra-sāman as the brahman's chant. Unto him this sāman causes to flow (return) sense-power, valour and sap (TMB XI.5.10 f). Similar is the significance of the Dakṣaṇidhana-sāman. Thus when Prajāpati created the beings, by means of this sāman, he put power and valour in them by means of its finale viz. *dakṣāya*. This sāman is sung on the seventh day of the Daśarātra of the Dvādaśāha. Thereby one puts power and valour into oneself (TMB XIV. 5.13). The Aṣṭādaṁṣṭra-sāmans are helpful to obtain power and valour if used on the third day of the Daśarātra of the Dvādaśāha-sacrifice. These sāmans are also described to be victorious and valourous (TMB XI.11.12). By means of Saṁśāna-sāmans, the Gods braced Indra up to sense-power, valour. Similarly the priests brace the sacrificer upto sense-power and valour using these sāmans in the Sautrāmaṇī-sacrifice (ŚB XII.8.3.26). By means of citra-sāmans, valour is put into the Puruṣa-brick which is laid down in the course of Fire-building ceremony. (ŚB VII. 4.1.22 ff).

A Stoma is a kind of singing a particular chant according to the number of verses chanted during the entire day of a soma sacrifice or a part of it.[8] Thus there are Trivṛt (nine-versed), Pañcadaśa (fifteen-versed) etc. stomas. This number is gained by way of repeating the basic verses. The stomas are also supposed to be powerful. Thus TMB II.5.4 identifies stomas with valour (*vīryaṁ vai stomāḥ*) and says that when one brings together the fifteen-versed, nine-versed and seventeen-versed stomas, one brings together valour there by (cp. TMB II. 11.2). In connection with the sacrifice named Rāj (King), it is said, "The other sacrifices amount to the metre (e.g. Sāhasra-sacrifice amounts Anuṣṭubh; i.e. the recitations of this sacrifice are in proportion of 32 which is the number of syllables in the Anuṣṭubh-metre: see TMB XVI.11.17 with Sāyaṇa's commentary) but this sacrifice amounts to the Ekaviṁśa-stoma (i.e. the recitations of this sacrifice are in proportion to twenty-one; and therefore this sacrifice amounts to the twenty-one-versed-stoma). The stoma is valour; on valour they inaugurate him" (TMB XIX.1.3). Among the different stomas, four stomas are compared to strong horses. They are said to be strongest of all the stomas- "When the kings undertake a journey, they yoke the strongest horses. The nine-versed, fifteen-versed, seventeen-versed and twenty-one-versed these are the strongest of the stomas. The chanter yokes these (in the Agniṣṭoma-jyotiṣṭoma-sacrifice) in order to reach the world of heaven" (TMB VI.3.15).

The nine-versed stoma is said to be identical with power and valour (JB III.89; III.309 etc.). The forty-four-versed stoma is to be used on the eighth day of the Dvādaśāha. Now the metre named Triṣṭubh has forty-four syllables and that metre is identical with the power of sense-organs and valour. Therefore by using this stoma also one becomes established in the power of sense-organs and valour (JB III.206; cp. 208).

The Pañcadaśa (fifteen-versed-stoma is particularly very often found to be identified with power, valour, might[9] etc. Thus TMB X.1.6. We read, "They call this stoma power and might (*taṁ caujo balam ityāhuḥ* - KS XXXVII.8; TMB XI.11.4; XIX.4.12; JB I.253; II.232; 407; III.21,22; AB VIII.4). In the sacrifice named Pakṣī (Bird), there are two fifteen-versed stomas to be used. The fifteen-versed-stoma is identical with power and valour (*ojo vai vīryaṁ pañcadaśaḥ*). One then gets power (TMB XIX.10.6). Similarly the Indrastoma-sacrifice is throughout fifteen-versed. The fifteen-versed stoma is power and valour and then the sacrificer thrives through power and valour (TMB XIX.16.4; cp. 7). In a similar manner by means of the use of Pañcadaśa-stoma in the sacrifices like Vighana (TMB XIX.18.3). Pañcadaśa-atirātra (TMB XX.10.1); Prajāpater Dvādaśa-saṁvatsara (TMB XX.6.3) etc., one obtains valour. Bhāradvāja desired, "May my progeny be the most powerful and the most valourous". He then saw the Pañcadaśa-stoma and having used it, obtained the desired progeny (JB II.217).

The reason why the fifteen-versed-stoma is described to be power and valour etc. seems to be sought in TMB VI.1.8 where stoma and Indra, Triṣṭubh, Kṣatra (warrior -) class all these power-substances are said to have sprung up from the breast and arms of Prajāpati.

There are in all six Pṛṣṭhas[10] viz. Rathantara, Bṛhat, Vairūpa, Śākavara, and Raivata. When any stotra is to be recited in its pṛṣṭha-form, then a sāman is to be enclosed as an embryo within some other sāman which as its Pṛṣṭha (i.e. back, flanks etc.) is chanted a number of times before and after the verses of the central sāman. In the Pṛṣṭhya-ṣaḍaha the above mentioned six Pṛṣṭhas are used serially. According to TMB IV. 8.7, the Pṛṣṭhas are identical with valour. Because there are Pṛṣṭhas in the Pṛṣṭhya-ṣaḍaha, the performers become established in the valour. The Ṣaḍrātra-sacrifice is to be performed in the manner of the Pṛṣṭhya-ṣaḍaha. This sacrifice was seen by Maruts who were desirous of being the most powerful and valorous. The performer of this sacrifice becomes the most powerful and valorous. The reason for this is that the Pṛṣṭhas are identical with power and valour and therefore when used properly, they help to obtain power and valour (JB II.297). In the Caturdaśarātra-sacrifice, the order of the days is as follows—an Atirātra, a threeday-rite in the normal order (Jyotis, Go, Āyus); a Pṛṣṭhy-ṣaḍaha (six-day rite), a three-day-rite in the reverse order (Āyus, Go, Jyotis), and an Atirātra. Here the Pṛṣṭhya-ṣaḍaha is in the middle. Now the Pṛṣṭhas are identical with power and valour. Thus the performers place power and valour in the middle (TS VII.3.4.3; cp. 7.3; 4.1.2; 2.3 in connection with the other sacrifices).

Metres are also supposed to be full of valour. The fire-pan is prepared with the help of metres; for metres are identical with valour (*vīryaṁ vai chandāṁsi*) and thus it is prepared with the help of valour (TS V.1.6.4; TĀ V.3.4). In the sacrifice which is performed by a joined group of sacrificers verses beginning with "*davidyutatyā rucā*" (ṚV IX.64.28-30; SV II.4-6) are to be used as the beginning tristich in the out-of-doors-laud. This tristich represents all the metres. "A joined group is, verily, devoid of sense-power and valour; the metres are sense power and valour *indriyaṁ vīryaṁ chandāṁsi*). One thus makes them possessed of these (TMB VI.9.26). Accordingly, different metres are at different places identified with valour, power etc. Thus the metre named Uṣṇih, is said to be identical with valour (*vīryam uṣṇik* JB I.309). Virāṭ is said to be identical with power (*ūrk*) (TB I.2.1.2). Similarly Jagatī is said to identical with might and valour (*balaṁ vai vīryaṁ jagatī* KB XI. 2). About Bṛhati and Triṣṭubh it is jointly remarked that they are full of valour (TMB IV. 4.9).

The metre Triṣṭubh appears specially to be a repertoire of power. It is very often identified with power and valour. On the seventh day of the Daśarātra of the Dvādaśāha-sacrifice, the introductory verse is in Triṣṭubh. "Triṣṭubh is power and valour (*ojo vīryaṁ triṣṭubh*). Having advanced in power and valour, they proceed". (TMB XIV.1.5 f). Similarly one who desires power and valour should sing the Sandhi-sāman in the Triṣṭubh-metre for it is identical with those (JB I.229). For such an identification of Triṣṭubh with power and valour see also MS II.4.4; III.2.4.6; 3.2; KS XI.3; 4; XXI.10; XXXIV.8). Sometimes this metre is identified with the sense-power and valour (*indriyaṁ vai vīryaṁ triṣṭubh*). Thus in the Sāvitrī-offering which takes place in the Aśvamedha-sacrifice, one has to make the saṁyājyā verses in the Triṣṭubh-metre for obtaining these (ŚB XIII.2.5.4; for this identification see also JB III. 206;208). In the morning litany of the Agniṣṭoma-sacrifice, a verse in Triṣṭubh-metre is recited". Triṣṭubh is identical with might and valour (*balaṁ vai vīryaṁ triṣṭubh*) and thus these are put in the sacrificer (KB XI.2; cp also XVI.1; 2; 4; 11; XVII.2; 9; XVIII.5). Sometimes this metre is identified merely with valour. In the second Trirātra (three-day-sacrifice) the verses of the morning litany are in the Triṣṭubh-metre; for it is identical with valour (*vīryaṁ vai triṣṭup*ṢaḍB III.7.4). In the Rājasūya-sacrifice, three verses beginning with *pavasvendo vṛṣā sutaḥ* (ṚV IX.61.28-30; SV II.128-130) are to be used. Even though these verses are actually in Gāyatrī, they have the characteristic of Triṣṭubh because they contain the word *vṛṣan* (= bull—a symbol of valour). The metre Triṣṭubh is identical with valour and by using these verses one gets consecrated in valour (TMB XVIII.8.13). According to some ritualists, the Prauga-śastra in the Mahāvrata-ceremony should be in the Triṣṭubh-metre. For Triṣṭubh is identical with valour and then the sacrificer becomes possessor of valour (AĀ I. 1.3). According to AB VI. 21, the metre Triṣṭubh, having made the performers go to the world of heaven does not fail; for it is the strongest of all (*vīryavattama*-). ŚB VII.5.2.24, Triṣṭubh is identified with *vajra* (thunderbolt) and thunderbolt with valour (*vīrya*-) and thereby the valorous character of Triṣṭubh is implied.

Along with Triṣṭubh, Gāyatrī is also said to be possessing valour. Thus according to TMB XX.16.8 "Gāyatrī and Triṣṭubh are the strongest of all the metres (*ete vava chandasam vīryavattameyad gāyatrī ca triṣṭup ca*"). Sometimes Gāyatrī alone is mentioned as identical with valour. In the Agniṣṭoma-sacrifice during the course of the midday-pavamāna-recitation, one sings the Āmahīyava-sāman with a finale, after one has sung a sāman in Gāyatrī-metre". For Gāyatrī is valour; the finale is valour; by valour one then augments valour (TMB VII. 2.13). In the New-and-Full-Moon-sacrifices, the enkindling (sāmidhenī -) verses addressed to Agni are in Gāyatrī-metre. Gāyatrī is identical with valour and one thus kindles the fire with valour (ŚB I.3.5.4). ŚB I.8.2.10, it is informed that Gāyatrī, having become a falcon brought soma which was in the heaven. Gāyatrī could accomplish such activities and therefore it was believed to be powerful.

Some other aspects of vedic recitation are also identified with valour. Thus according to KS IX.1, the Vibhaktis (particular forms with different case-endings of the name of the invoked deity),[11] are identified with valour (*vīryaṁ vai vibhaktayaḥ*). Puroruc-formula is generally used before drawing a soma-cup. But at the time of drawing the Pātnīvata-cup, this formula is not to be used. "For it is identical with valour; lest he should bestow valour on women" (ŚB. IV.4.2.11). On the second day of the Daśarātra of the Dvādaśāha-sacrifice, the stotriyā-verse beginning with *indramaccha sutā ime* (SV I.566. ṚV IX.106.1-3) is to be used for the sake of retaining the sense-power and valour (TMB IX.10.4). The verses of the out-of-doors-laud are identical with the sense-power, valour, sap and light of some deities (JB I.249). Some hymns[12] are also supposed to be full of valour, power. Thus the hymn beginning with the words, "*ābhātyagnir uṣasām*" (ṚV V.76) is to be used in the course of Pravargya-rite. It is in the Triṣṭubh-metre and because it is in the Triṣṭubh-metre and Triṣṭubh is identical with valour, valour is put in the sacrifice by means of this hymn (AB I.21). Similarly a hymn addressed to Indra and Viṣṇu is to be recited as an expiation in case soma being exceeded in the morning-pressing. For Indra is valour and Viṣṇu is sacrifice. The sacrificer then becomes established in valour and in sacrifice (TMB IX.7.4 f).

Apparently impossible and supernatural activities also can be performed with the help of music. Music can influence upon the superhuman potencies.[13] It has a magical power in it to work out wonders. Thus the Uśijs broke the rock by means of their words (*vacobhiḥ*) (ṚV IV.16.6). The Aṅgirases cut down (the fetters) with the help of a song (*arka* -) and a powerful hymn (*brahman* -). The god-invocation made by them proved to be successful (ṚV VI.65.5). Viśvāmitra[14] crossed the rivers viz. Vipāṭ and Śutudrī by the magical power of his songs. He addressed to the rivers "Stand-still O rivers on account of my soma-like speech for a moment" (ṚV III.33.5). He further said, "Listen unto the poet O sisters; he has come to you from distance by means of wagons and chariots. Bow yourself, be easy to be crossed over. Be with your streams under the wagon-axles O Rivers. "(ṚV III.33.9). Thereupon the chief of the river says, "O poet, we will obey your words; you have come from distance by means of wagons and chariots. I shall bend down myself like a milk-swollen mother (cow) (to the child-calf) and I shall submit you like a maiden to the lover". (ṚV III.33.10). According to JB III.238, Viśvāmitra made a stream of river shallow with the help of Vaiśvāmitra-sāman. One can easily remember the story of Moses from the Bible, *Exodus* XV. There we know that Moses and others, in order to cross the red sea sang and then with the divine intervention, the sea was divided.[15]

By means of music one can control not only water but also fire. Thus in the following story, Vatsa is told to have safely walked through fire by means of Vātsa-sāman. "Vatsa and Medhātithi were both sons of Kaṇva. Medhātithi reproached this Vatsa, "Thou art a non-brahmin, thou art the son of a Sūdra-woman". He answered, "Let us walk according to the rite through fire (to decide) which of us is the better brahmin". With the Vātsa (- sāman) Vatsa walked through the fire; with the Maidhātitha (- sāman) Medhātithi. Not even a hair of him (Vatsa) was burned by the fire". (TMB XIV.6.6). JB III.235, has practically the same story except a few changes. There,

Triśoka, instead of Vatsa is mentioned. JB III.198, however, it is expressly stated that Vatsa Kāṇva is the same person as Triśoka. Therefore even though the following may mention Triśoka, he can be understood as Vatsa. "The two sons of Kaṇva, Medhātithi and Triśoka contended about the sacred lore (*brahman*). They said, "Come, let us cross the flaming fire". They crossed the flaming fire. Triśoka crossed (unharmed); but of the other it scorched the eye-lashes. He (Triśoka) said to him (to Medhātithi), "I have vanquished thee". "No", said he, "Thou art the son of an asura-mother: even the deities have not wishes to touch thee. Then they said, "Come let us cross the water". They crossed the river Rathaspā flowing near by. Triśoka crossed it (unharmed) but of the other, the rims of his cart were moistened by the water of Rathaspā ..." (JB II.235).[16] The story runs further. But one thing is here notable. In this story, because the JB is going to prove the importance and significance of Maidhātitha-sāman, it has not directly stated that Triśoka could go successfully over fire and water by means of his own viz. Traiśoka sāman. But taking together the stories given by TMB and JB we can conclude that Vatsa who is also called Triśoka could cross fire and water with the help of his own power of melody.

Even the gods are strengthened by music and then they can perform heroic activities. Thus the praise-sung Indra, being *alone* kills *numerous* opponents (ṚV IV.17.19). The music of Vasiṣṭhas is specifically mentioned to have strengthened Indra. Thus ṚV VII.33.4, we read, "You O Vasiṣṭhas, put strength in Indra, (singing in) Śakvarī verse with loud voice (*yac chakvarīṣu bṛhatā raveṇendre śuṣmam adadhātā vasiṣṭhāḥ*)". The songs of Aṅgirases also strengthen Indra to do valorous activities. Thus, "Indra being sung by Aṅgirases, broke Vala; opened the firm (doors) of the mountains; removed the artificial walls ...." (ṚV II.15.18). A poet from the Kaṇva family addresses Indra in the following manner - "O you being carried by songs (*gir*-), whatever songs (*gir*-) and praise-songs (*uktha*-) there are for you, they always put strength (*śavas*-) in you". (ṚV VIII.

2.30). Vatsa Kaṇva refers to Indra's being strengthened by means of the songs of the Kaṇvas—"I adorn my songs by means of an old poem in the manner of Kaṇva, through which Indra held valour (ṚV VIII.6.11).

Like Indra, Ādityas also get themselves strengthened with the help of songs. Thus they are said to be "*ukthaśuṣma*—i.e. those who become powerful by means of praise songs" (ṚV X. 63.3).

The poet singers feel confident as regards the power of their songs effective on the gods. Thus ṚV III.42.4 a poet-singer says, "For drinking of soma, we call Indra with stomas and Ukthas. He will *certainly* come". Others are also aware of the power of the songs at the singers. Thus a singer is asked in ṚV I.127.10, "May your stoma be valid unto Agni".

Sometimes it is the gods who are said to be lending power unto the songs. Thus Soma goes putting good valour in the praisehymn (ṚV IX.20.7). ṚV IX.97.36, Soma is requested to increase (*vardhaya*) the speech (*vāc*) in strength. The valour of sāmans (*sāmavairya*) is said to be belonging to the divinities to which the verses upon which the sāman is based are addressed (JUB I.18.4.12).

Sāman is sometimes described to be *satya* (effective) (*satyaṁ vai sāma* KS XIV.7; MS I.11.7). JB III.185, in connection with the Gauṅgava-sāman a remark is made that this sāman praises the gods and therefore the benedictions of the sacrificer came to be true. Thus it seems that sometimes the magic and religion are mixed together. The sāmans cannot work independently. The favour of gods is required. And although everytime we do not get any mention of whether the power of the sāmans works independently or whether it requires the favour of gods, it can be generally said that both of these factors are mixed together in a complicated manner. Therefore the significanceo, of the vedic music can be conveniently named as magico-religious ones.

In short we may say that

(1) in the veda music is considered to be a power-sub stance.

(2) by means of it one can control natural phenomenon and perform miraculous deeds;

(3) the power of music is sometimes considered to be superior and sometimes inferior to gods; it can work sometimes independently and even upon gods; but sometimes it requires the help of gods for its effectiveness. Thus the power of music is magicoreligious.

REFERENCES

1. For the power of music see Schneider in Wellesz, *AOM*, p. 42,86, 259 etc., rf. also Abert, *Musikanschauung*, p. 156; *G. van der* Leeuw, *REM*, p. 405; Mowinkel, *Religion und Kultus*; p. 22. Among the Chinese the word Kong sufficed to designate the magic and *inter alia* the musical art: see Belvianes, *Sociologie de la musique*, p. 42, n. 1.
2. Hubert, Mauss, "Magic", *L' Année sociologique*, VII, p. 114.
3. James, *Priesthood*, p. 38.
4. Belvianes, *Sociologie de la musique*, p. 48.
5. See Bake in Wellesz, *AOM*, p. 199; rf. also Grosset, in Lavignac, *EnM*, I, p. 259 f.
6. Rf. Geldner, *Der Rigveda*, I. p. 201.
7. For the magical power of sāmans in general see Hillebrandt "Die Sonnwendfeste" in *Festschrift K. Hofman*, Erlangen, 1889, p. 22. 22 ff; S. Konnow, *Das Sāmavidhānabrāhmaṇa* Halle, 1893, p. 13; Bloomfield, "The god Indra and the Sāmaveda, "*WZKM*, XVII, 1903, p. 156 ff; Winternitz, *GIL*, I, p. 146 f.
8. Renou, *Vocabulaire du rituel védique*, p. 169.
9. cp. Gonda *O jas*, p. 19.
10. For Pṛṣṭhas see Eggeling, *SBE*, XLI, p. XX; Renou, *Vocabulaire*, p. 104.
11. Renou, *Vocabulaire*, p. 138.
12. cp. James, *Priesthood*, p. 38 "When for example the vedic priests in India filled with divine power (*brahman*) sang the hymns of the Ṛgveda, they were believed to exercise a constraining influence alike over gods and men at once coercive, persuasive and propitiative".
13. cp. Gonda, *Vision of the Vedic poets*, p. 125.

14. Rf. e.g. L. v. Schroeder, *Mysterium und Mimus im Rigveda,* p. 226 ff.
15. Rf. A. Cohen, in Lavignac, *EnM,* I, p. 67
16. For the Translation see Caland, *Pañcaviṁśabrāhmaṇa,* p. 367, n. 1.

CHAPTER IV

Music and Gods

Music is considered in the veda to be useful magicoreligiously. So the connections of music and gods are twofold. Sometimes music is considered to be more powerful than gods and it makes the gods behave according to the desire of the poet-singers and sometimes it is used in order to please the gods so that they may fulfil the desires of the poet-singers. Thus there is a fusion of magical and religious significances of the music in the veda. This will be illustrated by a detailed study of connections of music and gods.

Gods are requested etc. to come—Sometimes gods are requested by means of music to come. Sometimes, on the other hand, music is considered to have an attractive, dragging power. Gods being praised by the sāmans of Aṅgirases are expected to come near (*upa āgan* ṚV I.107.2). The Maruts are addressed, "Turn up finely towards the singer; the singer will sing these hymns (*brahmāṇi*) for you" ṚV I.165.14) Similarly Indra is requested, "Being well praised by us come here, O Indra, towards the hymns (*brahmāṇi*) of Mānya" (ṚV I.177.5). Elsewhere Indra is exhorted to come near (*upa yāhi*) the hymn as a knower (ṚV VII.28.1). ṚV X.104.6 also he is requested to come near to the hymns (*brahmāṇi*). Similar observations can be made in connection with another expression viz. *gir* (song). Thus a poet-singer says to Mitra and Varuṇa to come to the songs (*giraḥ*). The same is said to Aśvins also (ṚV VIII.57.4). ṚV II.6.6 Agni is entreated, "Come (*ā gahi*), O Agni, for the one who is praising you with a song (*girā*). Indra and Agni are requested to come on account of songs (*gīrbhiḥ* ṚV III.12.1). Elsewhere Aśvins are also requested to come on account of a ṛc, a song (*girā* ṚV VIII.27.5). Maruts are also addressed, "Come to the sacrifice, songs (*giraḥ*) and good praise, (*suṣṭutim* ṚV V.43.10). Aśvins are told ṚV VII.68.1 to come while enjoying (*jujuṣāṇāḥ*) the songs of their worshipper. Elsewhere also they are said, "These strengthening hymns and stomas are prepared for you by Gṛtsamadas; Come here enjoying them" (ṚV II.39.8). In the case of the vaṣaṭ-call also mention of enjoyment is found: "Come O Agni unto our invocation of gods enjoying the vaṣaṭ-call" (ṚV VII.14.3; cp. VII.15.6 where Agni is requested to come towards the vaṣaṭ-call and enjoy the songs (*giraḥ*). Similarly ṚV VIII.68.6 "Come (*ā gahi*) Indra enjoying our praise-hymn (*stoma* -)". ṚV VIII.38.6 a poet-singer says, "Come (*ā gatam*) O Indra and Agni and enjoy this my good praise (*suṣṭuti*-) in the Gāyatrī-metre". ṚV VIII.32.6, the singer says, "If you are taking delight (*varāṇaḥ*) in my praise-song, then come (*upāgahi*) from distance". ṚV III.43.3 one invokes Indra to come quickly (*tūyam*) to the sacrifice and says, "I am invoking you by means of thoughtful poems (*mati*-)" Aśvins who are described to be listeners of calls (*havanaśrutā*) are requested to come on account of visionic poem (*dhī*) and stomas (ṚV VIII.8.7). Elsewhere they are requested to come to the call (*havam*) of the singer (*jarituḥ* ṚV VIII.35.13-15). ṚV VIII.85.1 also they are addressed, "Come (*āgacchatam*) to my call (*havam*) you O Aśvins for drinking sweet soma".

Instead of requesting the gods to come, sometimes some other expressions are used; but then also the power of music in various forms is applied by the poet-singers in attracting the gods. Thus one addresses to Maruts, "Praised by visionic poems, hurry up (*iṣaṇyata*) towards here (O Maruts" ṚV V. 82.14).

The gods are attracted or dragged towards the music or the singer. But that is not enough. They are sometimes attracted to do some positive favour etc. unto the singer. Thus one says to Aśvins, "Enjoying the songs (*giraḥ*) come to (*upayātam*) us for good favour (*suvitāya* ṚV I.118.10). Similarly ṚV VI.32.4 Indra who is desirous of songs is requested to come (*prayāhi*) to the singer for doing good favour. Elsewhere Indra is addressed, "Praised, desiring for fame come you (O Indra) down with your favour towards me (*avasopa .... yāhyarvan*" ṚV

I.177.1). Indrāvaruṇā are also beseeched, "Come down (*arvāṅ āgatam*) to us with your divine favour (*daivyena avasā*) O heroes, listen unto my call if you enjoy it" (ṚV VII.82.2). In the next hymn also they are addressed, "The cry is raised upto the heaven O Indravaruṇā : Come down with favour O hearers of calls" : (ṚV VII.83.3). Aśvins are requested to come (*āgatam*) quickly towards the hymn to which they make good favour (*ni ṣu āviṣṭam* ṚV VIII.5.13). ṚV II.24.15 one asks for sons, "When having become powerful by means of the hymn (*brahman*-) O Brahmaṇaspati, you will come unto my call then give us sons".

The attractive power of music is expressed with the help of various expressions in the ṚV. The music *itself* turns, brings, or carries the gods to the singer. Thus ṚV I.135.5 we read, "May the visionic poems (*dhiyaḥ*) turn (*āvavṛtyuḥ*) you (O Indrāvāyū" ṚV I. 135.5). In connection with a stoma it is said, "May the stoma of our poems draw (*āyacchatu*) here; turn (*āvartaya*) your horses herewards" (ṚV IV.32.15) or "May these stomas drive (*cucyavīrata*) you herewards as (the wind) the clouds" (ṚV VIII.9.8); cp. ṚV VIII.1.29: my stomas have turned you (*āvṛtsata*) herewards at the time of morning, midday, and evening. Similar activity is also supposed to be done by the songs (*gir*-) also: "Make Agni inclined (*upa vivāsatam*) towards you by means of songs (*gīrbhiḥ*" ṚV VI.15.6). ṚV VIII.32.23 also a poet-singer expects that his song may draw (*āyacchantu*) Indra towards him. Indra is ṚV. VIII.77.13 also expected to be turned (*āvavartat*) by means of songs. A *brahman* (powerful hymn) also can "turn" the gods. Thus ṚV VI.17.13 it is said, "May this new hymn (*brahman*-) turn (*ā vavṛtyāt*) you herewards for doing favour". A *Brahman* sometimes indirectly does the work of bringing Indra. Thus ṚV VIII.2.27 it is said, "May the yellow horses yoked by means of a powerful hymn bring (*ā vakṣataḥ*) (Indra) herewards" In the case of *arka* (song) also it has been said, "This *arka* created by the Gotamas turns (*ā vavarti*) you (Indra) herewards for doing favour" (ṚV VIII. 88.4).

Music is many times found to be described as "carrying" the gods. Thus ṚV VI.21.2 one says "Praise that Indra who is to be carried by means of songs (*girvāhasam*)". Thus the songs seem to "carry" the god Indra; cp. also ṚV VI.24.6 where Indra is addressed as *girvāhaḥ* see also I.30.5; 139.6; VI.24.6; 2.30 etc. A *brahman* is also supposed to be a carrier of gods. Thus Indra is many times described as *brahmavāhas* i.e. one who is carried by means of hymns (ṚV I.101.9; III.41.3; V. 34.1; 39.5; VI.21.6; 45.4; 7) and as *brahmavāhastama* i.e. the best among those who are carried by hymns (ṚV VI.45.19). The praise-songs (*uktha* -) also carry the gods. "O Indra and Agni, carried by praise-songs (*girvāhasā*) by means of praise-hymns (*stoma* -) and all sings (*gir* -), O you listeners of calls come here for drinking of soma" (ṚV VI.59.10). For the word (*ukthavāhas* see also VIII.96.11; X.104.2 etc. Stoma is also a carrier of gods. Thus ṚV VIII.26.16 it is described to be *vāhiṣṭha* i.e. the best carrier. Similarly we read, "May our praise-hymn (*stoma* -), O Indra, be the best carrier (of the gods), go nearest to you". ṚV VIII.5.18 Aśvins are addressed, "May this *Stoma* of us carry you the best; may it go nearest to you".

Sometimes the *poet-singers themselves* attract the gods with the help of music. Thus ṚV VIII.9.9 we read, "When we drive (*acuccyuvīmahi*) you herewards O Aśvins by the praise-songs or by the song-speeches (*vāṇī*-) then give attention towards that singing of Kāṇva". ṚV VIII.4.2 also the power of music of Kaṇvas is mentioned, "The Kaṇvas drawing you with the praise-hymns turn you towards themselves by means of hymns (*brahmabhiḥ*)". ṚV VIII.61.8 the singers are confident that they will make Indra turn therewards (*ācakṛma*) for favour. ṚV IV.17.16 also the singer is equally confident of his power of music when he says, "We draw (*ācyāvayāmah*) Indra like a bucket from a well". On the other hand ṚV I.168.1 the singer hopes "May I turn (*āvavṛtyām*) you (O Maruts) by means of good songs (*suvṛktibhiḥ*) for the benefit of both the worlds".

Sometimes a *poet-singer* is told by someone else to use his musical power in attracting the gods. Thus ṚV VII.53.2 we read, "Make the two first born parents (viz. *Dyāvāpṛthivī*) sit upon the two seats of Order (*ṛta* -) by means of your newer songs". ṚV VIII.1.8 a poet-singer is told, "Sing a song loudly for him (Indra) by which Indra will come to sit upon the Barhis of Kāṇva and will break the fortresses". Some poet-singers are asked, "Make Agni turn (*ā kṛṇudhvam*) herewards by means of songs and obeisances" (ṚV IX.6.5). Elsewhere some other poet-singers are asked, "Lead (*prabharata*) the gods Jātavedas by means of divine visionic poems (*dhī*- ṚV X. 176.2).

The poet-singers call, invoke, *invite* the gods with the help of musical elements. In doing so they seem to be aware of the magnetic power of music and therefore they seem to be using that power in calling the gods. Thus ṚV I.47.10 the poet-singer says "By means of praise-song (*uktha* -) and songs (*arka* -) I call Indra here". ṚV III.42.4, the poet-singers feel sure that when they call him with the help of music, Indra will certainly come. Thus they say: "For drinking of soma we call Indra by means of the stomas and ukthas; he will come certainly (*kuvid āgamat*). ṚV IV.49.5 they call Indra and Bṛhaspati for drinking soma with the help of songs (*gir* -). Similarly "I invoke you (O Indra) herewards for drinking soma" (ṚV VIII.65.3). ṚV V.64.1 one invites Mitra and Varuṇa by means of a ṛc. ṚV VI.18.6 Indra is said to be invited by means of a visionic poem (*dhi* -). Sometimes the poet-singers invoke with songs (*gir*-). Thus ṚV VI.45.7 "I invite that priest, praiseworthy friend (= Indra) by means of songs like a cow for milking" or "I am praising the (godly) people by means of newer songs; may they come and listen—Mitra, Varuṇa, Agni. "Aśvins are invoked similarly by means of songs: "When we call you by means of songs ... then come here towards my call" (ṚV VIII.22.11 f). ṚV VIII.42.5 f another poet-singer addresses Aśvins, "As the poet Atri invoked you by means of songs, so I invoke you". ṚV VIII.52.6 Indra is invoked by means of praise-hymns (*stoma* -). Elsewhere "the seers call Agni by means of praise-songs (*uktha*)". AV VII.63 (65). 1 Agni is invoked, "We invoke Agni with praise-songs, from the highest station". By means of good songs (*suvṛkti* -) Indra is invoked at the time of dawn (ṚV X. 4.1). Sometimes the gods are invoked for doing some favour. Thus ṚV V.45.4, "I invoke you O Indrāgnī by means of hymns and speeches for favour". ṚV VIII.68.1, Indra is invoked by means of the Bṛhat-sāman for doing favour. Similarly ṚV X.141.3 we read, I invoke Soma, the king, Agni, Ādityas, Viṣṇu, Sūrya, Brahman and Bṛhaspati by means of songs for favour.

Music has its control over a large sphere. A singer believes, "Ou je suis entendu je commande".[1] Spatial distance cannot create any difficulty for the effectiveness of the music. The poet-singers therefore say that they would utter a formula for Agni in the performance of a sacrifice. They further describe Agni as" one who listens to us even from distance (*āre asme ca śṛṇvate* ṚV I.74.1). The singers attract and draw the gods even from afar by means of their musical power. ṚV VII.32.1 Śakti Vasiṣṭha addresses Indra, "Come to (our) feast even if you are at a distance; or if you are here then listen". In verse 4 also he requests Indra to come. The power of the music of Vasiṣṭhas in bringing Indra from distance is suggested in ṚV VII.33.3. In verse 2 it is stated that they brought Indra even from distance (*dūrāt*) by means of soma. In the 3rd verse the Vasiṣṭhas are praised as follows: "In the battle of ten kings Indra came for helping Sudās because of your hymn, O Vasiṣṭhas". In connection with an *ukthya* it is said to Indra, "If you are taking delight in my praise-song (*ukthya*-) come here even from distance (ṚV VIII.32.6). Similarly AV VI.35.1 a poet-singer says, "May Vaiśvānara come forth hither for our aid even from distance (*parāvataḥ*), unto good praises".

Music goes to gods: We saw above how music attracts the gods. Sometimes, however, it is said that music goes to the gods. ṚV V.42.15 a poet-singer expects, "May this stoma reach up (*udaśyāḥ*) to the crowds of Maruts; to the young sons of Rudra" (ṚV V.42.15). He further says: "May this stoma reach to the earth, space, trees and plants for the sake of wealth" (ṚV V.42.16). Similarly another poet-singer hopes, "May our stoma, the best carrier (*vāhiṣṭhaḥ*) (of the gods) be the nearest to you (O Indra) (ṚV VI. 45.30). For the sake of expressing the capacity of a poem-song to approach gods, it is aptly compared to a chariot: "May this bright poem (*manīṣā*-) -goddess go (*pra etu*) unto the gods like a well-shaped powerful chariot" (ṚV VII.34.1). Similarly ṚV V.43.8 a *gir*- (song) is compared to a messanger: "May the great, big, agreeable song go (*gantu*) like a messanger to the Aśvins for inviting them" (ṚV V.43.8). Many similar expressions of the going of a song to the gods are often found. Thus, "May this my song reach (*aṣṭa*) Indra and Varuṇa" (ṚV VII.84.5; 85.5). "May our songs go (*yantu*) to Indra" (ṚV VIII.71.10 f); May our songs reach (*nakṣanta*) you (O Indra) even from afar" (ṚV VIII.92.27); "May our songs reach (*nakṣanta*) to Agni" (ṚV VIII.103.1; may our songs enter (*ā viśantu*) you (O Indra) "(ṚV X.96.1) etc. ṚV VII.36.9 the praise-sound (*śloka*) is expected to go (*etu*) to Maruts. ṚV VI. 23.8 it is said, "May these calls (*havāsaḥ*) reach (*pra aśnuvantu*) the one who is invoked by many (i.e. Indra)". The ṛcs (verses) desire (*kāmayante*) him who awakes; the sāmans (melodies) approach (*yanti*) him who awakes" (ṚV V.44.14). Now it is Agni who awakes and therefore the ṛcs and sāmans approach Agni (ṚV V.44.15).

Music is not only expected to go to the gods, it is sometimes described as actually going or gone to them. Thus ṚV VI.47.14 it is said, "The songs (*gir*-), hymns (*brahman*-) hasten towards you, O Indra". ṚV III.51.2 the poet-singer says, "My songs approach (*upayanti*) Indra from all the sides." The songs and poems (*mati*-) go towards (*acchā yanti*) Agni asking for wealth (ṚV VII.10.3). The songs are sometimes compared to the rivers and their going to the gods is like that of the rivers to the sea. Thus "Into him (Indra) enter (*ā viśanti*) the songs strengthened by the praise-hymns like rivers to the sea" (ṚV VI.36.3). Similarly in the case of Agni it is said, "To you go (*īrate*) the songs making noise, like rivers to the sea" (ṚV VIII.s44.25). Some other expressions are also used for describing the approach of songs to the gods. Thus according to ṚV VII.18.3 the songs "have stood near" to Indra competing with each other. The songs which praise Agni are described to have stood near (*upa asthiran*) "him like sisters" (ṚV VII.102.13). Indra in the form of Laba says that a poem (*mati-*) has stood near to him as a bellowing cow near calf (ṚV X.119.4). W.P. Schmidt has rightly observed how poems are compared to cows and even are identified with them.[2] The praise-hymns (*stoma-s*) are metaphorically described as vessels of honey and are said to be going (*pra yanti*) to Agni (ṚV VIII.103.6). Elsewhere we notice that the praise-songs (*uktha-*) are said to have gone (*agman*) to Indra (ṚV IX.111.3). The same verb is used in the case of hymns (brahman-): These hymns desirous of you, have gone to you (O Aśvins) (ṚV VII.70.7; 71.6).

Gods enjoy Music

Gods are fond of music. They like music and enjoy it. The poet-singers sing and praise the gods with the intention that the gods may be pleased thereby and having become pleased they may grant gifts. The Sumerians used to think that gods charmed by the sweet tunes of citheras and flutes allow themselves to be touched by the prayers of men. Thus gods were supposed to have a taste for music.[3] Similarly the Syrians, in order to make the gods favourable used to accompany their prayers with the sounds of instruments.[4] The Vedic singers too were aware of the power of music which enchants gods, and pleases them. In this connection we find that numerous expressions are used in the Vedas to indicate that the gods desire music, like it, take delight in it and so on.

Gods desire: Gods are many times described as desirous of music. Thus Indra is very often addressed as being desirous of songs (*girvaṇas-* e.g. ṚV I.5.7; 10; 10.12). ṚV II.11.3 we know that Indra desires (*cākan*) praise-songs and praise-hymns belonging to Rudra. ṚV X.96.11 one says to Indra, "You desire (*haryasi*) a newer, newer beloved (*priya-*) thoughtful poem (*manma*)". ṚV X.105.1, it is indicated that he desires for a praise-hymn (*stotra*). Agni also desires songs etc. Thus, ṚV X.91.13 we read, "This newer good-praise (*suṣṭuti-*) I sing for him who desires (*uśate*) it". For the use of a form of the same root (*vaś*) see also ṚV IV.22.1. Agni's desires for music can be said to be implied in the following expression: "Sing a thoughtful poem (*manma*) and praise that god (Agni) who listens (*āśṛṇvate*)" (ṚV IV.3.3). Like Indra, Agni (ṚV I.45.2) and Soma (ṚV IX.64.16) are also described as "*girvaṇas*, desirous of songs." Not only the gods are said to be desirous of music, sometimes music also is said to be desirous of gods. Thus ṚV I.165.4, Indra boasts, "These praise-songs (*uktha-*) desire (*āśāsate*) me, expect me (*pratiharyanti*)".

mad-, mand: In order to indicate that gods are pleased by means of music, forms of various roots are used in the Veda. The root *mad* is one of those roots. In the Veda this root does not suggest any idea of intoxication etc. as it does mostly in the later Sanskrit literature, but rather it suggests the idea of extreme delight.[5] I, therefore, cannot accept *Keith's* translation[6] of AB III.38 in connection with the recitation of ṚV VI. 47. 1-4 (the Anupānīyā-verses) "The deities become drunk as it were in that the Hotṛ recites these verses." The translation should be rather as follows: "The gods are very much delighted in that the Hotṛ recites these verses." Music is supposed to offer extreme delight to gods. Thus ṚV I.51.1, the poet-singers are requested, "Make Indra delighted (*abhi mādata*) with songs". Elsewhere they are addressed similarly, "Making (gods) delighted (*madantaḥ*) with songs, make noise opressing stones like geese" (ṚV III.53.10). ṚV I.165.11 Indra says about a praisehymn (*stoma-*) that it made him delighted (*amadat*). The gods take delight (*mādayante*) together in the praise-hymn of Dyāvāpṛthivī, prepared by Āyu (ṚV III.54.2). ṚV III.64.1 the poet-singer hopes, "May the praise-hymns make you (O Indra) mad with delight (*ut-madantu*). ṚV X. 104.3 also he is requested to be delighted (*mādayasva*) by means of the poetic visions (*dhenā, dhī-*). Similarly Agni is ṚV X.140.3 requested to be delighted (*mādayasva*) by means of good-praises (*suṣṭutibhiḥ*).

The delight of music is sometimes closely associated with that of drinking of soma-juices. It is again to be born in mind that the soma-drinking has no connection with intoxication etc. but with an exalted delight. About Indra it is said, "The unpressed soma has never delighted (*mamāda*) Indra; nor the pressed soma without any powerful hymns" (ṚV VII.26.1). Similarly ṚV X.89.16 it is said that many soma-pressings and powerful hymns have delighted (*mandan*) Indra. Soma gave delight (*mamāda*) to Indra at each praise-songs (*ukthe ukthe*) (ṚV VII.26.2). Elsewhere Indra himself says, "Somas accompanied by praise-songs have delighted (*amandiṣan*) me" (ṚV X. 48.4). For the importance of music in the "satisfaction" of gods by soma, see under miscellaneous expressions.

Think, know (man-, vid- etc.): Another kind of expression indicating that the gods enjoy music is that they "think of" or "know" it. Thus Agni is praised as a thinker (*manotā*) i.e. an appreciator, enjoyer of a bright speech (*vacasaḥ*) (ṚV II.9.4). Agni knows (*veḥ*) the powerful hymns (ṚV II.5.3). ṚV IV.4.11 he is requested, "know (*cikiddhi*) (O Agni) this speech" (cp. V. 22.4; and "know (*bodhi*) O Agni this speech: ṚV VIII.43.27). Agni is a knower (*vidvān*) also of sāman (ṚV IV.5.3). ṚV V. 12.3 it is asked, "How will you, O Agni, be a knower (*navedāḥ*) of my new praise-song ? "Indra also knows or enjoys musical elements. ṚV IV.16.2 the poet-singer recites a praise-song (*uktha-*) a thoughtful poem (*manma*) for Indra who is described to be a knower (*cikituṣe*). ṚV VII.28.1 Indra is requested to come near unto the powerful hymn as a knower (*vidvān*). ṚV VII.22.3 he is requested, "know (*bodha*) well this my speech, the praise which Vasiṣṭha sings". ṚV VII.37.6 a poet-singer anxiously asks, "When will you O Indra know (*bubodhaḥ*) our speech?" but elsewhere another poet-singer is confident about his musical power when he says, "He (Indra) will certainly (*kuvit*) know (*vedat*) the songs" (ṚV VIII.96.10; cp. 11). ṚV VIII.69.4 a poet-singer is told, "Sing (*arca*) (about) Indra by means of a song as he will know (*vide*)". Other gods also "know" music. Thus Vatsa Kāṇva requests Aśvins to know (*bodhata*) his singing (ṚV VIII.9.9). ṚV VIII.35.4 another poet-singer requests them to know (*bodhata*) his call (*havasya*).

Maruts are ṚV V.55.8 similarly requested, "Be knowers (*navedasaḥ bhavatha*) O Maruts of whatever is spoken (*udyate*) or sung (*śasyate*) either old or new". While ṚV X.26.2 it is hoped about Pūṣan, "May he know (*ciketa*) good praises (*suṣṭuti-*), ṚV X.26.3 it is asserted that he docs know (*veda*) the good praises. Soma is described as "*vacovid* knower of speech" (ṚV IX.91.3). ṚV X.92.12 the Sun and Moon are requested to know (*bodhatam*) the song. ṚV X.114.1 it is remarked about the gods in general. "The gods knew (*viduḥ*) the song (*arka-*) along with the sāman."

prī: This is another root used to suggest that the gods enjoy music, are pleased thereby, love it etc. Thus, Soma is described as one to whom a praise-hymn is dear (*priyastotra*) (ṚV I.91.6). About a performer of sacrifice it is said that he "wants to please (*piprīṣati*) Agni by means of an oblation and praise-songs (*ukthaiḥ*)" (ṚV IV.4.7). Indra and Varuṇa are requested to be the lovers songs. "Be lovers (*pretārā*) of this visionic poem (*dhī-*) O Indra and Varuṇa as bulls of a cow". ṚV IV.68.9 a poet-singer is asked to sing (*pra-arca*) a beloved (*priyam*) poem (*manma*) poem for Varuṇa. ṚV X.54.6 a poem sung for Indra is also described as beloved (*priya-*). A song for Indra is also described as beloved (*priya-*). A singer (*jaritā*) is described to be dear (*priyaḥ*) to Indra. While giving the significance of the Vasiṣṭhasāman, TMB XII.12.10 says, "By means of this sāman Vasiṣṭha became dear to Indra. One who praises with this sāman also becomes dear to the deities". Similar is the case in connection with the Gāra-sāman". On (the verses beginning with) *idaṁ vaso sutam* ... (SV I.124), the Gāra- sāman (is to be sung). By means of this (sāman), Gara pleased (*aprināt*) Indra. Indra is pleased by means of this sāman" (TMB IX. 2.16). The sāman has something beautiful (*valgu-*) and dear (*priya-*) in it and JUB I.16.2.9f, it is said that Soma chose this part of the sāman. While uttering the vaṣaṭ-call, one should think of the deities; thereby one pleases (*prīṇāti*) them (GB II. 3.4).

raṇ, ram: Sometimes we find that the happiness of gods due to music is expressed with the roots *raṇ* and *ram*. Thus for example, about Indra it is said, "Indra becomes happy (*raṇyati*); where a singer (*arkaḥ*) sings (*āghoṣate*) his song (*ślokam*) resounding upto the heaven" (ṚV I.83.6). ṚV III.41.4, he is requested "At the time of soma-pressings, take happiness (*rārandhi*) in our praise-hymns, O Killer of Vṛta, take happiness also in praise-songs". ṚV VIII.12.18 it is said that he takes happiness (*raṇ-*) in the praise-songs (*uktheṣu*). ṚV VIII.32.6, he is requested, "If you become happy (*rāraṇaḥ*) by my praise-songs, then come here O Indra". Elsewhere the praise-singers say, "We shall, O Indra, make you happy (*raṇayāmasi*) in the praise-songs like the cows in willows. (ṚV VIII.92.12). ṚV X. 42.1 a poet-singer is told in the following manner: "Make Indra happy (*nirāmaya*), O Singer (*jaritaḥ*), by the Soma". ṚV V.74.3 Aśvins are asked, "Whose powerful hymns do you like (*raṇyathaḥ*) ?" ṚV I.147.1 it is asked about the gods in general, "How do the gods become happy (*raṇayanta*) in the right sāman". Thus gods become happy by means of music. Reciprocally music also becomes happy when it comes into contact with gods. Thus ṚV VIII.16.2 "The praise-songs (*uktha*) take happiness (*raṇayanti*) in him (Indra)".

juṣ: Many times we find the forms of the root *juṣ* to indicate that gods enjoy music. Thus ṚV I.12.2 Agni is requested, "Enjoy (*juṣasva*) this our praisehymn (*stoma-*) O Agni". Similarly ṚV III.15.2 "Get enjoyment (*juṣasva*) in my praise-hymn as in the birth of son (O Agni". cp. VIII.43.16). ṚV IV.2.20 he is requested to enjoy the ucathas (praise-songs). ṚV IV.3.15 Agni is requested to enjoy (*juṣasva*) the powerful hymns (*brahman-*). ṚV X.69.3 he is requested to enjoy songs (gir-) ṚV VII.15.6 he is hoped to enjoy (*juṣata*) songs. ṚV VI.5.6 he is requested to enjoy a sonorous thoughtful poem (*manma*) of the singer. Elsewhere he is requested to enjoy good hymns (*sūktāni*). ṚV X.122.2 Agni is requested to rejoice (*pratiharya*) by enjoying (*juṣāṇaḥ*) the speech (*vacaḥ*). ṚV X.150.2 he is requested to come enjoying (*jujusānaḥ*) sacrifice and speech (*vacaḥ*). The poet-singers made Agni joyful (*upo jujuṣuḥ*) by means of songs (*giraḥ*) (ṚV VIII.23.9). Indra is similarly requested to enjoy (*juṣ-*) the poem-songs of the poet-singers. Thus ṚV III.39.7 he is requested, "Enjoy (*juṣasva*) these songs (*gir-*) of a poet, O Indra" (cp. III.40.8). Elsewhere he is implored, "Eat our sacrificial cake and enjoy (*juṣayāse*) our songs as a wife-seeker a woman" (ṚV III.52.3; IV.32.16). Thus the musical enjoyment is compared to sexual enjoyment (cp. also ṚV III.62.8). ṚV III.51.6 Indra is entreated to enjoy the powerful hymns (*brahman-*) and songs (*gir-*). Similarly ṚV V. 29.15 he is requested to Enjoy the powerful hymns which are being created, and the new ones we have created. ṚV VII.22.3 he is requested to enjoy the powerful hymns at the time of a soma-feast. Indra who is addressed as desirous of songs (*girvaṇaḥ*) is exhorted also to enjoy the praisehymn "which swells like sea" (ṚV VIII.12.5). He is ṚV VIII.90.3 requested to enjoy the powerful hymns which are not too wonderful, just simple (*anatidbhutā*).[7] Elsewhere he is described as enjoying (*jujuṣāṇa-* ṚV VII.23.3; *juṣāṇa* - 24.4; cp. 29.2) the powerful hymns. ṚV VII.26.1 he is expected to listen (*śṛṇavat*) enjoyingly (*jujuṣat*) a heroic newer praise-song (*uktha-*) which is being created by a poet-singer. Elsewhere he is expected to get the songs arranged in such a manner that the poet-singers may sing songs enjoyable to him: "Whatever of us Indra enjoys (*juṣ-*) and desires (*vaś-*) may he make us arrange it: the powerful hymns (*brahman-*) praise-hymns (*stoma-*) and praise-songs (*uktha-*)" (ṚV IV.22.1). The praise-singers are ṚV VIII. 62.1 requested to carry for Indra a praise (*upastuti-*) which he would enjoy (*jujoṣati*). Indra does not like to enjoy a sacrifice devoid of powerful hymns (*brahman-*) (ṚV X.105.8). The Bṛhat-sāman is particularly said to be enjoyed (*juṣṭam*) by Indra (ṚV VIII.89.7). Aśvins also enjoy music. Thus a poet-singer says, "These strengthening, powerful hymns and a praise-hymn are prepared for you O Aśvins by the Gṛtsamadas. Come here enjoying them O heroes". The Aśvins are ṚV VII. 68.1 also requested to come enjoying the songs (*juṣethām*) the songs in ṚV VIII.35.6. Similarly elsewhere they are requested to enjoy (*juṣethām*) an emotional poem (*manīṣā-*), song (*gir-*)

and a good hymn (*suvṛkti-*) offered by the poet-singers (ṚV VII.70.7; 71.6; cp. 73.3 b). Some other gods and joint divinities are also supposed to be enjoying songs etc. Thus ṚV VII. 34.21 it is hoped, "May Tvaṣṭṛ enjoy (*prati-juṣeta*) our praise-hymns (*stoma-*)". ṚV VII.35.14 it is hoped that Ādityas, Rudras, Vasus will enjoy the newer, powerful, hymn being prepared. Maruts are expected to enjoy (*juṣanta*) a good hymn (*sūkta* ṚV VII.58.6). ṚV III.6.1 Uṣas and ṚV V.41.2 Mitra, Varuṇa, Aryaman, Āyu, Indra and Maruts are expected to enjoy the stoma (praise-hymn) of the poet-singers. The Vājas and Ṛbhus are requested to enjoy (*jujuṣṭana*) the most beautiful worth-seeing, ornament in the form of a stoma (ṚV IV.36.7). ṚV IV. 52.11, Indra with Maruts, Mitra with Tvaṣṭṛ and Aryaman are expected to enjoy a stoma. ṚV X.65.14, the Viśvedevas are expected to enjoy a *brahman* and *sūkta*. Similarly the joint divinities like Indrāvaruṇau (invocation of thoughtful poems: *mati*—ṚV VI.69.4); Indrāgnī (praise-hymns; *stoma*—ṚV VII. 93.1; good praise: *suṣṭuti-*, s. going on the path of the Gāyatrī-metre—ṚV VIII.38.6); and Mitrāvaruṇau (the powerful hymns: *brahman*—ṚV VII.61.6; and call: *hava*—ṚV VII.82.8) etc. are expected to enjoy (*juṣ* -) various musical elements.

śaṁ: Music is often blissful to the gods. The idea of blissfulness is expressed by the word *śaṁ*. Thus Indra says, "The powerful hymns (*brahman-*) and thoughtful poems (*mati-*) are blissful (*śaṁ*) to me" (ṚV I.165.4). ṚV VI.42.22 a poet-singer is told, "Sing (*gaya*) (a song) that will be blissful (*śaṁ*) to him (*Indra*)". The poet-singers desire that their songs will be blissful to the gods. Thus ṚV V.11.5 we read, "This sweetest speech (*vacaḥ*) is, O Agni, for you; may this emotional poem (*manīṣā-*) be blissful to your heart". Similarly ṚV VIII.74.8 a poet-singer says, "May it (the newer poem: *mati-*) be the most blissful (*śantamā*) agreeable (*caniṣṭhā*), lovable (*priyā*) to you (Agni)". In connection with Aśvins also another poet-singer says, "May the powerful hymns which increase (the strength of the listener *vardhanā*) which we have shaped out like chariots be the most blissful to Aśvins". (ṚV V.73.10).

Miscellaneous expressions: There are a few miscellaneous expressions indicating that the gods enjoy music, they like it etc. Thus ṚV IV.3.15 the poet-singer hopes, "May you (O Agni) be pleased in mind (*sumanāḥ*) with these songs (*arkaiḥ*). Gautama made Agni happy (*caniṣṭhat*) by means of a song (*girā*) (ṚV VIII.74.11). ṚV VIII.101.5 the poet-singers are requested to sing (*gāyata*) an agreeable (*chandyam*) praise-hymn (*stotra-*). About Soma it is said, "He becomes pleased (*modate*) by means of a song". ṚV IX.113.3 it is said that the praise-songs (*uktha-*) have delighted (*harṣayan*) Indra. ṚV X. 50.4 Indra is praised, "You became big (*mahān*) by means of a powerful hymn (*brahman-*). The "touch" of music is compared to that of a woman: "May the good praises (*suṣṭuti-*) touch to his (Agni's) heart as the desirous good-clothed wife the husband". Gods become pleased by songs, etc. and then do favour unto the singers. Thus Kāṇva pleased Indra by means of the Kāṇva-sāman and came into harmony (*saṁvid*) i.e. friendship with Indra. Whosoever sings this sāman becomes a friend of Indra (TMB IX.2.6). Music can "satisfy" and thereby "delight" the gods. Thus the vaṣaṭ-call is described as a vessel of the gods (*devapātra*) and when the Hotṛpriest utters the vaṣaṭ-call, he satisfies (*tarpayati*) deities by this vessel (AB III.5; GB II.3.1; cp ŚB I.7.2.13). Similarly JB III.58 the two Abhīśu-sāmans are described to be satisfying and thereby delighting the gods. Thus Abhīśu Śyāvāśvi desired that the gods should be satisfied by his soma. He then "saw" these sāmans and praised with them. Then the gods became satisfied of his soma. Therefore these sāmans are described as "satisfaction (*tṛpti-*" JB III.68). We have already noted above how the delight of music is associated with that of soma (see above *mad-*, *mand-*).

Thus we can say that the gods like music very much. The poet-singers make use of music for the sake of pleasing the gods and thereby getting the desired results granted by the gods. Moreover music is sometimes considered as a means for barter with gods as we shall detail now.

Music: A means of barter with gods: Many times the poet-singers barter by means of music with the gods. They offer their songs etc. to the gods and ask them to give various rewards in return. Thus there is a kind of "do-ut-des"[8] between the singers and gods. For example food is often demanded in return of music. ṚV I.165.15; 167.11 we read, "This is a praise-hymn (*stoma-*) this is a speech of poet Māndārya for you O Maruts. May food (*iṣam*) reach him". Indra is ṚV IV.16.21 addressed in the following way, "Praised in the past and being praised (now) give you (O Indra) food (*iṣam*) unto us, and the praise-singer". ṚV VII.68.9 Aśvins are addressed, "The poet of good thoughtful poems is singing hymns (*sūkta-*) for you, "May the cow strengthen him by means of food (*iṣā*) and milk". ṚV VIII.8.15 also they are requested, "Give thousand-coloured food (*iṣam*) dripping with ghee, unto him who, the seer Vatsa, strengthened you by means of songs (*gir-*). Sometimes *vāja* (power-substance viz. food) is expected from the gods in return of the music. Thus ṚV IV.32.9 we read, "The Gotamas O Indra have cried by means of a song so that you may give them *vāja*". Similarly, ṚV VI.50.6, "May Indra being praised (by a new *brahman-* powerful hymn) listen to our call and grant *vājas*". ṚV V. 65.3 Mitra and Varuṇa are praised, "I praise-sing (*upa brave*) you so that you may give *vāja*".

Sometimes some other things are expected from the gods in return of the music. ṚV I.171.1 favour and good inclination of Maruts are demanded in return of a beautiful song (*sūkta*) accompanied by obeisance. ṚV I.173.3 Maruts and Indra are requested to show favour (*mṛḷayanta*) unto the singers. ṚV VIII.6.32 also Indra is asked to enjoy the good praise (*suṣṭuti-*) of the poet-singer and to do favour (*ava*) generously unto him. ṚV I.182.4 Aśvins are asked to make each speech (*vāc-*) of the singer richly rewarded in him (*ratninī*) and to do favour (*avatam*) unto his recitation (*Śaṁsa-*). ṚV II.11.12 also they are requested, "We desirous of (your) favour prepare praise-songs; may we be destined for your gifts (*rāyo dāvane syāma*)". Elsewhere they are described as givers of various gifts (*citrarāti-*) to those who sing for them and praise them. ṚV V. 4.7 one expects wealth in return of the praisesongs, and oblations. "We shall worship you (O Agni) with praise-songs (*uktha-*) and with oblations; give us wealth (*rayi-*) desired by all and all the goods (*draviṇāni*)". Sometimes along with wealth (*rayi-*) some other things are demanded in return of the songs etc. Thus ṚV VII.93.4 wealth (*rayi-*) and fame (*yaśas-*) are asked for in return of songs (*gir-*). ṚV VI.65.4 wealth, good heroes (sons) and fame are expected. "Give unto the praise-singers wealth along with good-heroes (*suvīra-*) and wide-spread fame (*śravas-*)". ṚV II.9.5 also along with wealth food and good progeny are demanded: "Make, O Agni, your singer rich in food (*kṣumantam*) and lord of wealth with good progeny". ṚV V.41.5 a visionic song is expected to be prepared for wealth and favour. Elsewhere the poet-singers expect to be possessors of chariots as result of a visionic poem (ṚV IV.16.21; 17.21; 19.11; 20.11; 21.11; 22.11; 23.11; 24.11). ṚV I.182.3 one prays to the Aśvins to allow "light (*jyotis-*)" to the eloquent poet-singer. ṚV II.19.7, one prays for friendship in return of a praise-song. "We have released a praise-song (*ucatha-*) for you; may we obtain your friendship (O Indra); turn away the weapons of godless opponents". From Rudra one expects medicines (*bheṣaja-*) in return of praise (ṚV II. 33.12). Freedom from all the evil persons is demanded in ṚV V.25.3: "Pay attention to us;listen unto the call (*hava-*); make us free from all the evil persons O Agni". ṚV VIII.1.18 the desires of offsprings are expected to be fulfilled in return of a song for Indra. ṚV X.29.5 Indra is requested to steer to the other bank, those who have given many songs to him. Elsewhere one asks for immortality. "For the sake of immortality (*amṛtatva-*) I release this speech (*vācam*) as a stimulus (*jūti-*) to you (O Indra)" (ṚV III.34.2). The poet-singers are confident about the power of the stoma (praise-hymn) which they recite. Thus for example ṚV VII.15.4, it is said, "I have prepared a new praise-hymn for Agni, the falcon of heaven. He will *definitely* (*kuvit*) give good things to us". Agni is elsewhere addressed to be near (*antamaḥ*) to the praise-singers for blessedness (*svastaye* ṚV III.10.8). Bṛhaspati is described to be the most beneficent (*śaṁbhaviṣṭhaḥ*) to a praise-singer (ṚV V.42.7).

Thus it will be seen how music is supposed to be a means of barter with gods. The poet-singers sometimes request the gods to accept the songs and be pleased to give good things to the singers. Sometimes however they are confident that gods will definitely fulfil their expectations in return of the songs etc. Thus music is supposed to work magicoreligiously.

Music and gods helpful to each other: Music helps the gods in many ways. Gods also help the music in many ways.

Music strengthens the gods: Gods become strengthened when praise-songs are sung for them. Mbh V.18.17 Śalya informs Yudhiṣṭhira that the great persons acquire great strength when they are being praised (*saṁstūyamānā vardhante mahātmāno yudhiṣṭhira*). Elsewhere we find that Bṛhaspati praises Indra (Mbh V.16.13 ff). Then he is increased in strength (18) and becomes powerful (19). ṚV VIII.16.12 Vatsa, belonging to the family of Kaṇva says that Indra increases himself when praised. Various musical elements are used in praising the gods and then the gods become strengthened.

Gir- (song): Gods are often described or expected to be increased (in strength), aggrandised by means of songs. Thus one says to Agni, "You increase (*vardhase*) yourself (i.e. strengthened, inflamed) by a song" (ṚV II.1.11). Similarly one hopes, "May our songs (*giraḥ*) from which the praiseworthy Agni is born increase (*vardhantu*) him (ṚV III. 10.6). ṚV VIII.44.19 Similar expression is found: "May our songs increase you" (cf. also I.5.88; cp. VIII.44.22). While the poet-singers increase i.e. inflame Fire (Agni) by means of songs they increase another deity, Soma i.e. the juice of soma by means of songs. In both of these cases physical, material increase, growth is meant. Thus one says, "O Soma, we increase (*vardhayāmaḥ*) you by means of songs" (ṚV I.91.11). ṚV IX.26.6 soma is described as, "one who increases by means of songs (*girāvṛdh-*)" and ṚV IX. 61.14 one hopes, "May our songs increase (*vardhantu*) him (soma) (= ṚV VIII.92.21) as cows with younglings their calves". In connection with Indra also we read that he becomes increased i.e. strengthened by means of songs. Thus ṚV I.11.1: "All the songs have increased Indra (in strength)". Similarly ṚV VI. 44.13 describes Indra as "who was increased in strength (*vāvṛdhe*) by means of the old and new songs of the praising seers". ṚV VI. 44.6 Indra is described as "whom the songs increase in strength (*vardhayanti*)". Accordingly one requests Indra to be increased in strength (*vardhayasva*) by means of songs and then make the sun shine, allow the food to be increased, kill the enemy and release the cows (ṚV VI.17.3). ṚV VI.18.1 also it is said, "Praise him (Indra) (O Bharadvāja) and increase him, in strength (*vardha*) by means of songs". ṚV VI.37.5 one hopes, "May Indra be increased in strength (*vardhatām*) by means of songs;" compare also "May these my songs make you (Indra) increase in strength (*vardhantu*)" (ṚV VIII.3.3; cp. also 13.16; 92.21). ṚV III.53.1 Indra and Parvata are jointly addressed, "Enjoying our *iḍā*-offering be increased in strength (*vardhethām*) by songs". In connection with Rudra also we read, "Make Rudra increased in strength (*vardhaya*) by means of songs" (ṚV VI.49.10). One says to Mitrāvaruṇā also, "We want to increase you in strength (*vāvṛdhadhyai*) by means of songs (ṚV VI.67.1). ṚV X.104.7 form of another root is used in order to indicate the strengthening capacity of songs". The songs strengthen (*upabhūṣanti*)[9] Indra".

Brahman: Gods are sometimes described as increasing themselves in strength by means of *brahman* (a powerful hymn). Thus Agni and Soma are described as being increased in strength by means of a powerful hymn (ṚV I.93.6). ṚV V. 73.10 *brahmans* are described as "strengthening (*vardhana-*)". Cp. ṚV VII.22.7 where a poet-singer says, "I am preparing powerful hymns which make you increase in strength (*vardhanā*)". Cp. also ṚV VIII.62.4 "Come O Indra we shall prepare powerful hymns which increase (*vardhanā*) you in strength". ṚV VIII.1.3 a powerful hymn is expected to be increasing the strength of Indra for all the days. ṚV X.44.1,

Indra himself says, "I make out a powerful hymn increasing me in strength (*vardhanam*) for myself. "Elsewhere Indra is described as one "whom the powerful hymn increases in strength and whom does the soma" (ṚV II.12.14). Thus both soma and brahman strengthen Indra. The powerful hymns of Maruts increased Indra (*avardhan*) the power (*taviṣīm*) of Indra (ṚV V.31.10).[10] ṚV VII.19.11 Indra is requested, "Now increase yourself in strength (*tanvā vāvṛdhasva*) being incited by a powerful hymn (*brahmajūtaḥ*)".

Uktha: Similarly a praise-song (*uktha*) is also supposed to be increasing the gods in strength. Thus ṚV I.10.5 it is described as a "means of increasing (*vardhana-*) Indra in strength. The ukthas increased (*vāvṛdhuḥ*) in strength. ṚV VIII.95.6 we read, "We praise him Indra, whom the songs (*gir-*) and praise-songs (*uktha-*) made increase in strength (*vāvṛdhuḥ*)". In the next verse Indra is said to be increasing himself in strength (*vāvṛdhvāṁsam*) by means of pure (*śuddhaiḥ*) praise-songs (ṚV VIII.95.7). Soma also increases himself in strength (*vavṛdhate*) by means of praise-songs at the sacrifices (ṚV IX.18.4).

Stoma (*praise-hymn*): Stomas are also supposed to increase gods in strength. Thus Indra is described as one who is increased (*vāvṛdhe*), in strength by the praise-hymns ancient, mediaeval and new (ṚV III.32.13). Maruts are also described to have been big i.e. strengthened together (*samukṣanta*) by means of the praise-hymns (ṚV V.56.5). By means of a praise-hymn the praise-singer-seer strengthens (*pratibhūṣati*)[11] Aśvins and their chariot (ṚV V.75.1).

Miscellaneous: Some other miscellaneous details and some of the above-mentioned details of vedic music are jointly said to be increasing the gods in strength. Thus for example ṚV I. 190.1 it is said, "Increase, O Bṛhaspati, in strength newly with songs (*arkaih*)". ṚV VIII.44.2 Agni is requested to increase himself in strength by means of a thoughtful poem (*manmanā*). ṚV III.1.8 He is understood to be a bull and is described to have been increased in strength (*vavṛdhe*) by a poem (*kāvyena*).

Good poems (*suvṛkti*) increase Indra in strength (ṚV III. 55.1). The visionic poems (*dhītayaḥ*) speeches (*vāṇī-*) reach Indra increasing him in strength (*vardhayantīḥ* ṚV VI.34.1).[12] ṚV VIII.44.12 the poet-singer says, "Agni was increased (*vāvṛdhe*) by the singer by means of an old, thoughtful poem (*manmanā*)". Cp. also ṚV VIII.74.7f where Agni is requested to increase in strength (*vardhasva*) by means of new poems (*mati-*). According to ṚV X.113.8 the gods were increased in strength by means of a speech (*vacasyā-*) accompanied by soma (ṚV X.113.8). ṚV I.5.8 stomas and ukthas are said to have increased (*avardhan*) Indra in strength and it is hoped that songs (*girs*) also will increase (*vardhantu*) him in strength. Similarly many other musical elements are mentioned jointly to have increased various gods in strength (cf. ṚV VI.23.5; III. 38.4; VII.94.7; VIII.16.9).

Songs of particular persons: Sometimes the names of some particular persons, the songs etc. of whom have the power of strengthening the gods, are mentioned. Thus ṚV II.39.8 it is said, "O Aśvins, the Gṛtsamadas have prepared these powerful hymns (*brahman-*) increasing (you in strength) (*vardhanāni*) and the praise-hymn". Similarly in connection with the Gotamas it is said, "The Gotamas, bringers of praise-songs have increased (*avīvṛdhanta*) you in strength (O Indra)" (ṚV IV. 32.12). ṚV V.22.4 the power of Atris is described thus: "Artis increase (*vardhanti*) you in strength by means of praise-hymns (*stoma-*) O Agni". ṚV VII.77.6 Vasiṣṭhas are said to be increasing (*vardhayanti*) Uṣas in strength by means of their poems (*mati-*). By means of a praise-song (*uktha-*) Kaṇvas increase (*vardhayanti*) Indra according to ṚV VIII.6.11. Vatsa, belonging to the Kaṇva family is said to have increased Indra in strength by means of the praise-hymn (*stoma-*) (ṚV VIII.6.1). Elsewhere he is said to have done the same work by means of the songs (*gir-*) (ṚV VIII.8.8;15) and visionic poems (19). He is very much confident about the power of his praises and says, "So many seers have praised you and so many not praised you. O Indra you increase (*vardhasva*) yourself in strength only when praised by me" (ṚV VIII.6.12 cp. 18). The praise-hymns (*stoma-*) of Gaurīviti also increased Indra in strength (ṚV V. 29.11).

Strengthening for heroic activities: Gods are sometimes made increased in strength for the sake of accomplishing some definite heroic activity. Thus one addresses Indra, "Being increased in strength (*vāvṛdhānaḥ*) by praise-songs, you struck down, O Indra, that Dāsa who was considering himself to be immortal" (ṚV II.11.2). Similarly ṚV V.31.4, "The priests aggrandising Indra by praise-songs increased him in strength for killing the dragoon". ṚV VII.23.14, it is said, "Having listened unto my praise-hymn burn out the Rakṣases possessors of magical power, by means of your glow, O Agni". Similarly Agni is requested, "May Agni, the killer of Rakṣas, united with *mantra-* (formula) destroy the bad named".

Thus we observe that in the Veda musical praise is supposed to be a means of strengthening the gods. In describing this strengthening, forms of the root *vṛdh* are very often used. This root primarily denotes physical growth, increase etc. and secondarily, increase in strength strengthening etc. This strengthening of gods by music is often done with the intention that gods being strengthened may accomplish some heroic activities or activities fulfilling the desires of the poet-singers.

Some other ways in which music helps the gods: Music helps the gods in some other ways also. The Sun is requested ṚV VII. 62.2 to rise up, drawn by the praise-hymns and the Etaśa-horses. By means of sāman the sun was made to shine (ṚV VIII. 29.10). Atris beautify (*śumbhanti*) the gods by means of songs (ṚV V.22.4). The gods get their desired results fulfilled by means of music. They are said to have created Agni by means of a praise-hymn (*stomena*) (ṚV X.88.10). At the time of a contest between gods and Asuras, the gods desired to drown the Asuras into the sea. They then saw the Paurumudga-sāman and sang it. Thereby they could drown the Asuras into the sea (JB III.43). Similarly at another occasion they desired to get victory over the Asuras. Then they saw the Saṁjaya- (victory-) sāman and thereby got their desired result (JB III.132). Once they desired to obtain the food of Asuras. They obtained it with the help of Vājajit-sāman (JB III.151). Some individual gods also got their desired results with the help of music. When Prajāpati created the beings there was no food existing for them. So the hungry beings began to eat each other. Prajāpati then desired to remove their hunger. For that purpose he saw the Iṣovṛdhīya (Food-increaser) - sāman and fulfilled his desire (JB III.148). Indra desired to kill the Asuras having gathered them together (*saṁvṛtya*). Then he saw the Saṁvarta-sāman and did it (JB III.233). Indra desired glory (*śrī-*) which was in Prajāpati. He then saw the Hariśrīnidhana-sāman praised with it and obtained it (JB III.249).

The Gods sing: Many times the gods are described to be singing or performing music. TS III.3.2.1 gives details of music performed by gods. Thus Vāyu makes the hiṁkārs; Agni is the Prastotṛ-priest (i.e. he recites the prelude). Prajāpati is identical with the sāman (melody). Bṛhaspati is the Udgātṛ-priest (sings the udgītha). Maruts are the Pratihartṛ-priests (recite the response). Indra is identical with the finale (*nidhana*). ṚV V.41.2 we know that Mitra, Varuṇa, Aryaman, Āyu, Ṛubhukṣan, Maruts perform a praise-hymn (*stoma-*) along with obeisance for Rudra. Soma is said to be skilled in sāman: "Soma the poet skilled in sāman (*sāmanyaḥ*) goes making (*kṛṇvan* i.e. singing) a sāman to the sister of the friend as it were" (ṚV IX.96.2). Bṛhaspati is also said to be a singer: "With the friends who make noise (*vāvadbhiḥ*) like gooses, cutting the stone-bands, Bṛhaspati has made praise-tune (*prāstaut*) and sung (*ud-agāyat*)" (ṚV X.67.3). Indra is also well-known for his music. Thus his sāman is described as "unsurmountable (*duṣṭaram*)" (ṚV X.93.8). Indra is ṚV X. 112.9 requested to sing (*arca*) a loud song (*mahām arkam*). He dances[13] according to the measure of the Anuṣṭubh-metre (ṚV X.124.9). Agni knows the Gandharvical path of order (*ṛta*), i.e. the correct way of singing (ṚV X.80.6).[14] According to ṚV I.19.4 Maruts sing (*ānṛcuḥ*) a song (*arkam*). Similarly ṚV V.30.5 it is said : "These happy Maruts sing (*arcanti*) a song for you (O Indra)" (cp. V.31.5). Their powerful hymn increases Indra in strength (ṚV V.31.10). AV IV.15.4, one expects that the troops of Maruts would sing unto the god of rain (Parjanya).

The gods come under the influence of music : Music is thus helpful to gods. It is superior to gods. The gods come under the influence of music.[15] The praising-singer drives the shining Uṣas as a charioteer, with the ropes of speech (ṚV I. 113.17). They instigate (*hinvanti*) Soma by means of poems (*mati-*) (ṚV IX.107. 24). They make soma run on the barhis by means of a song (*gir-*) (ṚV IX.71.8). The wise poet-singers drive (*hinvire*) Agni to sit down for a feast (ṚV VIII.43.19). A singer can incite the gods (e.g. Maruts) by his newest song as a plougher the bulls (ṚV VIII.20.19). Music has a power with which one can have control over the gods. At the time of a competition between the two singers the condition of gods becomes the most pitiable and helpless. Thus once both Kutsa and Luśa invited Indra with their magically potent songs. Indra came to the call of Kutsa. Then he bound him on his testicles with one hundred straps. Then Luśa called him with the words *svavṛjaṁ hi tvām*..... (ṚV X.38.5). Then Indra having removed all the straps ran towards Luśa. Then Luśa called him with *indraḥ suteṣu* (ṚV VIII. 13.1). Then Indra came back to him. Luśa again called Indra with *hoyī hāva hoyī*. Indra then remained standing in between them and asked them to carry him by parts; "I shall drink of soma of one with my own self; and of the other with my greatness". On this they agreed and Indra partly consumed the soma of both (JB I.228). In this way the music is sometimes considered to be able to control the gods and is superior to them.

Gods help music—Sometimes, on the other hand, we also find that it is the gods who give inspiration[16] to the poet singers to prepare songs etc. and are thus superior to the music and musicians. Thus ṚV I.184.4, Aśvins are requested, "Spur (*hinota*) a praise-song (*stoma-*) of poet-singer Mānya".

Similarly it is expected, "May (Savitṛ) stimulate (*pracodayāt*) visionic poems "(ṚV III.62.10). ṚV IX.50.1 Soma is requested, "Stimulate (*condaya*) the noise of vāṇa (a musical instrument)". Elsewhere it is said about Soma that he, when being purified, instigates (*iṣyati*) speech (*vācam*)" (ṚV IX. 30.1). Similarly ṚV IX.95.5, he is requested, "Instigating (*iṣyan*) the speech (*vācam*) as the Upavaktṛ (the speech) of the Hotṛ, do you release, when being purified, a poem (*manīṣām*)". ṚV IX.96.7, Soma is said to have stirred (*prāvīvapat*) the speeches (*vācaḥ*), songs (*giraḥ*) and poems (*manīṣāḥ*) as a stream the waves.

Gods create hymns etc.: Gods are sometimes said to be creating hymns etc. Thus one says to Bṛhaspati, "You are the generator (*janitā*) of all the powerful hymns (*brahmāṇi*) (ṚV II.23.2). Indra is requested, "Create (*janayasva*) a new praise-song (*uktham*) by means of sacrifices" (ṚV VI.18.5). In connection with Agni also it is said, "May Vaiśvānara formulate (*cākḷpat*) a praise-hymn (*stoma-*) and a praise-song (*uktha-*)".[17]

Gods favour the songs: Gods are requested to do favour or are described as doing favour to the songs being made by the poet-singers. Thus Soma and Pūṣan are requested, "Favour (*avatam*) unto my visionic poem (*dhiyam*)" (ṚV II.40.5). Similarly ṚV III.62.8 Pūṣan is requested to do favour (*ava*) unto a visionic poem. Agni is requested to do favour (ava) unto the poet-singers at the time of preparing a song (*gāyatrasya prabharmaṇi*) (ṚV I.79.7). Indra is described as doing favour unto the poems (*avataṁ matīnām* ṚV II.46.4).

Gods strengthen the songs—We have seen above how songs etc. strengthen the gods. But sometimes it is the gods who are requested to strengthen or described as strengthening the songs etc. Thus ṚV III.29.10, it is said, "Increase (*vardhaya*) our song in strength". Compare ṚV X.141.6 : "You O Agni increase (*vardhaya*) our hymn (*brahman* -) and sacrifice in strength by means of Agnis". Similarly ṚV V.41.9 it is hoped, "May Āptya increase (*vardhāt*) our recitation (*śaṁsa* -) in strength". ṚV VI.23.6 it is said, "Indra has made the powerful hymns (*brahman-*) strength - (increasing) (*vardhanāni*). Elsewhere the River-goddesses are requested to increase (*vardhayanta*) the songs (*giraḥ*) (ṚV I.15.2). Soma is also requested to increase (*vardhaya*) songs of a singer (*jarituḥ*) in strength (ṚV IX.40.5; cp. 61.23).

Elsewhere some other expressions are used to indicate this strengthening capacity of gods. Thus ṚV VI.62.4 it is said, "Those Aśvins strengthen (*upabhūṣataḥ*) the thoughtful poems (*manman-*) of a newer singer". Addressing Indra one says, "May my powerful hymns (*brahmāṇi*) obtain vigour (*vājam*)" (ṚV VII.19.6). About soma it is said, "He goes putting good valour (*suvīryam*) in a praise-hymn (*stotre*)" (ṚV IX. 20.7). Ādityas, Rudras and Vasus are requested to make the (powerful) hymns (*brahman*) which are being sung strong (*jinvata*) (ṚV X.66.12). Indra and Agni are jointly requested to let the visionic songs (*dhiyaḥ*) swell (*pipyatam*)[18] in strength (ṚV VII.94.2).

Gods find the way for songs: The Gods are supposed to be helpful in finding out the way for songs etc. Thus Agni is requested, "Discover (*vinda*) O Vaiśvānara, path (*gātum*) for our powerful hymn (*brahmaṇe*) (ṚV VII.13.3). ṚV X.122.2 Agni is requested similarly, "Create (*eraya*) O Agni, the right path (*gātam*) for the powerful hymn (*brahmaṇe*)". Similarly one says to Soma, "Now prepare (*sādhaya*) the paths (*pathaḥ*) for a newer good hymn (*sūkta-*)" (ṚV IX.9.8). ṚV IX.91.5 also soma is requested, "Make out (*kṛṇuhi*) as previously the paths for a newer good hymn".

Some other expressions: There are some other expressions also which show how gods are helpful to the music. Thus Agni is requested ṚV VIII.20.2 to protect (*pāhi*) the songs (*giraḥ*) without any negligence (*aprayucchan*). The musical songs are prepared under the care of gods. Thus one requests to Indra, "Under your care (*abhiṣṭau*) the reciters of praise-songs (*ukthaśāsaḥ*) sing (*śaṁsanti*) the praise-songs (*ukthā*) (ṚV VII. 19.9). According to ṚV IX.2.7 the gods purify the songs: "The songs are being purified (*marmṛjyante*) by means of your power (*ojasā*) (O Indra)." AV VI.35.3 it is hoped that Vaiśvānara may extend brightness (*dyumnam*) and light (*svaḥ*) unto the praise-hymns and praise-songs. Bṛhaspati is described as the supreme lord of the powerful hymns (*jyeṣṭharājaṁ brahmaṇām*) (ṚV II.23.1). Agni is requested, "Teach (*ucchaśādhi*) now to me the powerful hymns (*brahmāṇi*) (ṚV VII.1.20; 25). It is the gods who gave a melody (*sāman*) to Nodhas kākṣīvat. That melody then came to be known as Naudhasa (TMB VII. 10.10).

Conclusions

1. Gods and music are closely connected with each other in the veda. 2. Music has an attractive power. So it attracts the gods. Music also goes to gods. One may please the gods with music and ask them to come. Gods are fond of music. They enjoy it. 3. One barters with gods by means of music and gets the desired results granted by them. 4. Music helps gods in many ways. Particularly it is often said that it strengthens them. Gods use music and get their desired results. They come under the influence of music and are sometimes inferior to music. 5. Sometimes, however, they themselves help the music in various ways and are superior to it. 6. Thus music has got a magicoreligious role in connection with the gods.

REFERENCES

1. Belvianes, *Sociologie de la musique*, p. 48.
2. Cf. for Sumerian thoughts on this subject, Virolleaud, in Lavignac, *EnM*, I, p. 38; for similar thoughts among the Chaldians see p. 43.
3. W. P. Schinidt, "Die Kuh auf der Weide", *IF*, 64, p. 1 ff.
4. Cp. Pelagaud, in Lavignac, *EnM*, I. p. 58.
5. Cf. Rahurkar, "Was Soma a spirituous liquor ?", *OT* II. (2-3) 1956, p. 131 ff.
6. Keith, *RBT*, p. 188.
7. For this word see my paper "Vedic *anatidbhutā*, Pali *anacchariyā*, *JUPHS*, 35, 1971, p. 31 ff.
8. For this formula see in general, G. van der Leeuw, "Die *do-ut-des* Formel in der opfer theorie, "*Archiv für Religionswissenschaft*, XX, 3-4, 1920, p. 241 ff.

9. For *upabhūṣ* - See Gonda, *Four Studies,* p.84.
10. Cf. Geldner, *Der Rigveda* II. p.30, see, however, the same, "Zur Erklärung des Rigveda", *ZDMG,* 71, 1917, p.319.
11. Cf. Gonda, *Four Studies,* p.77.
12. Cf. Gonda, *Vision of the vedic poets,* p.185.
13. L. Schroeder, *Mysterium und Mimus im Rigveda,* p.201.
14. Geldner, *Der Rigveda,* III. p.262.
15. Cf. Bergaigne *La religion védique,* I. p.297, Abert, *Musikanschauung,* p.59; James, *Priesthood,* p.38; Gonda, *Vision of the vedic poets,* p. 125; Padmapurāṇa, II. 46.21; 25.
16. Cf. Mowinkel, *Religion und Kultus,* p. 46; 117.
17. Cf. Whitney, *AV* I, p.307.
18. Cf. Renou, *ÉVP,* XIV, p.56.

CHAPTER V

Music and Sacrifice

Use of music in sacrifices

Sacrifice is the central part of the Vedic religion. It consists of many magico-religious phenomena. Music is one of those. It is used[1] during the course of the sacrificial performance in various ways. Numerous ṛc-verses and yajus-formulas are recited at the time of numerous activities in the sacrificial performance. Singing of sāmans is an essential part of the sacrifice in general and the Soma-sacrifices in particular. ṚV I.21.2, the priests are told, "Praise-sing those Indra and Agni (O priests) in the sacrifices". Elsewhere, the poet-singers say, "We shall make this (sacrifice) prosper O Agni, by means of praise-songs and praise-hymns" (ṚV IV.10.1). At the time of establishment of fires (Agnyādhāna) (Kātyāś IV.9.4 ff) and the fire-building ceremony (Agnicayana) (Baudhāśs X.49; Kātyāśs XVIII.3.1 ff) sāmans are sung. In the course of fire-building ceremony music is symbolically used as "bricks". Thus there are stoma-bricks (ŚB VIII.4.1.1 ff; 9); metre-bricks (ŚB VII. 5.2.42; VIII.2.3.7 ff; Baudhāśs X.45) to be laid down at this ceremony.

Many artificially created sacrifices differ from each other not so much on account of the manual activities but of the particular ways of recitations etc. Thus for example there is a two-day-sacrifice in which the first day is a Jyotiṣṭoma Agniṣṭoma and the second an overnight-sacrifice with all the stomas. This two-day-sacrifice is to be performed by one who wants to obtain heaven (TMB XX.11.1 ff). But there is another two-day-sacrifice, the second day of which is Āyus-over-night-sacrifice. This sacrifice is to be performed by one who is desirous of progeny (TMB XX.12.1 ff). These two sacrifices differ from each other in connection with the recitations therein rather than the other activities.

The use of music in various sacrifices is as follows:

In the Vājapeya-sacrifice, there is a race of chariots and at that time seventeen drums are beaten (cp. Kātyāśs XIV.3.14 ff etc.). The significance of this rite is told in the following way:—"The height (*varṣma*) of the speech went away from the gods. It entered the trees. That is the same speech which resounds in trees viz. in drums. Therefore, (the sound of) a drum supersedes all the other speeches (sounds)". When the drums are beaten, the highest speech and other speeches are obtained thereby (TB I.3.6.2; cp. ŚB V.1.5.6).

In the Aśvamedha-sacrifice playing upon lute takes place. "But indeed glory, royal sway departs from him who performs the Aśvamedha. When a man attains to distinction, lute is played to him ..... for lute is a form of glory. It is thus glory that they confer upon him" (ŚB XIII.1.5.1). There are two persons—a Brāhmaṇa and a Rājanya who sing and play upon lute every day for a year. Thereby, it is said that the performer gets both the brahman-splendour and the kingly power. The Brāhmaṇa sings during day-time and the Rājanya during night-time. The Brāhmaṇa sings "Such sacrifices he (the sacrificer) performed; such gifts he gave". The Rājanya sings, "Such war he (the performer) waged; such battle he won". Each of them sings three stanzas the total of which is six. "Six seasons make up a year; he thus establishes (the sacrificer) in the seasons or year" (ŚB XIII.1.5.2 ff; TB III.9.1.14; Māśs IX. 2.2.7; Baudhāśs XV.8f). Thus the music in the Aśvamedha-sacrifice is helpful for obtaining the brahman-splendour, kingly power, and for the sacrificer's establishment in the seasons of the year. In the same sacrifice there is another rite in which also music is performed. It is the "Pāriplava-ākyāna" i.e. the revolving, recurring or cyclic legend so called because in it there are ten such stories which are repeated on every tenth day during the year in which the Aśvamedha-sacrifice is performed. On every day the Adhvaryu asks the masters of lute-playing to play and sing of the performer-king along with the righteous kings of past. As the result of this singing, the sacrificer gets share of the same world with the righteous kings of past (ŚB XIII.4.3.1 ff). On the tenth day of the Pāriplava-rite ten sāmans are to be sung. (ŚB XIII.4.3.14). Thus music is a part of the Aśvamedha-ritual. Moreover, music seems also to be used during the Aśvamedha-sacrifice, not as a direct part of the śrautaritual but probably as a non-śrauta, popular rite. Thus in a performance of this sacrifice, many young women are mentioned to have sung and musical instruments like drums and conchshells, etc. are said to have been played upon (Mbh XIV.91.39).

In the Mahāvrata-ceremony also music is performed. Thus there is music in the form of beating drums (e.g. Satyāśs XVI. 6.7 ff. Kātyāśs XIII.3.15 ff), playing upon lutes and singing (e.g. Kātyāśs XIII.3.17 f) and dance of maidens (e.g. Kātyāśs XIII.3.21 ff).

Importance of music in the sacrifice

The importance of music is often emphatically mentioned in the Veda. Thus the recitation of hymns is so important in a sacrifice that without it no sacrifice can go to the gods. ṚV X. 105.8, One says to Indra, "No sacrifice without powerful hymns separately reaches you so that it may please you". Similarly sometimes it is said that a sacrifice without sāmans is not a sacrifice at all (*ayajño vā eṣa yo' sāmā* TS I.5.7.1; 8.1; TB II.1.5.6 f; cf. *nāsāmā yajño'stītyāhuḥ* - ŚB I.4.1.1). Therefore in a rite in which there is no direct singing of a sāman, efforts are made to show how indirectly, at least, sāman-singing is present there. Thus in the Darśapūrṇa-māsa-offerings, there is no direct singing of sāmans. But at the time of recitation of the kindling verse (Sāmidhenī-) one utters a verse beginning with *agna āyāhi vītaye* (O Agni, come here for the feast) and it is described as a form of the Rathantara-sāman. Further the recitation of the verse beginning with *taṁ tvā samidbhir aṅgiraḥ* (thee, with the kindling sticks, O Aṅgiras), is the form of the Vāmadevya-sāman and the recitation of the verse beginning with *bṛhadagne suvīryam* (the great powerful one, O Agni) is that the Bṛhat-sāman. Thus the recitation of these three verses symbolises the singing of three sāmans. Thus when one recites them one makes the sacrifice "with the sāman" (TS II.5.8.1 cp. II.5.7.1ff). ŚB I.4.1.1, another way of making the Darśa-pūrṇamāsa-sacrifices "with the sāman" is mentioned. According to that text, one should recite the kindling verses having made the hiṁkāra (the sound *hum*). "For no sāman is without the hiṁkāra (*na vā ahiṁkṛtya sāma gīyate*)". Therefore, the *hiṁkāra* is an essential part of a sāman, when one makes *hiṁkāra*, one sings sāman as it were. Moreover after each of the kindling-verses one should utter *OM* which also stands for a sāman. Thus the whole performance is symbolically made "with the sāman". Similarly in the Agnihotra-offering, there is no direct sāman-singing. But since, without sāman, a sacrifice is no sacrifice, efforts are made to make the Agnihotra "with the sāman", in an indirect way. Thus one ladles the offering-material four times. This is mystically, the form of the Rathantara-sāman. For the word *Rathantara* has four syllables. Similarly when one holds "up" the offering material, it is the form of Vāmadevya-sāman; for Vāmadevya is identical with the "middle-space (*antarikṣa-*)". One offers twice. This is the form of the Bṛhat-sāman; for the word Bṛhat is two syllabled. Thus the entire Agnihotra becomes, mystically "with sāmans" (TB II.1.5.6 f). The importance of the stomas is told by MS I.5.5 with the following remark—"It is no sacrifice in which no stoma is yoked (used)". In the Agnihotra-performance, there is no stoma. Therefore, the MS maintains that the prayer *"upaprayanto'dhvaram"* etc. which one makes in the Agnihotra, serves mystically as a stoma. (MS I.5.5; cp. KS VII.4; KPKS V.3; TS I.5.7.1).

Importance of music in the sacrifice is implied by associating music, sacrifice and gods together. According to AV VII. 54.1, ṚC and Sāman carry the offering to the gods (cp. SV I. 369). JB I.71, we read, "Therefore, wherever, priesthood is made by means of samans, *there* only, gods eat the most". Thus in order to please gods so that they may eat and enjoy the sacrifice, music is very much important. Similarly, according to ṚV I.83.6, "Indra rejoices there, where a singer sings his song resounding upto the heaven". Therefore, to Indra accompanied by Maruts, to Mitra, accompanied by Tvaṣṭṛ and to Aryaman oblations are given along with the praise-hymns (*stoma*) with the hope that they will enjoy them (ṚV VI.52.11). Similarly, ṚV VI.2.1, it is said to Agni, "People call you by means of sacrifices and *songs*". The sacrificer, who offers services to Agni in the form of sacrifice, sacrificial fuel, praise-songs (*uktha-*), songs (*arka-*) becomes immortal (ṚV VI.5.5). Compare ṚV V.72.1, "We sacrifice like Atri, for Mitra and Varuṇa, by means of songs".

The sāman-singing is so important in the Vedic sacrifices, that bad results accrue if one were to deviate from sāmans of a rite. Thus we read, "He who deviates from Sāmans (of a rite), to him bad luck will befall, after he has been consecrated (TMB XVIII.10.1; MS IV.4.10; TB I.8.8.3). TS II.5.7.1 sāman (melody)- singing is implied to be more important than the recital of ṛcs (verses) or yajus (formulas). Thus "(When) the gods (were performing the sacrifice, they) could not rest on the ṛc or the yajus. They could rest only on the sāman".

Elsewhere the recital of ṛcs is said to be more important than that of yajus and sāman. "Whatever of the sacrifice is done accompanied by a sāman or yajus that is loose; whatever by ṛc, that is firm (*yad vai yajñasya sāmnā yajuṣā vā kriyate śithilaṁ tad yad ṛcā tad dṛḍham*" TS VI.5.10.3-4). For the ṛcs and firmness see also KS XXIV.2. Sometimes importance of yajus is maintained. Thus, "whatever of sacrifice is done without a yajus-formula, it is unsuccessful (*vyṛddhaṁ vā etad yajñasya yad ayajuṣkeṇa kriyate*" ŚB XIII.1.2.1., TB II.8.3.2). According to MS III.6.5, sacrifice kept its beloved form in the yajus. Thus, "Sacrifice manifested itself, threefold. By one it rested upon the ṛcs by another one upon sāmans. What was the beloved form of the sacrifice, by it, is (the sacrifice) rested upon the yajus. (The sacrificial work) is performed with ṛcs, loudly; with sāmans also loudly, but with yajus silently; for there is the beloved form sacrifice there" (cp. KS XXIII.2).

The close connection of the Vedas with the sacrifice is obvious. Every ritual act is accompanied by some vedic text. Therefore ŚB V.5.5.10 it is said in an exaggerated manner :-

"This much is all the sacrifice, as much are the vedas (*etāvān vai sarvo yajñaḥ yāvāneṣa trayo vedaḥ*"). GB I.1.37 we read, "Sacrifice is acquired by and grasped as it were by the vedas (*vedair yajñaḥ abhipannaḥ grasitaḥ*)". Further GB I.1.38 says, "This sacrifice is based upon the vedas (*ayaṁ yajño vedeṣu pratisṭhitaḥ*)". As the rivers flowing to different directions, have different names, but when they go to the sea, they lose their names and are called only the "sea"; similarly all the Vedas along with all their ancillary literature, come to be called sacrifice (yajña-) when they meet with it (GB I.2.10). The gods are told to have followed the way of *Satya* (truth). The *satya* is then said to be the same as the threefold knowledge (*trayī vidyā*) i.e. the three vedas. The gods then spoke, "Let us spread the *satya* by performing the sacrifice (*yajñaṁ kṛtvedaṁ satyaṁ tanavāmahai*" ŚB IX.5.1.18). ŚB I.1.4.3 identifies the threefold knowledge with sacrifice (*saiṣā trayī vidyā yajñaḥ* and ŚB IV.6.7.1 says, "The threefold knowledge is used in a soma-sacrifice". In the story narrated in JB I.388, Prajāpati asks the gods to spread the sacrifice by means of the threefold knowledge (*trayeṇa vedena*).

While in most of the places, reference is found to the three Vedas only, GB (which belongs to the AV) is clearly active in mentioning the number four of the Vedas by including the Atharvaveda among the Vedas[2]. GB I.2.8 describes how four Vedas are nothing but the sacrifice itself. Thus the ṛc. forms the body of the sacrifice, the yajus is connected with its movements, the sāman with its lustre and the Bhṛgvaṅgirases (i.e. the Atharvavedic mantras) with the water. GB I.5.28, describes how sacrifice is projected by the four vedas. In this way all the four vedas are connected with the sacrifice.

Musical elements as limbs

The sacrifice is often metaphorically described to be a man,[3] and various elements of Vedic music are described to be the limbs of this sacrifice-man. Thus JB I.259, the out-of-doors-chant is described as feet; the four ājya-chants as thigh-bones; the three-metred midday-pavamāna-chant as the part below the navel; and the pṛṣṭhas as back (JB I.257; cp. 258). TMB VII. 3.7 describes the midday-pavamāna as the trunk of the sacrifice, the Gāyatrī-metre as the mouth, and the Gāyatra-sāman as the breath of the sacrifice. "When the Gāyatra-sāman is being chanted on Gāyatri-metre, breath is put into the mouth of the sacrifice". The Silent-praise (Tūṣṇīṁśaṁsa) is said to be the eye of the soma-pressing (AB II.32).

Sometimes sacrifice is supposed to be like a bird and various musical factors are said to be the limbs of this bird. Thus the Jyotiṣṭoma-Agniṣṭoma sacrifice is just like a bird. The Bahiṣpavamāna-stotra (out-of-doors-chant) is in the Trivṛt (nine-versed) - stoma and it is its (Jyotiṣṭoma-Agniṣṭoma-sacrifice) head. The other pavamānas are in the Pañcadaśa (fifteen-versed) - stoma and Saptadaśa (seventeen-versed) - stoma. They are the two wings. The Hotṛ's Ājyastotra is in the Pañcadaśa the pṛṣṭha-stotra is in the Saptadaśa and the Yajñāyajñīyastotra in the Ekaviṁśa (twentyone-versed) - stoma. They are the tail of this sacrifice-bird (ŚB X.1.2.7). Similarly when the fire-altar is built, one praises the built fire supposing it to be a bird, "Thou art a bird of fair feathers; thy head the Trivṛt-stoma; Thy eye the Gāyatra; thy breath the stoma; thy body the Vāmadevya-sāman; thy wings the Bṛhat and Rathantarasāmans; thy tail the yajñāyajñiya, thy limbs the metres; thy hoofs the altars; thy name the yajusformulas" (TS IV.1.10.5; cp. Baudhāśs X.15). JB I.173, the sacrifice is metaphorically supposed to be a cow, Yajñāyajñīyā-sāman is then the udder of the sacrifice-cow and the Gāyatra, Rathantara, Bṛhat and Vāmadevya are the teats of it.

AB III.31, the sacrifice is supposed to be a tree. The inserted verses (*dhāyyas*) and offering verses (*yājyās*) are just like "root" of this sacrifice-tree. If different inserted verses and different offering-verses are used, the sacrifice-tree becomes uprooted. For the inserted-verses as the "root" of the sacrifice see also AB III.32.

Elsewhere the sacrifice is described as a ship. In connection with Auśana-sāman and Kāva-sāman, it is said, "The ship which is driven by father and son remains uninjured. The sacrifice is the divine ship. These father and son drive it. The Auśana is forwards and Kāva afterwards. That is for the sake of uninjuredness of the sacrifice" (JB I.166). The Bṛhat and Rathantara-sāmans themselves are described as ships and it is added that these sāmans carry across the sacrifice (AB IV.14).

Sometimes the sacrifice understood to be a chariot and various musical factors are understood either as parts of this chariot or as draught animals. ṚV X.114.6, it is implied that ṛc and sāman are wheels of the sacrifice-chariot: "The wise men, having measured out the sacrifice thoroughly, make the chariot go by means of ṛc and sāman". JB III.9, it is said that the Bṛhat and Rathantara-sāmans being yoked carry the sacrifice. Here these sāmans are described as draught-animals. Similarly, JB III.370, glorifies the Trivṛt-stoma, by saying that it alone, being yoked "carries" the Dvādaśāha sacrifice. For stomas "carrying" the sacrifice see TMB II.16.3. TMB VI.3.15 directly compares the stomas with horses. "When the nobles undertake a journey they yoke the strongest of their horses. The nine-versed (Trivṛt), fifteen-versed (Pañcadaśa), seventeen-versed (Saptadaśa), and twenty-one-versed (Ekavimśa) are the strongest of all the stomas. The chanter yokes these in order to reach heavenly world".

Origin of music from sacrifice

For understanding the close connections of music and sacrifice, it will be helpful to observe how it is maintained sometime that music is originated from the sacrifice and sometimes that sacrifice is originated from music. Thus ṚV X. 90.9, it is said that from the primordial self-sacrifice of the Man, Ṛcs, Sāmans, metres and Yajus were born. According to ṚV X.71.3, the wise men followed the trace of speech (*vāc*) by means of sacrifice. Here the word "speech" implies the recitations of all kinds in the sacrificial performance. From the soma-cup called Upāṁśu, Trivṛt-stoma (ŚB VIII.1.1.5), and from the soma-cup called Antaryāma, the Pañcadaśa-stoma (ŚB VIII.1.1.8) is said to be made out. Similarly from the Śukra soma-cup, the Saptadaśa-stoma (ŚB VIII.1.2.2.), from the Manthin the Ekaviṁśa (ŚB VIII.1.1.5) and from the Āgrayaṇa, the Triṇava-trayastriṁśa-stoma (ŚB VIII.1.1.8) are said to be made out.

Origin of sacrifice from music

On the other hand we can give some references according to which the sacrifice has its origin in the music. Thus the Yajñāyajñīya-sāman is described to be the "womb" of sacrifice. Prajāpati created sacrifice from the Yajñāyajñīya-sāman (TMB VIII.6.3). The sacrifice named Ṣoḍaśī came into existence out of a manifestation of the Bṛhat-sāman. Thus once upon a time Indra and Bṛhat came together. The Bṛhat surpassed Indra through one of its manifestations. "Indra became afraid of this (manifestation) lest it (viz. the Bṛhat) should overcome him by means of it (the manifestation)". He (Indra) said, "Let this (manifestation) of you be the Ṣoḍaśī-sacrifice". It became the Ṣoḍaśī; This is its origin" (TMB XII.13.1). Upāṁśugraha is said to be made out of the Gāyatra-sāman (ŚB VIII.1.1.5). From the Svāra-sāman the Antaryāma-cup (ŚB VIII.1.1.8), from the Ṛksama-sāman the Śukra-cup (ŚB VIII.1.2.2), from the Aiḍa-sāman, the Manthin-cup (ŚB VIII.1.2.5), and from the Nidhanavat-sāman, the Āgrayaṇa-cup (ŚB VIII.1.2.8) are said to be born. Thus music is the origin of the sacrifice and sacrificial details.

If there are any hindrances in a sacrificial performance, and the sacrificial performances are stopped, music has an important role in restarting them. Thus once the sacrifice was carried away from the earth by the gods to the heaven. Then no sacrificial performance could be offered. Now both the gods and men depend upon each other. For men offer sacrifices to gods and gods, in return give rain and thereby food to men. Now when no sacrificial performance occurred, both gods and men began to starve. Being requested by gods, Ayāsya, a seer, restarted the sacrifice among men with the help of Ayāsya-sāman (JB III.216).

Music helpful to the sacrifice

Music is helpful to the sacrifice in many other ways also. The performance of the sacrifice should be a continuous, well-established, firm activity.[4] Music plays a distinct role in assuring the ideal nature of sacrifice in many ways.

Music keeps the "continuity" of the sacrifice intact. Thus on the second day of the Daśarātra of the Dvādaśāha-sacrifice, the Śyeta-sāman is sung. "A wedding of the two sāmans" viz. of the Śyeta and Naudhasa-sāman (the latter belongs to the preceding day) takes place here. For the finales of both of these sāmans are exchanged. This "wedding" is done for the sake of continuity of the sacrifice (TMB XI.9.5; cp. JB III.26). The Santati (continuity) - sāman also serves similar purpose. Thus it is to be sung on the seventh day of the same rite for connecting that day with the sixth. The continuity of the sacrifice is preserved thereby (TMB XIV.3.7 f; cp. JB III.182). Bṛhat and Rathantara-sāmans are described to be the "continuities" of the broken sacrifice (*vicchinnasya yajñasya santatyau*" JB II.213). This means that these two sāmans join the sacrifice if it is broken, discontinued etc. in any way, and make it continuous. The Yadvāhiṣṭhīya-sāman joins the ninth and tenth days of the Daśaratra of the Dvādaśaha-sacrifice. Once Agni was not willing to carry the oblations offered to the gods, from the ninth day towards the tenth day. The gods desired, "May Agni carry the oblations for us. They saw this sāman and praised with it". Then, as one may cross over by means of a ship, in the like manner Agni carried over the oblations from the ninth day towards the tenth day". Thus this sāman is for the sake of continuity of sacrifice (JB III.269). The verse *ehyūṣo bravāṇi te* (SV I.7, ṚV VI.16.16; SV II.55-57) contains the word *ehi* (come hither). And this word serves for calling near the third day (of the Daśarātra of the Dvādaśāha); for continuity. Therefore the verse is used on the second day (TMB XI.11.2).

Similarly in the Daśarātra of the Dvadaśaha, the Āyāsya-sāman joins together the seventh day which is gone amiss (*vibhraṣṭa*) as it were (TMB XIV.3.22).

Many times music is said to be useful in giving firm foundation (*pratiṣṭhā*)[5] to the sacrifice. In the Agniṣṭoma-sacrifice, at the time of the midday-pressing the Yaudhājaya-sāman with three finales,[6] is to be sung. By means of this sāman with three finales, the midday-pressing gets firm foundation (TMB VII. 3.21). In the same sacrifice at the time of the third pressing, Āndhīgava-sāman with its finale in the middle and the word *iḍā* at the end is to be sung. If there would not be such a sāman the third pressing would be foundationless (TMB VIII.5.12). On the third day of the Daśarātra of the Dvādaśāha-sacrifice Antarikṣa (intermediate region) - sāman is sung. Now this day has the intermediate region as its deity. So by singing that sāman, the sacrifice gets firm foundation (TMB XII.3.19). In the course of the performance of the third three-day-period of the Dvādaśaha-sacrifice, Gāyatrapārśva-, Santani-, and Saṁkṛti-sāmans are sung. When the three-day-period of this sacrifice was shattered the gods healed (made firm) it by means of these sāmans: by means of the Gāyatrapārśva they propped it; by the Santani, they connected it, by the Saṁkṛti they brought it into good order. The two preceding three-day-periods are well-established. But this one (i.e. the third three-day-period), becomes well-established, well-founded by these sāmans only (TMB XIV.9.27). By reciting verses beginning with *yajñā yajñā vo agnaye* (through sacrifice on sacrifice in honour of Agni, SV I.35), in the course the Ārbhava-pavamāma-laud, one establishes sacrifice into the sacrifice (TMB XI.5.2). The Yajñāyajñīya-sāman gives foundation to the sacrifice in numerous ways. Thus TMB VIII.6.1 f, it is told, "The gods divided among themselves the sacred lore; what sap of it was left over, that became the Yajñāyajñīya-sāman ...... By chanting the Yajñāyajñīya-sāman, one established the sacrifice in the sap of the sacred lore". According to TMB VIII.6.3 the Yajñāyajñīya-sāman is a womb. By chanting this sāman, the singers establish the sacrifice in its womb. TMB XI.5.28 identifies this sāman with vāc (speech). When this sāman is sung, the sacrifice becomes founded on vāc. By means of the Yajñāyajñīya-, Nārmedha-, Dāśaspatya-, Viśoviśīya and Vāravantīya-sāmans, sacrifice is established on lustre (*haras*) (JB I.170). The Vāravantīya-sāman is identical with this earth; the foundation. So, when on the sixth day of the Daśarātra of the Dvādaśāha-sacrifice, Vāravantīya sāman is used as pṛṣṭha, it serves then for establishing the sacrifice on the earth (JB III.155).

Music is supposed to give firm support (*dhṛti-*) to the sacrifice. Various sāmans are therefore sung in order to give support to the sacrifice. Thus on the second day of the Daśarātra of Dvādaśāha, sāman named Śaṅku (Pin) is used for giving support to the sacrifice. "Whatever is not supported therein, one supports by means of this sāman (TMB XI.10.12). Similarly the Ābhīśava-sāman used on the fourth day supports that day (TMB XII.9.15 f). The verses beginning with *vṛṣā pavasva* (SV I.469; RV IX.65.10-12; SV II.153-155) are to be recited on the seventh day for supporting it (TMB XIV.3.1f).

The music "props (*utthambh-*, *viṣṭambh-*, *ārabh-*)" the sacrifice in various ways and numerous expressions are used to suggest this idea. Thus the Saubhara-sāman is to be sung on the fourth day of the Daśarātra of the Dvādaśāha. This sāman is described as the splendour of the Bṛhat-sāman. For when Indra hurled his thunderbolt on Vṛtra by means of the Bṛhat-sāman, the splendour of Bṛhat went away and it became the Saubhara-sāman (cp. TMB VIII.8.9). "The fourth day is gone down as it were (*pannam iva*)" For the preceding days have their pṛṣṭha-laud on the longer verses viz. Bṛhatī-verses each of which contains thirty six syllables. On this fourth day, however, the pṛṣṭha-laud is on Virāj-verses each of which contains thirty syllables. Therefore, this fourth day is fallen as it were. The Saubhara-sāman which is, mystically, nothing else than the splendour of the Bṛhat-sāman (which is based on verses in the Bṛhatī-metre) props up (*uttambhayati*) this day (TMB XII.12.8; JB III.82). This same day is propped up also by the Traiśoka-sāman. JB III.72, it is said, "This day goes down as it were. By means of the Traiśoka sāman, by means of a larger metre, one props it up". The third day of this same sacrifice was also once collapsed. Gods propped (vyaṣṭabhnuvan), it by means of the Viṣṭhambhas (name of certain stobhas propping the sāman (TMB XII.3.10).

Another expression used with similar purport is *ārabh-* (to keep fast)". Thus when Yajñāyajñīya-sāman is sung, the sacrifice is established and kept fast (TMB XI.5.28). On the seventh day of the Daśarātra of the Dvādaśāha-sacrifice, Sauparna-sāman is sung. In this connection, the following story is told. Once sacrifice went away from the godṣ. It wandered in the form of a well-winged (suparṇa) bird. Gods kept it fast (*ārabhauta*) with the Sauparṇa-sāman (JB III.147; cp. TMB XIV.3.10). According to JB III.182, Sauparṇa-sāman is used on this day because the sacrifice is "gone away" on this day and so it is necessary to keep it fast. This sāman is useful for this reason. The recitation of the verses belonging to Viṣṇu viz. *pavitre dhāraya sutaḥ* ... on the second day in the same rite is also for the sake of keeping the sacrifice fast. "For sacrifice is Viṣṇu". (JB III.129)

Indra has a great importance in the sacrifice. He is called the deity of sacrifice (*indro vai yajñasya devatā* ŚB I.4.1.33 etc.). Therefore, efforts are to be made to make the sacrificial performance "with Indra (*sendra* -)". Many sāmans are sung with this purpose. Thus once Indra, loathing the third pressing, went away. The Gods, by means of the Śyāvāśva-sāman and especially by its *stobha* viz. *aihāyi ehiyā* (these are the chanting forms of *ehi* "come hither") called him back. Then he returned. Therefore the Śyāvāśva-sāman is to be sung for making the third pressing "with Indra" (TMB VIII.5.11; cp. JB I.164). Similar is the significance of the Nihava-sāman. When Indra went away from the third pressing, thinking that it is drunk out and loathing it, the Viśvedevas brought him back with this sāman and particularly with the words *āyāhi āyihi* (come, come). So also when this sāman is sung, Indra comes back and does not want to go away. Thus the sacrifice becomes "with Indra" (JB III.268). The Kāleya-sāman is said to be identical with soma. Indra, who is well known for its addiction to the soma-drink, rushes towards this soma in the form of the

Kāleya-sāman being sung, like a cow the calf of which is bound elsewhere, rushes towards it, lowing. And thus, by means of the Kāleya-sāman also one makes the sacrifice "with Indra", "with god" (JB I.164).

Music puts "sap (*rasa*-)", "delight (*mada*-)" in the sacrifice. When the Adhvanya draws the Mahāvratīya cup of soma, Udgātṛ sings the Mahāvrata-sāman and puts sap by means of it in that cup. The Mahāvrata-sāman, is identical with all the sāmans. Thus he puts sap with all the sāmans. The priest called Hotṛ also puts sap in it by means of the great recital. "This great recital is identical with all the ṛc-verses. So he puts sap in it by means of all the ṛc-verses" (ŚB X.4.1.13). The purpose of singing the Mādila-sāman is also to put sap, delight in the soma. Thus the gods desired to make their soma full of sap and delight. Then they discovered this sāman and got delight of the soma. Similarly by singing this sāman, one puts sap and delight in the soma (JB III.222). Verse containing the forms of the root *mad,* to delight are recited in the course of sacrifice with special intention of putting sap and delight in the sacrifice. Thus on the prāyaṇīya-day of the Dvādaśāha-sacrifice, at the time of reciting the ārbhava-pavamāna, the verses beginning with *yaste madaḥ* .... and recited. They contain the word *madaḥ* (delight). Now *mada* is the same as sap (*rasa*-). The third pressing is drunk out as it were. So by reciting these verses one puts sap and delight in the third pressing and makes it swell (JB III.28). Similar significance of recitations of other verses containing the forms of root *mad* is told in JB III. 53; 119; 159; 191; 220 etc. At the end of the Fire-building-ceremony, the great Litany (Mahaduktha) is recited. By means of it, the vital sap is put in the built up Fire (ŚB X.1.1.1 ff).

Music is sometimes useful for the sake of making the sacrifice "entire".[7] Thus in the Aśvamedha (horse) sacrifice, the Acchāvāka's sāman is Saṅkṛti. This it is argued, "The Aśvamedha-sacrifice is an extensive sacrifice [8] 'Who knows', they say, 'if all of it is done or not ?'. In that the Acchāvāka's sāman is Saṅkṛti, it serves to make the horse (*aśva*-) whole, to make it entire (*paryāptyai*); to prevent interference (TS V.

4.12.3). In the Ārbhava-pavamāna-laud of the fourth day in the Daśarātra of the Dvādaśāha, verses beginning with *pari priyā divaḥ kaviḥ* (SV I.46; ṚV IX.9.1,3,2) are sung. They contain the word *pari* (round). The fourth day is the end (of the catūrātra). Therefore, these verses serve to make this day "entire" (TMB XII.11.1). The same is the significance of the use of the verses beginning with *parīto ṣincatā sutam* (SV I.512; ṚV IX.107.1-3; SV II.663-665) in the midday-pavamāna on the ninth day of the Daśarātra in the Dvādaśāha (TMB XV.3.3).

Music is sometimes said to be useful for adaptation (*kḷpti*) of the sacrifice. Thus the Yaudhājaya-saman, with three finales is helpful for the same of adaptation of the three soma-pressings (JB I.124; III.15). The same is the significance of the Āgneya-sāman with three finales (JB III.100) as well as of Aiḷata-sāman with three finales (JB III.210).

It is supposed that music protects the sacrifice. Thus ṚV V. 44.9, it is said, "The soma-pressing at which a thoughtful poem (*mati-*) is extended, does not perish (*na riṣyati savanaṁ yasminnāyatā (matiḥ)*". Here the root *riṣ*, to perish is used along with *na* and means - does not perish, i.e. remains safe and secure. Elsewhere the word *ariṣṭi* which is also derived from the same root is used. Music is used for protection (*ariṣṭi-*) of the sacrifice, for keeping it intact, safe, and secure.[9] Thus the sāman named Ariṣṭa is useful for the safety (*ariṣṭi-*) of the sacrifice. Here the name of the sāman and its result have a magical connection. So whatever harm has been created by the faulty praise, faulty recitation etc. that is to be removed by means of this sāman and the sacrifice is to be protected. Even the gods sang this sāman for the same result (JB III.55). The Auśana - and Kāva-sāmans are described to be like strings, of the sacrifice. They close up the divine case (*devakośa-*). Therefore, they are to be sung for keeping the sacrifice safe (TMB VIII. 5.16). On the third day of the Daśarātra of the Dvādaśāha, Paurumudga-sāman is recited. "When this day, once, collapsed, it was pursued by the Ogres. The gods by means of the Paurumudga-sāman repelled the ogres from it" (TMB VIII. 5.16. In the fire-building-ceremony, verses in Gāyatrī-metre, addressed to Agni are to be recited. The Hotṛ marches reciting, behind the bricks carried by attendants. He thus marches defending the sacrifice by means of the metres from behind (ŚB VIII.3.2.9).

The sacrifice is sometimes metaphorically described to be a jar or a cloth. Any mistake in the sacrifice is like a hole, cleft (*chidra*) etc. For the sake of getting the desired result of the sacrifice, it is essential that there should not be any cleft in the sacrifice. Music has a helpful function in this respect. It makes, when properly used, the sacrifice "without cleft (*acchidra-*)". Thus a sāman itself is called Acchidra (without a cleft). This sāman is to be sung on the eighth day of the Daśarātra of the Dvādaśāha. "By means of the Acchidra-sāman, gods covered up whatever cleft there was in this day. Therefore, it has this name (TMB XIV.9.36). The fifth day in the same performance is described by JB III.91 like a cleft. When praises are made with the Yaṇvasantani-sāman, in the beginning of the midday-pavamāna-recital of the same day, the day becomes, "cleftless" (JB III.91). In the Agniṣṭoma-sacrifice, Yaudhājaya-sāman with three finales is to be sung. For there are three clefts in the three soma-pressings of that sacrifice. For after each pressing, there is a savanīya-puroḍāśa (a sacrificial cake connected with the pressing) which creates disjoinment between the recitations of pavamānalaud corresponding to each pressing (cp. Nidānasūtra II.11). By means of the Yaudhājaya-sāman, with three finales, those clefts are covered (TMB VII. 3.19) and then the sacrifice becomes cleftless. In the Yajñāyajñīya-sāman the line *uta trātā tanūnam* is short of one syllable. Therefore, some ritualists raise objection: This is a cleft in the sacrifice. "If one does not cover it, at the time of singing this saman there remains a cleft in the Yajñāyajñīya-sāman; when the Yajñāyajñīya-sāman has a cleft, the sacrifice leaks ... "Therefore according to some ritualists the word *vāc* (speech) and according to some others the word *go* (cow) is to be inserted in the line mentioned above. Then the number of syllables becomes adequate and no defect, no cleft remains. According to some other ritualists there is no need of *insertion*. Since the word *vāc is* to be used as the finale, it does the function of joining (JB I.178).

The significance of the Dhāyyās (inserted verses) is similar one. Thus AB III.18, we read, "Wherever the gods observed a breach in the sacrifice, that they closed up (*api dadhuḥ*) by the inserted verses; that is why the dyāyyās are so called. With a sacrifice without breach does he sacrifice who knows thus ... ; just as he continues putting together a garment with a needle, so does he continue with these (verses) putting together the breach in the sacrifice who knows thus".

Sacrifice becomes damaged if there are any mistakes. Music "cures" and "invigorates" the sacrifice in such cases. Thus the seventh day of the daśarātra of the Dvādaśāha is "gone amiss" as it were. Therefore many sāmans the purpose of which is do the work of a redṛess (*bheṣaja*) are sung on this day. Thus the Ayāsya-sāman (JB III.186), Vaikhānasa-sāman (JB III.190), Jarābodhīya-sāman (JB III.197) and Sauśravasa-sāman (JB III. 202) are "redresses" as it were and they cure the sacrifice. This same day which is, gone amiss as it were is "invigorated (*samdakṣ* -) by means of the Dakṣoṇidhana-sāman (JB III. 192). On the fourth day of the same rite, verses, beginning with *pavasva dakṣasātaye* are sung in the midday-pavamāna-laud for invigorating that day (JB III.66).

We detailed above a few ways in which music helps the sacrifice. There are many other miscellaneous ways in which music is helpful to the sacrifice. Thus a four-day-sacrifice named Caturvīra, the Acchāvāka's sāman (or the fourth pṛṣṭha-laud) of the first day is the Kāleya, of the second the Mādhucchandasa; of the third the Raurava; and of the fourth the Samanta. By using different sāmans on different days every day is endowed with a different *strength* (TMB XXI. 9.15). Music gives *illumination* to the sacrifice. Thus the chandoma-days of the Dvādaśāha are described as darkness as it were. By means of the Bhāsa (light) - sāman they are made shining (TMB XIV.11.15). The Sabha (having brightness) sāman also serves to make the sacrifice bright (JB I.160). TMB VII.5.6 mentions Sapha-sāman which is the same as Sabha.

Although the meaning of the word Sapha is not clear, it can be conjectured that the Sapha also has the same significance as the Sabha. Recitation of verses is used for getting *control* over the sacrifice. Thus on the fourth day of the Daśarātra of the Dvādaśāha-sacrifice, verses beginning with *pibā somam indra* (SV I.398; ṚV VII.22.1-3; SV II.277-279) are recited. For this day is "long-drawn" as it were. The recitation of these verses is for getting control over it (TMB XII.10.1). Śyena-sāman is to be sung on the sixth day of the Daśarātra of the Dvādaśāha. Śyena i.e. falcon is the swiftest of the birds. Therefore, it is able to *convey* (*saṁpāraṇa*-) this day (TMB XIII.10.14; JB III.159). The Vāravantīya-sāman is also used on the sixth day. "The pṛṣṭhas become old as it were when the performers come upto the sixth day. Now in an old man, there is no semen (no generation-power). As there is the Vāravantīya-sāman, that is for the sake of *"generation (prajātyai) of the further sacrificial rites"* (JB III.155). ṚV VII.12.11, it is said, "The embryo of sacrifice has grown up by means of stomas of Indra". ṚC and Sāman help the sacrifice to be *complete.* Thus the performer go upto the end of the sacrifice by means of the ṛc and sāman (ŚB III.1.1.12). Music *increases* the sacrifice in strength. Therefore AV V.26.12, Aśvins are requested to come, increasing the sacrifice by means of the Vaṣaṭ-call. The sacrifice is "*led*" by means of the music. Thus ṚV X.114.7, it is said, "The wise persons lead forward the sacrifice sevenfoldly, by means of speech".

It will be thus clearly seen how music helps the sacrifice in various ways.

Music helpful to the performers of sacrifice

Music is helpful to the performers of the sacrifice also. It helps them to *know* the sacrifice. The recital of the two hymns viz. ṚV X.61, and 62 is useful for knowing the sacrifice (*yajñasya prajñātyai*) (AB V.14). Thus the Aṅgirases were falling into confusion whenever they used to reach the sixth day of the Dvadaśāha. Nābhānediṣṭha, on the suggestion of his father went to them and made them recite these two hymns.

Thus these two hymns make the sacrifice known to the sacrificers. Thereby they know heaven also (AB V.14). Similarly, in the same sacrifice, in order to know the third day *vācaḥ sāman* is useful. Thus "Niṣkirīyas (once) performed a sacrificial session. They did not know (the practice of the) third day. Chanting this sāman, the speech came drifting near to them; through it (i.e. this sāman) they learnt (the practice of the) third day". (TMB XII.5.14). When the sacrifice had run away from gods, it was obtained back by them with the help of the Praiṣas (directions) and Purorucs. They then made it known by means of Nivids (AB III.9). In this way music helps the performers to know the sacrifice.

Music helps the performers of sacrifice in a "profane" way also. It "entertains" the priests during the intervals in the various acts of the sacrifice. Thus Mbh XIV.90.39 Gandharvas, skilled in vocal music are said to be entertaining the priests at the time of intervals in the sacrificial deeds (*gandharvā gītakūśalā vṛtteṣu ca viśāradāḥ / ramayanti ca tān viprān yajñakarmāntareṣvatha //*)

Music for expiations

We have seen above, how music protects the sacrifice, removes breathes, in it, "cures" it etc. in this connection it will be pertinent to give a few details of how music is used in the expiatory rites in the sacrifice. Music removes the defects or mistakes in the sacrifice and brings order in it. The divine musicians Gandharvas are said to have pointed out defects in the sacrifice being performed by seers and thereby to have rendered a great service to the correct performance of the sacrifice (ŚB XI.2.3.7f).

The expiations are performed when some mistakes occur in the sacrificial performances. They make the sacrifice defectless. To sing sāmans is an important element of the expiations. Thus if the soma-trough is burst at the time of the midday-pressing, the saman with vaṣaṭ-call as its finale is to be sung. For the vaṣaṭ-call is the foundation of the sacrifice and by singing such a sāman, one gives foundation to the sacrifice

(TS VII.5.5.3; cp. Kātyāśs XXV.12.22). According to TMB, in this case one should use the Śrāyantīya-sāman as the Brahman's chant. For "milked out as it were, emptied out is he whose trough bursts; in that the Śrāyantīya is used as the Brahman's chant, One braces (*saṁśrīṇāti*) oneself again fully with progeny, cattle, and sense-power". (TMB IX.6.8). Then one should apply the sāman based on Anuṣṭubh verses addressed to Viṣṇu. This sāman should have the word *vaṣat* as its finale (TMB IX.6.9; cp. Māśs III.6.11). Then Vāravantīya-sāman should be sung as Agniṣṭoma-sāman (TMB IX.6.11; cp. Māśs III.6.11).

Similarly if Soma is left over from the moving-pressing, Gāyatra-sāman is to be sung on the verses in which the Maruts are invoked and which begin with "*asti somo ayaṁ sutaḥ* (SV I. 174; ṚV VIII.94.4-6; SV II.1135-1137). If the soma is left over from the midday-pressing, the Gaurivīta-sāman is to be sung on the verses in which the Sun is invoked, and which begin with *baṇmahān* ...... (SV I.276; ṚV VIII.101. 11-12, SV II.1138-1139). If soma is left over from the third pressing then the Gaurivīth-sāman is to be sung on the verses addressed to Viṣṇu Śipiviṣṭa (TMB IX.7.1 ff; cp. Kātyāśs XXV.13.1 ff; Māśs III.7.9; JB I.350).

During the act of pressing the soma also if one of the stones is broken expiation is to be made by means of singing the sāman of Dyutāna of the Maruts. For the stones belong to the Maruts. By singing this sāman, one makes the stones thrive (TMB IX.9.13 f; cp. JB I.353; KPKS 48.14; Kātyāśs XXV.12.15; Māśs III.6.10).

The Gauṣūkta and Āśvasūkta-sāmans are to be sung as an expiation by one who has "accepted too much". If one accepts too much (in the form of Dakṣiṇās, sacrificial gifts given to the priests) then one has to perform the Punaḥstoma-sacrifice. In that sacrifice the above-mentioned sāmans are used (TMB XIX.4.10f). The Vāmadevya-sāman is described as a pacification of whatever is sung or recited wrongly. Similarly it is further described as a "roller (*mulya*)" which makes the ground even (JB III.301). Gobhilagṛyasūtra I.9.29, prescribes the singing of Vāmadevya-sāman at the end of each domestic rite for purification and expiation.

Recitation of verses also has an expiatory significance.[10] Gods having killed the Asuras considered themselves to be impure. They desired to be pure and then to go to the heaven. Then they saw the verses beginning with *punānas soma dhārayā* and purified themselves thereby (JB I.121). When in a soma-sacrifice, soma is being carried to the place of sacrifice if the soma-cart produces any noise of creaking, expiation is to be made by reciting the verse—*svaṁ goṣṭhaṁ avadatam* (VS V.17) (ŚB III.5.3.17). During the course of the Darśapūrṇamāsa-offerings, no profane word is to be spoken. But if one speaks such a word, then expiation is to be made by reciting a ṛc or yajus addressed to Viṣṇu (ŚB I.1.4.9). If the priest Brahman breaks silence and utters any profane word then also expiation is to be done by a ṛc or yajus addressed to Viṣṇu. For Viṣṇu is identical with the sacrifice and by using a text addressed to Viṣṇu, one obtains hold on the sacrifice (ŚB I.7.4.20). If the cow, the milk of which is used in the Agnihotra-offering, is united with the calf and being milked calls aloud, one has to recite *suyavasād bhagavatī* .... (ṚV I.164.10) (AB V.27).

Utterances of the vyāhṛtis etc. are also important in expiations. The vyāhṛtis viz. *bhuḥ bhuvaḥ and svaḥ* are described as "the all-expiatory (*sarvaprāyaścitti-*)" (AB V.32; ŚB XII.4.1.8; JB I.53; JUB III.4.3.3 etc.). They can be used for any unknown mishap (JB I.358; AB V.32) or for both the known and unknown ones (ṢaḍB I.6.17). If Agnihotra-milk is spoiled, then one should pour some water while uttering the vyāhṛtis (ŚB XII.4.1.6-8; JB I.53f). The function of the vyāhṛtis is to 'join' the sacrifice which gets itself "broken" when some mishap occurs (cp. JUB III.4.3.3; AB V.32).

The Pratigara (response given in a high tone by the Adhvaryu-priest after a recitation of the Hotṛ) is also expiatory. Thus it atones for the breathing done by the Hotṛ during the recital. When the Hotṛ breathes during a recitation evils spirits are supposed to attack on the sacrifice. By means of the Pratigara they can be excluded from the sacrifice (ŚB IV.3.2.6).

It will be thus noticed how various musical elements help the sacrifice by removing the defects, when it is used as a means of expiation.

Music to be performed carefully

The use of music in the sacrificial activities is to be made carefully and without any mistakes. As in the case of other sacrificial details, in the case of the music also it must be remembered that any mistake will not only create an hindrance in obtaining the desired result, but it will also create some positive harm to the performers.[11] Music has its useful power only when it is performed correctly.[12] Thus music is double-natured. If used in a correct manner it leads to good results and if used wrongly, it gives bad results.

There are certain rules about the recitation of verses. They are to be followed strictly. Otherwise there is some harm. The invitatory and offering-verses of the upasad-offerings must be of the same metre. If they were of different metres there would be swelling on the neck of the sacrificer. The sacrificer will have boils. Therefore both of these verses must be of the same metre (AB I.25). In the course of the out-of-doors-chant-singing, a Retasyā-verse in the Gāyatrī-metre is to be sung. One should sing it watchfully (*adhīyan*),[13] as it were. If one were to sing it without watchfulness, dead children will be produced (JB I.260).

At the time of recitation, great care must be taken in uttering the words correctly, in the prescribed manner. If some undue words are spoken in the procedure of the recitation, then some harm is likely. Thus at the time of singing the Yajnāyajñīya-sāman one should utter the words *O yirā ihā* ... If one were to utter *O girā gira* ..., then Vaiśvānara Agni would swallow (*giret*) the sacrifice. If one were to utter *O yirā yirā*, one would lose all the food and would become "dry (*rūkṣa-*)". For *yirā* is nothing but *irā* and *irā* means food. And one would then put food into the mouth of Vaiśvānara Agni (JB I.175). Similarly in the same saman, one has to utter (*puprim vayam* ... If one utters *pra prā vyam*, then one will die before the time. On the contrary, if one recites in the correct manner Agni releases one from death (JB I.176).

At the time of singing sāmans also care should be taken for the correctness. Thus at the time of singing the Rathantara-sāman, the modifications (*stobha-*) are to be made on the syllables of the verses (on which this sāman is to be sung) themselves. For this sāman is identical with Agni and Agni is nothing but death. So, if the modifications were made out-side the syllables of the verses, the sacrificer would be thrown in the mouth of the fire. Similarly, the Rathantara-sāman is like the sea. So if the modifications are made out-side the syllables of the verses, one will be drowned in the sea (JB I. 332). The Vāmadevya-sāman is to be sung without breathing upto the Pratihāra-utterance. For the Vāmadevya is identical with breath. If one breaks this rule, one will be devoid of the breath. Moreover, this sāman is not to be sung in imitation of someone else. If it is sung so, there is a fear of being his dependent. Therefore it must be sung independently (JB I. 333). In the over-night-sacrifice, one should not depart from the Nārmedha-sāman. For this sāman belongs to Indra and Agni. The day belongs to Indra and night to Agni. Therefore this saman is a form of day and night. If one departs from this sāman, one departs then from day and night. Therefore one should not depart from the Nārmedha-sāman in the over-night-sacrifice (JB I.188). Similarly one should not depart from the Kāva-sāman. If one does so, one gets skin-disease and bad fame (JB I.169).

There are many other miscellaneous rules to be observed in the course of various recitations. If one commits any mistake, it is dangerous. Thus the Uṣṇih-and Kakubh-verses are identical with breaths. So one should not make vaṣaṭ-call while reciting them. Otherwise the breaths would be put in the fire. This means that the verses in these metres should not be used as yājyā (offering-verses), to accompany a burnt offering. At the end of a yājyā, the vaṣaṭ-call is pronounced. So if the vaṣaṭ-call is to be accompanied with the verses in Uṣṇih and Kakubh-metres, the breaths are put in fire as it were (TMB VIII.5.5).

Similarly at the time of reciting the Retasyā-verse, no hiṁkāra should be produced. For recitation of the Retasyā-verse is a generation-process as it were. The hiṁkāra is a thunderbolt as it were. So if the hiṁkāra is made the semen will be discontinued. (JB I.259). The ṛc and sāman have equal importance. They also are connected with generation. Therefore if mere ṛc is recited without sāman, then there will be in a child, bones without flesh. If, however, sāman without ṛc is sung, there will be mere flesh and no bones. One should therefore recite ṛc covered with sāman. Therefore covered with hair, skin and flesh, a man is born (JB I.259). The hymns viz. Nābhānediṣṭhīya (ṚV X.61; 62), Vālakhilays (ṚV VIII.49-59), Vṛṣākapi (ṚV X. 86) and Evayāmarut (ṚV X.87) are said to be sung together. If anyone of these is omitted, the sacrificer himself becomes omitted. If the Hotṛ omits the Nābhānediṣṭhīya, he will omit the sacrificer's seed; if the Vālakhilyas, then his breath; if the Vṛṣākapi, then his body; if the Evayāmarut, then he will remove him from foundation (AB V.15). At the time of reciting the Nivids, the Hotṛ should not pass over a sentence. If he passes over, he will make a break in the sacrifice. Then the sacrificer will be worse (AB III.11). Similarly the sentences of the Nivids should not be inverted. If that is done, the sacrificer becomes confused. Further, no two sentences of the Nivids should be united. If that is done, the sacrificer dies and so on (AB III.11).

Thus we observe that music is to be used in the sacrificial performances very carefully. The mistakes in its use are dangerous.

Antipathy of sacrifice to music

Although music of vocal and instrumental type is prescribed to be used in sacrifice and although as observed above, it helps sacrifice in many ways we see sometimes a kind of antipathy of sacrifice to music also maintained in the Vedic texts. Thus JB II.69, mentions a battle between Death and Prajāpati. In this battle, the sacrificial utensils were the weapons. Prajāpati's army consisted of whatever is praised with the sāmans, recited with the ṛcs and performed with the yajus-formulas. The army of Death consisted of whatever is sung with Vīṇā, whatever is danced, and whatever is performed in vain. Here we find that music and sacrifice stand against each other. Music is, moreover, grouped together with the vain acts done in the sacrifice. ŚB III.2.1.18, it is said that as an heritage of Prajāpati, Gods obtained sacrifice and Asuras the speech (*vāc*). Here it is noteworthy that speech is connected with Asuras. At the end of the tenth day in the Daśarātra of the Dvādaśāha-sacrifice Gāyatra-sāman is sung. This sāman is identical with mind. So it is to be sung in the mind only. By means of this mental singing, one fulfils all that is unfulfilled. "Whatever Gods could not fulfil of the sacrifice with speech, they fulfilled it with mind" (JB III.305). Thus we note that the mind is implied to be superior to speech. ŚB III.5.2.46, explicitly denies the use of any sāman at the time of the avabhṛthabath in the Varuṇapraghāsa-rite. (cf. KātyəśsIV.3.5). At the time of other Avabhṛtha-baths, sāman *is* sung. It is a rule that those who have consecrated for a long sacrificial session should aviod all kind of dance, songs, and instrumental music. (ĀŚS XII.8). Sacrifice, it is said, becomes pierced as it were by the ṛcs and sāmans in the same manner as the earth is pierced by ploughs. Therefore, a sterile cow is to be killed for the sake of pacification of the sacrifice. Thus as a roller makes the earth even, in the same manner, this cow makes the sacrifice pacified.

In this way we sometimes observe the contrast between the sacrifice and music. It, however, seems that music is to be used in sacrificial ritual according to the prescribed rules. Any unprescribed music is to be avoided in the sacrifice. If there is any likely danger from the prescribed music itself, then there is, a provision of pacifying the danger, in the ritual itself.

Conclusions

We can conclude in the following way:

(a) Music is immensly used in the Vedic sacrifice; It is an important, essential and constitutory part of the sacrifice.

Many forms of Vedic sacrifice are products of merely particular way of singing employed in them.

(b) Music helps the sacrifice by making it continuous, well-established, well-supported, entire, well-protected and defectless.

(c) Music is double natured. It can be useful or harmful. Therefore it must be used carefully.

(ḍ) Sometimes music and sacrifice stand in contrast to each other.

This also indicates the double-nature of music.

REFERENCES

1. For the use of music in the ritual in general see Combarieu *La musique et la magie*, p. 12, 150, 260, 332. Gunkel, Zscharnack (ed.) *RGG, IV.* 298; Meyer, *Trilogie*, II. p. 75, n 1; Mowinkel, *Religion und Kultus*, p. 108 f; Cuisinier, *La danse sacrée*, p. 21f; W.O.F. Oesterley, *Sacrifices in ancient Israel*, (New York, 1937), p. 193f. Kraeling, Mowry in Wellesz, *AOM*, p. 291, M. Courant, in A. Lavignac, *EnM*, I. p. 267.
2. For the activity of the GB in pushing up to the front the Atharvaveda, See Bloomfield, *The Atharvaveda*, p. 29.
3. See my thesis: *Sacrifice in the Brāhmaṇa-texts.*
4. *Ibid.*
5. For this term see *Gonda, Saṁjñāvyākaraṇa*, I.
6. This sāman has no finales in the proper sense of the term. But three parts of the verse itself are taken as finales: *sā 234 sī; dā* 234 *sī; ṇyā* 345 *yāḥ*
7. Cp. Mowinkel, *Religion und Kultus*, p. 108 f. "Die ältesten riten und Kulthandlungen sind zumeist genau, wie es bei der magischen Praxis der Fall ist, Symbolhandlungen *die der Ergänzung durch das Wort bedürfen.*
8. *utsannayajña*: for this term see my paper in *JOIB*, XVIII.3 March 1969, p. 179f.
9. For the positive meaning implied by the negative expressions, see Renou *BSOAS*, 10, p.15, Gonda, *Four Studies*, p.95ff.
10. Cf. Gonda, "Indian Mantra" *Oriens* 16, 1963, p. 266 f.

11. For the importance of correctness and danger of the mistakes in music of Nāradīyaśikṣā I.1.4 ff;
Belvianes, *Sociologie de la musique*, p. 50 f;
A. Bake in Wellesz, *AOM*, p. 199;
H.G. Farmer, in Wellesz, *AOM*, p. 259;
Gonda, *Stylistic repetition*, p. 27. Hastings, *ERE*, IX. p.12:
In many of the Omana Societies a fine was imposed if a member made mistakes in singing.
12. Cf. G. van der Leeuw, *REM*, p. 423; Webster, *Magic*, p. 96.
13. Caland, *JB in Auswahl*, p. 101 f.

CHAPTER VI

Some Musical Elements

(A) WORDS

It is well-known that in primitive weltanschauung power leading to the good or bad results is attributed to the words. Thus G. van der Leeuw has observed, "a word is always a charm; it awakens power either dangerous or beneficent".[1] The words which are used to express one's desired result are supposed sometimes to be producing the desired result by themselves.[2] We see this phenomenon in the Vedic texts[3] very often.

A *pratipad* containing a particular word has a particular result. Thus in the out-of-door-laud, the tristich beginning with *agna āyūṁṣi pavase* (SV II.868-870; ṚV IX.66.19-21 should be taken as the opening tristich (*pratipad*) for those sacrificers among whom somebody is dead. Now, this verse contains the words *āyūṁṣi* (lives). "One, by saying *āyūṁṣi* puts life into them who are living" (TMB VI.10.1 ff). When two sacrificers are performing some soma-sacrifices simultaneously, the udgātṛ should take the tristich containing the word *vṛsan* (bull) as the opening one, in the recital of the out-of-doors-land. "Indra is a bull (*vṛṣan-*)". Thereby the sacrificer whose Udgātṛ has used the above mentioned tristich, appropriates Indra from the morning-pressing of the other sacrificer (TMB IX.4.3). In the Out-of-doors-land of the sixth day of the Daśarātra in the Dvādaśāha-sacrifice, the tristich beginning with the words *jyotir yajñasya pavate* (SV II.381-383; cp. ṚV IX.86.10-12) is the opening tristich. In it the word *jyotis* (lustre) is used; and thereby the sacrificer as well as his grand-son obtain lustre (TMB XIII.7.1f).

The word which is used as the finale (*nidhana*) of a sāman is significant. Thus the sāman named Vaitahavya Okonidhana has the word *okas* (house) as its finale. In this context the following story is narrated. The gods removed the Asuras from each "house" by means of this sāman. "One who knows this removes one's hateful enemy from each house" (JB I.214). It is further told that Vītahavya Āśrayasa, being driven out of his dominion wandered for a long time. He could obtain "house" by means of this melody by making the word *okāya* as its finale (JB I.214). The Kāṇva-sāman is to be sung in an overnight (atirātra) - rite. Kaṇva, the son Nṛṣad was wandering without any firm foundation for a long time. He wanted to have a firm foundation. Then he saw this melody and sang with it. He made the word *rantāya* (for repose). One who has no firm foundation is without any repose as it were. "The night is quivering as it were and this melody (which is to be used in an overnight-rite is repose as it were". Then he (Kaṇva) obtained repose (JB I.216). On the third day of the Daśarātra in the Dvādaśāha-sacrifice, the Sāman named Mahāviṣṭambha is sung. In that Sāman the word *diśaḥ* (quarters) is to be used. Thereby, one holds the quarters firmly (TMB XII.4.21). In the midday-pressing of the Agniṣṭoma-sacrifice the sāman named Vasunidhana is to be sung. This sāman has the word *vasu* as its finale. According to the Brahmanical ideology, the cattle are identical with *vasu.* So by singing this sāman, one becomes established in the cattle (TMB VII.10.16).

The verses with the help of which the sāmans are sung, must contain some words with which the result is mystically connected. Thus on the sixth day of the Daśarātra of the Dvādaśāha-sacrifice the verses beginning with *pra va indrāya vṛtrahantamayā* are used. These verses contain a reference to killing of Vṛtra and therefore they are helpful in killing one's enemy and getting victory (JB III.172). In the verses of another sāman named Nānada, the word *hari* (yellow horse) which, in the Brahmanical way of thinking is nothing but *haras*(glow), is used. Thus when Indra, desirous of killing Vṛtra, went to Prajāpati to seek some help, he gave him the Nānada-sāman, without the word *haras.* Then Indra could not be successful in killing Vṛtra. Indra then again went to Prajāpati. Prajāpati gave him the *haras* (glow) of the seven hotrās.[4] Then Indra could vanquish Vṛtra. Therefore the chanters chant verses containing, the word *hari* (viz. *upa no haribhiḥ stutam..* (SV II.

378-380; ṚV I.84.1; 3;2) (TMB XII.13.4 ff; cp. JB I.203). The Ārṣabha sāman, is based on the verses beginning with *abhi tvā vṛṣabhā sute*. Indra, desirous of becoming a bull (i.e. the best) of all the beings, saw this sāman and having praised with it, obtained the desired result. The verses on which this sāman is based contains the word *vṛṣabha* (bull) and thus the result is connected with word used (JB I.222). Pūrvatitha Ārcanānasa desired to obtain a lot of cattle. He discovered the Pauravatitha-sāman and praised with it. That sāman was based on verses containing the word *sahasra* (thousand). So he obtained a thousand of cattle (JB I.227).

In the course of the Vedic ritual some verses in which the words derived from the root *mad* "to be delighted" is found, are prescribed to be recited. When these verses are recited sap (*rasa*), which is identical with the delight according to the Brāhmaṇa-texts is believed to be put in the sacrifice. Thus at the evening-pressing on the third day of the Daśarātra of the Dvādaśāha-sacrifice the stotriyā-verses of the second ukthya-laud contain verses beginning with *taṁ te madaṁ gṛṇīmasi* (SV I.383; ṚV VIII.15.4-6; SV II.230-232). The third pressing is possessed of delight and sap. One then thus puts delight and sap in it (TMB XII.6.3). The same is the reason why the verses beginning with *asāvyaṁśur madāya* (SV I.473; ṚV IX.62.3-5; SV II.358-360) are used in the Ārbhavapavamāna-laud in the third pressing of the fifth day in the Daśarātra of the Dvādaśāha-sacrifice (TMB XIII.5.1; cp. also XIV.5.1; 11.1; XV.11.1). In the third-pressing of the prāyaṇīya-day in the Dvādaśāha-sacrifice, verses beginning with *yaste mado vareṇyaḥ* are to be sung in the Ārbhava-pavamāna-laud. For the third pressing is "sucked out" as it were; and by means of these verses (containing the word *madaḥ*) "sap" is put in it. Then the third pressing becomes swollen, full of sap etc. (JB III.28; cp. JB III.159; 227; 265; 268).

There are some verses containing some words due to which the obtainment of food is said to be possible. Thus at the time of the midday-pavamāna-laud of the third day of the Daśarātra of the Dvādaśāha-sacrifice, verses containing the word *andhas* (food), viz. *ucā te jātam andhasā* .... are to be recited. Thereby one gets food (JB III.40). On the eighth day of the same rite also verses containing the word *andhas* viz. *punāhīndrāya pātave tava tya indro andhasā* are to be recited for the sake of obtainment of food (JB III.209). In the Vājapeya-sacrifice, the chief aim of which is to obtain food,[5] verses containing the word *andhas* viz. *purojitī vo andhasaḥ* .... are to be recited. The priests thereby make the sacrificer rich in food (JB II.195). In the course of the same sacrifice, the priest brahman, while sitting on the chariot-wheel sings, *aganma vājaṁ vajibhiḥ* .... These verses contain the word *vāja* which means food. Therefore, the recital of these verses is helpful for obtainment of food (JB II.193). Similarly on the sixth day of the Daśarātra of the Dvādaśāha-sacrifice, the recital of verses containing the word *vāja* (food) viz. *pavasva vājasātaye* leads one to get food JB III.129). On the second day of the same rite verses beginning with *pavasva madhumattamaḥ* (SV I.566; ṚV IX. 106.1-3; cp. SV II.44-46) are used in the ārbhava-pavamāna -laud. The word *madhu* occurs in those verses. "*Madhu* is identical with food". Therefore the sacrificer gets food thereby (TMB XI.10.3).

There are some verses containing some words due to the recital of which one gets cattle. On the third day of the Daśarātra of the Dvādaśāha-sacrifice, the verses *ṛtasya dhītim* .... which contain the word *gāvaḥ* (cattle) are recited. Thereby one gets cattle (JB III.46). Similarly on the fourth day the verses beginning with *ā pavasva mahīm* are used (JB III.60); on the fifth day the verses beginning with *adhiṣṇubhiravīhām* .... are used (JB III.97); on the sixth day the verses beginning with *svadanti gāvaḥ* are used (JB III.119) and so on. All these verses contain the word *go* (cattle) in some form. Recitations of these verses lead one to obtain cattle. On the sixth day the verses beginning with *yat te soma citram uktham* which contain the word *citram* (variegated) are to be used. "The cattle are indeed variegated and this day is identical with cattle". Therefore one gets cattle thereby. In the Dvādaśāha-sacrifice, the priest named Maitrāvaruṇa recites the hymn *sadyo ha jāto vṛṣabhaḥ* ... (ṚV III.48) which contains the word *vṛṣabha*(bull). Because it contains the word *vṛṣabha*, it helps to obtain cattle (AB VI.20). When three persons are performing a sacrificial session, the opening tristich of the out-of-doors-laud should be *asṛkṣata pravājinaḥ* ..... (ṚV IX.64.4 ff). These verses contain the word *go* (cattle) and *aśva* (horse) and the performers then get cattle and horses (JB I.94).

There are many other numerous results which are obtained by reciting the verses which contain the words having some correspondence with the results. Thus in the Vājapeya-sacrifice, the verses to be recited at the time of the morning pressing, contain the word *śukra* (bright) and *jyotis* (light). One then obtains, by these verses light and brahman-splendour (TMB XVIII.7.2). On the fourth day of the Daśarātra of the Dvādaśāha-sacrifice, the verses beginning with *agniṁ vo vṛdhantam* (SV I.21; ṚV VIII.102. 6-8; SV II.296-298) which contain the word *vṛdhantam* (growing powerful) are to be recited. By reciting these verses, the priests make the sacrificer grow powerful (TMB XII.12.1f). On the tenth day, the verses beginning with *kayā naścitra* ..... (SV I.169; ṚV IV.31.1-3; SV II.32-34), are used in the recital of the first pṛṣṭha-laud. There is the word *ka* (in *kayā*), which according to the vedic texts stands for Prajāpati. By using these verses, one obtains Prajāpati (TMB XV.10.1). The recitals in the Indrastoma-sacrifice are based on the verses addressed to Indra. Thereby the sacrificer gets sense-power (*indriya*: a mystic connection between the words *Indra* and *indriya* is implicit here) and valour (TMB XIX. 16.5). After the soma-plant is purchased, the Udgātṛ sings verses containing the word *janat*. Thus these verses contain a reference to *generation*. The Udgātṛ then generates the sacrificer thereby (JB I.199). On the tenth day the verse *yata indra* ... is used. In that verse Indra is requested to kill the hateful enemies (*vi dviṣo vi mṛdho jahi*). By singing this verse one indeed kills the enemies according to JB III.264.

Thus we find that in the Vedic thought the utterance of words has a magicoreligious significance. Sometimes the words are supposed to work out the result directly. Sometimes the prayer is made to gods to do that work (see for example JB III.264 mentioned in the above paragraph). Thus the words are power-substances in Vedic thought; but at times the grace of gods is required for the sake of obtainment of desired result.

REFERENCES

1. G. van der Leeuw, *REM*, p. 404; cp. Mowinkel, *Religion und Kultus*, p. 109 f; Farmer in Wellesz, *AOM*, p. 259; also Combarieu, *La Musique et la magie*, p. 126.
2. Webster, *Magic*, p. 73: "But words or actions intended to show what was to be done, would by constant repetition often come to be regarded as potent in themselves and so would acquire a magical character.
3. For the power of words in the Vedic ritual see Bake in Wellesz, *AOM*, p. 199; cp. Keith, *RPV*, p. 393, Gonda, *Ojas*, p. 26; the same, "Indian *mantra*", *Oriens* XVI, 1963, p. 244 ff; 255; 268.
4. Namely the functions of the following priests—Hotṛ, Maitrāvaruṇa, Brāhmaṇācchaṁsin, Acchāvāka, Potṛ, Neṣṭṛ, Āghīdhra.
5. See my paper "Apropos of the Vājapeya", *JUPHS*, 31, 1968, p. 31 ff.

(B) VAṢAṬKĀRA

Vaṣaṭ-call and sacrifice

The Vaṣaṭ-call is[1] pronounced at the time of offering some oblations. This expression is used at the end of a yājyā (offering verse). The origin of vaṣaṭ-call according to ritual texts, is in the need of carrying the oblations to the gods. Thus once the oblations did not go to the gods. Then Prajāpati thought over how to make them go to the gods. Then he extracted two syllables out of the Gāyatri-metre. Then the two-syllabled Vaṣaṭkāra came into existence and through it the sacrificial offerings began to go to the gods (JB III.113). It is a rule that one should offer either simultaneously with the vaṣaṭ-call or after it has been pronounced; but in any case *not before* it. If one were to offer before the vaṣaṭ-call, the offering would be lost; it would fall on the ground. It would be *lost* like seed not poured *into* the womb. Therefore the offering must be made either simultaneously with the vaṣaṭ-call or after it has been pronounced (ŚB I.7.2.13f). The importance of this exclamation in sacrifice is described in high words in the vedic texts. Thus TS VII.5.5.3 praises it as being the firm foundation of the sacrifice (*vaṣaṭkāro vai yajñasya pratiṣṭhā* cf. KS XXXIV.4) and therefore if the soma-trough is broken at the time of the midday-pressing, a sāman which has the vaṣaṭ-call as its finale should be sung. Thereby the sacrifice gets firm foundation. The vaṣaṭ-call takes care of sacrifice as can be seen from the following story. Thus once metres did not stand to serve the sacrifice. The vaṣaṭ-call then being angry cut the head of Gāyatrī (MS II.5.7; cf. KS XIII.8; TS III.5.7.1). The oblations without any vaṣaṭ-call or svāhā-call do not reach to the gods (KB XII.4; cf. further under *vaṣaṭ-call and gods*). Thus one can get here an idea about the importance of vaṣaṭ-call in the sacrifice. In elevating the vaṣaṭ-call, JB I.250 describes it to be the navel (*nābhi-*) of the sacrifice. Elsewhere the Uttarakurus are mentioned to be complaining. "The Kurus and Pāñcālas partake of soma upon which no *vaṣaṭ*-call is uttered (JB I.113). Thus there seems to be a rule that one should partake of the soma upon which vaṣaṭ-call is uttered. Efforts of making soma "consecrated by vaṣaṭ-call (*vaṣaṭkṛta*) can be seen in the following expiation-rite. Thus if the soma-trough bursts, the sāman which contains the word *vaṣaṭ* as its finale should be made the brahman's chant. "The soma of him whose trough bursts is spilled as it has not been consecrated by the vaṣaṭ-call; in that the brahman's chant is the one that has the word vaṣaṭ as its finale, his soma becomes consecrated by the vaṣaṭ-call" (TMB IX.6.1-2; cp. JB I.352).

Vaṣaṭ-call in the abhicāra-rites—The vaṣaṭ-call has got a special significance in the abhicāra-rites (sorceries) performed against some enemy. In a sorcery-rite the sāman with the word vaṣaṭ as finale should be used as the brahman's sāman. For the word vaṣaṭ is the god-arrow (*deveṣu-*). So this is a kind of throwing an arrow upon the enemy (TMB VIII.1.1f). In the Śyena-sacrifice which is of the nature of black magic, the sāman with *vaṣaṭ* as its final is to be used (ṢaḍB III.8.7). According to ĀŚS IX.7 in this sacrifice one should make the vaṣaṭ-call as if one were cutting (the enemy mentally). The gods went near the Asuras by means of a low-voiced (*upāṁśu*) offering and slew with the thunderbolt viz. vaṣaṭ-call whichever they wished of the Asuras. So in the Darśapūrṇamāsa-offerings the two prayers (viz. invitatory and offering ones) are to be muttered in a low voice; but the vaṣaṭ-call at the end of the offering-verse is to be pronounced loudly. Then by means of that vaṣaṭ-call, the thunderbolt, the sacrificer kills his enemy (ŚB I.6.3.28). In order to destroy the sorcery performed by one's enemy one uses the following formula in which the vaṣaṭ-call is described as a thunderbolt (*vajra*). "The sorcery of him who wants to kill me, O Fire, of the enemy who is either near to me or far from me, I smite it with vaṣaṭ-call, the thunderbolt" (TB II.4.2.3f). AB III.6 also the vaṣaṭ-call is said to be a thunderbolt. The Hotṛ should think[2] of him whom he hates, when about to say the vaṣaṭ-call. He thereby hurls the thunderbolt against him.

The vaṣaṭ-call gives the good or bad results according to the way of its pronounciation. Thus there are three kinds of vaṣaṭ-calls viz. *vajra* (thunderbolt), *dhāmacchad* (hider of his abode) and *rikta* (empty). The vaṣaṭ-call which the Hotṛ makes aloud and forcibly is the *vajra;* it he hurls as a missile at the rival who hates him. This vaṣaṭ-call is to be pronounced by him who has enemies. The vaṣaṭ-call which is even, continuous, and without loss of any part of the verse is *dhāmacchad.* On it depend the off-spring and cattle. Therefore it is to be pronounced by one who is desirous of offspring and cattle. The vaṣaṭ-call in which the *ṣaṭ* is pronounced in an inaudible voice, is *rikta.* One who pronounces it becomes worse because of it (AB III.7). Similarly if the Hotṛ wants that the sacrificer after sacrificing should remain as he was before sacrificing, then he should utter the vaṣaṭ-call in the same voice in which he utters the ṛc. if he wants to make him worse, then he should utter the ṛc in a raised voice and the vaṣaṭ-call in a depressed one. And if he wants to make him prosper, then he should recite the verse in a depressed voice and utter the vaṣat-call, in a raised voice (AB III.7). Thus by means of a particular way of pronouncing the vaṣaṭ-call the Hotṛ can do good or bad of the sacrificer.

In the abhicāra-rite performed by means of the Daśahotṛ-formulas KS IX.16 prescribes vaṣaṭ-call to be used and points out, "This is the cruel (*krūra-*) part of speech viz. the vaṣaṭ-call (*etadvai vācaḥ krūraṁ yad vaṣaṭkāraḥ*)". According to TB in such a rite vaṣaṭ-call should be made by means of such words which can be described as "cruel (part) of the speech (*vācaḥ krūram*)" e.g. *khaṭ, phaṭ, jahi* etc. (TB II.2.1.7; see Sāyaṇa's commentary). The same kind of vaṣaṭ-call is to be made in the Rāṣṭrabhṛt-offerings of the abhicāra-type performed with the Rāṣṭrabhṛt-formulas (TS III.4.8.5).

The dangerous nature of the vaṣaṭ-call can be seen also from the following rule; one should not utter the vaṣaṭ-call at the time of the recital of a verse in the Bṛhatī-metre. For "the other metres are created for the sacrifice, the Bṛhatī-metre for autocracy (*svārājya-*) only". If one utters the vaṣaṭ-call in connection with Bṛhatī one will place the cattle in fire as it were (KS XXXIV.7; cp. JB I.120). Thus the vaṣaṭ-call is as dangerous as fire. JB I.352 identifies the vaṣaṭ-call with fire and

MS IV.6.7 identifies it with Vaiśvānara-fire. Vaṣaṭ-call is also said to be identical with one who shines i.e. the sun and thereby with death. Therefore when one offers after the vaṣaṭ-call has been pronounced, "One consecrates (the sacrificer) after death and causes him to be born from out of it, and he (the sacrificer) is delivered from that death". Thus the vaṣaṭ-call is connected with both the mystical death and mystical generation of the sacrificer (ŚB XI.2.2.5). It is of double-nature.

Vaṣaṭ-call : a power substance

The vaṣaṭ-call is considered to be a power-substance. Its identification with vajra[3] (= powerful = thunderbolt) is significant from this point of view. Power is double-natured and vaṣaṭ-call, a power-substance is also double-natured. It can be dangerous if it is not duly pacified. Therefore one has to pacify the dangerous nature of the vaṣaṭ-call. One should mutter *bhūr bhuvaḥ* before the words *ye yajāmahe* and after the vaṣaṭ-call the following words: *ojaḥ sahaḥ saha ojaḥ svaḥ* (strength is might; might is strength; light). Thus one quietens the thunderbolt both in the front and behind. "Strength and might are the most dear forms of the vaṣaṭ-call; verily with them one quietens it" (KB III.5; cp. AB III.8; GB II.3.5). Here powerfulness of the vaṣaṭ-call as well as the pacification of its dangerousness is well mentioned. ŚB I.3.3.13 f a story is given. Agni was afraid of the vaṣaṭ-call the thunderbolt and gods protected it with the paridhi (surrounding) - sticks. Therefore, in order to protect Agni from the dangerous vaṣaṭ-call, it is to be enclosed with the paridhi-sticks. According to another story, Indra hurled thunderbolt on Vṛtra. The two syllables in the vaṣaṭ-call were the two crooked cyclical parts (*cakrau*) of that thunderbolt. Therefore the vaṣaṭ-call is the thunderbolt. Whosoever will touch it, will touch the thunderbolt (JB I.113). Here also the powerfulness and dangerousness of the vaṣaṭ-call are suggested.

Vaṣaṭ-call and generation

The vaṣaṭ-call is mystically connected with generation. Thus at the time of uttering the vaṣaṭ-call, "One pronounces the syllable *vauk.* For the vaṣaṭ-call is speech (*vāc*) and speech is identical with seed; hence one casts seed thereby; one then pronounces *ṣaṭ* (six); the seasons are verily six (*ṣaṭ*); one thereby casts seed into the seasons and the seasons cause that seed so cast to spring up here as creatures. This is the reason why he pronounces the vaṣaṭ-call. The reason why an offering is to be made simultaneously with the vaṣaṭ-call is based on the generation-idea. Thus the offering is like pouring the seed. The seed should be poured *into* the womb. When the offering is offered simultaneously with the vaṣaṭ-call the seed becomes poured exactly into the womb and not outside (ŚB I.7.2.13). There is a rule that the Hotṛ-priest should not utter anything improper until his vaṣaṭ-call. For, "by the vaṣaṭ-call, he pours the sacrifice into the fire as seed into the womb; for fire indeed is the womb of the sacrifice; from thence it is brought forth" (ŚB I.5.2.11; cp. 14).

Vaṣaṭ-call and food

JB I.113 identifies these two (*annaṁ vai vaṣaṭkāraḥ*) and suggests that the Vaṣaṭ-call is an instrument for obtaining food.

Vaṣaṭ-call and the gods

The vaṣaṭ-call has got some special importance because the gods like it very much. Food is given to the gods by means of it. ŚB IX.3.3.14 we read, "By means of the vaṣaṭ-call and svāhā-call food is given to the gods (*vaṣaṭkāreṇa vā vai svāhākāreṇa vā devebhyonnaṁ pradīyate*"). The gods live on two breaths of speech (*vāc*) viz. *svāhā* and vaṣaṭ-call (ŚB XIV.8.9.1). According to KB XII.4, "The offerings which are offered without any vaṣaṭ-call or svaha-call, do not reach the gods (*na ha vaita āhutayo devān gacchanti yā avaṣaṭkṛtā vāsvāhākṛtā vā bhavanti*"). ŚB IV.6.7.6 the vaṣaṭ-call is said to be connected with the gods more closely than the svāhā-call: "Whatever is offered with svāhā but without vaṣaṭ that belongs to speech (and not to the gods). ŚB I.5.2.13 and AB III.5 describe the vaṣaṭ-call as the vessel of gods (*devapātra-*) and suggest that gods consume the offerings through it. One satisfies the gods by means of it. In

ṚV VII.14.3, Agni is requested, "Come, O Agni, enjoying our vaṣaṭ-call unto invocation of gods". ṚV VII.15.6 he is requested to come towards the vaṣaṭ-call. Viṣṇu is also requested to enjoy the oblation with vaṣaṭ-call: "I make for you, O Viṣṇu, the vaṣaṭ (call) out of my mouth. Enjoy then my oblation O Śipiviṣṭa" (ṚV VII.99.7; 100.7). Aśvins are requested to come increasing the sacrifice with vaṣaṭ-call. (AV V.26.12). It will be thus seen how the vaṣaṭ-call is supposed to be magicoreligiously significant.

Indirect way of vaṣaṭ-call

Sometimes instead of directly uttering the vaṣaṭ-call, it is to be uttered in an indirect way (*parokṣa-*). In the course of the fire-building-ceremony, during the twelve Prospering - (Kalpa) offerings, at the end of the twelfth formula, one utters *stomaśca ..... veṭ svāhā*. Here instead of *vauṣaṭ, veṭ* is pronounced. "The veṭ-call is verily the same as the vaṣaṭ-call in an indirect manner; food is given to the gods either by means of the vaṣaṭ-call or svāhā-call. One thus gratifies Agni by both the vaṣaṭ- and svāhā-call" (ŚB IX.3.3.14). At the time of sprinkling water upon the earth collected for preparing a fire-pan (*ukhā*) one utters a verse which itself contains the word vaṣaṭ. Therefore at the end of this verse there is no direct vaṣaṭ-call as is generally the case. Since the word vaṣaṭ is already pronounced, "If one directly utters the vaṣaṭ-call as usual, the vaṣaṭ-call will be exhausted; if one does not utter it, then the evil beings (*rakṣas-*) will kill the sacrifice: (Therefore) one says *vaṭ*; verily one thus utters the vaṣaṭ-call in an indirect manner. Thus neither one's vaṣaṭ-call is exhausted, nor the evil beings kill the sacrifice" (TS V.1.5.2; cp. KS XIX.5; KPKS XXX.3). Thus the vaṣaṭ-call is significant for gratifying the gods, for destroying the enemy, for protecting the sacrifice from the evil beings etc. Therefore one has to utter it at least in an indirect way.

Cosmic nature

The vaṣaṭ-call has a cosmic nature. Thus one utters *ṣaṭ* (six) while pronouncing the vaṣaṭ-call. "There are six seasons. One thus puts the seasons in order; and one gives firm foundation to them". (AB III.6). According to KB III.5, by the word *ṣaṭ* (six) one pleases (*prīṇāti*) the seasons which are six in number. Various worldly sounds are described mystically to be the vaṣaṭ-calls of the Brahmayajña (sacrifice to the brahman i.e. the study of the Vedas). "When the wind blows, when it lightens, when it thunders and when it rumbles; whence he who knows this should certainly study when the wind is blowing, when it lightens, thunders or rumbles and so as not lose his vaṣaṭ-calls" (ŚB XI.5.6.9). At the time of sprinkling water upon the earth collected for preparing the fire-pan (*ukhā*) one utters, "To him O goddess be *vaṣaṭ*, with thee". "Now the seasons are six and the thus bestows rain upon the seasons and there-fore in all the seasons it rains". (TS V.1.5.1f; MS III.1.5; cp. KS XIX.5; KPKS XXX.3). According to TĀ II. 14.1 the thunder of clouds (*stanayitnu-*) is identical with the vaṣaṭ-call of sacrifice. Here the vaṣaṭ-call is closely connected with rains.

Conclusions

1. The vaṣaṭ-call is very important in the sacrifice. It is called "the foundation of sacrifice". 2. It has many magicoreligious significance - it pleases the gods by giving food to them it helps the sacrificer for obtaining food, protecting the sacrifice from evil beings, killing his enemy etc. It has also got cosmic significances. 3. It is a power-substance and is of double-nature. It can be helpful, it can be harmful.

REFERENCES

1. Weber, *IS* IX.256 derives the word *vaṣaṭ* from *vakṣ* to grow, increase ("May it prosper, or agree with you") and Eggeling, *SBE*, XII, p. 88, n. 2, from *vah* to carry ("May he - Agni carry it - the oblation - up"). The latter explanation seems to be acceptable (cp. Minard, *Trois énigmes*, I, p. 102).
2. For the power of thinking rf. Webster, *Magic*, p. 79: "In the opinion of many primitive people the human will can be projected mentally in a given direction and bring about the result desired by the operation".
3. For *vajra* and power see Gonda, *Viṣṇuism*, p. 52.

(C) HIMKĀRA

The *hiṁkara* is a sound introductory to a litany and consists generally of *him* or *hum.*[1] In the vedic texts numerous significances are attached to the *hiṁkāra*. It is considered to be of double nature, giving good and bad results. Here I propose to study the magicoreligious significances of the *hiṁkāra.*

ŚB II.2.4.11f, origin of the hiṁkāra is told. Agni, Vasu and Sūrya having come into existence from Prajāpati, desired to create something. "They enclosed a piece of ground and sang praises in Gāyatrī-stanza without *hiṁ*-sound. Then a cow came into existence. The cow, having seen these three, produced the sound *hiṁ*. Heretofore the sāman was without the *hiṁkāra*. These gods come to know the hiṁkāra now. Obviously, the sound *hiṁ* is inserted in the Vedic chant in imitation of cow and this has been told in the above story in a mythological way. Some other texts also support this point. Thus on the fourth day of the Daśrātra of the Dvādaśāha, at the time when the Virāja-sāman is being sung, fire is produced from churning sticks on the right thigh of the Udgātṛ-priest. "For from the right side the seed is discharged". When the fire has been produced, then hiṁkāra is to be made. "Therefore, when a young calf is born, the cattle make the *hiṁ*-sound over it (sniff at it)" (TMB XII.10.12). Here a macrocosmic fact is explained on the basis of a microcosmic practice. But the real explanation is likely to be the reverse one. Thus the ritual *hiṁ*-sound must be an imitation of the sound of cattle. According to JUB I.3.1.4f, Prajāpati gave the hiṁkāra as food to the cattle. Therefore they wander producing this sound. Similarly KS XXVII.9 it is told: Prajāpati, having created the beings made the *hiṁ*-sound at them. The Āgrayaṇa-soma-cup is identical with Prajāpati. Because one makes the *hiṁ*-sound after having drawn the Āgrayaṇa-cup, therefore, a cow makes the *hiṁ*-sound at the calf newly born. "The sacrificer who offers the Agnihotra has to observe the vow of behaving like animals (*paśu-vratena bhavitavyam*)". Silent as it were the animals are born. Therefore they are purified for the sacrifice (*medhya-*).

As he (the sacrificer) has to approach his wife without speaking, he becomes still more purified for the sacrifice. He should approach her having uttered the *hiṁ*-sound. In this way as it were the animals approach; for the sake of sacrificial purity" (MS I.8.7). Thus from this passage also it will be clear that the ritualistic hiṁkāra has its origin in the imitation animals. It is an animalism[2] which occurs many times in ritual. Similarly a sacrificer having come back after some journey should smell the head of his son. At that time he utters among other words, the following words: "I utter the hiṁkāra over thee with the hiṁkāra of kine". He utters the hiṁkāra thrice over his head (ŚāṅĀ IV. 11). Here the imitation of kine is directly stated.

The hiṁkāra is an important element of a sāman. Thus ŚB I.4.1.1 says, "Sāman is not sung without the hiṁkāra (*na vā ahiṁkṛtya sāma gīyate*)". After the fire-building is completed, sāmans are sung. "One sings having made the hiṁkāra. Then only the sāman becomes complete" (ŚB IX.1.2.34). Thus the hiṁkāra is the completeness of the sāman. It is the glory (*śrī*) of the sāman (JUB I.1.4.6; cp. JUB III.3.2.3). TMB VI.8.7 the hiṁkāra is said to be the "sap (*rasa*-)" of the sāman. Therefore, when one holds the prastāva, at the time of Bahispavamāna, after having made the sound *hiṁ*, one begins the chant after moistening the verses with the sap as it were. When a praise-hymn is sung accompanied by the hiṁkāra, power and sap are put in it. For hiṁkāra is identical with power and sap (*ūrg vai hiṁkāraḥ* ŚāṅĀ II.1). Because the hiṁkāra is so important in singing a sāman, it is sometimes said to be equivalent to the sāman itself. Thus when the horse of the Aśvamedha-sacrifice makes the *hiṁ* sound, it is supposed that the horse has sung a sāman itself (ŚB XIII.2.3.2; cp. TB III.8.22.2). The soma-cup called Āśvina becomes mystically accompanied by a sāman by means of merely the hiṁkāra (MS IV.6.1). Not only the priests connected with the sāman-singing perform their activities with the hiṁkāra, but also the priests reciting other vedic texts e.g. the Hotṛs, Adhvaryus, and Brahman perform their activities having uttered the hiṁkāra (GB II.3.9).

The hiṁkāra is especially significant for obtaining food. JUB I.1.3.4 identifies the hiṁkāra with the moon and the moon with food. Thus it implies the identification of the hiṁkāra and food. By means of the hiṁkāra one obtains food (JUB I.10.1.3). Prajāpati having created the beings, gave them food by means of the hiṁkāra. Udgātṛ, who is identical with Prajāpati, similarly gives food to the beings with the hiṁkāra (JB I.88). According to JB III.214, Prajāpati gave food to the beings by means of the verses accompanied by the hiṁkāra therefore when the Gāyatra-sāman accompanied by hiṁkāra is sung, food is obtained. The Śākala-sāman with two hiṁkāras is to be employed on the fifth day of the Daśarātra of the Dvādaśāha. "The hiṁkāra is identical with food; for with the word *huṁ* food is given" (JB III.93). On the eighth day of the same rite, the Vāmadevya-sāman with two hiṁkāras is sung for the sake of obtainment of food (TMB XIV.9.22). For the identification of food and the hiṁkāra see also JB I.315. Food is given even to gods by means of the hiṁkāra (JB I.246).

The hiṁkāra is closely connected with generation also. Thus at the time of recitation of kindling verses (*sāmidhenī-*) the hiṁkāra is to be made. Thereby off-springs are born (TS II.5.7.1). ŚB I.4.1.2 an explanation of the generative power of the hiṁkāra is found: "The hiṁkāra is breath (*prāṇa-* masc.) because it is indeed breath; one cannot therefore pronounce it when one closes one's nostrils. One recites verses with speech (*vāc-* fem). Speech and breath are a productive pair. Thereby a productive pair is formed at the outset". Elsewhere also the hiṁkāra is said to be generative. Thus at the time of reciting the out-of-doors-chant, in the Agniṣṭoma-sacrifice, the hiṁkāra is to be made. The hiṁkāra is Prajāpati, the verses of the out-of-doors-chant are women. By holding after the hiṁkāra has been made the Prastāva, one effectuates a productive pairing at the beginning of the sacrifice in order that the sacrificer may procreate (TMB VI.8.5). In the same sacrifice, the Adhvaryu makes the Udgātṛ look at the sacrificer's wife. This rite has clearly a bearing upon generation. At this time, hiṁkāra is to be made. "For after the hiṁkāra, the seed implanted" (TMB VIII.7.13). The Mahāvrata-day-ceremony is well-known for its connection with fertility[3]. This day begins with hiṁkāra. "For the hiṁkāra is a bull (male) and ṛc is a female. They make a pair at the beginning of the hymn for the sake of generation. One who knows this prospers with children and cattle"(ĀĀ I.3.1). On this day the priests like Adhvaryu, Maitrāvaruṇa, Brāhmaṇācchaṁsin and Neṣṭṛ utter the hiṁkāra simultaneously. "Therefore a man is produced "contagious" one". They utter hiṁkāra after the Udgātṛ has uttered it. Therefore the limbs are in control of the body (JB II.407). The Kāṇvāyanas are said to have created the animals by means of hiṁkāra (JB I.226).

Sometimes however the hiṁkāra is supposed to be anti-generative. The Retasyā-verse is specially connected with generation. At the time of reciting this verse one should not utter the hiṁkāra. For, "The hiṁkāra is thunderbolt ..... If he should make the hiṁkāra he would with the hiṁkāra, with the thunderbolt, divide the ejaculated seed" (SaḍB II.1.5). JB I. 100 it is said that if one were to utter the hiṁkāra, one would "discontinue (*vicchindyāt*)" the implanted seed, by means of the thunderbolt in the form of the hiṁkāra (cp. JB I.259; 315).

The hiṁkāra is described to have an apotropaeic significance. The sacrifice is a generation activity par excellence. The evil spirits are on the other hand notorious for the disturbance they create to the generation activity. So the removal of these spirits is essential for the sake of safe and secure generation[4]. By the hiṁkāra, as the thunderbolt, Ayāsya pushed the Asuras away from this world. He said to them, "Go ye far". That is a world named *afar* They went to it. These Asuras then were irretrievably defeated (JUB II.3.2.3f). The Hotṛ should recite the sāmidhenī (kindling) verses having made hiṁkāra. For hiṁkara is the thunderbolt. He kills the evil of the sacrificer by means of this thunderbolt. The hiṁkāra is to be made three times; for the thunderbolt is threefold. The gods also removed the Asuras by means of the threefold thunderbolt (KB III.2). Similarly at the time of the recitation of the morning-litany (*prātaranuvāka*) the hiṁkāra is made for killing away the evil of the sacrificer (KB XI.1). One can throw away one's rival from this world by means of the hiṁkāra (JUB II.3.2.9).

Hiṁkāra and breath (*prāṇa-*) are closely connected. ŚB IV. 2.2.11, it is said that by means of the hiṁkāra breath is put in the speech (*vāc-*). Thus when the speech became exhausted, gods infused breath in it. Then by means of that breath she rose again. Elsewhere the hiṁkāra is identified with breath (*prāṇo vai hiṁkāraḥ*). Therefore one cannot utter the hiṁkāra after having closed one's nostrils (ŚB IV.2.2.11; cp. I.4.1.2). For the identification of the hiṁkāra and breath see also MS IV.6.4; ŚāṅĀ II.1).

The hiṁkāra has a cosmic significance. It has been many times identified with the seasons. Thus when a sāman is described to be a year, the hiṁkāra is said to be identical with the spring-season. "Therefore, animals came together in the spring continually uttering *hiṁ* (JUB I.12.1.2; cp. I.3.2.7). Similarly JUB I.18.3.9, the hiṁkāra is said to be the wind (Vāyu) (cp. 1.18.4.4) and elsewhere in the context of description of sāman as rain, it is said to be the wind that precedes rain (JUB I.3.2.9; 12.2.1). Similarly the hiṁkāra is said to be the East (JUB I.10.1.2), the unrisen Sun (JUB I. 3.2.4), the Moon (JUB I.11.1.5), the Mind (JUB I.3.3.5; 11.1.3) Prajāpati (TMB VI.6.5ff).

The hiṁkāra is significant in many other respects. Its importance in the sacrifice is suggested by an henoistic remark that it is uttered at the "beginning" of the sacrifice (GB II.3.9). The hiṁkāra has the power of reviving the sacrifice. "The sacrifice is killed as it were when soma is pressed; the animal is seized, and the oblations are cooked. Prajāpati verily smells over them by means of hiṁkāra; for the sake of keeping the sacrifice lifefull, for obtaining it, for making it powerful (GB II.3.9). In the sacrificial performance it has a pacificatory significance. On the fifth day of the Daśarātra of the Dvādaśāha, the Vāmadevya-sāman with two hiṁkāras is sung. Whatever "cruel" has been done after the recitation of the Śakvarī-verses, that is pacified by means of those two hiṁkāras (JB III. 132). The hiṁkāra is described to be a wooden shovel of brahman (powerful recitation). "Just as one desires to dig up anything with a wooden shovel, so with the hiṁkāra, one digs up brahman on the Mahāvrata-day" (AĀ I.3.1). Further, the hiṁkāra used on the Mahāvrata-day also serves to discriminate the divine and human speech (AĀ I.3.1).

Conclusions

Thus we conclude: 1. The hiṁkāra seems to be originated in the animalistic imitation of the *hiṁ*-sound of cattle. 2. It has been connected with food, generation and removal of evil spirits. 3. It is a power-substance with double nature : benefi cent and maleficent.

REFERENCES

1. Rf. Renou, *Vocabulaire*, p. 175.
2. For animalism see my paper "Animalism in Ancient India" *JOIB* XXI, 1972, p. 191 ff.
3. See Mahāvrata in my work *Sacrifice in the Brāhmaṇa-texts.*
4. Rf. Meyer, *Trilogie*, I. p. 136.

(D) MUSICAL INSTRUMENTS

In the Vedic literature we find some musical instruments are mentioned. Thus ṚV X.135.7 it is said that in the house of the death-god Yama, a wind-instrument named Nāḷī is being blown. Vāṇa which is likely to be another wind-instrument is mentioned e.g. in ṚV I.85.10 and Maruts are said to be blowing it. TMB V.6.12 ff however, Vāṇa appears to be a string-instrument like a lute, for here we get a reference to its hundred strings. ṚV VIII.69.9 the instruments like Gargara (Drum ?), Godhā and Piṅgā (some string-instruments) are mentioned. The origin of the musical instruments is considered to be divine one. Thus it is Prajāpati who is told to have created the musical instruments from the sacred syllable *om* (GB I.1.21).

Musical instruments possess many magicoreligious significances. Particularly important in this respect is *dundubhi* (drum). It has an effective role at the time of war (for more details see under "music and war"). At the time of the chariot-race in the Vājapeya sacrifice seventeen drums are beaten (ŚB V.1.5.6. cp. Māśs VII.1.2.22 etc.). The sound of the drums is described by ŚB V.1.5.6 as the "supreme speech". By means of their sound one obtains the supreme speech (cp. TS VII. 5.2.9). According to TS VI.1.4.1 speech went away from the gods and entered into the trees. It is the same speech which speaks through the musical instruments like Dundubhi, Tūṇava or Vīṇā (cp. MS I.11.6 KS XIV.7; KPKS XXXVI.1). The beating of drums occurs in the course of the Mahāvrata-rite also. There also it is connected with the obtainment of speech. Thus in that ceremony drums are beaten at all the corners of the great altar. Thereby the speech in the trees is obtained (TMB V.5.18). In the same ceremony two wind-instruments viz. Nāḍī and Tūṇava are played upon and they are also helpful for obtaining the speech from the trees (KS XXXIV. 5). In the same sacrifice the earth-drum is also beaten. Behind the Āgnīdhrashed, a hole is made in the ground, half inside and half outside the great altar. Over this hole an ox-hide with the hairy side above is stretched (Drāhyāśs X.3.1-3; cp. Māśs VII.2.7.9; Āpśs XXI.18.2-3). Then this earth-drum is beaten for the sake of obtaining the speech that is in the earth (TS VII. 5.9.3; KS XXXIV.5; TMB V.5.19). The sound of lute (Vīṇā) serves to obtain the speech in the cattle (KS XXXIV.5). According to JB II.404, there are, in the Mahāvrata-ceremony, sounds of the following musical instruments - small Parimāds, Karkarīlute, bottle-gourd, Vakrā, Kapiśīrṣṇīd, Aiṣikī, Apaghāṭalikā, Vīṇā, Kaśyapī, earthen drum covered with the skin of a bull, a hundred-stringed harp and drums put in the air. These all kinds of sounds are to be made for the sake of obtainment of the whole speech. The play on Vāṇa (harp) in the Mahāvrata-rite is helpful for obtaining full life and strength. For, Vāṇa has a hundred strings. "Man is of (i.e. possesses normally) a hundred (years) of age and a hundredfold strength; verily they find support in age and strength" (TS VII. 5.9.2; cp. KS XXXIV.5; TMB V.6.13).

Lute is supposed to be auspicious and a symbol of glory (*śiriyā vā etadrūpaṁ yad vīṇā* TB III.9.14.1). Therefore during the Aśvamedha-sacrifice, there is a play on Vīṇā for the sake of reobtainment of glory which is supposed to have gone away due to the performance of this sacrifice (ŚB XIII.1.5.1; TB III. 9.14.1).

Thus it will be seen that in the veda the musical instruments were considered to be having many magicoreligious significances.

(E) METRES

In any sacrificial performance verses of various kinds are recited. These verses are composed in some metres. The ritualists of the Vedic age give very much importance to the metres. They go on speculating in mystic manners on metres in general and individual and on their magicoreligious significances. Now we shall study the metres on the basis of Vedic speculations and try to illustrate the doctrine of metres in the Veda.

Etymology of the word chandas (metre)

Etymology of the word *chandas*[1] is given by the Vedic texts in three ways. In two of them the root is the same viz. *chad*. But the meanings differ. Thus the vedic texts derive the word from the root *chad* either meaning "to cover etc.", or "to please, to seem good etc". Thus to illustrate first way of etymology, we may refer to TS V.6.6.1 where it is said, "Prajāpati built the fire (-altar). It kept being razor-edged. The gods in terror, did not approach it; they clothing (*chādayitvā*) themselves in the metres (*chandas-*) approached it and that is why the metres have that name". Similarly, JB I.283f, this word is derived from the root *chad* to cover. Thus Prajāpati created the gods. Afterwards death was also created. Prajāpati advised the gods to protect themselves from death by means of bringing together metres. Then the Vasus, Rudras, Ādityas and Viśvedevas brought together Gāyatrī, Triṣṭubh, Jagatī and Anuṣṭubh respectively, entered into them and covered (*chad-*) themselves thereby. Now because the metres (*chandāṁsi*) covered the gods and protected them from death, therefore the metres are called *chandas*- (cp. JUB I.4.4.1 ff). Similarly ChāU I.4.2 derives the word *chandas* from the root *chad* to cover. Thus the gods afraid of death entered into the threefold science. They covered (*acchādayan*) themselves with metres. "Because (they) covered themselves with these, that is why the metres are called *chandas*". AĀ II.1.6 also derives the word similarly. "His (of man) hair are Uṣṇih, his skin the Gāyatrī; his flesh, Triṣṭubh, his sinews Anuṣṭubh his bones Jagatī, his marrow Paṅkti and his breath Bṛhatī. Since he is covered (*channaḥ*) with the metres, therefore, the metres are so called. Nirukta VII.12 also the word is derived from the same root (*chandāṁsi chādanāt*). From this kind of etymology the meaning of the word *chandas* appears to have been "protecting formulas". According to Vināyaka's commentary on Śāṅkhāyana Brāhmaṇa, XI.5 from the word *chandas* "protection of the text through metres" is to be understood (*paśavo yathā gṛhasthaṁ chādayanti dīnatvacchādanāt tathā chandāṁsi varṇāṁśchādayanti saṁghātaniyamena bahirbhāvanivāraṇāt*). The etymological attempts of the Vedic texts in connection with the word *chandas* imply the magical significance of metres viz. covering and protecting from fearful things. As far as the actual sense of the word chandas (metre) the explanation of Vināyaka seems to be acceptable.

Another way of deriving the word *chandas* observed in the vedic texts is from the root *chad* meaning "to please", "to seem good" etc.[2] According to MS III.4.7, the gods after having killed the Asuras became afraid of death. Then they saw the metres and entered into them. With everything that pleased (*acchandayat*) them they covered (*acchādayanta*). That is why the metres are called *chandas.* Here both the meanings of the root *chad* are mentioned and the metres are connected with both the activities. ŚB VIII.5.2.1 we read, "Prajāpati, having freed himself from evil, death, asked for food ..... The gods gave him that food, these bricks relating to the metres; for the metres are cattle; and cattle are food. They the metres pleased (*acchandayan*) him and in as much as they pleased him, they are called *chandas*". From this etymology, the word *chandas* seems to mean "the pleasant, lovely aspect of a song".[3] This etymology also throws light upon the magicoreligious significance of metres of pleasing the listeners, particularly the gods.

A quasi-etymology of the word *chandas* is found at TB II. 2.8.6f. Thus according to this text, "The Gods, after having killed (pressed) Soma said, "We have killed the one who was the best of us. Let us produce it again. They then produced (*sū-*) it by means of metres; that is why metres are so-called. Here it is not clear from what root the word is derived. Apparently the text derives it from the root *sū* to impel, produce etc. In that case the etymology is obviously unsatisfactory. It, however, implies a magicoreligious significance of *chandas* viz. to impel (the gods), to produce etc.

Number of syllables and of feet of the metres

In the Vedic literature the number of syllables and of feet of a metre have their own significance. The number of syllables and feet is supposed to be powerful in various respects.

The Gāyatri-metre is said to be of eight syllables. Its everyfoot has eight syllables (*aṣṭākṣaraṁ ha vā ekaṁ gāyatraṁ padam* BṛhU V.15.1). This number very often serves as measurement of some ritual details. Thus on the ninth day of the Daśarātra of the Dvādaśāha-sacrifice a group of eight verses (SV II.616 ff) is to be recited in the out-of-doors chant. "Eight-syllabic is a Gāyatrī-verse; Gāyatrī is strength and brahman-splendour; One obtains strength and brahman-splendour thereby". (TMB XV.1.8). The Bharadvājasya Adārasṛt-sāman has eight-syllabled finale. The Gāyatrī is eight-syllabled; cattle have eight hoofs; therefore this sāman helps to obtain cattle (JB III.248). In the Dīkṣaṇīyeṣṭi of the Agniṣṭoma-sacrifice, the cake for Agni is to be baked on eight potsherds. For Gāyatrī is eight-syllabled and it is the Agni's own metre (AB I.1). In the morning-recital of the same sacrifice, if the sacrificer who is performing the sacrifice is called abusingly, a non-brahmin or is ill-spoken of and seized with defilement, then eight hundred verses are to be recited. "For Gāyatrī has eight-syllables; by means of Gāyatrī, the gods smote away the evil, the defilement; verily thus by Gāyatrī he (the Hotṛ) smites away the evil, the defilement" (AB II.17). The sacrificial post should have eight corners. For Gāyatrī is eight-syllabled; Gāyatrī is the forepart of the sacrifice; the post is also the forepart of the sacrifice; therefore, it should be eight-cornered (ŚB III.6.4.27).

Sometimes attempts have been made in the Vedic texts for mystically explaining why Gāyatrī is eight-syllabled. Thus according to a story Prajāpati, in the beginning, created waters; from waters he created foam; from foam, clay; from clay, sand; from sand, pebbles; from pebbles, stone; from stone, metal ore; and from ore gold. Now that which was created was flowing; and in as much as it was flowing (*akṣarat*), a syllable (*akṣara-*) resulted therefrom; and in as much as it flowed eight times, the eight-syllabled Gāyatrī was produced (ŚB VI.1.3.1 ff). Thus here a mystical explanation of why Gāyatrī has eight syllables is given. Similarly a mythological story of the number eight of the syllables of Gāyatrī is given by AB III.25 ff. According to that text, soma[4] was at first in the yonder world and gods tried to obtain it with the agency of metres. All the metres at that time, were of four-syllables only. First Jagatī went to bring soma. But she went only half way, felt weary and having lost three syllable came back. Similarly Triṣṭubh went and came back having lost one syllable. Gāyatrī, however, made a successful expedition and brought not only the soma but also the syllables lost by the other two metres and became the eight-syllabled metre (cp. with some differences TS VI.1.6.1-2; TMB VIII.4.1; ŚB IV.3.2.7).

Sometimes, however, Gāyatrī is said to be nine-syllabled. Thus in the Ātithyeṣṭi a cake is to be baked on nine potsherds. The reason is that the Ātithyeṣṭi is the front half of the sacrifice. Similarly Gāyatrī also is the front half of the sacrifice. Gāyatrī has nine syllables i.e. the eight which are in the verse and one more (*om*) which is added to it (ŚB III.4.1.15).

The Triṣṭubh metre is often said to be eleven-syllabled (KS XIX.12; XXI.12 etc.) and this number also serves as a measurement of many sacrificial details. In the case of rebuilding of the fire-altar, eleven Lokampṛṇā-bricks are to be laid down. "*Triṣṭubh* has eleven syllables and Triṣṭubh is valour. Thus one builds the fire-altar *with* valour" (KS XXII.2). When the sacrificial post is being anointed, seven verses are to be recited. Out of them the first and last are to be recited three times each. Thus the number becomes eleven. Triṣṭubh has eleven syllables. It is moreover identical with the thunderbolt of Indra. "Thus with those whose abode is Indra he prospers who knows thus" (AB II.2). In the animal-sacrifice which is a part of a soma-sacrifice, a cake is to be baked on eleven potsherds. "For Triṣṭubh is eleven-syllabled. It is Indra's metre viz. Triṣṭubh; animals belongs to Triṣṭubh; one thereby puts animals in his (sacrificer's) animals" (MS III.10.2). In the Rājasūya-sacrifice, at the time of midday-pressing the Hotṛ recites a hymn beginning with *janiṣṭhā ugraḥ* (ṚV X.13). This hymn contains eleven verses. "The Triṣṭubh contains eleven syllables. The Rājasūya is connected with Triṣṭubh; Triṣṭubh is might, power, strength; Rājasūya is might, power, strength" (AB VIII.2). Similarly in this sacrifice eleven royal sāmans are to be used. The significance of this number eleven is also similar (TMB XVIII.10.7).

The Jagatī-metre is often said to be containing twelve-syllables (*dvādaśākṣarā jagatī*) (JB I.141; TMB VI.3.13 etc.). This number also serves as a measurement in the sacrifice. Thus according to the opinion of some, the Āhavanīya-fire is to be laid down at the distance of twelve steps from the Gārhapatya-fire. "For of twelve syllables indeed consists the Jagatī-metre. Hence thereby he (the sacrificer) ascends to the heaven by means of Jagatī (ŚB I.7.3.25). In the course of fire-building-ceremony twelve bricks called Chandasyā are to be laid down in the middle layer. "For Jagatī is twelve syllabled; Jagatī is identical with cattle, cattle is food; the middle layer is the middle; thus food is held in the middle" (ŚB VIII.3.3.3). In the Agniṣṭoma-sacrifice at the time of the evening pressing the call of the Hotṛ consists of seven syllables (viz. *adhvaryo śoṁsāvom* "O Adhvaryu, let us two recite"). The Adhvaryu's reply consists of five syllables (viz. *śoṁsāvo daivom.* "Let us two recite, O divine one"). "This makes up the twelve syllables; Jagatī has twelve syllables; verily thus they place Jagatī in front at the third-pressing" (AB III.12). The Plava-sāman has a twelve-syllabled finale. Jagatī is twelve-syllabled and is identical with cattle. Therefore the Plava-sāman with twelve-syllabled finale also serves to obtain cattle (JB III.195).

The Virāṭ-metre is ten-syllabled (*daśākṣarā virāṭ* TMB VI.8.2; XIII.7.8 etc.) and this is also a measurement of many sacrificial details. In the course of the New and Full moon-sacrifices, after the sacrificial grass is spread ten utensils are to be placed on it. Those ten utensils are following: winnowing basket (*śūrpa-*), agnihotra-ladle (*agnihotrahavaṇī-*), wooden sword (*sphya-*), Potsherds (*kapālāni*), wedge (*śamyā-*), black antilope-skin (*kṛṣṇājina-*), mortar and pestle (*ulūkhalamusale*) and the large and small millstones (*dṛṣadupale*). The utensils are here measured by Virāj which has ten syllables (ŚB I.1.1.22). The process of the Agnihotra-offering is also measured by the Virāj-metre. "Twice one offers in the fire, twice one wipes (the spout of the spoon), twice one eats (of the milks) and four times one ladles. These are ten acts; there are ten syllables in the metre Virāj and the sacrifice is Virāj (ŚB II.3.1.18). At the time of purchasing soma-stalks, the Adhvaryu metes out them ten times. For soma is of Virāj-nature (ŚB III.3.2.17). Again, the soma is to be bought with ten objects; for Virāj consists of ten syllables and soma is of Virāj-nature (ŚB III.3.3.18). The number of the Spṛt-bricks (ŚB VIII.4.2.13) and that of Virāj-bricks (ŚB VIII.5.1.5) both of which are laid down in the fire-building-ceremony is ten. Here also the ten-syllabled Virāj is mentioned as a measurement. On the Viṣuvat-day of a year-long sacrificial session the Bhāsa-sāman with ten stobhas is to be sung as the Agniṣṭoma-sāman" The Virāj has ten syllables; Virāj is food; for the sake of obtaining food" (JB II.390).

Gāyatrī is sometimes said to be twenty-four syllabled and then the number twenty-four of all the three feet is taken into consideration together. By this number also Gāyatrī works as a measurement of sacrifice. In the Catuṣṭoma-sacrifice, the Agniṣṭoma-laud is twenty four-versed "Gāyatrī has twentyfour syllables; Gāyatrī is identical with light and brahman-splendour". Then light and brahman-splendour can be obtained (TMB XIX.5.8). The same is the significance of using two twenty-four-versed pavamānas in the first Apaciti-sacrifice (TMB XIX.8.2). At the time of establishing the fires a cake on eight potsherds is offered to Agni Pavamāna, Agni Pāvaka, and Agni Śuci. Thus there are twenty four potsherds in all. "Gāyatrī has twenty four syllables; Gāyatrī is Agni's own metre. Thus one establishes Agni with his own metre" (ŚB II.2.1.17). The sacrificial altar is twenty-four steps broad in front. "For Gāyatrī has twenty-four syllables; Gāyatrī is the fore-part of the sacrifice" (ŚB III.5.1.10). For the animal-sacrifice in the course of fire-building-ceremony twenty four enkindling verses are to be used. "For Gāyatrī is twenty four-syllabled; Agni belongs to Gāyatrī; as great as Agni is as great as is his measure by so much one kindles him" (ŚB VI.2.1.22). Similarly Triṣṭubh is sometimes said to be forty four-syllabled (*catuścatvāriṁśadakṣarā triṣṭubh*). The metre Triṣṭubh serves as a means of measurement in the sacrifice by this number. Thus if the sacrificers desire to possess power (*ojaskāmāḥ*) they should be forty-four in number and get themselves consecrated for a sacrificial session. "The Triṣṭubh-metre has forty four syllables; Triṣṭubh is power and valour; they then obtain power and valour (KS XXXIV.9). Jagatī has in all forty eight syllables (*aṣṭācatvāriṁśadakṣarā jagatī*) and this number also serves as a measurement in the sacrifice. At the time of Vasordhārā-offering, in the course of fire-building one offers forty-eight offerings. "For Jagatī is forty-eight-syllabled; the cattle belong to Jagatī; one thus obtains cattle" (KS XXI.11). On the ninth day of the Daśarātra in the Dvādaśāha-sacrifice, forty-eight-versed stoma is used. This also helps to obtain cattle because Jagatī is forty-eight-syllabled and is identical with cattle (JB III.242). In the Aśvameda-sacrifice there are forty eight offerings. In this connection also the same significance is given (ŚB XIII.1.3.8). Similarly the significance of the number forty-eight of the men bound to the central post at the time of human-sacrifice is the same (ŚB XIII.6.2.5). The thirty-syllabled Virāj (*triṁśadakṣarā virāj*) also serves as a measurement of some sacrificial details. The fire-altar for a soma-sacrifice should be thirty steps broad behind. "For the Virāj-metre consists of thirty syllables; by means of the Virāj, the gods obtained a firm footing in this world and even so does he (the sacrificer) now, by means of Virāj obtain a firm footing in this world" (ŚB III. 5.1.8). On the place where the fire-altar is built up, one has to sow the seeds of all the herbs. Earlier to this fifteen jarfuls of water is poured and after this also fifteen jarfuls of water is poured. This makes the number thirty. "The Virāj-metre consists of thirty syllables; Virāj is the whole food; thus he (the Adhvaryu) puts the whole food into him (the sacrificer)" (ŚB VII.2.4.25). In the course of the Aśvamedha-sacrifice thirty Audgrabhaṇa-offerings are to be offered". Here also the significance is the same (ŚB XIII.1.7.4).

Some other metres also become measurements of the sacrificial details by the total number of syllables in each of them. Thus the Anuṣṭubh-metre has thirty two syllables and this number is a measurement of some sacrificial details. In the Rājasūya-sacrifice, while gathering the waters for consecration, one draws sixteen cups and offers sixteen offerings. "This makes thirty two. Anuṣṭubh has thirty two syllables; speech is identical with Anuṣṭubh; as much is the speech, one gets consecrated thereby" (MS IV.3.10). The sacrifice of thirty-two days is to be performed by one who desires to get cattle. "For these days are identical with Anuṣṭubh; Anuṣṭubh is of thirty-two syllables; Anuṣṭubh is speech; four-footed are cattle (Anuṣṭubh has four feet); through the speech, through these days, one holds cattle" (TMB XXIII.28.2 ff). Similarly the number thirty six of the Bṛhatī-metre (*ṣaṭtriṁśadakṣarā bṛhatī*) is a measurement of some sacrificial details. Thus in the Fire-building-ceremony, in the middle layer, the Bṛhatī-bricks are put. On each of the southern, western and northern sides, twelve bricks are put. Thus they become thirty six. There are thirty six syllables in Bṛhatī; Bṛhatī is identical with autocracy; one who knowing thus puts the bricks gets autocracy (KS XX. 11; cp. MS III.2.9; TS V.2.2.4 f; ŚB VIII.3.3.8). The Dvādaśāha-

(twelve-day) sacrifice is mystically said to be one of thirty-six days. "For one is consecrated for twelve days; one performs Upasads for twelve nights; having passed twelve days continuously, having born anew, having shaken clear his body, pure and purified one goes to the gods. Thus the twelve-day sacrifice is (mystically) one of thirty-six days." Bṛhatī has thirty-six syllables; the twelve-day sacrifice is the way of Bṛhatī (AB IV.24).

The counting of the number of syllables in a metre is not always very strict and objective. Whenever a particular number of syllables comes into existence even by combination of two verses of different metres, then the metre having that particular number of syllables comes into existence. Thus in the course of the Ṣoḍaśī-sacrifice, the hotṛ interwins the metres. He mixes the verses in Gāyatrī (ṚV I.161.1-3) with the verses in Paṅkti (ṚV I.82.1; 3-4). When Gāyatrī (24 syllables) and Paṅkti (40 syllables) are mixed together, then two Anuṣṭubh (32 plus 32) verses come into existence (AB IV.3). The Hotṛ priest similarly mixes verses in Uṣṇih (28) and Bṛhatī (36). One Uṣṇih and one Bṛhatī also form two Anuṣṭubhs (AB IV.3). Similarly according to JB II.89, six Gāyatrīs (6 X 24 = 144) are equivalent to four Bṛhatīs (4 X 36 = 144) and three Jagatīs (3 X 48 = 144).

A very interesting statement in the mysticism of the number of syllables of metres is as follows: "Metres are not different by reason of one syllable nor yet by two" (AB I.6; cp. ŚB XII. 2.3.3). Therefore the Virāj-metre is said to be mystically containing the powers of five metres. "In that it has three feet, it is (mystically) Uṣṇih and Gāyatrī (which also have three feet each. In that it has eleven syllables (this refers to ṚV VII.1.3 and 18. Otherwise Virāj has ten syllables) it is Triṣṭubh; in that it has thirty-three syllables it is Anuṣṭubh (which has thirty-two syllables). *For metres are not different by reason of one syllable nor yet two.* In that it is Virāj that is its fifth (power)" (AB I.6; and cp. KB XXVII.1).

Number of feet

We saw above the significances of the number of *syllables* in various metres. The number of feet of the metres is also significant and becomes very often a measurement of the sacrificial details. Thus Gāyatrī has three feet (*tripadā gāyatrī* TS III.2.9.1). The Adhvaryu's response to the Hotṛ's call at the time of the morning-pressing consists of three syllables viz. *ukthaśāḥ*. For Gāyatrī has three feet and the morning-pressing belongs to the Gāyatrī-metre (TS III.2.9.1). Similarly the Triṣṭubh-metre which has four feet (*catuṣpadā triṣṭubh*) becomes a measurement in sacrifice. Thus the Adhvaryu's response to the Hotṛ's call at the time of the midday-pressing consists of four syllables viz. *uktham̐ vāci*; for Triṣṭubh has four syllables (TS III.2.9.1). On the third day of the Daśarātra in the Dvādaśāha-sacrifice, a sāman consisting of five verses is to be sung at the time of out-of-doors-chant. "For Paṅkti has five feet; food is fivefold (viz. *aśyam, peyam, khādyam, lehyam, coṣyam:- Sāyaṇa*); for the sake of obtaining food" (TMB XII.4.6). Similarly, Śakvarī-metre, having seven feet (*saptapadā śakvarī*) becomes a measurement in the sacrifice. Thus the Adhvaryu's response to the Hotṛ's call at the time of the third-pressing consists of seven syllables viz. *uktham̐ vācīndrāya.* "For Śakvarī has seven feet" (TS III.2.9.4). In the Agnihotra-performance, one praises Agni standing nearby, with seven verses. "For Śakvarī has seven feet; cattle belong to Śakvarī; one obtains thereby cattle" (MS I.5.6). While singing the Yaṇvasantani-sāman the Prastāva must be recited three times. The finale also is to be sung thrice and the Pratihāra is to be pronounced once. Thus the number seven is made. "For Śakvarī has seven feet" (JB III.92).

In this way we observe that (1) the number of syllables and of the feet of metres is very much significant particularly because it serves as a measurement in many sacrificial details; (2) one gets some good results by maintaining this measurement supplied by the metrical number; (3) the theory of numbers is rather loose and must be understood mystically.

Number of metres

Although there are many metres, at different places,[5] different numbers of metres are specifically mentioned. Instead of mentioning the exact and actual number of the metres, the ritual texts often mention a number which will suit their mystical speculations of the ritual. The sacrifice is a proportionate, well-measured activity. Among the guiding principles of sacrifice there is one to keep the measurements of sacrifice intact. The numbers of metres vary according to the context because the ritualists want to support the particular measurements in the ritual on the basis of those numbers.

Thus for example, sometimes the number of metres is said to be three. JB I.120 informs us, "Three metres verily carry the sacrifice viz. Gāyatrī, Triṣṭubh and Jagatī". Similarly ŚB XII. 2.2.21 it is said that there are three metres (cp. JB II.360). Here reference is also made to the number of three pressings of soma. Now, these three metres are one by one put in contact with the three pressings viz. the morning-, the midday-, and the third (cp. e.g. JB I.266). And it is quite in keeping with the importance of these three metres that the number of metres themselves is mystically told to be three. At the time of churning out fire, one addresses Fire with the words, "Be born after the Gāyatrī metre, ... Triṣṭubh; .... Jagatī ....". Having mentioned this KS XXVI.7 remarks, "These many are the metres (*etāvanti vai chandāṁsi*)" (cp. KPKS XLI.5). KPKS XXX. 5 and XLVI. 5 repeat this remark in connection with the soma-cups. "The Aindravāyava-cup belongs to Gāyatrī, the Śuktra to Triṣṭubh and the Āgrayaṇa to Jagati". For the number three of the metres see also KS XXV. 9; KPKS XL.2.

Sometimes, however, the number of the metres is said to be four. To the above three metres, then, the Anuṣṭubh-metre is added. Thus JB I.300 we read, "Four metres are the carriers of sacrifice; Gāyatrī, Triṣṭubh, Jagatī and Anuṣṭubh" (cp. JB II. 431). AB III.47f it is said that Gāyatrī, Triṣṭubh, Jagatī and Anuṣṭubh, these many only are the metres. The other remaining metres are, according to AB dependent on these metres;

for these four metres are used most prominently in the sacrifice. This number four of the metres also sometimes becomes a sacrificial measurement. While digging the earth for making the fire-pan, one has to take the spade with four verses. Having prescribed this, TS V.1.1.4 remarks, "For four are the metres" (cp. MS III.1.2). Similarly the clay for preparing the fire-pan is to be gathered with four verses because the metres are four (TS V.2.3.4). At the time of Saṁsava (confusion of soma-pressings which happens when two non-friendly sacrificers perform a soma-sacrifice simultaneously and at the places not separated by a river or mountain) offerings are given to four metres because these many only are the metres (KS XXXIV.4). At the time of the Vājapeya -sacrifice when the horses are running the race, four formulas are to be recited over them; for, four are the metres (TB I.3.6.5).

At times number of the metres is said to be five and to the metres mentioned above, Paṅkti-metre is added. The audgrabhaṇa-offering in the Agniṣṭoma-sacrifice is to be performed by means of a verse in the Anuṣṭubh-metre. The ritual texts, however, show that this verse contains mystically, the characteristics of all the five metres. Thus, it has one foot of seven syllables and three of eight syllables. Out of the seven syllables of the first foot, three syllables are to be attached to the first foot of the eight syllables. Then the latter becomes a foot of eleven syllables i.e. of a Triṣṭubh-metre-verse. The remaining four syllables are to be added to the eight syllables of the second eight-syllabled foot. Then it becomes a foot of twelve syllables i.e. of a Jagatī-metre-verse. The third of eight-syllabled foot is by itself a foot of Gāyatrī-metre-verse. The word *svāhā* which is added to this verse is to be understood as the fifth foot. Then the verse becomes a Paṅkti-metre-verse. Having shown this, the texts say that these are the metres (KS XXIII.2; KPKS XXXV.8).

Sometimes the number of metres is said to be six and then the metre named Kakubh enters into the list. Thus in the recitation of the morning-litany in the Agniṣṭoma-sacrifice six meters viz. Gāyatrī, Jagatī, Triṣṭubh, Kakubh, Anuṣṭubh and Paṅkti are changed into Bṛhatī-metre according to MS IV.5.3. Here the number of metres is mentioned to be six. At the time of "Creeping" for the out-of-doors-chant[7], the brahman-priest creeps as the sixth. For the metres are six. So he kills away the evil beings by means of the metres (JB I.86). Similarly at the time of singing the Rathantara-sāman, one modifies (*stobhati*) six syllables; for the metres are six in number (JB I.131).

Sometimes the number of metres is said to be seven and then Bṛhatī is added to the above six metres. In ŚB IX.3.1.23 and JB III. 86, it is said, "There are seven metres increasing by four (syllables respectively)". The order of these seven metres each of which has four syllables more than the earlier, is as follows—Gāyatrī (24 syllables), Uṣṇih (or Kakubh 28), Anuṣṭubh (32), Bṛhatī (36), Paṅkti (40), Triṣṭubh (44) and Jagatī (48). Many times this number serves as a measurement. Thus in the dīkṣā-ceremony, the sacrificer is purified by seven stalks of darbha-grass; For the metres are seven in number (TS VI.1.1.8; MS III.6.3; KS XXIII.1). On the seventh foot-step of the cow with which soma is to be bought, an offering is to be made; for there are seven verses and metres are identical with speech. One thus obtains the whole speech by means of this offering (MS III.7.6). The sacrificial post to which the victim is bound, should be according to some, seven cubits long. For the sake of making a form of metres (KB X.1). In the Agniṣṭoma-sacrifice one sings an ājya-laud consisting of seven verses and obtains all the metres; for there are seven metres (KB XIV.2). The gods invoked Indra in the morning by means of seven metres. Therefore one has to recite the morning-litany with verses in seven metres each increasing by four syllables (TB I.5.9.7). In the Vājapeya-sacrifice, there are seven Vājaprasavīya-offerings; for there are seven metres; One then obtains food by means of all the metres. (MS I.11.8; KS XIV.8). According to some ritualists, the lotus-garland which is to be worn by the sacrificer at the time of the Daśapeya-sacrifice in the Rājasūya should consist of seven lotuses; for, they argue, that the metres are seven. Since the sacrifice is extended by means of metres, when one wears such a garland, one wears the sacrifice itself as it were (JB II.200). By performing the seven-day sacrifice, one obtains lordship of speech. For the metres are seven and they are the whole speech (JB II.301). One obtains the world of autocracy (*svārājya*) by means of these sacrifices because the metres are seven and they are identical with the world of autocracy (JB III.301).

Thus we observe that the number of metres is told differently at different places and it varies from three to seven according to the requirements of ritual mysticism. The number of metres has numerous significances, the chief of them being to serve as a measurement of the sacrificial details.

Now let us study the relations of metres and sacrifice more closely.

Metres and Sacrifice

That the metres (i.e. the verses composed in the metres) are used in the sacrifice is directly stated by MS II.4.5. "Verily all the metres are used in the sacrifice (*sarvāṇi hi chandāṁsi yajñe prayujyante*)". Similarly some other expressions are also used to imply this point. Thus it is sometimes said, "By means of metres, verily, the sacrifice is stretched (*chandobhir vai yajñas tāyate* JB II.431; cp. JB II.200; ŚB XII.2.2.17). According to JUB IV.12.1.8, the metres and sacrifices are inseparable from each other: "Wherever there is the sacrifice, there are the metres and wherever the metres, there will be the sacrifice "The Dvādaśāha-sacrifice is said to be possessing all the metres (*sa eṣa sarvacchandā yajño yad dvādaśāhaḥ* JB III.369). The metres are sometimes supposed to be like animals carrying the sacrifice to the gods. Thus ŚB IV.4.3.1, it is said, "The metres are verily the (draught) animals of the gods. "The metres satiate the gods and the gods satiate them. It is further said that by means of drawing the Hāriyojana-soma-cup, one really satiates the metres (ŚB IV.4.3.2). For the concept of metres "carrying" the sacrifice to gods see also AB III.47, ŚB I.3.4.6 etc.).

Sacrifice is often mentioned to be a man and the metres are sometimes described as the limbs of the body of that sacrifice-man. Thus MS III.1.1, Gāyatrī is said to be the mouth of sacrifice (*gāyatrī yajñamukham* cp. KS VIII.8; TS V.3.3.4; TMB VII.3.7). Sometimes Gāyatrī is said to be the fore-part of the sacrifice (ŚB III.4.1.15; 6.4.27; 7.1.28). According to JB I.250, Gāyatrī is the navel of the sacrifice-man. Elsewhere Gāyatrī, Bṛhatī and Anuṣṭubh are said to be the three bellies of the sacrifice (JB I.311). TMB VII.5.4, the Uṣṇih and Kakubh-metres are said to be the nostrils (*nāsike*) of the sacrifice. "Therefore, although being the same metre (Uṣṇih: 8 + 8 + 12; Kakubh: 8 + 12 + 8) they convey in different ways the sacrifice; therefore, from each of the nostrils although they are similar, the two breaths (out-breathing and in-breathing) issue in a different way.

Sacrifice is sometimes said to be born out of the metres. Thus AB IV.3, it is said, "The Ṣoḍaśin (sacrifice) is verily fashioned out of all the metres (*sarvebhyo vā eṣa chandobhyaḥ sannirmito yacchoḍaśī* cp. also AB IV.4). JB I.250, it is said that Gāyatrī generates the sacrifice which ends with *iḷā* and which has seven navels. Anuṣṭubh is also said to have generated the sacrifice (JB III.285). According to JB III.317, Jagatī created the Dvādaśāha-sacrifice. When the sacrifice departed from the gods, the gods obtained it back by means of the Brāhmaṇa and metres (AB III.45). Sometimes however, we find that metres are said to be born out of the sacrifice. Thus ṚV X.90.9 the origin of metres is said to be from sacrifice.

The close association of the metres and sacrifice is evident from the following examples. The sacrificial horse in the Aśvamedha-sacrifice is said to be belonging to the Anuṣṭubh-metre (ŚB XIII.2.2.19). The built up Fire - (altar) is said to be identical with the metres in general (ŚB X.5.4.7). Sometimes the built up fire (- altar) is said to be belonging to the Gāyatrī-metre (ŚB VII.2.1.16; 3.2.9; 4.1.41; X.1.4.11). According to AB IV.23, the Dvādaśāha-sacrifice is identical with the Gāyatrī-metre. The sacrifice in general is also said to be belonging to

Gāyatrī (ŚB XII.2.2.11; JB II.431). ŚB IV.2.4.20 identifies the sacrifice with Gāyatrī (cf. ŚB IV.2.4.21;22). Elsewhere, sacrifice is said to be belonging to the Virāj-metre (JB II.431). Some soma-cups are also said to be belonging to various metres. Thus the Aindravāyava-cup belongs to Gāyatrī; the Śukra to Triṣṭubh and the Āgrayaṇa to Jagatī (e.g. KS XXX.2; KPKS XLVI. 5). AB IV.24 Dvādaśāha-sacrifice and the Bṛhatī-metre are identified. JB III.6 remarks, "It is verily the Anuṣṭubh-metre being extended when the Dvādaśāha is being extended". Sometimes sacrifice in general is said to be identical with Anuṣṭubh (TS V.1.3.6; KS XIX.3). KS XXXIII.6 identifies the sacrifice in general with the metres in general. ŚB III.9.3.9 identifies the after-offerings with the metres in general. Thus it will seem how sacrifice and metres are closely connected with each other.

Priests and metres also have close connections with one another. Thus according to JB I.319, the Maitrāvaruṇa-priest belongs to Gāyatrī; the Brāhmaṇācchaṁsin to Triṣṭubh and the Acchāvāka to Anuṣṭubh. KS XXVI.9 identifies priests and metres (*chandāṁsi vai ṛtvijaḥ*). Thus when the sacrificer selects the priests he, mystically, selects metres also. When one selects the Hotṛ one selects Jagatī; in this way the Hotṛ and Jagatī are identical. Similarly Agnīdh and Paṅkti, two Adhvaryus (viz. Adhvaryu and Pratiprasthātṛ) and Aticchandas; Maitrāvaruṇa and Gāyatrī; Brāhmaṇācchaṁsin and Triṣṭubh, Potṛ and Uṣṇih; Neṣṭṛ and Kakubh, Acchāvāka and Anuṣṭubh are implied to be identical (cp. KPKS XLI.7; MS III.9.8).

Metres are sometimes mystically, if not actually, put in contact with the sacrifice. Thus in the Fire-altar building-ceremony the Chandasyā-bricks ('metres' bricks) are laid down (ŚB VII.5.2.42; VIII.2.3.7 ff; 3.3.1 ff; 5.2.1 ff; 6.2.1 ff; cp. KS XX.2; KPKS XXXI.17). The lump of clay for preparing the fire-pan is to be deposited on the black antelope's skin. It is to be deposited on the hair-side. For the hair are metres. Then Agni becomes deposited on metres (ŚB VI.4.1.6). In the course of the Fire-altar building-ceremony, the sacrificer wears a golden plate. It is sewn up in a black-antilope's skin with the hair inside. For the hair are metres and the metres are able to sustain the golden plate (ŚB VI.7.1.6; for similar cases cp. ŚB IX.3.4.10; XII.8.3.3; XIV.1.2.2). The sacrificer who has been consecrated becomes an embryo as it were. At that time he mystically enters the metres (ŚB III. 2.1.6). At the time of Upayājas (connected offerings), the animal which is killed at the time of the animal-sacrifice is addressed, "Go to the metres" (ŚB III.8.1.16).

In many of the sacrificial activities one takes help of the power of metres. One makes merely a mention of the metres while performing an activity and supposes that by referring to the metres one will indeed acquire the power of metres. Thus when in the course of the Aśvamedha-sacrifice, the queens anoint the horse, the following formula is used: "Let the Vasus anoint thee with the Gāyatrī-metre; let the Rudras anoint thee with the Triṣṭubh-metre; let the Ādityas anoint thee with the Jagatī-metre" (TS VII.4.20.1; MS III.12.19; KS-Aśva IV.9; VS XXIII.8; ŚB XIII.2.6.4 ff. TB III.9.4.6f). Similarly the lump of clay out of which the fire-pan is to be made is addressed thus: "May the Vasus Aṅgiras-like fashion thee by means of the Gāyatrī-metre; ..... May the Rudras ...... Viśvedevas .... Anuṣṭubh-metre (TS IV.1.5.3f; MS III.7.6; VS XI.58; ŚB VI.5.2.3ff). At the time of fumigating the fire-pan similar words are uttered in which fumigation is expected to be done by means of metres (TS IV.1.6.1; cp. MS III.7.6; KS XVI.5; Baudhāśs X.6). KS XIX.7 aptly remarks in this connection, "The fire-pan is prepared by means of the metres; fumigated by means of the metres; baked by means of the metres (*chandobhirvā eṣā kriyate chandobhir dhūpyate chandobhiḥ pacyate*)". At the time of fencing round the fire-altar with three lines also the work is expected to be mystically done by means of the metres (TS I.1.9.3; MS I.1.10; IV.1.10; KS I.9; XXV.5; KPKS I.9). In the Pravargya-ceremony, the two lifting sticks are to be taken with the words; "The Gāyatrī-metre thou art; the Triṣṭubh-metre thau art". Then the sticks become taken by means of these metres (ŚB XIV.2.1.16).

Sometimes, however, the metres behave in an antipathetic way with the sacrifice. Thus once metres did not agree to co-operate with the sacrifice (MS II.6.7; KS XIII.8). Nothing is told about how the reconciliation took place between them afterwards. But from this incident it can be concluded that metres are of double-nature. They may co-operate with the sacrifice or not.

Metres and soma-pressings

Metres and the soma-pressings are closely associated with each other.[8] Thus ŚB XIV.1.1.17 identifies Gāyatrī with the morning-pressing, Triṣṭubh with the midday-pressing and Jagatī with the third pressing. Many times morning-pressing is said to be "belonging" to Gāyatrī, midday-pressing to Triṣṭubh and third-pressing to Jagatī (KS XXII.3; ŚB XI.5.9.7; JB I.263; 265; 266; 284; III.57; ṢaḍB I.4.12; ChāU III.16.1; 3; 5). JB I.280 says that Gāyatrī is the excellence (*jyaiṣṭhya-*) of the morning-pressing. Therefore whatever metre may be used at the time of that pressing, it is called, mystically, Gāyatrī. Similar are the cases of Triṣṭubh and Jagatī in connection with the midday-pressing and third-pressing respectively. Prajāpati told Puruṣa Nārāyaṇa to hold on to Udgātṛ from behind at the chanting of the Bahiṣpavamāna-laud, which occurs at the time of the morning-pressing with the words, "Though art a falcon formed of the Gāyatrī-metre I hold on thee; bear me unto well-being". The same action is to be done at the time of the midday pavamāna at the midday-pressing with the formula, "Though art .... an eagle .... Triṣṭubh-metre". Again at the time of Ārbhava-pavamāna at the third pressing, the same action is to be done with the formula, "Thou art a Ṛbhu formed of the Jagatī-metre.... " (ŚB XII.3.4.3 ff; cp. formulas in AV VI.48.1 ff). Here also the three metres and the three pressings are put into contact. For the connection of Gāyatrī, Triṣṭubh and Jagatī with the three pressings see also Agnipurāṇa 336.6 f[9]; AB III.13 gives a mythological explanation why these three metres are connected with three pressings. Once, Prajāpati distributed sacrifice and metres to the gods. He allotted Gāyatrī to Agni and Vasus at the morning-pressing and Jagatī to Viśvedevas and Ādityas at the third-pressing (for these gods, pressings, and the metres see also ŚB IV.4.1.18). JB I.288 another mythological explanation is found. According to that explanation, Gāyatrī brought from the heaven the morning-pressing; Triṣṭubh brought the midday-pressing and Jagatī brought the third-pressing (cp. ŚB IV.3.2.7 ff).

The association of the three metres with the three pressings mentioned above must be understood in a very broad sense. Although the morning-pressing which is "carried" by the Gāyatrī-metre alone (ŚB IV.2.5.20f) and therefore can be legitimately called *gāyatra* i.e. belonging to the Gāyatrī-metre, the cases of midday-pressing and of the third-pressing are not so simple. Thus in the midday-pressing verses other than those in Triṣṭubh-metre and in the third pressing verses other than those in the Jagatī-metre also are recited. Thus in the midday-pressing which is called Traiṣṭubha, verses in Triṣṭubh, Gāyatrī and Bṛhatī-metres and recited. Similarly in the third-pressing which is described as Jāgata, verses in Jagatī, Gāyatrī, Uṣṇih, Kakubh and Anuṣṭubh-metres are used. (ŚB IV.2.5.20).

Thus the connection the three metres with the three pressings must be understood in a mysterious way and not literally. In the midday-pressing although metres other than Triṣṭubh are used, those metres are also to be mysteriously understood as Triṣṭubh. Thus out of the twenty-eight syllables of the Kakubh-metre, one should separate twenty syllables and add them to the twenty four syllables of the Gāyatrī-metre. Then the number forty four i.e. that of the Triṣṭubh metre is obtained. The remaining eight syllables are to be added to the thirty-six syllables of the Bṛhatī-metre. Then again we get the number fortyfour i.e. that of Triṣṭubh. Thus even though there are some metres other than Triṣṭubh in the midday-pressing they are all mystically converted into Triṣṭubh (JB I.242). Similarly the third-pressing can be mystically shown to be consisting of the Jagatī-metre alone. Actually six metres viz. Gāyatrī, Uṣṇih,

Kakubh, Anuṣṭubh, Jagatī and Bṛhatī are used in the third-pressing. Out of the twenty four syllables of Gāyatrī twenty are to be added to the twenty eight syllables of the Kakubh metre and then the number forty eight which is that of the Jagatī-metre is obtained. The remaining four syllables are to be added to the twenty eight syllables of Uṣṇih and then this number comes to be thirty two. There is already the Anuṣṭubh metre with thirty two syllables and it is to be divided into two parts of sixteen syllables each. Thus to the above-mentioned number thirty two, one of these sixteen-syllabled parts is to be added. Then we get the number forty eight of the Jagatī. The remaining sixteen syllables are to be added to the thirty six syllables of the Bṛhatī-metre of the Yajñāyajñīya-sāman. Then a fifty two-syllabled Jagatī comes into existence. The additional four syllables in this Jagatī are identical with the quadrepeds. Thus the third-pressing mystically belongs only to the Jagatī-metre even though other metres are used at its time (JB I.242).

The connection of the particular deity with the particular soma-pressing is based on the connection of the particular metre with the particular soma-pressing. Thus Gāyatrī has eight syllables in each foot. The Vasus are eight in number. Therefore, in the morning-pressing this deity, viz. Vasu is associated with each syllable. Similarly Triṣṭubh has eleven syllables in each foot. The Rudras are eleven in number. Therefore in the midday-pressing Rudras are associated with the syllables. Similar is the case of the third pressing which belongs to Jagatī which has twelve syllables in a foot. The Ādityas are twelve and therefore, in the third-pressing Ādityas are associated with the syllables (JB I.141). Prajāpati and Indra obtained worship from the gods by means of the performance of the Apaciti (Worship) sacrifice. For the morning-pressing of this sacrifice amounts to Gāyatrī which is eight-syllabled. The Vasus are eight. Thus Prajāpati and Indra obtained worship from Vasus. In the same manner they obtained worship from Rudras who are eleven and from the Ādityas who are twelve by means of the eleven-syllabled Triṣṭubh-metre to which the midday-pressing amounts and by means of the twelve-syllabled Jagatī to which the third-pressing amounts, respectively (JB II.101).

The close connection of the metres and the soma-pressings is sometimes significant in determining some ritual details. Thus at the time of the morning-pressing the Maitrāvaruṇa-priest recites verses in Gāyatrī because the morning-pressing belongs to Gāyatrī (AB VI.9). Similarly at the first turn of the morning-pressing, soma is to be pressed eight times. For Gāyatrī consists of eight syllables and the morning-pressing belongs to Gāyatrī (ŚB IV.1.1.8). Further, at the midday-pressing, verses in Triṣṭubh are recited; for the midday-pressing belongs to Triṣṭubh (AB VI.11). At the time of the third-pressing, verses in Jagatī-metre are to be recited at the beginning; for this pressing belongs to Jagatī (AB VI.15). At the time of each soma-pressing, all the soma-sap must be poured out, offered and drunk. But if soma is left over from the morning-pressing, an expiation is made with a sāman based on verses in the Gāyatrī-metre; for the morning-pressing belongs to the Gāyatrī-metre (TMB IX.7.1f).

We saw above the association of Gāyatrī with the morning-pressing, of Triṣṭubh with the midday-pressing and of Jagatī with the third pressing. But to this normal position, there are some exceptions. Thus the midday-pressing is sometimes said to be belonging to the Kakubh-metre because Kakubh is used in it (JB I.180). TMB IX.7.6 f, one is asked to use the Gaurīvita-sāman based on the verses in Bṛhatī as an expiation, if the soma is left over from the midday-pressing; for the midday-pressing belongs to the Bṛhatī-metre. According to JB I.180, the third-pressing is connected with the Anuṣṭubh-metre because it is used in it. In an henoistic way, Gāyatrī is praised to be alone carrying all the three pressings. Thus ŚB IV.3.2.10 quotes an opinion according to which Gāyatrī itself, became the metres like Triṣṭubh, Jagatī etc. by increasing the number of syllables. Therefore it is Gāyatrī alone that carries all the three pressings. TS VI.4.11.4, some ritual thinkers ask, "Why does Gāyatrī, being smallest of all the metres carry all the pressings"? The answer is, "The Āgrayaṇa-soma-cup is the calf of the Gāyatrī-metre; verily turning back towards it, it carries all the pressings. Therefore, a cow turns back towards the calf which is taken away". Similarly we read "Gāyatrī verily carries the morning-pressing, Gāyatrī the midday-pressing and Gāyatrī the third-pressing". It is further added that one who know this, possesses fame and name upto his old age. Thus Āruṇi once boasted, "I know verily the Gāyatrī-metre carrying all the pressings. Therefore, my fame and name do not depart from me upto the old age" (JB I.289). The real reason why Gāyatrī is said to be carrying all the pressings seems to be in the fact that in morning-pressing all the verses are in Gāyatrī. The first chants in the midday-pressing and in the third-pressing are in Gāyatrī. This is told by means of a mythological story in TMB VIII. 4.2. "Triṣṭubh and Jagatī said to Gāyatrī, "Let us join thee". She (Gāyatrī) asked, "What will result therefrom for me"? "What thou wishest" they said. She replied, "To me must belong the whole morning-pressing and I must have the lead of the other two pressings". Therefore the whole morning-pressing belongs to Gāyatrī and the other two pressings are introduced by it.

As regards the metres and sacrifice in general we may conclude that they are closely associated. The metres however are of double-nature. Although they are mostly helpful to the sacrificial performance they can sometimes go against it.

Metaphorical descriptions

The metaphorical descriptions of metres can imply the way in which the metres are supposed to execute their power. Therefore a study of such descriptions is fruitful. Metres are very often supposed to be draught animals. They are yoked to sacrifice which is a cart or chariot as it were and then the metres "carry" the sacrifice. Thus ṚV X 114 9 it is asked, "Who knows the yoking of the metres"? ŚB I.8.2.8 metres are said to be the draught animals of gods (*paśvavo vai devānāṁ chandaṁsi*). "As they (animals) when yoked, here, convey (burdens) for men so in like manner, the metres being yoked, *convey* the sacrifice to the gods" (cp. ŚB IV.4.3.1). TMB XIX.5.11 also metres are described to be draught animals. According to ŚB IV.2.5.20, Gāyatrī *carries* the morning-pressing, Triṣṭubh *carries* the mid-day-pressing and Jagatī *carries* the third-pressing. Compare JB I.120 where it is said, "Three metres verily *carry* the sacrifice viz. Gāyatrī, Triṣṭubh and Jagatī". Elsewhere four metres are said to be *carrying* the sacrifice and Anuṣṭubh is added to the above three (JB I.300; II.431).

JB III.313 f, the stomas are said to be the divine chariots and the metres the divine horses. The gods having *yoked* these horses to those chariots, went to the heaven. AB IV.27 compares the metres to horses and oxen. Thus it is said: "Just as in the world men go with relays of fresh horses or oxen, so with relays of fresh metres they (the performers) go to the world of heaven when he (the Hotṛ priest) transposes the metres in the course of the Dvādaśāha with transposed metres".

Sometimes the metres are said to be like birds. The metres, it is supposed, carry the sacrificer to the heaven, in the form of birds. Thus AB IV.23 it is said, "He who knows Gāyatrī as possessed of wings, of eyes, of light, and of brilliance, goes to the world of heaven with Gāyatrī as possessed of wings, of eyes, of light, and of brilliance". ŚB XI.4.1.8 also Gāyatrī is described to be a golden-coloured bird with brilliant wings and as carrying the sacrificer to the world of heaven (cp. ŚB XI. 4.1.16). For the Gāyatrī-metre as a bird with brilliant wings see also KS XXXIV.8. Elsewhere it is said that Gāyatrī having become a falcon brought soma from the heaven (ŚB III. 9.4.10).

TB I.5.12.5, the metres are supposed to be like a chariot. Thus Prajāpati said (to the metres), "Be a chariot for me O metres: By means of you I shall go by this way. For him Gāyatrī and Jagatī became the wheels (wings); Uṣṇih and Triṣṭubh became the sidepoles; Anuṣṭubh and Paṅkti became the horses; Bṛhatī became the seat. Riding this chariot, he went". The knower of this also enjoys the same kind of chariot.

The metres are magically powerful. From the above mentioned metaphorical descriptions it will be seen how they *carry* those who use them to some good results. Even the gods, as we shall see use the metres as a means to obtain some kind of results. It will be however, also seen that metres and gods are closely associated or even identical with one another. One uses a particular metre which is closely connected with a particular god for that god only and propitiates and pleases him. Thus an idea of pleasing the metres is at times supposed to be a means of pleasing the gods who ultimately grant the desired result to the performers.[10] Thus in the ultimate analysis we have to understand the metres as significant not merely magically but rather magicoreligiously. Let us now study the relations of metres and gods.

Metres and the gods:

The metres and gods are very closely connected. The metres *carry* the sacrifice to the gods (ŚB I.3.4.6). They are described to be the houses of the gods (*chanāṁsi vāva devānām gṛhāḥ*). Thus "Gāyatrī is eight-syllabled; the Vasus are eight. The Vasus become the house-holders by means of Gāyatrī. Triṣṭubh is eleven-syllabled; The Rudras are eleven; therefore the Rudras become the house-holders by means of Triṣṭubh. Jagatī is twelve-syllabled; the Ādityas are twelve; Therefore, the Ādityas become the householders by means of Jagatī. The Viśvedevas become the house-holders by means of Anuṣṭubh (no reasoning is given)". (JB I.280). The Virāj-metre belongs to all the deities (*sarvadaivatyaṁ vā etaccandaḥ yadvirāṭ* ŚB XIII.4.1.13) and the case of the Anuṣṭubh-metre is also the same (*sarvadevatyo vā anuṣṭup* JB III.63). Sometimes metres are described to be the wealth and the cattle of gods (*chandāṁsi vai devānaṁ vāmaṁ paśavaḥ* TS V.3.8.1; MS III.2.6; 3.2). The verses in the Uṣṇih-metre are said to be the fortresses of gods (*devapurā vā eṣā yaduṣṇihaḥ* JB I.227). According to JB I.188, gods collected the sap of metres just as the bees collect the sap of flowers. Gods enjoy the metres and the metres become exhausted (*yātayāma-*). When the Hotṛ-priest recites the morning-litany, he makes the metres fresh (ŚB III.9.3.10). By means of the Pratigara, the Adhvaryu makes the metres fresh (ŚB IV.3.2.5).

Metres are sometimes identified with gods. If another sacrificer is performing a soma-sacrifice simultaneously, then one has to begin the morning-litany at the midnight i.e. before the normal time. So that one wins all the speech, all the metres and thereby all the deities: "For metres, verily are identical with all the deities (*chandāṁsi vai sarvā devatāḥ*)" and thus one takes hold of all the deities (JB I.342; for the identification of metres, stomas etc. with the deities see also JB I.332; II.350). ŚB III. 9.3.9 metres are identified with the early coming gods [*chandāṁsi devāḥ prātaryāvāṇaḥ* (cf. MS IV.5.3)].

Gods took the help of metres in defeating Asuras many times. Thus JB I.342 we read, "Gods verily defeated the Asuras by means of metres". They won their breath by means of Gāyatrī; eye by means of Triṣṭubh, ear by means of Jagatī and speech by means of Anuṣṭubh (JB I.99). Further they drove them away from this world by means of Gāyatrī, from the middle region by means of Triṣṭubh, from the heaven by means of Jagatī and from the cattle by means of Anuṣṭubh (JB I.99). Gods, led by Viṣṇu removed the Asuras by means of metres (KS XXXII.5; cp. XIX.11). At some places it is said that both the gods and Asuras were possessing metres. But gods conquered the metres of Asuras and conquered them. "The monosyllabic metre was the lowest one in possession of the gods, the heptasyllabic their highest; the enneasyllabic one was the lowest of the Asuras, the metre of the fifteen syllables was their highest. The gods and the Asuras were contending with each other. Prajāpati having become of Anuṣṭubh-nature, took place between them. The gods and Asuras called him to join them and he joined the gods. Then the gods throve and the Asuras perished .... By means of monosyllabic metre the gods took away the metre of fifteen syllables belonging to the Asuras. By means of the disyllabic metre, the metre of fourteen syllables; by means of the trisyllabic metre, the metre of thirteen syllables; by means of the four syllabic metre, the metre of twelve syllables; by means of the five syllabic metre, the metre of eleven syllables; by means of the six syllabic, the metre of ten syllables; by means of the seven syllabic, the metre of nine syllables. By means of the eight syllables (of the Anuṣṭubh-metre representing Prajāpati), they took away the eight syllables of the Asuras" (TMB XII.13.27). In this way the gods conquered the metres of Asuras (cp. JB I.192f; 196f; 205). The gods not only obtained the metres of Asuras by means of their own metres, but they also obtained the world of Asuras (cp. TS VI.6.11.5; MS IV.7.5). Indra, accompanied by other gods removed the Asuras from the three pressings of the soma-sacrifice (JB I.197 f).

Gods used the metres in removing darkness, death, night. Thus when the gods were afraid of these, they protected fire by means of metres. The Vasus protected it by means of Gāyatrī, the Rudras by means of Triṣṭubh and the Ādityas by means of Jagatī (KPKS V.3). Gods tried to protect themselves from death and evil by means of metres. "Prajāpati created the gods. After them, death and evil were created. These gods coming to Prajāpati asked, "Why evil after us"? he said to them, "Bring together the metres; enter these each one at one's proper place; then you will be separated from death and evil. The Vasus brought together Gāyatrī; they entered it. It concealed them. The Rudras brought together Triṣṭubh .... The Ādityas brought together Jagatī .... The Viśvedevas brought together Anuṣṭubh ..." (JUB I.4.4.1ff; cp. JB I.283 f).

Metres proved to be useful to gods at the time of reaching to the heavenly world or even obtaining all the worlds. MS III. 2.3 it is said, "By means of metres, verily, gods came to the heavenly world (*chandobhir vai devāḥ svargaṁ lokam āyan*; cf. KS XX. 1; KPKS XLVI.5; cp. TS V.2.3.4; ŚB III.9.3.10; IV.3.2.5;). Sometimes however, Bṛhatī alone receives the credit of this kind of help. Thus ŚB XII.2.3.1 it is said, "By means of Bṛhatī the gods obtained the heavenly world (*bṛhatyā vai* (*devāḥ*) *svargaṁ lokam āpnuvan*" cf. XII.3.3.13). According to ŚB III.5.1.9, the fire-altar should be as broad as thirty-six steps on the eastern side. For Bṛhatī has thirty-six syllables. Gods obtained the heavenly world by means of Bṛhatī. So by making the fire-altar in this way, one reaches the heavenly world. The other metres, it is said, could not help the gods in reaching the heaven. But Bṛhatī could. This has been told by TMB VII.4.2: "The gods said to the metres, "Through you let us reach the heavenly world". They employed Gāyatrī; through it they did not reach it; they employed Triṣṭubh ...; Jagatī ......; Anuṣṭubh; through it they nearly reached it. Then they squezzed out the essences of the quarters and added (these essences as) four syllables to Anuṣṭubh". Then they obtained not merely the world of heaven but all the worlds (cp. JB I.120). Satobṛhatī is a kind of the Bṛhatī-metre having three feet of twelve syllables each. Sometimes the gods are said to have obtained all the worlds by means of Satobṛhatī (TMB XVI.11.8f). TMB VIII. 5.7, gods are said to have gone to the world of heaven by means of a verse-quarter-Virāj (i.e. a group of ten verse-quarters mystically called Virāj because Virāj has *ten* syllables). At the time of carrying the sun towards the heaven also gods took the help of metres (TMB XII.10.6). When the gods obtained the world of heaven, they desired that others should not reach it. Therefore, they again took the help of metres. They mixed together the metres in order to make the world of heaven unrecognisable (MS IV.7.5).

Gods obtained great help from the metres at the time of discovering the sacrifice which had run away, from them. Thus we read, that the Sacrifice, the food, ran away from the gods. The gods said, "Sacrifice, the food, hath left us; this sacrifice, this food; let us search for". They further decided to search o·· the sacrifice by means of the Brāhmaṇa and the metres .... (AB III.45).

Metres are sometimes connected with Agni in various ways. Thus metres are said to be clothes of Agni (*chandāṁsi vā agner vāsaḥ* MS III.1.5; KS XIX.5; KPKS XXX.3). The metres are according to KS XX.1 a beloved form of Agni (*eṣā vā agneḥ priyā tanūḥ yacchandāṁsi*; cp. TS V.1.5.3. *sarvāṇi* (*catvāri* TS V.2.1.2) *chandāṁsi khalu vā agneḥ priyā tanūḥ*). Metres are said to be the place of origin of Agni (*chandāṁsi vā agneḥ yoniḥ*) (KS XIX.10; XX.4; KPKS XXX.8; XXXI.6). KS XX.5 teaches us that Agni reached the northern altar by means of metres. TS V.7.9.3, says that fires (fire-altars) are built by means of metres because metres and fires are identical. ŚB IX. 2.3.44 metres are mentioned to be seven beloved seats of Agni.

Among the gods, Agni stands in special connection with the Gāyatrī-metre. In the divine, primordial sacrifice, Gāyatrī became the co-yoked (helper) of Agni (ṚV X.130.4). It is noteworthy that some ritual prescriptions are based on this connection of Agni and Gāyatrī and his connection has some magicoreligious significance. Many times the following remark is made: "Agni verily belongs to Gāyatrī. Agni's metre is Gāyatrī (*gāyatro vā agnir gāyatracchandāḥ*)". This remark is made by KB I.1 after having prescribed that verses in Gāyatrī-metre should be employed at the time of establishing fires (*agnyādhāna*) (cp. MS I.6.8). Similarly this remark is made by the same text when it prescribes that the fire-enkindling-verses at the time of New and Full-moon-offerings should be in Gāyatrī-metre (KB III.2; for this remark see also KB IX.2; XIX.4). A similar remark is also found in KS XX.5 *gāyatro'gnir gāyatracchandāḥ* when it is a matter of putting down of a ghee-filled spoon made of Kārṣmarya wood in the course of Fire-building-ceremony. This action is also to be done with a verse in Gāyatrī. For Agni belongs to Gāyatrī; Agni's metre is Gāyatri. Then one propitiates Agni by means of his own metre. The same remark is repeated in KS XXIX.4; MS IV.8.6; TS III.5.4.4 in connection with the Udavasānīyā-offering. At the end of the Agniṣṭoma-sacrifice, this offering is to be made by means of a cake baked on eight potsherds. For Gāyatrī has eight syllables; Agni belongs to Gāyatrī; Agni's metre is Gāyatrī; one thus propitiates Agni with his own metre. Here there is the idea of *propitiating* a god and thus the idea of religion seems to be mixed with the idea of magical power of metres. For Agni belonging to Gāyatrī etc. See also KS IX.13; MS I.5.5; 7.4; III.9.5). Sometimes we read following expressions like *Jāyatro'gniḥ* (MS III.3.2; KS XX.1; XXI.5; 7; XXII.2) or *gāyatram agneśchandaḥ* (AB I.1; ŚB II.1.4.14; 2.1.17; cp. II.3.4.32) or *gāyatraccandā agniḥ* (TMB XVI.5.19 cp. VII.8.4). Sometimes Gāyatrī and Agni have been identified with each other (ŚB I.8.2.13; III.9.4.10; VI.6.2.7).

Agni is connected with the Anuṣṭubh-metre also and KS XXX.3 says : Anuṣṭubh is a beloved form of Agni (*anuṣṭubh vā agneḥ priyā tanūḥ*).

Indra has a special connection with the Triṣṭubh-metre. ṚV V. 29.11 it is said, "Indra, by means of speech in the Triṣṭubh-metre, distributed the sky". "In the primordial, divine sacrifice, Triṣṭubh was the share of the sacrificial day for Indra" (ṚV X.30.5). ŚB VI.6.2.7 identifies Indra with Triṣṭubh (*indrastriṣṭubh*). Indra, after having killed Vṛtra chose his portion in which Triṣṭubh was included (AB III.21). Similarly TS I.7.11.2 we read, "Indra, by means of eleven syllables won the Triṣṭubh-metre" (cp. MS I.11.10; MS XIV.4). Triṣṭubh is, AB II.2, described as the thunderbolt of Indra. According to AB III.13, Prajāpati assigned the Triṣṭubh-metre to Indra and Rudra. Elsewhere we read, "By means of the Triṣṭubh-metre Indra obtained worship from Rudras at the midday-pressing" (JB II. 101). KS XI.3 has a similar story. In that story it is told that Bṛhaspati offered a sacrifice to gods in the house of Indra with verses in Triṣṭubh. Therefore all the other gods then recognised the supremacy of Indra. The Indra-Triṣṭubh connection also has a ritualistic, magicoreligious significance. Thus in the Mahāvrata-ceremony, by using the Prauga-laud in the Triṣṭubh-metre, one propitiates Indra by his own metre. For "Of Indra is this metre viz. Triṣṭubh" (ŚāṅĀ I.2). Similarly by reciting one hundred verses in Triṣṭubh-metre on this day, one propitiates Indra by his own metre for the same reason (ŚāṅĀ II.16). In the course of the Fire-altar-building-ceremony a curds-filled spoon of udumbara-wood is to be put down with a verse in Triṣṭubh; for Triṣṭubh belongs to Indra and food also belongs to Indra; one thus obtains food belonging to Indra (KS XX.5; KPKS XXXI.7, cp. ŚB VII.4.1.42). Even a verse or foot of it not in Triṣṭubh, but containing the word Indra, should be regarded as having a form of Triṣṭubh. Such is the case of the line (*indrasya kāmam akṣaran* JB III.206).(For Indra and Triṣṭubh-connection see also KS XIX.8; KB XXII.7).

Indra takes the help of many metres other than Triṣṭubh in accomplishing his task. Thus at the time of killing Vṛtra, Indra got the help of many metres. According to JB III.110f Indra killed Vṛtra by means of Śakvarī, Ṣaṭpadā, Paṅkti, Anuṣṭubh and Triṣṭubh having gathered them together. Elsewhere it is said that Indra hurled thunderbolt against Vṛtra by means of Uṣṇih and Kakubh-metres (cf. JB I.158, III.295; TMB VIII. 5.2). According to JB I.193f, Indra killed Vṛtra by means of Śakvarī-metre. Indra followed after a female evil doer named Dīrghajihvī, having raised the thunderbolt in the form of Anuṣṭubh-metre (JB I.163).

Metres are sometimes very closely connected with Prajāpati. The origin of metres is said to be from Prajāpati. Thus "When Prajāpati was relaxed, the cattle having become metres went (came) out from him". (ŚB VIII.2.3.9). According to AĀ III. 2.6 Prajāpati, the year after creating creatures, relaxed. He put himself together by means of the metres. Thus here Prajāpati seems to have created the metres for his own use. According to JUB I.4.4.1ff he advised the gods to create the metres and protect themselves from death and evil and they did accordingly. Quite in agreement with AĀ II.2.6 (see above) where Prajāpati is said to have put himself together, AB II.18 says "Prajāpati's limbs, verily are these metres (*prajāpater vā etānyaṅgāni yacchandāṁsi*)". Sometimes Prajāpati and metres are said to be identical (*prajāpatir vai chandāṁsi* MS IV.5.3; 7.5; cp. ŚB VI.2.2.33; 3.1.11: "Prajāpati, verily is all the metres: *sarvāṇi chandāṁsi Prajāpatiḥ*)". The ascription of particular metres to particular gods has been done by Prajāpati. Thus AB III.13 it is said, "Prajāpati assigned to the gods the sacrifice and metres in portions. He allotted Gāyatrī at the morning-pressing to Agni and Vasus; Triṣṭubh to Indra and Rudras at the midday-pressing, Jagatī to the Viśvedevas and Ādityas at the third-pressing ..". In this story further it is said that Prajāpati created the metre Anuṣṭubh and that became his own metre. Thus of all the metres, Anuṣṭubh is many times specially connected with Prajāpati and is said to be his own metre (*svaṁ chandaḥ* AB III.13). KS XXIII.2; KPKS XXXV.8: "Anuṣṭubh verily is Prajāpati's own metre: *anuṣṭubh vai Prajāpateḥ svaṁ chandaḥ*". This connection of Prajāpati and Anuṣṭubh has some ritual significances. Thus the Audgrabhaṇa-offering in the Agniṣṭoma-sacrifice is to be offered with a verse in Anuṣṭubh. For sacrifice is identical with Prajāpati and Anuṣṭubh is Prajāpati's own metre. Then the sacrifice becomes established on its own metre. (KS XXIII.2; KPKS XXXV.8). While MS III. 6.5 says that the metre Anuṣṭubh belongs to Prajāpati (*prājāpatyam*) JB I.197, II.95, TS VII.4.4.1 it is said that Prajāpati belongs to Anuṣṭubh (*ānuṣṭubhaḥ*). Some texts identify Prajāpati and Anuṣṭubh (*prajāpatir vā anuṣṭubh* TMB IV.8.9; JB I.290; II.86; III.309; cp. TS III.4.9.7).

Metres are sometimes described as goddesses. Thus MS IV. 3.5, it is said, "Metres are goddesses .... Thus Anumati is Gāyatrī, Rākā is Triṣṭubh; Sinīvālī is Jagatī; Kuhū is Anuṣṭubh". Whosoever performs a soma-sacrifice, his metres become exhausted (*yātayāma*). By offering oblations to these goddesses, one makes the metres sapful and fresh (*ayātayāma* cp. MS IV.3.6; KS XII.8; TS III.4.9.4f; KB XIX.7). Since metres are identical with these goddesses and also with offsprings and cattle, by offering oblations to these goddesses, one gets offsprings and cattle (TS III.4.9.1f; cp. MS IV.3.5; KS XII.8). For the identification of metres and these goddesses see also ŚB IX.5.1.39).

Sometimes the word *gna* (woman or wife, particularly in plural meaning wives of the gods) is used to indicate the goddesses and the metres are identified with them. Thus at the time of fumigating the fire-pan, one says, "May the wives (bake) thee". TS V.1.7.2 interprets this by identifying the wives with metres and it is the metres that are requested to bake the fire-pan (cp. MS III.1.8; KS XIX.7; ŚB III.5.4.7).

The Sun seems to be specially connected with the Bṛhatī-metre. "By means of the out-of-doors-chant, the gods carried the Sun to the world of heaven. They then fixed it at midday by means of Bṛhatī. Therefore, they sing at the midday-pressing Bṛhatī (part); for it is the (metre) that props up the sun at midday" (TMB VII.4.7). ŚB XII.8.3.24 says, "Established in Bṛhatī, in glory, in establishment, verily this sun shines". ŚāṅĀ II.17 says, "He belongs to Bṛhatī, this one who shines". KPKS IV.7 also says that the sun belongs to Bṛhatī.

Rudras are connected with Triṣṭubh. Thus GB II.2.9 says, "Triṣṭubh is the wife of Rudras" (cp. MS I.9.2; KS IX.10; TĀ III. 9.1). Rudras supported Agni by means of Triṣṭubh (KS VII.6; KPKS V.5). In order to protect themselves from the death, the evil, Rudras brought together the Triṣṭubh-metre and concealed themselves in it (JUB I.4.4.4). At the time of fencing around the fire one addresses to Agni, "May Rudras fence you round by means of Triṣṭubh" (MS I.1.10; KPKS XXXIX.1).

Many other gods also are associated with some metres. Thus in the primordial, divine sacrifice, Savitṛ united himself with Uṣṇih, Soma became concealed with Anuṣṭubh and the praise-songs (*uktha*). Bṛhatī supported the speech of Bṛhaspatī (ṚV X.130.4); the Virāj-metre was the glory of Mitrāvaruṇā and Jagatī entered into Viśvedevas (ṚV X.130.5). In Yama all the metres like Uṣṇih, Gāyatrī etc. are put (ṚV X.14.16). Maruts are addressed as follows: "When the poets poured a Triṣṭubh-feast, then you were shining on the mountains" (ṚV VIII.7.1). This place seems to refer to the midday-soma-feast which is in special connection with Tristubh. KB XVI.3 mentions Anuṣṭubh as Soma's metre. JB II.131 Bṛhaspatī is said to be belonging to the Gāyatrī-metre. Indra and Agni are said to be the deities of metres in general (*asti vai chandasāṁ devatendrāgnī* (ŚB I. 8.2.16). ŚB VI.5.2.3 ff Vasus are connected with Gāyatrī, Rudras with Triṣṭubh, Ādityas with Jagatī and Viśvedevas with Anuṣṭubh (cp. ŚB VI.5.3.10; 4.17).

Metres are double-natured. So they can sometimes go against the gods. Thus according to a story, metres once ran away from the gods. For they were desirous of some share in the sacrifice. They said, "We shall not carry your shares, the oblations". Gods then attributed the four-times ladled libation to them and thus made them share-holders of the sacrifice (KS XVIII.19; KPKS XXIX.7). Thus about the connection of the metre and gods we conclude that the metres are double-natured power-substances and although mostly they cooperate with gods and are very closely associated with them they can sometimes go against the gods; Moreover, the metres are magicoreligiously significant in their connections with the gods.

Metres and Sāmans

Metres and sāmans are closely connected with each other in various ways. Sometimes they are mentioned to be food of each other. JB II.384, the sāmans are said to be food of Anuṣṭubh and Anuṣṭubh is said to be food of sāmans. There can be one sāman based on the verses of numerous metres. Thus the Agniṣṭoma-sāman is one; but it is based on verses of numerous metres. "Therefore one man thrives in many ways". Here also the idea of metres being the food of sāmans is implied.

The sāmans are sometimes said to have their origin in the metres. Thus according to TB II.3.2.3 Prajāpati created Gāyatrī from the mind. From Gāyatrī he created all the other metres and from the metres he created sāman. Elsewhere it is said that Prajāpati created the Gāyatra-sāman from the Gāyatrī-metre (ŚB VIII.1.1.5); the svara-sāman from the Triṣṭubh-metre (ŚB VIII.1.1.8), the Ṛksama-sāman from the Jagatī-metre (ŚB VIII.1.2.2), the Aiḍa-sāman from the Anuṣṭubh-metre (ŚB VIII.1.2.5) and the Nidhanavat-sāman from the Paṅkti-metre (ŚB VIII.1.2.8). TMB VII.8.8ff, Prajāpati is said to have seen Gāyatri as a womb. He then thought of creating Pṛṣṭhasāmans out of this womb. He then created the following Pṛṣṭhasāmans: Rathantara, Bṛhat, Vairūpa, Vairāja, Śakvarīs and Revatī. TMB XV.10.5, Gāyatrī is said to be the womb of

Rathantara-sāman. JB I.299, tells us how various gods created various sāmans with the help of metres. Thus Agni, Indra, Viśvedevas and Prajāpati created the Svāra-sāmans, Nidhanavat-sāmans, Aiḷa-sāmans, and Ṛksama-sāmans with the help of Gāyatrī, Triṣṭubh, Jagatī and Anuṣṭubh respectively.

Metres and speech (vāc)

These two also are connected with each other. ṚV IX.113.6 the Brahman-priest is said to be singing the speech which is metrical (*chandasyā*). ṚV IX.103.3 seven speeches of the seers are said to have cried for Soma and it can be assumed that these are nothing but the seven metres. Many times metres and speech are said to be identical. KS XXXVI.3 it is said, "Metres are speech (*chandāṁsi vai vāk*" cp. MS III.7.5; IV.8.8: *chandāṁsi vāk*; cp. also MS III.10.7. "Speech is metres *vāg vai chandāṁsi.* Similarly JB II.301 Metres are identical with the whole speech *chandāṁsi vai sarvā vāk*" and ŚB VIII.7.3.8; IX.5.1.53 "Speech is identical with all the metres *vāgu vai sarvāṇi chandāṁsi*"). The seven metres increasing by four syllables are described as the ascendances of speech. Thus when the performers of sacrifice use metres increasing by four, they ascend the speech as it were (JB II.367). Sometimes metres are said to be born out of speech. ŚB III.3.1.1 it is said, "When from speech the metres were born, the one consisting of seven feet viz. Śakvarī was the last (highest) of them" (cp. III.9.2.17).

Sometimes individual metres are also identified with the speech. Thus Gāyatrī is said to be identical with speech (*vāg vai gāyatrī* KS XXIII.5; KPKS XXXVI.2; CHU III.12.1). The metre Anuṣṭubh is specifically connected with the speech (vāganuṣṭubh; KB XI.2; ŚB X.3.1.1; JB I.188; 269; TMB XII. 13.15; ŚāṅĀ II 15; *vāgvā anuṣṭubh*: AB I.28; ŚB I.3.2.16; JB II. 425; TMB VIII.7.3 etc.). In the Vrātyastoma-sacrifice the Pratipad-verse should be in Anuṣṭubh. For Anuṣṭubh is identical with speech (*vāc*). Those who are leading the life of Vrātyas are devoid of speech as it were. For they speak impure speech. But when the Pratipad in Anuṣṭubh is used, they prosper in speech (JB II.221). In the Agniṣṭoma-sacrifice, the last verse of the Yajñāyajñīya-chant is to be transformed into Anuṣṭubh. And because A. is identical with speech, one becomes firmly established in speech thereby (TMB VIII.7.3). Thus the *vāc* and A. identification is ritually significant. According to JB II.326, the speech desired to be large and then became the Anuṣṭubh-metre.

Henoistic praise of some metres

Some metres have been henoistically praised in the vedic texts. Thus at different places different metres are treated to be of the highest importance. This praise has many significances. Anuṣṭubh metre is very often described to be the supreme of all the metres. In the Aśvamedha-sacrifice the Pratipad (opening Tristich) is in Anuṣṭubh. For "Anuṣṭubh is the supreme of all the metres (*paramā vā eṣā chandasāṁ yadanuṣṭup*), the fourfold stoma is the supreme of all the stomas; the three-night-sacrifice is supreme of all the sacrifices; the house is the supreme of all the animals; verily by the supreme, one makes the sacrificer go to the supreme state" (TS V.4.12.1; cp. ŚB XIII.3.3.1). Elsewhere Anuṣṭubh is described as the bestness (*jyaiṣṭhyaṁ vā anuṣṭubh* TMB VIII.7.3). MS IV.5.1 it is described as the height of the metres. The context is of collecting waters for the consecration of a king in the Rājasūya-sacrifice. In this collection, the rain water is also collected. This water is taken with a verse in Anuṣṭubh, because it is the height (*varṣma*) of the metres. The Adhvaryu priest thereby leads the sacrificer to the height (MS IV.5.1). In the same context Anuṣṭubh is also said to be identical with all the metres (*anuṣṭubh vai sarvāṇi chandāṁsi*). When one takes the above-mentioned water with an Anuṣṭubh-verse, one takes it with all the metres as it were (MS IV.5.1). For Anuṣṭubh being identical with all the metres see MS III.1.4; KS XIX.10; KPKS XXX.8; TB I.7.5.5 etc. The reason why Anuṣṭubh is said to be identical with all the metres can be sought in the following story. Thus Keśī Dārbhya took over the Ahīna Āśvatthi's function of Purohitaship for Keśī Sātyakāmī. Then Ahīnas asked Keśī Dārbhya, "Keśin, knowing what have you removed the king from me"? Keśī replied, "We worship the Anuṣṭubh-metre as identical with all the metres". His statement was based on the following mystic calculation: Gāyatrī is eight-syllabled; Triṣṭubh eleven-syllabled; Jagatī twelve-syllabled; the finale of the Yajñāyajñīya-sāman viz. *vāc* is one syllabled. Thus totally we get the number of thirty-two syllables. Anuṣṭubh is thirty two syllabled. Thus Anuṣṭubh stands for all the metres; is identical with them (JB I.285). Anuṣṭubh supersedes all the metres (*anuṣṭubh sarvāṇi chandāṁsi paribhūḥ* KS XXX.1; CP. KS XIX. 3). AB III.15 it is described as the furthest distance (*paramā parāvat*). Many times it is described as the end of all the metres (*anto vā anuṣṭup chandasām* JB III.60, 76; 296; cp. II.95).

The metre named Aticchandas is also praised henoistically. Thus it is said to be identical with all the metres. Thus soma-stalks are to be meted out with a verse in the Aticchandas-metre. For that metre is identical with all the metres and thus that soma becomes meted out mystically with all the metres (ŚB III.3.2.11; cp. TS VI.1.9.4; MS III.7.4). At the time of Avabhṛtha-bath at the end of a soma-sacrifice, the Prastotṛpriest sings a sāman in the Aticchandas-metre. For it is identical with all the metres (ŚB IV.4.5.7; MS IV.8.5). In the course of the Rājasūya-sacrifice, after the symbolic looting of cows the sacrificer steps down from the chariot with a verse in Aticchandas. For it is identical with all the metres (ŚB V.4.3.22; cp. TB I. 7.9.6). In the Pravargya-rite also the Prastotṛ-priest sings a sāman in Aticchandas for the same reason (ŚB XIV.3.1.11). For Aticchandas being identical with all the metres see also ŚB IV.6.9.13. Sometimes Aticchandas is said to be superior to all the other metres. Thus according to ŚB VIII.2.4.5, "Aticchandas is a covering metre (*chadiśchandaḥ*). It covers (includes) all the metres. ŚB VIII.6.12.2 it is said that A. being only one is beyond all the metres (*ekā hyeva sā sarvāṇi chandāṁsyati*). On the central day of the Aśvamedha-sacrifice, at the midday-service, the opening tristich of the Marutvatīya śastra is in the

Aticchandas-metre. "For outstanding indeed is this Aticchandas amongst metres; and outstanding is the Aśvamedha amongst sacrifices" (ŚB XIII.5.1.9). In the Ekatrika-sacrifice the Gāyatrapārśvasāman is to be sung in Aticchandas. "For A. surpasses all the other metres (*aticchandā vai sarvāṇī chandāṁsyabhibhavati*" JB II.127). For Aticchandas as superior to all the other metres see also JB II.48; 392; 412; TMB V.2.11). The reason why it supersedes the other metres is, "No other metre has as many syllables (as Aticchandas has" JB III.315). KB XXV.13 A. is said to be the best and biggest of the metres. Many times A. is described as the height (*varṣma*) of the metres. Therefore, when the Adhvaryu metes out the soma-stalks with a verse in A. he makes the sacrificer the height of his equals (TS VI.1.9.4; MS III.7.4; KS XXIV.5; KPKS XXXVII.6). For A. as the height of the metres cf. also TS V.2.1.5; 2.2.; 3.8.3; TB I.7.9.6.

Sometimes Gāyatrī is praised henoistically. Thus Gāyatrī is said to be "bestness (*jyaiṣṭhyam*" JB II.346; 353; 361). According to AĀ I.4.1 it is the beginning (*agram*) of the metres. According to JB II.227 it is both the beginning and bestness of the metres (*gāyatrī vai chandasāmagraṁ jyaiṣṭhyam*). Therefore the Vrātyastoma-sacrifice of the Kaniṣṭha-vrātyas should be in Gāyatrī-metre. So that it leads those Vrātyas to be at the beginning and to the bestness (JB I.227). TMB VIII.4.2ff it is told how Gāyatrī is identical with all the metres. Thus Triṣṭubh and Jagatī requested Gāyatrī to allow them to join it. Triṣṭubh joined it with three syllables and then Gāyatrī itself became Triṣṭubh. Jagatī then joined to this new Triṣṭubh with one syllable and then the new Jagatī came into existence. Thus Gāyatrī itself became Triṣṭubh and Jagatī; Therefore, it is identical with all the metres (For these three metres only are mystically all the metres). In Mbh VI.32.55 Lord Kṛṣṇa says, "Among the metres I am Gāyatrī" and thus G. is one of the manifestations (*vibhūti-*) of Lord Kṛṣṇa. G. and Virāṭ are said to be the most valiant of all the metres (*ete ha khalu vai chandasāṁ vīryavattame yad virāṭ ca gāyatrī ca* JB II.335; cp. 339).

Some other metres are also praised henoistically. Thus MS III.4.6 Virāj is said to be identical with all the metres (*virāḍ vai sarvāṇi chandāṁsi*). ŚB VI.2.1.30 Jagatī is said to be all metres (*jagatī sarvāṇi chandāṁsi*). According to TMB XXI.10.9 of all the metres Jagatī has reached the highest thriving (*jagatī vai chandasāṁ paramaṁ poṣam puṣṭā*). J. is also said to be the bestness (*jyaiṣṭhya-*) of all the metres (JB II.286). Sometimes Śakvarī is said to be the highest (*parārdhyā*) of all the metres created from speech (ŚB III.3.1.1; 9.2.17).

Metres have a cosmic character according to the vedic texts. Thus the whole world is said to be divided into two parts viz. one that is metrical and the other that is non-metrical (KB III. 2). But some other times the whole world is said to be connected with the metres. Thus according to Chāu III.12.1. "All this whatever has come into existence is Gāyatrī". All the beings are said to be identical with the metres (*prajāśchandāṁsi* JB I.277). In accordance with the arrangement and releasing of the metres, the beings are changed (*chandasāṁ kḷptim vimuktimanu prajāḥ kalpante* JB I.178). The worldly occurrences are dependent on the magicoreligious significance of the use of metres in the ritual. Thus in the Aśvameda (horse-sacrifice) three verses in Anuṣṭubh viz. SV II.366-368 are used. Now three Anuṣṭubhs (3 X 32 = 72) make four Gāyatrīs (4 X 24 = 72). Therefore, when one uses three Anuṣṭubhs one uses mystically four Gāyatrīs. Because one use three Anuṣṭubhs therefore the horse stands on three feet and because one (mystically) uses four Gāyatrīs; therefore the horse runs on all four feet (TS V.4.12.1; cp. ŚB XIII.3.3.1). In the New and Full-moon-sacrifices, after uttering a Gāyatrī-verse (24 syll.), as an invitatory formula, one offers with a Triṣṭubh-verse (44 syll.). Therefore, the lower teeth are smaller and the upper ones are broader. Both the Saṁyājyās are in the same metre. Therefore the molars are of equal size (ŚB XI.4.1.13). Thus many factors of the macrocosm depend on the microcosmic use of the metres (see also JB I.254).

Metres have been connected with the worlds in various ways. Thus TMB VI. 3.9 identifies the worlds with the metres (*ime vai lokā etāni chandāṁsi*). Thus the earth, the middle world, and the heaven are said to be identical with Gāyatrī, Bṛhatī and Triṣṭubh respectively. At the time of the midday-pavamāna-laud in the Agniṣṭoma-sacrifice one sings praises with the help of metres and this is for the sake of keeping the worlds joined. Thus the ritualistic use of the metres keeps all the worlds in contact with each other. According to TS V.4.6.4, Virāj holds the earth and the middle region (*virājā imau lokau dhṛtau*). Elsewhere the earth, middle world and heaven are said to be identical with Gāyatrī, Triṣṭubh and Jagatī respectively (JB I. 339; cp. KS XIX.1; KPKS XXIX.8; TS V.2.1.1). JB I.286, the following story is given: "When the metres divided their shares in the worlds, Gāyatrī shared this world (i.e. the earth); Triṣṭubh the middle world and Jagatī that world (i.e. the heaven)". KB VIII.9 it is said, "This world belongs to Gāyatrī ... the middle world to Triṣṭubh .... and that world to Jagatī". The earth has been sometimes identified with Gāyatrī (ŚB I. 4.1.34; IV.3.4.9; TMB VII.3.11); and sometimes with Jagatī (ŚB XII.8.2.20). ŚB I.8.2.11 gives the reason why the earth is Jagatī. Because this universe (*jagat*) is based on this (earth), therefore, this earth is Jagatī (cp. ŚB VI.2.2.3). MS II.5.10 identifies the earth with Virāj. The world of heaven is also identified with some metres. Thus I.7.2.15 the heaven is identified with Triṣṭubh. Sometimes Bṛhatī and heavenly world are identified (JB II.7; III.258; ŚB X.5.4.6 etc.). All the metres in general are also identified with heaven (*chandāṁsi vai svargo lokaḥ* - JB II.224; 381).

Meters and castes are sometimes mystically connected. Thus AB I.28 connects Brāhmaṇa, Rājanya and Vaiṣya castes with Gāyatrī, Triṣṭubh, and Jagatī-metre. Therefore at the time of bringing forward the fire a verse is to be recited in a metre either of these three metres according to the caste of the sacrificer.

Metres are sometimes supposed to be identical with the year or seasons. Thus TS II.4.3.2 Gāyatrī is identified with the year (*saṁvatsaro vai gāyatrī*). ŚB VI.4.2.10 identifies Bṛhatī with the year. For in a year there are twelve full-moon-days, twelve eighth days (after the full-moon-days) and twelve new-moon-days. This makes the number thirty-six and Bṛhatī also has thirty-six syllables. Therefore Bṛhatī is the year (see also ŚB XII.2.3.1). Sometimes Gāyatrī is connected with spring, Triṣṭubh with Summer, Jagatī with the rainy-season, Anuṣṭubh with the autumn and Paṅkti with winter (KPKS XXV.9; KS XVI.19; MS II.7.19; TS IV.3.2.1ff; ŚB VIII.1.1.5ff; 2.2ff). Metres are also described to be born out of the seasons. Thus Gāyatrī, Triṣṭubh, Jagatī, Anuṣṭubh and Paṅkti are said to be born out of the spring, summer, rainy season, autumn, and winter respectively.

The sun is described to be belonging to the Bṛhatī-metre (KPKS IV.7). The sāman which is to be sung after the consecration of the sacrificer in course of the Sautrāmaṇī-sacrifice is in Bṛhatī. "Established in Bṛhatī the sun shines". Similarly the sacrificer shines when the sāman in Bṛhatī is sung (ŚB XII. 8.3.24).

Metres are also identified with the directions; e.g. ŚB IX. 5.1.39 *chandāṁsi vai diśaḥ*. According to TS V.2.1.1. the directions belong to the Anuṣṭubh-metre.

Thus the metres have a cosmic character and this cosmic character is important for the magicoreligious significance of the use of metres in the ritual.

While recapitulating the important points in the study of metres in the Vedas we must note that metres are considered to be very much important in the sacrifice in which there are numerous recitations or songs which are in some metres. The metres are considered to be power-substances. But they work magicoreligiously rather than only magically. They help the sacrificial performance in many ways the chief of which is that they often become a measurement of the sacrifice which is a measured activity par excellence. The metres are helpful to gods. Gods often use the metres for their own purposes. But one also uses particular metres for particular gods in order to propitiate them. The metres are so closely connected with gods that they are often identified with them and it seems sometimes that the power the metres possess is nothing but divine power. Metres are an essential part of the vedic music as can be seen from their close relations with sāmans and speech. They have a cosmic significance. The metres are, however, of double-nature[11] and can sometimes go against the sacrifice as well as against the gods.

REFERENCES

1. On this subject see Weber *IS* VIII. 2ff;
2. Hauer, *Yoga*, p. 26, derives the word *chandas* from the same root and according to him it originally meant an enticing magical song.
3. Weber, *IS*, VIII, p. 8 accepts this etymology; cp. the same *IS*, I. 29, n; cp. also Wackernagel-Debrunner, *AG*, II. 2.222; Mayrhofer, *Woerterbuch*, I. 404.
4. For this legend cf. Bloomfield, *JAOS*, XVI, p. 1 ff.
5. Cf. Weber *IS*, VIII, p. 13 ff.
6. Cf. my paper "Pāṅkta-yajña" in *Ṛṣikalpanyāsa*, English section p. 22.
7. Cf. Caland, Henry, *L'Agniṣṭoma*, p. 171.
8. Cf. Bloomfield, *JAOS*, XVI. 4ff; Oldenberg, *SBE*, XLVI, p. 301.
9. *prātaḥsavanayogayaṁ tu chando gāyatramāśritaṃ /*
   kaṇṭhe mādhyandinayutaṁ madhyamaṁ traiṣṭubhānugam /6/
   ....tāraṁ tārtīyasavanaṁ śīrṣaṇyaṁ jāgatānugam /7/
   Agnipuraṇa 336.6 f.
10. For the role of gods in granting the result of the sacrifice to the sacrificer see my paper, "Yajñaphala āṇi deva" *Ānandavana*, I.2 (April, 1973), p. 57 ff.
11. Metres are sometimes looked down. They are considered as dirty. Thus Mbh XIII.85.19 metres said to be born out of Prajāpati's sweat and therefore dirty (*svedācchando malātmakam*).

CHAPTER VII
Gandharvas and Apsarases

The Gandharvas and Apsarases form a semi-divine genus. The exact character of the Gandharvas is very difficult to determine because their descriptions particularly in the Ṛgveda[1] are rather vague. But the Vedic literature in general gives a good deal of information about the Gandharvas and Apsarases which can throw sufficient light on their good and evil traits. The Gandharvas show themselves, according to Oldenberg,[2] "bald als gütig und hilfreich, bald als feindlich" but not only the Gandharvas the Apsarases are also double natured. Now follows a study of them.

Even though the Gandharvas (and Apsarases) are well-known as divine musicians in the latter literature, the ṚV does not possess any clear reference to their relation with music[3], even though ṚV X.177.2 suggests indirectly their relation with music. "The bird (viz. the Sun) holds speech by means of mind. The Gandharva informed it in the mother-womb". Thus the Gandharva here seems to possess and declare the speech and thereby seems to be connected with music. Similarly ṚV X.11.2 says "As the Gandharvī, the water-woman has made noise, she would protect my mind at the time of the noise of the singers"[4] (Cf. AV XVIII.1.19). Thus the female Gandharvī has also some connection with music. AV II.2.5 the Asparases are described as noisy (*klandāḥ*). Elsewhere in an apotropic formula one says to them: "Where are your swings green and whitich where the cymbals and lutes sound together thither go away; ye Apsarases; ye have been recognised" (AV IV.37.5).

The Gandharvas have a cosmic nature in the Veda. ṚV X. 139.5 describes the heavenly Gandharva, Viśvāvasu as a traverser of space (*rajaso vimānaḥ*).[5] He stands erectly on the vault of heaven (ṚV X.123.7). His abode is in the heaven (AV II.2.1). He is often described as *divya* (heavenly) and is requested to purify the thoughts (VS IX.I;XI.7; XXX.7; TS I.7.7.I; IV.1.1.2; MS I.11.1. KS XIII.14; XV.11; ŚB V.1.1.16; VI.3.1.19). In the AV the heavenly Gandharva is described as the lord of world and then requested to make favour (AV I. 2.1f). The Gandharva is closely connected with the celestial light. The sun is sometimes described as Gandharva.[6] Thus ṚV IX.85.12 describes the sun-rise as the rise of Gandharva: "The Gandharva has risen to the sky exhibiting all his forms. His ray flashed in bright glow. He has enlightened both the worlds" ŚB VI.3.1.19 says: This sun is indeed the heavenly Gandharva (*asau vā āditya divyo gandharvaḥ* cp. ŚB IX.4.18: *sūryo gandhavaḥ*). The Gandharvas are said to be twenty-seven (VS IX.7, TS I.7.7.2; KS XIII.14; ŚB V.1.4.8) and this leads us to suppose that they were considered as the 27 Nakṣatras.

While the Gandharvas are closely connected with light, the Apsarases are closely connected with water.[7] A watery-woman (*apyā yoṣā*) is mentioned in ṚV X.10.4 alongwith Gandharva and it can be assumed that she is an Apsaras. Similarly ṚV X. 11.2, a female Gandharvī is described as watery-woman (*apyā yoṣaṇā*) who cannot be anyone else than an apsaras. Sea is the abode of the Apsarases (*samudra āsāṁ sadanam* AV II.2.3). They are brought to depart from the vicinity of men and go to some river or a bank. (AV IV.37.3). The goddesses accompanying Gandharvas are described to be closely connected with among others, clouds (AV II.2.4). When Purūravas was searching for Urvaśī who had left him, he saw that the Apsarases, along with Urvaśī were swimming in the form aquatic birds (*ātayaḥ*) (ŚB XI.5.1.4; cp. ṚV X.95.9).

The Gandharvas have a special connection with Soma. Sometimes they are said to be the protectors of Soma[8] and sometimes they are said to be robbers of Soma. Thus the Gandharva (i.e. the Sun) guards the place of Soma and protects generations of gods (ṚV IX.83.4; For Gandharvas as guards of soma see also ŚB III.6.2.9; 9.3.18; JB I.287). ṚV IX. 85.12 it is said that the divine Gandharva stands erect on the vault of heaven, observing all the forms of Soma. The

Gandharvas received Soma, which was increased by rain and brought by the daughter of Sun. They then put sap in it (ṚV IX.113.3). Through the mouth of the Gandharva the gods drink Soma. The Gandharvas in general are said to be soma-drinking[9] (*somya* AV IV.34.3). Suvāc, Nabhrāṭ, Aṅghāri and Bambhāri were the Gandharvas who were in charge of protecting Soma. The metres, however, carried the Soma away and thus the Gandharvas were deprived of the share of Soma. The Gandharvas then changed their names and then obtained the share (MS III.8.10). In another story the Gandharvas are said to be protectors of Soma. The metres tried very hard and obtained the Soma from them (Cp. TS VI.1.6.1 ff; MS III. 7.3.4; KS XXIII.10; XXIV.1; KPKS XXXVII.2; AB III.25; ŚB III. 2.4.1 ff; 3.1.13 ff.[10] This Soma was robbed by a Gandharva named Viśvāvasu. Then the gods obtained it by means of speech (TS VI.1.6.5; 11.5; Cp. ṚV IX.113.3 KPKS 37.1, AV I.27). When the gods were sacrificing with Soma, the Gandharvas came there and asked for a share in the soma-sacrifice. They requested gods to appoint them as Soma-keepers on the earth, as they were in the heaven. This request was granted by the gods. So the Gandharvas became the Soma-sellers on the earth (ŚB III.6.2.18f). From this story it appears that the Gandharvas used to consider Soma as their privilege and that they were jealous possessor of it. Because, the Gandharvas were sometimes looked down as evil beings their representatives on the earth viz. the Soma-sellers[11] were also looked down. Thus in the procedure of a soma-sacrifice soma is to be bought from a soma-seller. But afterwards that soma-seller is to be beaten and driven out as it were (Cf. Kātyāśs VII.8.27). A Brāhmaṇa is expected not to sell Soma (e.g. Mbh. XII.80.4ff) and this shows that the position of the Soma-sellers was very low. This also illustrates the low position of the Gandharvas, the divine soma-sellers. The low position of the Gandharvas can be seen also from their connection with the Śudras. Thus if persons belonging to various castes perform their duties prescribed for the caste correctly, then they reach various divine worlds. Thus the Brāhmaṇas get the world of Brahman, the Kṣatriyas that of Indra, the Vaiśyas that of Maruts and the Śudras that of the Gandharvas (Viṣṇudharmottarap. I.107.58f; Cp. Vāyup. VIII.175; Garuḍap. I.4.36; 49.24 ff. Mārkp. XLVI.78).

The connection of Gandharvas with sacrifice is two-fold and illustrates their double nature. Thus sometimes they are described as opponents of sacrifice and sometimes as well-wishers of it or closely associated with it. AV IV.37.8 f they are described to be "eaters of oblations (*havirad-*)" which are offered to some of the deities. Therefore Indra is requested to kill them. It seems that Gandharvas are here supposed to be like some evil beings antipathetic and troublesome to the sacrifice. Elsewhere however, they appear to be very helpful to the sacrificial institution. Thus ŚB XI.2.3.7f, following story is told "When the seers were performing a sacrifice, Gandharvas came near them. They looked on thinking that surely they have done too much here and they have done too little there. And when the sacrifice was completed, they pointed it out to them .... Now wherever they had done too much it was like a hill and wherever they had done too little, it was like a pit". Here the Gandharvas appear to be pointing out mistakes so that they may be corrected and the sacrifice may be well performed. Thus they are helpful to the sacrificial performance. The close connection of the Gandharvas and sacrifice can be seen from the following examples. They are, metaphorically speaking nothing else than the firehearths (*dhiṣṇya*) and firepriests (ŚB III.6.2.9; cp. JB I.287). After Soma was taken away from them by gods they became the soma-sellers and thereby participated in the sacrificial performance (ŚB III.6.2.17 ff). According to ŚB IX.4.1.2 ff, when Prajāpati was dismembered, couples went forth out of his body in the form of Gandharvas and Apsarases. Therefore, in the course of the fire-building-ceremony, when the Rāṣṭrabhṛd-homa is performed, offering to the Gandharvas and Apsarases are offered. Thus the Gandharvas and Apsarases get sacrificial offerings also. The sacrifice named Aupaśada is described to be belonging to the Gandharvas and Apsarases. They have a share in that sacrifice (TMB XIX.3.2). Many times the sacrifice is identified with Gandharvas and the sacrificial gifts (*dakṣiṇā-*) with the Apsarases (*yajño gandharvas tasya dakṣiṇā apsarasaḥ* TS III.4.7.1; MS III.12.2; KS XVIII.14; KPKS XXIX.3; VS XVIII.42). According to Vāyupurāṇa 68.37 ff, Pravāhī generated the Gandharvas, the best singers, at a sacrificial performance. Thus, the Gandharvas have their origin in the sacrifice. In the Mbh the Gandharvas skilled in vocal music are mentioned to be singing and thereby amusing the priests during the intervals of the sacrificial activities in the course of the Aśvamedha-sacrifice being performed by Yudhiṣṭhira (*gandharvā gītakuśalā vṛtteṣvatha viśāradāḥ / ramayanti ca tān viprān yajñakarmāntareṣvatha* // XIV.90.39). In the sacrifice performed by Nahuṣa's father, the Gandharvas sang Sāmans and the Apsarases danced (Vāyu p. II.31) Thus the Gandharvas and Apsarases are connected with and helpful to the sacrifice in numerous ways. But it must be remembered that sometimes they are considered to be antagonistic to the sacrifice.

The Gandharvas and Apsarases are closely connected with each other. The Gandharvas are sometimes described as the lovers of the Apsarases. Thus Vena, a Gandharva is described as the lover (*jāra*) of an Apsaras and she is described to be smiling on him (ṚV X.123.5). Elsewhere the Gandharvas appear to be the husbands of Apsarases. Thus AV IV.37.12, one addresses the Gandharvas, "Apsarases are your wives, O Gandharvas, and you are the husbands" (see also AV IV.37.7). Similarly some Apsarases are said to be the wives of Viśvāvasu Gandharva and he is asked to go to them (AV XIV.2.35).

Gandharvas and Apsarases are sometimes supposed to be evil genii. One therefore seeks to pacify them by means of praising them and paying obeisance to them (e.g. AV II. 2.1 ff). Sometimes one tries to remove them. They are sought to be removed by means of an apotropaeic herb named Ajaśṛṅgī. One says addressing that herb: "By thee do we expect the

Apsarases, the Gandharvas, O Goat-horned one! drive the demon; make all of them disappear by means of (thy) smell" (AV IV.37.2). Further he says "Of the hitherdancing, crested Gandharva, lord of Apsarases, I split the testicles; I bind fast (?) the member" (7). Elsewhere one takes the help of a gem named Śatavāra for removing them away: "With the Śatavāra I ward off a hundred of ill-named ones (f) a hundred of the Gandharvas and Apsarases and a hundred of dog-like ones (f)" (AV XIX.36.6). Elsewhere one prays to Earth, "What Gandharvas, Apsarases (there are) and what *arāyas, kimīdins,* the *piśācas,* all demons, them do thou keep away from us O earth". Elsewhere they are requested to run away (AV IV. 37.12; XIV.2.34; 35). AV XIV.2.36 the magician priest claims that he has made the Gandharva go away.

One of the reasons why the Gandharvas and Apsarases are looked down and expected to go away is that they are too much adicted to the sensual pleasures. They seem to be fond of flower-garlands and adornments as TĀ III.10.3 indicates it (*gandharvāpsarobhyaḥ sragalaṅkaraṇe*). They are specifically connected with odour. Thus AV XII.1.23 we read, "What odour of thine O Earth came into existence which the herbs, which the waters bear, which the Gandharvas and Apsarases shared, with that do though make me odorous". Viṣṇudharmottarap. III.301.20 says that all the fragrances belong to the Gandharvas.[12] A person who sprinkles fragnant water on Viṣṇu becomes happy in the company of Gandharvas for ten thousand years (Viṣṇudharmottarap. III.341.28f; cp. 131). Similar result of the company of the Gandharvas can be obtained by offering fragrant things to a guest (Viṣṇudh. p. III.314.2). Not only (Gandharvas and apsarases are connected with) fragrance, they are connected also with beauty of the form (*rūpa*). Thus in the course of the detailing how different beings worship the same Divine person under his different names ŚB X.5.2.20 says, "The Gandharvas (worship it) under that of form (*rūpa*)[13] and Apsarases under that of fragrance (*gandha*)". The same text elsewhere says, "the Gandharvas and

Apsarases are busy with sweet fragrance (*gandha*) and beauteous form (*rūpa*) (*atho gandhena ca vai rūpeṇa ca gandharvāpasarasaś caranti*" ŚB IX.4.1.4). Even though the exact etymologies of the words Gandharva and Apsaras are doubtful, it may be noted that they are sometimes connected with *gandha*[14] (fragrance) and *Apsas* (in the sense of beauty)[15] respectively. TS III.4.7.3 the Gandharva is identified with *kāma* (desire) in general. Further, the Gandharvas are often mentioned as very much desirous of women[16] (*strīkāma vai gandharvāḥ*: TS VI.1.6.5; MS III.7.3; KS XXIV.1; KPKS XXXVII.2; AB I.27. cp. KB XII.3: *yoṣitkāmā vai gandharvāḥ*; ŚB III.2.4.3). The gods were knowing this weak point of the Gandharvas. Therefore when they wanted to get back Soma which was robbed by Viśvāvasu Gandharva from Gāyatrī-metre, the gods sent the speech (*vac* fem.) to the Gandharvas. The speech came back alongwith Soma. The Gandharvas being desirous of speech, agreed to give Soma, if the gods would give them the speech. The gods agreed to allow them to use her. They themselves woed her by means of music. The Gandharvas woed her by means of Vedas. But she turned to Gods; for women love one who sings (*tasmād gāyantaṁ strī kāmayate* TS VI.1.6.6; KS XXIV.1; KPKS XXXVII.2; Cp. MS III. 7.3: *tasmād gāyan striyāḥ priyaḥ*; for this story cp. also ŚB III. 2.4.2 ff). On another occasion also the gods took advantage of this weakness of the Gandharvas viz. their desire for women. Thus when the head of the sacrifice was struck off, its sap, running, entered the waters. The Gandharvas watched this. The gods realised the likely danger from side of the Gandharvas that they would rob the sap of the sacrifice. Therefore the gods said among themselves "The Gandharvas desire women; let us go together with the wives. The Gandharvas will surely hanker after the wives; and we shall carry off that sap of the sacrifice free from danger and injury". It happened exactly as the gods planned. Then the gods obtained the sap of Soma back (ŚB III.9.3.18 ff; cp. KB XII.3). Thus the lust of the Gandharvas for women is clearly seen in this story also. A Gandharva named

Urṇāyu desired to obtain Apsarases. Then he saw Aurṇāyava-Sāman and sang with it. Then he could obtain any Apsaras (JB III.76). This story also illustrates the lustry nature of the Gandharvas. The Gandharvas are attracted to the earthly women also. It is supposed that the Gandharvas assuming various forms fasten up women. Thus from AV IV.37.11, we know that a Gandharva takes the form of a dog; another of an ape; another of an all-hairy boy; another becomes pleasant to look at. In this way a Gandharva fastens up women (*gandharvaḥ sacate striyaḥ*). In the Vedic literature we often meet with the expression meaning "a maiden seized by Gandharva (*kumārī gandharvagṛhītā*" AB V.29; KB II.9 etc. for this see further). Moreover, the Gandharva appears to be a rival of the husbands in connection with the wives.[17] Thus according to ṚV X. 85.40 and AV XIV.2.3 Soma obtains any girl first, then the Gandharva then Agni becomes her husband and the human husband is the fourth one only. In the next two verses (41 and 42) it is said that Soma gives that maiden to the Gandharva; Gandharva to Agni and Agni to the human husband (see also Padmapurāṇa VI.120.6: *romakāle tu samprāpte somo bhuṅkte tu kanyakām / rajaḥkāle tu gandharvo vahnistu kucadarśane //* cp. *Agnipurāṇa* 165.19: *pūrvaṁ striyaḥ surair bhuktāḥ somagandharvavahnibhiḥ / bhuñjate mānuṣāḥ paścānnaitā duṣyanti kenacit //*; See also Garuḍapurāṇa I. 59.19; Viṣṇudharmottarap. II.33.17; Bṛhatsaṁhitā 74.7). Thus the Gandharvas have women as their share (Cf. AV VIII.6.19 where they are called *strībhāga-*). After a marriage, during the first nights which the young pair has to pass in chastity, there lies a stick between the two and it is a symbol of Gandharva Viśvāvasu who prevents the husband from possessing the wife (Cp. ĀpGS III.8.9 and the commentary on it).[18] The verses ṚV X.85.21 and 22 are addressed to Viśvāvasu Gandharva in which he has been praised and requested to leave the newly married woman. He is further asked to take hold of another unmarried girl. "Get up from there; because she has now a husband; I pray Viśvāvasu with homage and songs; search another one who still lives in the house of her father; mature one; who is naturally destined to be your share; be mindful of him (21); Get up from there O Viśvāvasu; we pray you by means of homage; search out another maiden; allow the married woman to be with her voluptuous husband"(22). Thus due to this woman-seaking nature the Gandharvas are removed away and are looked down. AV IV.37 is addressed to a herb Ajaśṛṅgī and the herb is requested to kill the Gandharvas and Apsarases by means of its odour (AV IV.37.2).[19] AV XIV 2.9 contains a prayer in which the Gandharvas and Apsarases are requested to please unto the bride and not to injure the bridal-car as it is driven. Thus the Gandharvas and Apsarases are feared lest they would create harm. The Apsarases as well as Gandharvas are notorious for their sensuality, and seductive nature. Thus AV VI.130.1 connects Cupid (Smara) with the Apsarases. One of the Apsarases viz. Urvaśī expresses her sensuality openly when she says to her lover Purūravas "Dreimal des Tages stachst du mich mit der Rute und liszest mir wenn ich kein Gelüste hatte reichlich zukommen"[20] (ṚV X.95.5; cp. ŚB XI.5.1.1). The Apsarases sing in order to seduce the ascetics etc. Thus an Apsaras named Menakā sings in order to seduce Viṣṇuśarmā (Padmap. II.3.6. cp. also for similar seductive significance of music II.24.6). The Gandharvas also do similar work with their music. Indra sent Gandharvas for the sake of disturbing the penance of Mārkaṇḍeya (Bhāgavatap. XII. 8.6). Sakka, before visiting the Buddha sends Pañcasikha, a Gandhabba for the sake pleasing the lord by means of his music (cf. Sakkapañhasutta in the Dīghanikāya).

A further reason why the Gandharvāpsarases are removed is that they seize men and women and make them insane. AV IV.37.12 one prays to the Gandharvas not to fasten on men. AV II.2.5. the Apsarases are said to be "mind-confusing (*manomuhaḥ*)". TS III.4.8.4 we read, "It is the Gandharvas and Apsarases who madden him who is mad (*gandharvāpsaraso vā etam unmādayanti ya unmādyati*)". A Rāṣṭrabhṛt offering is therefore to be made to the Gandharvas and Apsarases so that one may become free from madness when they are pacified (TS III.4.8.4 f). AV VI. III is a prayer to be used for relief from insanity. In that hymn, among other deities, the Apsarases are prayed to make one free from madness "May the Apsarases give thee again; may Indra again, may Bhaga again, may all the gods give thee again that thou mayest be made same". The daughter (BṛhUp. III.3.1) and the wife (BṛhUp. III.7.1) of Pānañcala Kāpya are described as "seized by Gandharva (*gandharvagṛhītā*)". This seizure may be nothing else than hysteria. Viṣṇudharmottarap. I.231.36f we get a description of the madness due to the seizure by a Gandharva. Thus "A man maddened by a Gandharva becomes overwhelmed with joy and dances after having listened to any sound of vocal or instrumental music or after having come into contact with a ford, garden, or a bank of a river, fragrance or garlands etc. He wanders according to his will". Such a man can be cured by worshipping the Gandharvas by means of fragrances, garlands, and various kinds of songs and instrumental music (38). Thus the Gandharvas are of double-nature. They can create madness and cure it also. Moreover it is the double-natured music which in the final analysis is supposed to make man insane and sane. Among the Greeks, we get references to the religious madness the chief symptom of this disease consisted therein that the possessed man supposed to hear the sound of Aulos and used to dance.[21] The Greeks also believed that by means of music mental diseases can be cured.[22] In the mediaeval period also similar beliefs prevailed. Thus many thinkers like Johannes Cottonius etc. maintained the power of music moderating madness.[23]

The Gandharvas and Apsarases are closely connected with fertility and sterlity and are double-natured in this respect also. The Gandharvas and Apsarases are rightly described by Meyer as fertility spirits and erotic genii.[24] They are connected with sterlity also. Thus TMB XIX.3.2. says, "The Gandharvas and Apsarases rule over man's possession of progeny or want of progeny (*gandharvāpsaraso hi manuṣyasya prajāyā vā aprajastāyā veśate)*". The Aupaśada sacrifice which belongs to these genii and in which they have a share in the soma-draught is to be performed by one who is desirous of progeny. When this sacrifice is performed, the gratified and pleased Gandharvas and Apsarases grant progeny to the performer (TMB XIX.3.2). Gandharvas helped Varuṇa to reobtain his virility. Thus AV IV.4.1 one addresses to a plant: "Thee that the Gandharvas dug for Varuṇa whose virility was dead, thee here we dig penis-erecting herb". In the Aśvamedha-sacrifice one pleases the Gandharvas by means of penis and the Apsarases by means of testicles of the killed horse (TS V.7.15.1; KS 53.5). Thus the Gandharvas and Apsarases are closely connected with genetical organs and this connection is in keeping with their character as fertility-genii. The Gandharvas are sometimes supposed to be harmful to embryos[25] and new-born children. Therefore a prayer is made for their removal. Thus AV VIII.6.19, it is said, "They who suddenly make die those that are born, who lie by the (woman) who has newly given birth (*sūtikā*)[26] the Gandharvas who have women as their share, let the Brown One drive, as the wind a cloud". Sometimes the Gandharvas and Apsarases are closely associated with trees and herbs.[27] This association implies that they can be considered as vegetation-genii and in this respect also they must have *played* an important role in the fertility of earth. AV XIV.2.9 mentions the Gandharvas and Apsarases who stand upon the forest trees. Trees like Nyagradha, Udumbara, Aśvattha, and Plakṣa are said to be the houses of the Gandharvāpsarases. Therefore for one who is mad, offerings with the woods of these trees are made to the Gandharvāpsarases in order to cure him (TS III.4.8.4). While removing the Gandharvāpsarases away, by means of the Ajaśṛṅgī-plant, one addresses the Apsarases to go back to that place where there are trees like Aśvattha, Nyagrodha etc. (AV IV.37.4). All the herbs on the earth are mystically identified with the Apsarases named Svāśir. Now these Apsarases (herbs) desired to be numerous, to pervade all this world. Then they saw the sāman named Svāśirām arka. They sang it and got their desire fulfilled (JB III.226).

The Gandharvāpsarases are closely connected with play of dice. It may be a further reason why they are sometimes removed; for the dice-play was considered to be evil (see for example in ṚV X.71). The hymn AV VII .109 (114) along with VII.50 and IV.38 is to be used for success in gambling, according to the Kauśikasūtra 41.13. In the Agnyādheya - (fire-establishment) ceremony when the sacrificer hands the Adhvaryu the anointed dice, for winning .(at play) the Somakrayaṇī cow the same hymns are to be used according to the Vaitānaśs VI.10. Thus AV VII.109 (114) is closely connected with the dice-play. In this hymn there are many references to the dice as well as to the Gandharvas and Apsarases. In the first stanza the prayer-maker says that he anoints the Kali dice with ghee and makes it powerful. In the second stanza the prayer-maker requests Agni to carry ghee for Apsarases. In the next stanza it is said, "The Apsarases revel in a joint revelling, between the oblation-holder and the Sun. Let them unite my hands with ghee; let them make the rival-gambler subject to me" (AV VII.109.3). Further in the fifth stanza we read, "He who made this riches for our playing, who the taking (?) and leaving of the dice—that god enjoying this libation of ours—may we revel a joint revelling with the Gandharvas". The Apsarases not only help a dice-player, but also themselves love the dice (*akṣakāmāḥ* AV II.2.5). They take delight in the dice (*yā akṣeṣu pramadante* AV IV.38.4). They dance with the dice[28] (AV IV.38.3). TS III.4.8.2 identifies the Rāṣṭrabhṛt-offerings, which are to be offered at the dicing places (TS III.4.8.4) with the Gandharvāpsarases.

A further reason why the Gandharvāpsarases are condemned can be seen in their connection with death and death-gods. Thus TS III.4.7.2f, the Gandharva is said to be identical with death. The Gandharvāpsarases are said to be the parents of Yama (the god of death) and his sister Yamī (ṚV X.10.4).[29]

Further the Gandharvāpsarases who are of double nature are connected with some other double-natured genii. Thus the Gandharvas are mentioned to be the subjects of Varuṇa (ŚB XIII.4.3.7; cp. ĀŚS X.7), who is double-natured. Similarly Vrātyas, (another double-natured genie) are connected with Gandharvas and Apsarases. Thus in the Puruṣamedha (human sacrifice) a Vrātya-person is offered to the Gandharvāpsarases (VS XX.8; TB III.4.5.1)[30] Such connections also explain the low position of the Gandharvāpsarases.

In the Dharmasūtras, Gṛhyasūtras, and Smṛtis eight forms of marriages are described and the Gāndharva marriage is one of them (ĀŚG I.6; BaudhāDhSū I.11; GautamaDhSū IV.6-13; Manusmṛti III.21ff; Yājñavalkyasmṛti I.58ff etc.). The Gāndharva form of marriage is based on mutual love (e.g. Manu. III.32). Now the Gāndharva form of marriage is sometimes considered to be rather of inferior type and sometimes as the best. Thus Manusmṛti III.24. prescribes only the Brāhma, Daiva, Ārṣa and Prājāpatya for a Brāhmaṇa and thereby indicates that the remaining forms including the Gāndharva are not worthy to be *prescribed* even though they *occur* in the world. According to the Baudhāyanadharmasūtra I.11.6, the Brāhma is the best kind of marriages. The Kāmasūtra III.5.1.28 similarly implies that the Brāhma is the best kind of marriages because it is based on sacred law (*dharma*). However it further expresses its own opinion viz. the Gāndharva is the best form of marriage. "For, the aim of marriage, after all, is love; (So) even though the Gāndharva is in the middle position in the hierarchy, it *is* honoured (*vyūḍhānāṁ hi vivāhānām anurāgaḥ paraṁ phalam / madhyamo' pi hi sadyogo gāndharvas tena pūjitaḥ* // Kāmasū. III.5.1.29). The text further says that because this kind of marriage is happy, without any disturbances, without any efforts for selection and is based on love, it is the best (III.5.1.30: *sukhatvād ababuklesād api cāvaraṇādiha / anurāgātmakatvācca gāndharuvaḥ pravaro mataḥ* // cp. *Mbh* I. 67.4 *vivāhānāṁ hi rambhoru gāndharvaḥ śreṣtha ucyate*). Viṣṇudharmottarap. III.239.7 says, however, that the Gāndharva and Rākṣasa are the forms of middle order i.e. neither good not bad (*gāndharvo rākṣasaścaiva madhyamau parikīrtitau*).

In conclusion we may say that the divine musicians viz. Gandharvāpsarases are considered to be double-natured; helpful as well as harmful. Taking into consideration, however, their harmful character more seriously, they are often repelled as the evil beings like demons etc. Taking into consideration that they can execute their power through rendering help to men, they are sometimes honoured and worshipped also.

REFERENCES

1. Rf. Oldenberg, *Religion des Veda* p. 244.
2. Rf. Oldenberg, *Religion des Veda,* p. 248.
3. Cp. Macdonell, *Vedic Mythology,* p. 137.
4. Rf. Pischel in Geldner, Pischel, *Vedische, Studien,* I. 186; Geldner, *Der Rigveda,* III. p. 137.
5. Cp. Gonda, *The Vision of the Vedic Poets,* p. 91.
6. For the connection of Gandharva and Sun cf. Kuhn, "Gandharvas and Kenturen", *Zeitschrift für vergleichende Sprachforschung* I, 1854, p. 518 ff.
7. For the connection of Apsarases and water see Holtzmann, *ZDMG,* 33, 1879, p. 635, 641.
8. Cf. Kuhn, *ZVS* I, 1854, p. 521 cp. *Gonda, Ṛgvidhāna,* p. 14, n. 5.3; for Gandharvas and Soma see also V. Schroeder, *Mysterium und Mimus,* p. 59.
9. Whitney, *Atharvaveda-saṁhitā,* I, p. 206.
10. For this story see Weber, *IS,* VIII. p. 31. Oldenberg, *ZDMG* 37, 1883, p. 67ff.
11. Hillebrandt, *VM,* I, p. 380.
12. For the connection of Gandharvas and fragrances in the Buddhist literature see Saṁyuttanikāya III. 250ff.
13. For Gandharvas connected with *rūpa* see also Bhāgavatap. II. 3.6 One can obtain *rūpa* (beauty) by worshipping the Apsarases: Viṣṇudharmottarap. III. 221.38.
14. Cf. Macdonell, *Vedic Mythology,* p. 137.
15. Weber *IS* XII, p. 135. n. 3.
16. Cf. Kuhn, *ZVS,* I, p. 525 ff; Meyer, *Trilogie* I, p. 34 n. 2.
17. Cf. Oldenberg, *Religion des Veda,* p. 249.

18. Cf. Winternitz, *Hochzeitsritual*, p. 88.
19. See Meyer, *Trilogie*, III, p. 177.
20. Geldner, *Der Rigveda*, III. 300, Cf. Meyer, *Trilogie*, I, p. 34, n. 2.
21. Abert, *Lehre von Ethos*, p. 62.
22. Abert, *Lehre von Ethos*, p. 6.
23. Abert, *Musikanschauung* p. 156, 163, 100 etc.
24. Cp. Meyer, *Trilogie*, I, p. 34, n. 2; cp. Hillebrandt *VM* I, p. 378.
25. Cp. Meyer, *Trilogie*, I, p. 136; Gonda, *Religionen Indiens* I, p. 101.
26. Cf. Sāyaṇa: *abhinavaprasavā*. Whitney translates the word *sūtika* as "pregnant". I follow here Sāyaṇa.
27. For the association of spirits of words and those of sounds see Combarieu, *La musique et la magie*, p. 122f.
28. Cf. v. Schroeder, *Mysterium und Mimus* p. 389, n. 1.
29. Cf. v. Schroeder, *Mysterium und Mimus* p. 59; 282. On p. 477 v. Schroeder considers the Gandharvas to be spirits of dead.
30. Rf. Hauer, *Vrātya* p. 54.

CHAPTER VIII

Results of Music

(A) MUSIC AND RAIN

Music and rain are very much connected with each other in the belief of primitive men.[1] Primitive men often make use of music in the magic rites for producing rain.[2] They believe that music has a magic power in it for bringing rains. Thus in the Mara tribe of the Northern Australia, the rain-maker goes to pool, and sings over it his magic song. After that he throws water all over himself, scatters it about and returns to the camp. It is believed that rain would follow this rite.[3] The Garo of Assam, at the time of drought perform an animal-sacrifice. They pour gourds of water over their priest until he is thoroughly drenched. At the time of this ceremony drums are beaten and wind-instruments are blown. Then rain showers.[4] Similarly in the vedic literature we get many references to the belief that music is a means of obtaining rain. Singers and many elements of Vedic music are associated with rain. This association also implies that music causes rain.

Singers are supposed to bring rain by means of their songs. Therefore, ṚV V.83.1, a praise-singer is asked to sing nicely for Parjanya (Rain-god). Similarly, ṚV V.42.14, a poet-singer is requested, "O, singer, the praise should now reach that thundering roaring Lord of blessings, who with clouds, water and lightening wanders, moistening both the worlds". The effect of the songs of singers is indicated in ṚV I.167.6; the Maruts place the young maiden (i.e. lightening according to Sāyaṇa's commentary), when the singer, having pressed Soma, sings a song (*arka*). Udgātṛ the chief priest of the Sāmaveda, must have been supposed to be a rain-bringer. He is said to be identical with the rainy season (*varṣā udgātā*) and it is further remarked: "When it rains hard, a sound as that of a sāman is produced" (ŚB XI.2.7.32). At the time of choosing the priests, in connection with the Udgātṛ-priest, the sacrificer says, "*parjanya udagātā* (Udgātṛ is Rain)" (Māśs II.1.1.4; Āpśs X. 1.14). Similarly when the sacrificer notifies the priests to invite him to partake of the soma, he utters the same words in respect of Udgātṛ (ṢaḍB II.5.5). In the course of a sacrificial session, the Adhvaryu has to consecrate the Udgātṛ. Having prescribed this, ŚB XII.1.1.3, remarks, "The Udgātṛ is Parjanya (god of Rain). From Parjanya, rain is produced. He (Adhvaryu) thus connects the rain with the plants. No person should be consecrated between the Brahman and the Udgātṛ. For in that case, rain would be separated from plants; there will not be any rain". (ŚB XII.1.1.3; cp. GB I.4.3). When the Udgātṛ sings the Gāyatra-sāman based on *uccā te jātam andhasaḥ ....* (ṚV IX. 61.10); when he utters *divi sad bhūmyā dade* (ṚV IX.61.10b), he makes rain fall from the sky (JB I.81). The Pavamāna-lauds are like Agni (Fire), Vāyu (Wind) and Āditya (Sun). When Prajāpati gives rain, the food to the beings, he covers these (Agni and other) as it were. The Udgtīṛ is identical with Prajāpati. He should sing the Pavamāna-lauds, "having covered" them as it were. When he sings the Pavamāna, the Udgātṛ "covers" the sacrificer and himself with food. Ample rain falls there (JB I.274).

Some hymns are associated with rain. Thus in the course of the Agniṣṭoma-sacrifice, Aponaptrīya-hymn (ṚV X.10) is to be recited. It should be recited "continuously". "Parjanya comes to rain continuously for the offspring when one, knowing thus recites this (hymn) continuously". Thus the use of this hymn is to be made according to AB II.19, for the obtainment of rain.

In the Ṛgveda IV.57.5, it is said, "Enjoy this speech (*vāc-*) O Śuna and Sīra. That liquid which you have prepared in heaven, sprinkle this earth with it". Elsewhere Devāpi makes request to Bṛhaspati, "Lay shining speech (*vācam*) in the mouth for us, O Bṛhaspati, which is diseaseless (mistakeless), and quick and by means of which we shall win rain for Śantanu" (ṚV X.98.3). In ṚV X.98.7 it is further told that Bṛhaspati gave speech to Devāpi. This speech is described as that which obtains rain (*vṛṣṭivani*).[5] Nirukta II.10 has prescribed the whole hymn (ṚV X.98) to be used by one who desires rains. Similarly, ṚV VII.101.5, the poet-singer says, "This speech (*vacas*) is for Rain; may it be in his heart. May he enjoy it; may there be pleasant showers". Ṛgvidhāna II.326-327 it is prescribed that ṚV VII.101 and 102 should be recited for the sake of rains.[6] ṚV VII.102.1, it is said, "Sing loudly for Parjanya (god of rain) .... may he give us willow" ṚV VII.102.1 and 2 are to be used in an offering of rice for Parjanya by one who is desirous of rain, according to Māśs V.2.5.19f. About ṚV VII.103 which is well-known as Maṇḍūka-sūkta, Nirukta IX.6 informs us that Vasiṣtha, desirous of rain, sang this hymn (*vasiṣṭhaḥ parjanyakāmaḥ tuṣṭāva*). Thus the recitation of this hymn seems to be a kind of rain-magic. AV IV.15.3, the God of Rain is requested, "Do thou (O god of rain) make the singer see the clouds; let gushes of water rush up here and there; let gushes of rain gladden the earth. Let plants of all forms be born here and there". In the next verse, it is said, "Let the troops of Maruts sing unto thee O Parjanya, noisy here and there. Let gushes of rain go down the earth" (AV IV.15.4). Kauśikasūtra (XL.1ff) prescribes this hymn along with AV VII. 18 to be applied in a rite for procuring rain.

Some sāmans are connected with the obtainment of rain. Thus the Śyāvāśva-sāman can bring rain. Once Śyāvāśva, the son of Arcanānas was taking part in a sacrificial session. His jealous fellow-sattrins (co-performers) wanted to kill him and brought him to a desert. Then he saw this sāman and by means of it created rains (TMB VIII.5.9).

Once upon a time the rain retired from these worlds. Ayāsya, by means of the two Āyāsya-sāmans caused it to fall. He who praises with these two sāmans causes the rain to fall (TMB XI.8.11). Similarly, on another occasion, when rain had receded from these worlds, Prajāpati caused it to fall (*acyāvayat*) by means of the Cyāvana-sāman. He who praises with this sāman, causes rain to fall (TMB XIII.5.13). Here the magical connection between the verb *acyāvayat* (caused to fall) and the name of the sāman Cyāvana is noteworthy. In the rain-giving power of sāmans, the finales (*nidhana-*) play an important role. Thus about the Saubhara-sāman it is said that Prajāpati gave food, rain, to the hungry beings by means of this sāman (TMB VIII.8.14-17). He who desires for rain, for food, and for the world of heaven, should chant the Saubhara-sāman with *his* as its finale (TMB VIII.8.18f). Similarly, according to JB I.186, one who is desirous of rain, should sing Saubhara-sāman and use the word *his* as its finale. In connection with the Traita-sāman, following story is told. "Āptyas who were going at ease,[7] through forests, became thirsty. In the dry land, they found a well. Neither Ekata nor Dvita, liked to descend in it. Trita, however, descended in it. Those two drank water and became satisfied. Then, having closed (the well) by means of a wheel of a chariot, they went away on bulls. He (Trita) desired, "May I get out from this; may I get help. Then he saw this (viz. Traita) sāman and praised with it. He made the words, *sam indubhhiḥ* its finale. Rain having fallen made him float over to the top. He floated over the chariot-wheel with which he was covered" (JB I.184). Thus here also special importance of the finales in the rain-magic can be observed. One can, however, stop the rain with the help of finale of a sāman. Thus in connection with the Āmahīya-sāman the following story is told: Prajāpati created the beings which remained hungry. They asked for food and then gave them food by means of the Āmahīyava-sāman *without* finale. Then it rained ceaselessly. So in order to stop the rain he saw (discovered) the finale (viz. the word *stauṣe*) and when he pronounced it, the rains stopped. By means of this finale rain can be made to fall and cease. When one wants rain, one should sing this sāman without the finale and when one wants to stop it, one may pronounce the finale (JB I.117). For the connection of finale with cessation of rain see also ChāUp. II.3.2.

A sāman carries the name Vārṣāhara which means "that which brings rain" (ŚB XIV.3.1.26; Māśs IV.4.24; ṢaḍB III. 8.10).

Sometimes the process of rain-falling is metaphorically described as the sāman in general. Thus we read in JUB I. 12.2.1, "Now this is the sāman in Parjanya (rain). The wind which precedes is its *himkāra*; when it causes to float together, that is the *prastāva*; when it thunders, that is the *udgītha*; when it lightens, that is the *pratihāra*; when it rains that is the *nidhana*. That is the sāman in Parjanya. He who knows the sāman in Parjanya, to him, verily, Parjanya sends rain". Similarly, at another place, Prajāpati is said to have given sāman in the form of the sun to the beings created by him. On being requested to make it (sun) "near" (to the beings) he transferred the sun into seasons. Then Prajāpati is said to have made the rainy season the *udgītha*, which is the most important part of the sāman (JUB I.3.2.7; cp. JUB I.12.1.4 "The rainy season is the *udgītha*; the rainy season sings as it were").[8] Being similarly requested again, Prajāpati transformed the sun i.e. sāman into Parjanya (rain). "He made the preceding wind the *himkāra*; the thunder-clouds the *prastāva*; the thunder the *udgītha*; the lightening the *pratihāra*; the rain the *nidhana*". (JUB I.3.2.9-3.1). In ChāUp. II.3.1f, one is advised to meditate on the fivefold sāman in the form of rain. "The preceding wind is the *himkāra*; the formation of clouds is the *prastāva*; what rains is the *udgītha*; the lightenning and thunder are the *pratihāra*; The cessation is the *nidhana*. It rains for him and he causes it to rain, he who knowing this meditates on the fivefold sāman in the rain". ChāUp II.15.1, the Vairūpa-sāman is described to be "woven in rain" in the same manner. Elsewhere one is advised to meditate on the fivefold sāman in all the waters: "When a cloud forms, that is the *prastāva*; when the waters flow to east, they are the *udgītha*; when they flow to west, they are the *pratihāra*; the ocean is the *nidhana*" (ChāUp. II.4.1).

Instrumental music has been often mentioned to be connected with rain. When the Bṛhat-sāman took birth out of waters, the noise of rain followed its birth. Therefore, at the time of the Bṛhat-stotra drums are beaten; and then rain is about to fall (JB III.118; cp. I.143). At the time of ascending the risings (*roha-*) of the Bṛhat-sāman, one who is desirous of water should strike upon the water-jar (JB I.136). Thus the noise of instruments seems to bring out rains.

By using the Viṣṭuti (method of repetition) named Parivartinī in which *hum* 1, 2, 3; *hum* 1, 2, 3, *hum* 1, 2, 3, is the schema, one causes the rain fall (TMB II.2.2). The same is the result of another Viṣṭuti named Kulāyinī in which following is the schema: *hum* 1, 2, 3,: *hum* 2, 3,1; *hum* 3, 1, 2 (TMB II.3.5). The Viṣṭuti named Udyatī (schema: *hum* 1, 1, 1; *hum* 2, 2, 2; *hum* 3, 3, 3) is useful for sorcery against an enemy; but when it is used no rain falls (TMB II.1.4). Thus music has twofold effect according to its use. It can bring rain. It can delay it.

Some other miscellaneous elements are also connected with rain. For one who is desirous of rain, the Tristich beginning with *prāsya dhārā akṣaran* (SV II.1115-1117; ṚV IX.29.1-3) should be made the opening one (*pratipad*) at the time of reciting the out-of-doors-chant. By the words *prāsya dhārā ...* one causes rain to fall from the heaven and by the following words viz. *vṛṣṇaḥ sutasya* one causes it to fall from the intermediate region (TMB VI.10.15f). Once these worlds became separated from each other. Then no rain came down from the heaven to the earth. Nor any food offered by men went to the heaven. Now "the gods live on whatever is given from here; and the men live on whatever is given from there". Then both the gods and men remained hungry. At that time Prajāpati used the verses *uccā te jātam ......* (ṚV IX.61.10ff) as the beginning tristich (*pratipad*). With the words *uccā .... andhasaḥ* (ṚV IX.61.10 a) he carried the oblations upwards and with the words *divi sad bhūmyā dade* (ṚV IX.61.10 b), he made rain fall from the sky (JB I.116). Thus here also the words of a beginning tristich are connected with the rain-fall. The recitation of the concluding verse of the morning litany can produce good or bad results for the sacrificer according to its recital either before or after the sun-rise. If it is recited exactly at the dawn, when the sun is neither risen nor unrisen the sacrificer does not either prosper or become poor. But in that case, as a co-effect, rain falls heavily (JB I.213). The Vyāhṛtis (sacred utterances) are also connected with rain. Thus one who is desirous of rain, should utter *āpo vāyur āpo vāyuḥ*, before the Vāmadevya-sāman. Then it really rains (JB I.333). About some other Vyahṛtis it is said that gods made use of them for procuring rains. Thus "with '*O Śrāvaya* the gods sent forth the east wind; with '*astu śrauṣaṭ*' they caused the clouds to flow together; with '*yaja*' they sent forth the lightening; with '*ye yajāmahe*' the thunder; with the vaṣaṭ-call they caused it to rain" (ŚB I.5.2.18). AB II.41, connects the offering verse (yājyā) with rain. "The offering verse is verily identical with rain and lightening; lightening, verily gives rain and food; (when one recites the offering verse) one puts lightening in order". If a student of Sāmaveda follows the rules of studentship, Parjanya gives rain for him according to his (student's) desire (Gobhilagṛhyasūtra III.2.29).[9]

From the above details the following points emerge: (1) Musicians and music are supposed to be possessing the power of bringing rains. In the veda, they are closely associated and identified with rain. (2) Music can procure rain. It can also stop the rain once started. It can even prevent the rain-fall totally. Thus it is double-natured. (3) Some times one seeks to please the gods by means of music and it is the gods who give rain. This shows how music works magicoreligiously.

REFERENCES

1. For music and rain rf. e.g. Gunkel, Zscharnack, *RGG*, IV. 276; *Belvianes, Sociologie de la musique*, p. 45.
2. Combrarieu, *La musique et la magie*, p. 35ff; Hastings *ERE*, VIII. 260 (a)
3. Frazer, *Golden Bough*, p. 64, 65.
4. Webster, *Magic*, p. 50; cp. p. 51, 78.
5. Cf. Bergaigne, *La religion védique* ...... I. p. 298.
6. Cf. Gonda, *Ṛgvidhāna*, p. 60; cf. also the same "The so-called secular, humorous and satirical hymns of the Ṛgveda, *Orientalia Neerlandica*, Leiden, 1948, p. 312.

7. The text reads *sāte nayataḥ*. I have emended it as *sātena yataḥ* and translation is based on emendation.
8. *udiva varṣaṁ gāyati*—I do not accept Oertel's translation (*JAOS*, 16, 1896, p. 112). "One sings the *udgītha*, through the year (*varṣa*) as it were". For, JUB I.12.1.1 ff every such sentence refers to a *season*; therefore this sentence also must refer to a season viz. the rainy one.
9. Cf. Oldenberg, *Religion des Veda*, p. 420ff.

(B) MUSIC AND FOOD

Music is closely connected with fertility, growth of crops and obtainment of food.[1] Various aspects of Vedic music are said to be powerful enough to give food to the performers. The Vedic texts sometimes identify a particular aspect of music with food and thereby imply that that musical element is a means of obtainment of food.

Sāmans are very often said to be identical with food and the singing of them is prescribed to be used by one who is desirous of food. The Sāman in general is said to be food of gods (JB I.71). When the Udgātṛ, sitting upon a chair of Uduṁbara-wood (which is identified with strength) sings sāmans, he puts strength in the sāman i.e. in the food of gods (TMB VI.4.13) and thereby strengthens the gods. Therefore, wherever there is the priesthood *with* sāman, gods eat there much (JB I.71). JB II.39, Sāman in general is said to be identical with food (*annaṁ vai sāma*). Prajāpati, after having created all the beings gave them sāman as their means of livelihood (SVB I. 1.6). The gods live on that part of sāman which is sung in the highest note; the men on their part sang the first of the remaining notes; the Gandharvas and Apsarases in the second; the cattle in the third; the Fathers and those "Who are sleeping in the eggs" in the fourth; the Asuras and Rakṣases in the fifth and the herbs and trees and whatever other world, that lives on what is sung in the last note. "Therefore, they say, the Sāman verily is the food, for he (Prajāpati) gave it to them as a means of livelihood (SVB I.1.8). Thus all the beings subsist on sāman. JUB I.3.1.1 ff, following story is told. When Prajāpati created the beings, they became hungry and were desirous of food. Then they beleaguered him on all sides. Prajāpati then said to them, "Verily, one Veda have I created for food-eating viz. (That of) sāman; that I will furnish to you". Then he gave *hiṁkāra* to the animals; *prastāva* to men; *ādi* to the birds; *udgītha* to the gods and *pratihāra* to the beasts of the forest (JUB I.3.1.1 ff).

Some individual sāmans are also said to be identical with food. Thus the Rathantara-sāman is said to be identical with food (*annaṁ vai rathantaram* AB VIII.1). Therefore, in the Manustoma-sacrifice, Rathantara-sāman is used as *pṛṣṭha*. And because it is identical with food, it also serves to obtain cattle (JB II.170). According to JB I.135, gods crossed over (*tṛ-*) i.e. defeated the Asura-rakṣases which were called *rathāḥ* by means of the Rathantara-sāman. Further, JB I.136 it is said that hunger is *rathā* and food is Rathantara. Hunger is "killed" by means of food. Thus the gods killed hunger by means of food in the form of the Rathantara-sāman, and ascended to the heaven. Āndhīgava-sāman is also identical with food and therefore it is to be used in the Vājapeya-sacrifice for obtaining food (JB II.195). Similarly Pṛśni-sāman is identical with food (JB II.14). Gods call food by the name "Pṛśni" (TMB XII. 10.25). Rājana and Ilānda-samans are said to be "directly (*sākṣāt*)" identical with food. The Rājana-sāman is identical with food because it is five-fold and food is also fivefold. The Rājana is fivefold either because all the five parts of it are to be repeated five times or on account of the five times repeated *stobha* (*hum, hum, hum, hum, hum*) or on account of the five finales (*vāg, iḍā, suvar, bṛhad, bhā*). Food is also fivefold: eating (*aśyam*), chewing (*khādyam*), sucking (*coṣyam*), licking (*lehyam*), and drinking (*peyam*) (TMB V.2.7). Ilānda-sāman is directly identical with food because the word Ilānda is mystically nothing but *Irānna* and Irānna means drink (*irā*) and food (*anna*) (TMB V.3.2). The Gaurivīta (JB I.125) and Dairghaśravasa (JB III.14; 257), are also identical with food.

Many stories tell us how Prajāpati gave food to the beings created by him with the help of a particular sāman. Thus the first food was also created by Prajāpati with the help of a saman, at the time of creation. Take for example the story of the origin of Āmahīyava-sāman. Prajapati created the beings without any food. The beings became hungry and ate each other. Then Prajāpati thought of how the beings would not eat him. Then he saw the Āmahīyava-sāman and gave them food by means of it (JB I.116; cp. TMB XV.4.5). Similar is the case of Vājadāvarya-sāman. Thus when Prajāpati created beings, they were without food. They ran to Prajāpati. He then gave food to them with this sāman (JB III.147; cp. TMB XIII.9.13). Prajāpati himself used a sāman called Devasthāna for preserving food. Thus, when he created food it flew away with fear of directions (*diś*). Prajāpati desired to preserve it. Then he saw the Devasthāna-sāman and preserved the food from all the directions (JB III.256).

Gods also use the power of sāmans in obtaining food. Thus when the gods and Asuras were contesting in connection with food, gods desired to obtain the food belonging to the Asuras. Then they saw the Vājājit (food-winning) - sāman and having praised with it, got their desire fulfilled (JB III.151; cp. TMB XIII.9.21; JB II.194). On another occasion of similar contest also, gods won the food in possession of the Asuras. Still a great part of food called *Gūrda* was remaining with the Asuras. Then the gods saw the sāman named Gūrda, praised with it and obtained that food (JB III.171). Agni once desired to be "eater of food". Then he saw the Āgneya-sāman, praised with it and became "eater of food". For, this sāman is obtainment of food" (JB III.100).

Seers and other personalities obtained food by means of sāmans. Once food went away from these worlds. A seer named Ayāsya caused it fall from the other world, by means of two Āyāsya-sāmans (TMB XI.8.12). By means of the Ihavad Vāmadevya-sāman, Vāmadeva became the chaplain (*purodhā*) of food (TMB XIII.9.27). Bṛhaduktha, the son of the woman called Vamrī obtained the chaplain's office of food by means of the Bārhaduktha-sāman (TMB XIV.9.38). Similarly, the Śāktyas obtained food by means of the Śāktya-sāman (JB I.215), Dīrghatamas by means of the sāman named Dīraghatamaso'rkaḥ (JB III.259; cp. TMB XV.3.34) and Cyavana by means of the Cyāvana-sāman (JB III.128). Pañcavājas Kautsa wanted to drink both the human and divine liquids. He saw the Pañcavāja-sāman and got his desire fulfilled (JB III.229; cp. TMB XIV.11.27 where the sāman is named as Kautsa). Dīrghaśravas, a kingly seer, being expelled from his realm by his enemies, wandered about for a long time and became hungry. Then he saw the Dairghaśravasa-sāman and by means of it obtained food from all the sides (TMB XV. 3.25). JB III.257, adds that Dīrghaśravas praised Agni with this sāman. Agni, then made everything for him full of honey and food. Elsewhere it is said that Indra gave food to Bṛhadgiri, by means of the word *atha* of the Traikakubhya-sāman (JB I.86). Thus gods play sometimes an important role in giving food to the singers. Not merely through the magical power but through the magical power accompanied by the grace of gods, one obtains the desired result. Thus magic and religion are mixed together here.

The Vedic texts, on the basis of the stories given above and similar ones try to maintain that because the sāmans were used by particular ancient personalities they got food. Similarly the sacrificers will get food if they make use of these sāmans in the prescribed manner in their sacrifices.

There are many other sāmans which also are prescribed to be used in various sacrifices for the sake of obtaining food; but in their cases no stories are told. Thus the Arkapuṣpa-sāman is used in the Dvādaśāha-sacrifice and the Vājapeya-sacrifice. "Food is called "*arka-*" by the gods and its flavour (is called) "flower (*puṣpa-*)". He who in lauding has applied the Arkapuṣpa-sāman obtains food with flavour" (TMB XV.3.23; cp. JB II. 194). JB II.14 and III.256 precribe this sāman for obtaining food belonging to forest. The sāman named Agneḥ arkaḥ (JB III.191) and the sāman named Svāśirām arkaḥ (JB III.226) are also useful for obtaining food, because *arka* is identical with food. The Soma-sāman is also useful for obtaining food. For Soma is royal power (*kṣatra*). "A royal man (*kṣatriya*), verily, is the giver of food". Therefore this sāman can give food to the user (JB III.191).

The *nidhana* (finale) of a sāman is often said to be powerful in giving food to the users. Thus the sāman which has the word *madhuścut* as its finale is useful for obtaining the highest kind of food. For *madhu* (honey) is the highest kind of food (TMB

XIII.11.18). The Vairūpa-sāman with five finales (viz. *diśam, viśam, has, aśvā, śiśumatī, īṭ, iḍā*) is connected with food. For food is five fold. Therefore, this sāman is helpful for retaining food (TMB XII.4.5f). One who is desirous of food should sing the Saubhara-sāman and make the word *ūrk* (power) its finale (JB I.186). The Yaudhājaya-sāman has its finale in the middle. By means of the Pavamāna-laud all the food would be given to gods. But the finale of this sāman which is a part of the Pavamāna-laud preserves some food for human beings (JB I. 124). Food, it is said, nourishes the beings in the middle (cp. AB V.3). Therefore, the sāman, having its finale in the middle, serves to obtain food. The Kāleya-sāman which has the word *iḍā (Iḷā)* as its finale is also useful for obtaining food. For iḷā means cattle and food. By means of this sāman food is given to the beings (JB I.305).

Some sāmans have the last vowel being *svarita,* and this itself becomes their finale. Such sāmans are also connected with food. The *svaras* are the food of sāmans and when a sāman with *svara* as its finale is sung, then food is obtained (JB I.112). The Auśana-sāman is sung with its last vowel being *svarita.* By means of *svara,* food is given to the gods (*svareṇa vai devebhyo' nnādyaṁ pradīyate*). Thus food is given to the gods thereby (TMB VII.3.25f; JB I.127). Similar purpose is served by the Kāva-sāman which has also the last vowel *svarita* (TMB XI. 5.26).

Many times the hiṁkāra (the sound *hum* produced at the time of singing sāmans) is connected with food. Thus when, at the end of the out-of-doors-chant, the hiṁkara is produced, food is given to gods (JB I.246). Prajāpati gave food to the beings with the verses *having* the hiṁkāra. Therefore, by means of the Gāyatrapārśva-sāman, which *has* the hiṁkāra, food is given to the sacrificer (JB III.214). In this way, the hiṁkāra is connected with the obtainment of food. Śakala, who was desirous of food, practised penance and saw the Śākalya-sāman. Having praised with this sāman he got his desire fulfilled. This sāman is *with* the hiṁkāra. "The hiṁkāra is identical with food; (*annaṁ vai hiṁkāraḥ*); for with the word "yes" (*hum*) food is given". Therefore this sāman helps in obtaining food (JB III.93). The Vāmadevya-sāman with double hiṁkāra also is useful for obtaining food (TMB XIV.9.22).

The stomas are also useful to obtain food. ŚB IX.3.3.6 identifies stomas with food (*annaṃ vai stomāḥ* cp. MS III.4.2). In the course of the fire-altar-building-ceremony, there are stoma-offerings and because the stomas are identical with food, the Adhvaryu-priest, by offering those offerings, consecrates the sacrificer with food (ŚB IX.3.3.6). The seventeen-versed stoma is specifically said to be identical with food (JB II. 332). One who is desirous of food should perform an Agniṣṭut-sacrifice all the lauds of which are seventeen-versed. "For the seventeen -versed stoma is food; Agni is a bestower of food. Agni bestows food on him" (TMB XVII.9.1f). Here it will appear that magic and religion are mixed. The stoma does have a food-giving power because it has been identified with food. But here the role of a god (Agni) is specifically mentioned. Thus magicoreligious significance of the Vedic music can be directly observed on the basis of such passages. In the sacrifice named Jyotis, the midday-pavamāna-laud begins with the verses in Gāyatrī and is followed by the pṛṣṭhas on seventeen-versed stoma. "The Gāyatrī is the mouth; the seventeen-versed stoma is food; one thereby puts food in one's mouth" (TMB XIX.11.4). Because there is a seventeen-versed stoma in the Vighana-sacrifice, one obtains food thereby (TMB XIX. 18.3). A sacrificer desirous of food should perform an Atirātra-sacrifice which has seventeen-versed stoma (TMB XX.10.1). According to JB II.387, the Pṛṣṭhya-ṣaḍaha which forms a part of the Twelve day-sacrifice is identical with the body and the seventeen-versed stoma is identical with food. So if the seventeen versed stoma were removed from the Pṛṣṭhya-ṣaḍaha, food would be removed outside the body and then the sacrificer and the priests would remain hungry. Therefore, this stoma must be applied in the Pṛṣṭhyasadaha.

The Stobhas (modifications) like *hāu, hāi* etc. are said to be identical with food (*annaṁ vai stobhāḥ* JB I.332). On the

Viṣuvat-day of the Gavāmayana-sacrifice, Bhāsa-sāman with *ten* stobhas is to be sung. "Virāj-metre has *ten* syllables, Virāj is food; for the sake of obtainment of virāj, food" (JB II.390).

Certain stobhas are called Viṣṭambhas (props). They are the following: - *matsva, ojaḥ, sahaḥ, balam, indraḥ, vayaḥ, bṛhat, ṛtam, svaḥ, jyotiḥ, dadhe,* each followed by *hā.*[2] These Viṣṭambhas are also connected with food. Thus on the fourth day of the Daśarātra of the Dvādaśāha, Virāja-sāman is to be sung. At the time of singing it, when the Prastāva (Prelude) is sung, one should apply the Viṣṭambhas (props). "One thereby puts food into one's own mouth; for the Prastāva is the mouth (= beginning of the chant). Ten times one props; of the ten syllables is the Virāj. Food belongs to Virāj; for obtainment of food: thirty times one props; for obtaining more food". (TMB XII.10.7 ff).

The recitation of some verses is regarded as helpful for obtaining food; The Sūdadohas-verse (i.e. ṚV VIII.69.3), is according to SāṅĀ II.1, identical with food and when it is sung, the joints of the body become joined by food. The verses beginning with *pavasva vājasātaye,* are to be used on the sixth day of the *Daśarātra* of the Dvādaśāha. These verses contain the word *vāja* which means food and are therefore helpful in obtaining food (JB III.129). Similarly the verses like *tenāpavasvāndhasā* .... (JB III.28), *uccā te jātamandhasah* ... (JB III.40), *purojitī vo andhasā* ... (JB II.195; III.79); *punāhīndrāya pātave* ... (JB III.209) are to be sung on different days of the Dvādaśāha-sacrifice. They contain the word *andhas* which means food. Therefore they are useful for obtaining food. On the eighth day of the Daśarātra of the Dvādaśāha-sacrifice a complex of five verses (SV II.555-559; ṚV IX.50.1ff) is sung. "The Paṅkti-metre is of five feet (of five verse-quarters) five-fold is food; so they serve to obtain food" (TMB XIV.7.7).

Some metres are also said to be useful for obtaining food. Thus the Paṅkti-metre is said to be identical with food. Some ritualists, on this basis, prescribe that the Prauga-śastra should be in Paṅkti-metre; so that one will get food (AĀ I.1.3).

The metre named Virāj[3] has a special connection with food.[4] The Saṁyājyā-verses of the Dīkṣanīyā offering should be in Virāja-metre, if the sacrificer is desirous of obtaining food. "For Virāj is identical with food (*annaṁ vai virāṭ*)" (AB I.5). In the Mahāvrata-performance, the verses in Virāj-metre (ṚV VII.22.1-6) are sung. "For Virāj-verses are food and serve to win food" (AĀ I.5.2). For food and Virāj see also TMB XII. 10.20; 13.18; JB I.229; III.363 etc. Not only the Virāj-metre but whatever is ten in number, that is also helpful for obtaining food. For the Virāj has ten syllables in each foot; and Virāj is connected with food. Thus all the things connected with the number ten are useful for obtaining food. On the sixth day of the Daśarātra of the Dvādaśāha-sacrifice, there is a complex of ten verses to be sung. Because the number of verses is ten and it is connected with Virāj and thereby with food, this complex of ten verses serves to obtain food (TMB XIII.7.8).

Some other miscellaneous elements of the Vedic music also appear to have a magical power of giving food to the users of them. Pratipad (the beginning triad of verse) is connected with obtainment of food. Thus one who is desirous of food should use the verses beginning with *agna āyūṁṣi pavase* as a Pratipad (JB I.193). Nivids (formulas inserted in the middle or at the end of a Śāstra, accompanying the midday and third pressing) are connected with food. Therefore when a nivid is used in the middle of the Marutvatīya-Śastra, food is placed, as it were, in the middle of body (KB XV.3). It is further told that according to some ritualists, Nivids are identical with food (KB XV.3;4). Certain ways of uttering the vaṣaṭ-call is named as *antaḥsri*. At the time of pronunciation of this kind of vaṣaṭ-call, one closes one's lips and utters the call at a loud toneful pitch. By pronouncing such a vaṣaṭ-call, one becomes an eater of food (ŚB XI.4.2.11). The *mandra* (soft) part of a sāman is identical with food and whosoever sings it, becomes a food-eater (JUB I.16.2.6). Dance is also connected with obtainment of food.[5] In the Mahāvrata-ceremony, slave-girls dance around the Mārjālīya-fire, with waters on their heads beating the ground with their feet and singing "This is honey". TS VII.5.10.1 comments on this, "Honey is the chief food of the gods. Verily they win the chief food".

Singers are also connected with food. Thus in the Ṛgveda II.9.5, Agni is requested, "Make the singer (O Agni) rich in food (*kṣumantam*)".[6] Udgātṛ sits on a seat of Udumbara-wood. "Udgātṛ is verily identical with Prajāpati and Uduṁbara is power. He, Prajāpati, taking support in the power, distributes power, food among the beings" (JB I.72). JB I.71, sāman is said to be the food of gods and the Udgātṛ is supposed to give food to the gods by means of his singing. Therefore, it is added, that gods eat much wherever priests perform *with* sāman (cp. TMB VI.4.13). A man is not really born until he does not perform a sacrifice. When he sacrifices, he takes birth. The Udgātṛ causes him to enter the Sun, by means of uttering *om*. By means of the next syllable *vāc* (speech) he gives him the Moon, which is equal to eatable food and imperishableness (JUB III.3.4.9).

It will be thus observed that in the Vedic literature music and musicians are considered to be powerful of giving food. The music is sometimes said to be the food even to gods. Not only gods but all beings depend on the food in the form of music. Thus music is the cosmic food according to the veda. Music works magicoreligiously. Sometimes it is directly stated that by means of music one obtains food; but sometimes it is said that the music is used for praising the gods and the gods, when pleased give food to the sacrificers etc. Thus it has a magicoreligious significance of giving food.

REFERENCES

1. See in general Combarieu, *La musique et la magie,* p. 109; 298; Seeman, in *Handwoerterbuch der deutschen Aberglaubens,* VI.648, 649; Meyer, *Trilogie,* I, p. 122 etc; *Jewish Encyclopaedia,* IX118 etc.
2. Caland, *Pañcaviṁśa-brāhmaṇa,* p. 293.

3. For the various meanings of the word - Virāj, see Renou, *JA*, 240, p. 141ff; Gonda, *Viṣṇuism*, p. 167; the same, *Ancient Indian Kingship*, p. 115f and *Loka*, p. 27, n. 7.
4. For Virāj and food see Mauss, *Mélanges d'indianisme, ... a Lévi*, p. 333ff.
5. Meyer, *Trilogie*, I. p. 57, n. 1 and the literature there.
6. Cf. Ludwig, *Der Rigveda* I, p. 225; Grassman *Worterbuch*, 369.

(C) MUSIC AND CATTLE ETC.

In the Vedic literature, music is many times mentioned as a means of obtaining cattle and other animals. Some of the musical elements are even identified with cattle very often.[1] It is well-known that cattle were objects of desire, a kind of wealth for the Vedic people. The Vedic people believed that by singing various items of music they could obtain cattle.

Many sāmans are identical with cattle. By singing them, one obtains cattle. Thus Vāmadevya-sāman is identical with cattle (*paśavo vai vāmadevyam*) and its use is to be made for obtaining cattle (JB I.333; II.194; cp. III.26; 49; 71; 157; 189; 219; 261; TMB XI.4.8; XIV.9.24 etc.). Similarly one should praise with Samanta-sāman; for it is identical with cattle and then one gets cattle (JB III.186). The same is the case of the Raurava-sāman (TMB VII.5.8). Bṛhadrathantara-sāmans (TMB VIII.7.1) Vairūpa-sāman (TMB XIV.9.8) Surūpa-sāmans (TMB XIV. 11.11) and Rayiṣṭha-sāman (TMB XIV.11.32).

Many Sāmans were seen (prepared) by various seers etc. in order to get cattle thereby. Thus Aśva Sāmudri desired to obtain cattle and to have plenty of them. Then he saw the Āśva-sāman and got his desire fulfilled thereby (JB III.14). Pṛthu Vainya desired to produce himself for the sake of kingdom of all the cattle. He succeeded in this by means of the Pārtha-sāman (JB III.24 cp. TMB XIII.5.20 according to which Pṛthu Vainya obtained lordship of both the domestic and forest animals). Mṛgayu Deva obtained lordship of both the village-animals and forest-animals with the help of the Mārgīyava-sāman (JB III.212). Hārāyaṇa Āṅgirasa obtained both cows and horses by means of Hārāyaṇa sāman (JB III.217). Prajāpati obtained one-hooted animals by means of Rauhiṇaka-sāman (JB II.14). Vatsa-Kāṇva obtained animals without hair and without ears immediately after having sung with Kāṇva-sāman (JB III.198). Thus it appears that various kinds of animals or cattle can be obtained by means of various sāmans. Hungry Devatithi was wandering together with his son. He found gourds in the forest. He approached them with the Daivātitha sāman. The gourds then appeared to him having become spotted cows. Thus by means of the magical power of this sāman he turned gourds into the cows (TMB IX.2.19; cp. JB I.226 where this sāman is named as Maidhātitha). According to TMB XV.10.12, Medhātithi Kāṇva created two-uddered cows out of an Asura called Vibhinduka (cp. JB III.234). Similarly many other seers obtained cattle with the help of their sāmans. Thus Śāktyas obtained cattle by means of Śāktya-sāman (JB I.215), Pūrvatithi by means of Paurvatitha (JB I. 227), Andhīgu by means of Āndhīgava (TMB VIII.5.12); Vadhryaśva Ānūpa by means of Ānūpa-sāman (TMB XIII. 3.17), Virūpa Āṅgirasa by means of Vairūpasāman (JB III. 209); Harivarṇa by means of Hārivarṇa-sāman (TMB VIII. 9.4); Kārṇaśravasa Āṅgirasa by means of Kārnaśravasa-sāman (TMB XIII.11.15).

The specific *forms* of the different animals were created with the help of music. Thus Prajāpati created the animals. But he could not recognise their forms (for all the animals were of the same form). Then he saw the Surūpa ("Wellformed") sāmans and gave them their forms (JB III.223).

The Bṛhat and Rathantara-sāmans are distinctly connected with cattle. Thus cattle came into existence, according to JB I. 294, 297, immediately after these sāmans. Sometimes cattle are divided into two groups. Some are called Bārhatas (belonging to the Bṛhat-sāman) and some Rāthantaras (belonging to the Rathantara-sāman (JB II.84).

Some sāmans are helpful in preserving the cattle. Prajāpati created cattle. They went away from him. He desired, "May they not go away from me; may they return to me". Then he saw the Śyeta sāman and praised with it. He used the word *vasu* as it finalc. Now, "Cattle are *vasu* (wealth)". Therefore, the cattle returned to him. "The cattle return to him and do not go away from him who knows this" (JB I.148; cp. TMB VII. 10.16). The same story is told in connection with Sabha-sāman (JB I.160); Jyāyasa-sāman (JB III.218); and Rayiṣṭha-sāman (JB III.230). In JB III.91; Prajāpati, in the same condition desired,

"May I hold fast (*yam-*) the cattle in myself". Then he saw the Yaṇvasantani-sāman and got his desire fulfilled. Here, the word *Yaṇva* is mystically connected with the root *yam*. The Udgātṛpriest is identical with Prajāpati and therefore he also holds fast the cattle by means of this sāman. Prajāpati, according to JB III.213, created cattle and on their not willing to acknowledge him, the cattle went away. Then he desired, "May the cattle return. May they acknowledge me". Then he saw the Saṁjñāna-sāman and got his desire fulfilled. Similarly, according to TMB XV.5.34, Prajāpati created cattle but they went away. Then he called after them with the words *śrudhiyā ehiyā*. Then they returned. In order to make cattle return, this sāman is to be used (TMB XV.5.34).

The sāmans which have the word *iḷā* as their finale (*nidhana*) are specially considered to be helpful for obtaining cattle. Vajra Āṅgirasa was desirous of cattle. He practised penance and saw the Vajra-sāman. He praised with it and made *iḷā* its finale. "Cattle are identical with *iḷā*". Then he obtained cattle (JB III.15). Similarly, Purumudga Āṅgirasa was desirous of cattle. He practised penance and saw the Paurumudga-sāman. He praised with it and made *iḷā* its finale. Then he obtained cattle (JB III.43). Similar stories are told in connection with the Aṣṭādaṁṣṭra (JB I.191); Gauloma (JB III.163); Pauruhanmana (JB III.215); Surūpa (JB III.233); Sādhya (JB III.72) etc. sāmans.

By means of many other sāmans, having *iḷā* as the the finale one becomes "established in cattle". See e.g. Kāleya (JB I. 155); Nārmedha (JB I.191); Āṣṭādaṁṣṭra (JB III.34); Raurava (JB III.50); Sauparṇa (JB III.183); Vaiyaśva (JB III.221); Dharma (JB III.231); Vaiśvāmitra (JB III.239) etc.

The Soma-sāman is with one and half *iḷā* (*adhyar dheḍam*) as its finale. Thus it ends with it *iḍā*[2] and it also helps to get cattle (JB III.191). Ariṣṭa-sāman is to be sung with three iḷās as its finale. And since *iḷā* is identical with cattle, one obtains cattle thereby (JB III.35).

The Hārivarṇa-sāman has four-syllabled finale. Cattle have four feet. Therefore, this sāman is to be sung for the sake of obtaining cattle (JB III.55). The same is the case of Iṣovṛdhīya-sāman which also has a four-syllabled finale (JB III.148). Goṣūkta and Aśvasūkta-sāmans have five-syllabled finale. The cattle belong to Paṅkti (five-feet-metre). Therefore this sāman is to be used for obtaining cattle (JB III.252). Plava-sāman has twelve-syllabled finale. The Jagatī-metre has twelve syllables. Jagatī is identical with cattle. Therefore one gets cattle by means of that sāman (JB III.195).

The Śyeta-sāman has the word *vasu* (wealth) as its finale. The cattle are *vasu* (wealth). Therefore, one who uses this sāman, establishes himself in cattle (TMB VII.10.15; cp. JB I. 148). In connection with the Aidāvasunidhana-sāman following story is told. A seer named Asu, was without cattle. He desired to obtain cattle. He saw the Aidāvasunidhana-sāman. He made the words *idaṁ vasuḥ* (this wealth), the finale of that sāman. Therefore the sāman got its name. Now cattle are wealth (*vasu*) and therefore he obtained cattle thereby (JB III. 265). Babhru Kumbhya desired to produce himself along with cattle. Then he saw the Bābhravya-sāman and praised with it. He made the word *gvābhiḥ* (along with the cattle) its finale and then he produced himself along with cattle (JB III.250).

In the Govikarta chandoma-pavamāna-sacrifice, the stomas containing both the even and odd number of verses, are to be used. By means of the odd-number-versed stomas, one obtains village-animals and by means of the even-number-versed stomas, one gets forest-animals (JB II.275). JB III.304, however, considers the even-number-versed stoma as *"apaśavaya"* i.e. not capable of giving cattle and therefore an odd number versed stoma should be used. It prescribes the nine-versed stoma on the tenth day of the Daśarātra of the Dvādaśāha-sacrifice. Thereby one gets cattle and progeny. Jamadagni wanted to have cattle as well as progeny. He saw the seventeen-versed stoma and by using it, got his desire fulfilled thereby (JB II.218). In the Pakṣī-sacrifice, two seventeen-versed stomas are used. The seventeen-versed stoma is identical with cattle; one thereby wins cattle (TMB XIX.10.7 cp. the use of this stoma in Manustoma-sacrifice TMB XIX.14.6). The use of twenty-one-versed stoma in the Aptoryāma-sacrifice is also helpful for obtaining cattle (TMB XX.3.2).

Metres are sometimes identified with cattle (e.g. TS V. 3.8.1). In the Apaciti-sacrifice, both the biggest and smallest metres are used. Since the metres are identical with cattle, one gets thereby the biggest and smallest cattle (JB II.103). In the twenty-five-day-sacrifice, the metres in which each following metre is bigger by *four* syllables than the preceding one, are used. The cattle have four feet. Therefore this serves to obtain cattle. Some individual metres are specially mentioned to be useful for getting cattle. Thus according to some, the Prauga-śastra in the Mahāvrata-ceremony should be in the Jagatī-metre. "For the cattle belong to the Jagatī-metre; one thereby becomes possessor of cattle". (AĀ I.1.3). At the time of Fire-altar-building-ceremony, metres are also laid down as "bricks". Among these bricks, Jagatī-bricks are laid down for the sake of obtaining cattle. For the cattle belong to Jagatī (TS V.3.8.2). At the time of Sviṣṭakṛt-offering of the Dīkṣaṇīyeṣṭi which is a part of the Agniṣṭoma-sacrifice, one who wants cattle, should use Jagatī-verses as invitatory and offering verses (AB I.5). JB II.273 connects the minor (*kṣudra*) animals with Jagatī.

Gāyatrī-metre is also connected with the obtainment of cattle. Thus according to some ritualists, the Eight-day-sacrifice should be performed by one who wants to obtain cattle. "For Gāyatrī has eight syllables. Cattle have eight hooves; cattle are identical with Gāyatrī; and this sacrifice amounts to Gāyatrī" (JB II.311).

The cattle are sometimes described as "belonging to the Bṛhatī-metre" (*bārhatāḥ paśavaḥ* e.g. AB IV.3). Thus the first Vighana-sacrifice, amounts to *Bṛhatī*. For in all there are 216 verses. This number can be divided by 36 (Bṛhatī has 36 syllables). Therefore this sacrifice should be performed by one who is desirous of cattle (TMB XIX.18.4; cp. XIX.19.3).

TS VI.1.8.1 identifies the Śakvarī-metre with cattle (cp. also TMB XIII.5.18. etc.).

The recitation of verses can be useful for obtaining cattle. The verses containing the word *go* (cow) are specifically important for obtaining cattle. Thus the verses beginning with *ṛtasya dhītim* .... are to be recited on the third day of the Daśarātra of the Dvādaśāha-sacrifice. They contain the word *go* (cow). This recitation is therefore useful for obtaining cattle (JB III.46; cp. for similar verses used for obtaining cattle JB III.48; 51; 97; 119; 136; 149; 162 etc.). The verses containing the word *citra* (bright) are also helpful for obtaining cattle. "For cattle are of bright appearance (*citrarūpāḥ* JB III.101). JB I.323 identifies cattle with ṛc (verse).

Similarly recitation of various hymns (*sūkta*) is useful for obtaining cattle. Anurūpa-hymn is that which is chanted at the beginning of a śastra. Now this hymn is, according to JB III. 206, identical with cattle. On the 8th day of the Daśarātra in the Dvādaśāha-sacrifice, an Anurūpa-hymn of five verses is to be sung. "Paṅkti-metre is with five feet. Cattle belong to Paṅkti. These chandoma-days are identical with cattle". Therefore the recitation of such a hymn is helpful for obtaining cattle (JB III.206). On the tenth day of the same rite the hymn beginning with *eṣa devo amartyaḥ* is to be recited as an Anurūpa-hymn. Because this hymn is identical with cattle, this helps to obtain cattle (JB III.241).

Many other miscellaneous elements of Vedic music are prescribed for obtainment of cattle. The gods Agni and Soma, are requested to give nourishment (*poṣa-*) of the cattle unto him who worships them by means of a song (speech : *vacas*) (ṚV I.93.2). Similarly Paryāsa, i.e. the final piece of some śastras is to be sung for the sake of supporting the offsprings and cattle (e.g. JB III.21; 34; 61; 86; 176; 206). Likewise, the Ājyastotras (TMB VII.2.6, XIX.2.6; 5.4; JB II.273); Vaiśvadeva-śastra (KB XVI.3); Ukthas (JB I.201; II.84; 296; 300; 377; 387; TMB VII.8.8); Viṣṭutis (method of repetition of chant in a stotra) (TMB II.2.3; III.4.3; 8.2); hiṁkāra (JB III.213; JUB III.3.3.2), Pṛṣṭhas (JB II.84; 274; TMB XXV.1.5; 2.3) etc. are connected with obtainment of cattle.

Thus we find that many elements of the vedic music are said to be identical with cattle and are prescribed to be used by one who wants to obtain cattle.

REFERENCES

1. For the close connections between the animals in general with music see Seeman, in *Handwörterbuch der deutschen Aberglaubens,* VI. 682; see also Meyer, *Trilogie,* II. 178.
2. Rf. Caland, *JB in Auswahl,* p. 243, n. 23.

(D) MUSIC AND MEDICINE

Peoples of different parts of the world suppose that music has a medicinal power in it. Many times it is used in various magical rites for curing a diseased person.[1] A malady is considered to be caused by some evil spirits.[2] Now music has apotropaeic capacities. It can remove the evil spirits and thereby cure maladies.[3] Thus among the Chinese people in olden times, dances and songs used to be executed by a troop of performers masked as animals and led by a wizard. This performance used to take place for driving away disease.[4] Similarly in Congo, in curing-ceremonies, in order to remove the bad spirit, chants are sung and dances are performed before the hut of the patient.[5] In Greek mythology Asklepios is said to have cured his patients by means of chants.[6] So also in ancient Greece music was practised as an ingredient of magical medicine.[7] The initiation festivals of the Phrygian deities used to be performed sometimes for curing and the means employed in them, principally, used to be dance and music.[8] Hebrews also ascribed curing power to music. Thus Saul (I. *Sam.* 16.14-19; 23) and Elisa (2 *Kings* 3.15) are told to be cured with the help of music.[9] In the Islamic ideology also medicinal properties of music were recognised.[10] In the mediaeval period, Theophrast derived the conception of music as a means of cure from the ancient Ethos Theory.[11] Producing non-sensical sounds[12] or drone-sounds[13] as well as playing upon instruments[14] is practised in curing ceremonies. In the Veda also there are numerous examples illustrating the close connections of music and medicine.

AV XI.8.4 the sāmans are described as "remedies *(bheṣaja-)*" and they are praised: "We praise the sacrifices, the sacrificer, ṛc-verses, and sāmans which are remedies". Thus it is implied here that sāmans have some medicinal properties. Similarly many individual sāmans are described to be possessing the power of disease-removal. Thus for example TMB VIII.6.12, the Bṛhat and Rathantara sāmans are said to be identical with the out-breathing and inbreathing. So they are to be sung for the sacrificer who is suffering from a lingering disease. "For gone forth, verily, are the out-breathing and in-breathing of him, who suffers from a lingering disease". The out-breathing and in-breathing are then put into the sacrificer when these sāmans are sung. The Traiśoka-sāman is to be sung as a sāman of Brahman, also for the sacrificer who is suffering from a lingering disease (TMB VIII.1.8). About this sāman the following story is told: "These worlds (earth, intermediate region, and sky) were once joined; they languished. Indra, by means of this sāman removed their langour .... " (TMB VII.1.9 cp. JB III.72). Then it is remarked, "Hurt by langour, verily, is he who suffers from a lingering disease. In that the Brahman's sāman is the Traiśoka, he removes from him the langour". By means of the Sauśravasa-sāman, Suśravas joined the head of his son which was cut down by Indra (TMB XIV.6.8; cp. JB III.198 ff). The Ādityas gave the yonder sun, in the form of a white horse as a sacrificial fee to a seer named Ayāsya. As soon as he had accepted it, it went amiss.[15] By means of the Āyāsya-sāman, Ayāsya strengthened himself. Therefore, the Āyāsya-sāman is to be used for healing and appeasing the evil influence (TMB XVI.12.4f).

Even gods take the help of music in curing themselves. Thus Prajāpati's eye swelled and fell. Then he desired to have the eye-sight back. He then saw the sāman which came to be known as Śaiśava and praised with it. Then he got the eye-sight back. This sāman is called *cakṣuṣya* (helpful for eyes). "One who knows thus does not lose one's eye-sight upto old age". (JB III.102). Similarly, Indra got his power of hearing by means of the Kārṇaśravasa-sāman. Thus, "Indra, having hurled thunderbolt at Vṛtra, and suspecting that he had not killed him (Vṛtra) remained confounded. His ears joined together. He could not listen thereby. He desired, "May I not be a deaf; may I listen with my ears". Then he saw this sāman. He praised with it. Then he became a non-deaf; he could then listen with ears. He said, "Indeed, I listened with my ears". Therefore, the Kārṇaśravasa is so called. He becomes a non-deaf, listens with his ears, who knows thus" (JB III.163). At another time Indra has some eye-disease and it was cured by means of the Tvāṣṭrī-sāman. Thus "When Indra was suffering from a disease of eye, the other beings could not cause him to sleep; (but) the daughters of Tvaṣṭṛ brought sleep to him by means of this (i.e. Tvāṣṭrī) sāman ..." (TMB XII.5.19). The Atharvan-mantras in general are described as a "remedy of gods (*bheṣajaṁ vai devānāṁ atharvāṇaḥ*)". And the Ātharvaṇa-sāman in the Anuṣṭubh-metre-verses is useful as a remedy to cure diseases (TMB XVI.10.9f; cf. XII.9.10). Thus the gods also make use of the magical power of music in curing themselves. For the sake of curing their devotees also the gods take the help of music. See for example the story of Ākūpāra- sāman. "There was (once) a female Aṅgiras named Ākūpārā. As the skin of a lizard, so was her skin. Indra, having thrice cleaned her by means of this sāman made her sun-skinned" (TMB IX. 2.14)[16]. Similarly, "Cyavana, the son of Dadhyañc, was beloved of Aśvins. As he became of old age, they by means of this (viz. Vīṅka-) sāman, shook (*vyaṅkayatam*) him in the water and made him young again" (TMB XIV.6.10). Thus gods take the help of the magical power music in curing themselves or their devotees.

On the other hand we also find that sometimes man pleases gods with music, and then the gods by their *own* power cure the devotee. Thus Kāśīti Saubhara, when he was practising a sacrificial session, became ill. He desired to "kill away" the illness. Then he saw a sāman which came to be known as Kāśīta and praised the deity of wind with it. The wind cured him (JB III.266). Here we find that one uses music as a means to please a god and then that god, being pleased favours his devotee by granting him the desired result.

Some opening tristiches (*pratipad-*) are connected with curing. Thus the tristich beginning with *ā no mitrāvaruṇā* (SV II.13-15; ṚV III.62. 16-18) should be used as opening one for him who is suffering from a lingering disease. "Gone away are the out and in-breathing of him who suffers from a lingering disease. Mitra and Varuṇa are the out and in-breathing. Out and in-breathing are thus put in to him" (TMB VI.10.5 f). According to JB I.96, for a person suffering from a lingering disease a Tristich belonging to Agni and Varuṇa is to be used. "Seized by Agni and Varuṇa is he who is suffering from a lingering disease". When a tristich belonging to Agni and Varuṇa is used, one becomes free from Agni and Varuṇa" (JB I.96). Elsewhere it is said that for a person who is ill, the Tristich beginning with *agna āyūṁṣi pavase* (SV II.868-870; ṚV IX.66.19-21), is to be used as the opening tristich. For when one is ill, one's body goes to Agni and breathing to Vāyu. When this *pratipad* is recited, one's body unites itself with breath because of Agni, the purifier (JB I.92; cp. TMB VI. 10.1ff). There is an opening tristich (*pratipad-*) for curing animals,[17] and herbs also. Thus the tristich beginning with *sa naḥ pavasva* (SV II.2; 3;1; ṚV IX.11.3;2;1) should be used as the opening one in a year in which the great God (i.e. Rudra) slays cattle. By the words *sa naḥ pavasva śaṁ gave* (be thou purified for the weal of our cow) one purifies one's quadrepeds; by the words *śaṁ janāya* (for the weal of our people) one heals the bipeds; and by the words *śam arvate* (for the weal of our runner) one heals one's one-hoofed animals. In the year in which the Great God slays cattle, the herbs are also smeared with poison as it were. By saying *yacchaṁ rājannoṣadhībhyaḥ* (for the weal of, O King, our herbs), one makes the herbs which ripen uncultivated and those that ripen cultivated palatable for oneself (TMB VI.9.6 ff).

The recitation of some hymns is regarded as cure for diseases. Thus AV I.23.4, the priestly medicine-man speaks, "By means of a powerful hymn (*brahman-*) I have made the white mark disappear". This hymn is to be used for removing leprosy. Similarly, AV. II.10.1 the priestly medicine-man speaks, "From Kṣetrīya (disease), from Perdition (*nirṛti-*), from hatred (*druh-*) do I release thee; from Varuṇa's fetter. Free from guilt I make thee by means of a powerful hymn (*brahman-*); may Heaven and Earth be propicious to thee".

Here it is noteworthy that although the priestly medicine-man is confident of his magic formula, nevertheless he requests the deities viz. Heaven and Earth for propitiation. This propitiation-formula is the refrain of the entire AV II.10. Similarly ṚV X.97 is a charm against disease, addressed to medicinal herbs. There also the priestly medicine-man prays to the Herbs (which are the deities of the formula), "Make Favour (*prāvata*) (O Herbs) unto my this speech" (ṚV X.97.14). ṚV II.33.12, Rudra is requested, "Being praised by us give medicines unto us". Thus sometimes the recitation alone is considered to be powerful to cure the diseases and sometimes gods are pleased with the help of recitations so that they may remove the diseases. Thus music works magicoreligiously.

Some other miscellaneous elements of the Vedic music also are said to be powerful enough to cure diseases. Thus at the time of singing the Traiśoka-sāman, which is meant for curing a person suffering from a lingering disease, one utters the word *divā* (by day). "*Divā*, verily is the dawning, he makes it dawn upon him (the sacrificer)" (TMB VIII.1.13). This means that the diseased person becomes cured and sees the next day. The Sarvasvāra-sacrifice which has throughout the *svāra* kind of finale (i.e. of the musical notation 5, 6, 5) is said to be useful for curing. Thus one who wishes, "May I go to the yonder world without having any disease" should perform a nine-versed Agniṣṭoma which is of Sarvasvāra type (TMB XVII. 12.1). The metre named Gāyatrī is also helpful for curing. Thus the Āyus (life) - sacrifice performed as an overnight-rite is prescribed for one who is suffering from a lingering disease. For this rite amounts to Gāyatrī in the following way. This rite amounts to Gāyatrī in the following way. In this rite, in all 448 verses are sung. A Gāyatrī-verse has twenty-four syllables. If we divide 448 by twenty-four, the result is 28 Gāyatrīs and two feet of Gāyatrī. Thus the rite amounts to the Gāyatrī-metre. Now the Gāyatrī-metre is identical with "breath" and this rite is "life". Thus one brings into the sacrificer life and breath both together (TMB XVI.3.5f). Similarly Virāj metre is also connected with curing. Thus the second Sādyaskra-sacrifice is prescribed for one suffering from a lingering disease. For this rite amounts to Virāj, because it has in all 120 verses and this number is divisible by ten, the number of syllables in the Virāj-metre. Now, "food goes away from him who is suffering from a lingering disease and Virāj is food". Therefore, by performing this sacrifice, one puts food in the body of the diseased sacrificer and then the sacrificer becomes cured (TMB XVI. 13.3). Mere repetition of the sacred names of the Lord Viṣṇu e.g. Acyuta, Ananta, Govinda etc. is described to be a medicine by itself. It destroys all the diseases according to Viṣṇudharmottarapurāṇa I.196.32 *(acyutānantagovindanāmoccāraṇabheṣhajat/ naśyanti sakalā rogāḥ satyaṁ satyaṁ vadāmyaham //)*. Here also magic and religion are mixed together.

It can be thus concluded that in the Vedic literature music is closely associated with curing. Sometimes music alone is said to be powerful to cure. But sometimes it is the gods who being pleased with music are said to be curing the diseased. Thus the attitude of vedic literature is magicoreligious.

REFERENCES

1. For the Magical power of music in curing diseases see in general - Hastings, *ERE*, IX, 16 (a); Gunkel, Zscharnack, *RGG*, IV. 216; Seeman, in *Handwörterbuch der deutschen Aberglaubens* VI. 683 ff; Belvianes, *sociologie de la musique*, p. 134 ff; Schneider, in Wellesz, *AOM*, p. 40; W.K.L. Guthrie, *Orpheus and Greek Religion*, London, 1952 (reprint) p. 68, n. 25.
2. See my "Cāturmāsya-sacrifices researched" *JUPHS*, 31, 1969, p. 60.
3. Belvianes, *Sociologie de la musique*, p. 135.
4. Rf. Pickon in Wellesz, *AOM*, p. 104; For music & medicine in China see also Courant in Lavignac, *EnM*, I. p. 185.
5. Combarieu, *La musique et la magie*, p. 77; cp. Belvianes, *Sociologie de la musique*, p. 135.

6. Belvianes, *Sociologie de la music,* p. 136; Similarly Thaletas cured Sparte, with the help of musique - Combarieu, *La musique et la magie,* p. 82.
7. I. Henderson in Wellesz, *AOM,* p. 376; cf; p. 401f; cp. also Combarieu, *La musique et la magie,* p. 81.
8. Cf. Rhode, *Psyche,* p. 286.
9. Saalschutz, *Musik bei der Hebraern,* p. 16.
10. Farmer, in Wellesz, *AOM,* p. 434.
11. Abert, *Musikanschanung,* p. 162.
12. Schneider, in Wellesz, *AOM,* p. 3.
13. V. Belaiev, "The Folk-music of Georgia", *The Musical quarterly,* XIX, 1933, p. 423.
14. *Belvianes, Sociologie de la musique,* p. 135.
15. To accept a horse is dangerous see Caland, *Die Wunschopfern,* no. 24; 166.
16. Cf. for Parallels to this legend, Oertel, *JAOS,* XVIII, p. 26 ff.
17. For music curing the animals see Combarieu *La musique et la magie,* p. 109.

(E) MUSIC AND LONG LIFE

Many musical elements are said to be useful in obtaining long life. Thus on the fourth day of Daśarātra of the Dvādaśāha-sacrifice the Ātiṣādītya-sāman is prescribed to be sung. This sāman is identical with life; therefore, it is to be sung for obtainment of life (TMB XII.11.16). The singers should utter its finale until their breath fails. Thereby they get long life (TMB XII.11.17; JB III.79). Similarly on the sixth day of the same sacrifice, Bharadvājasya loma-sāman is to be sung. For the sake of obtainment of long life. For this sāman is called "long"; and "life is also long". Therefore, this sāman is useful in obtaining long life (TMB XIII.11.13). In the Agniṣṭoma-sacrifice the Paurumīḍha-sāman is to be sung if the sacrificer is desirous to get a long life (JB I.151). In the chanting of the Yajñāyajñīya-sāman, one chants the following words in which the word *āyu* (life) occurs: *ūrjo napātaṁ sa hyāyumā.* Here if the Udgātṛ were to utter *nāyumā* (not possessing life), instead of *hyāumā* (possessing life), the sacrificer would lose his life. Now when he utters *hyāyumā,* he puts life in himself as well as in the sacrificer (JB I.177). On the Mahāvrata-day, the Prauga-śastra should be, according to some ritualists, in the Uṣṇih-metre. "For life is identical with the Uṣṇih-metre; the sacrificer then possesses long life" (AĀ I.1.3).

(F) MUSIC AND GENERATION

Music has both creative and destructive powers. In the Vedic texts we find both kinds of powers ascribed to music. Its creative[1] power is expressed by the Vedic texts by describing it to be helpful for getting progeny. Now we shall see how musicians and music are significant for generation.

The musicians are specifically supposed to be possessing the generating powers. Thus the heavenly musicians viz. Gandharvas and Apsarases are told to be the controllers of human fertility or sterility (*gandharvāpsaraso vai manuṣyaṣya prājāyā vā veśate*) and therefore, the Aupaśada-sacrifice is to be performed by one who desires to get progeny (TMB XIX.3.2). In the epics and Purāṇas, Gandharvas and Apsarases are often described as singing and dancing after the birth of a great hero. Thus when Bharata was born, the drums of gods resounded. Apsarases danced (Mbh. I.624*.1ff). When Arjuna was born the Gandharvas sang and the Apsarases danced (Mbh. I.114.43ff). Similarly they sang and danced when Devakī conceived Kṛṣṇa (Viṣṇupurāṇa V.3.5).[2] Plato informs us that wise women used to relieve the pains of child-birth by singing magic chants.[3] Udgātṛ, who is the chief of the Sāmaveda-priests has a distinct bearing on the generation. Thus he has been very often identified with Prajāpati—the lord of offsprings. ŚB IV.3.2.3, he is said to be Prajāpati while the Hotṛpriest is described to be a female. The reason why the Hotṛ is described as female is that he recites ṛcs. The word *ṛc* (fem.) is a woman and therefore the Hotṛ being mystically identical with ṛc is a female. "When the Udgātṛ chants, then he, who is nothing but Prajāpati implants seed in the female Hotṛ, the ṛc". Afterwards, in the same sacrifice he exchanges looks with the wife of the sacrificer; for he is Prajāpati (the Lord of off-spring) and the wife is woman. That forms a productive pair (ŚB IV.4.3.1; cp. TS VI.5.8.6; KS XXVI.1; TMB VIII.7.12f).[4] The sāman (melody) is considered to be seven-fold, and by means of it, the Udgātṛ it is said, generates the sacrificer as well as himself for seven times out of his own body (JUB III.6.6.4). When he sings the Bahiṣpavamāna-laud, he pours the sacrificer in the form of seed (JB I.253). JB I.259, he is identified with Prajāpati. The text describes the importance of singing both the *ṛc* and the sāman. The Udgātṛ pours seed as Prajāpati. When he recites the Retasyā-verse, he pours himself in the form of seed. If he were to recite the verse without sāman, then there would be only bones and no flesh at all in a man. If sāman alone were to be sung then there would be flesh alone and no bones at all. As he recites the verse equipped with sāman, therefore a man is born covered by hair, skin, and flesh (JB I.259; cp. ṢaḍB II.1.1). In a sacrificial session of one year, Udgātṛ, generates the sacrificers and gives them to the Hotṛ-priest (JB II.24). According to JB III.8, he, like Prajāpati, creates the beings by means of ten days (in the Dvādaśāha-sacrifice). He sings the Virāj-sāman with "repeated push (*anutunnam*)" for the sake of generation: for from the repeated push, seed is implanted (TMB XII.10.11; JB III.70). On the *right* thigh of the Udgātṛ, fire is produced through the process of churning with wooden Araṇis. For, from the right side, the seed is discharged (TMB XII.10.12; JB III.70). Not only the Udgātṛ, but the other priests belonging to the Sāmaveda, are also connected with generation. Thus when the Prastotṛ, Udgātṛ and Pratihartṛ recite their portions mentally, they pour seed as it were. And when the Hotṛ recites the Caturhotṛ-formulas, he generates the seed which has been implanted (KS IX.15). ṚV II.9.5, Agni is requested, "make the singer a lord of wealth accompanied by good progeny". Thus sometimes the singers themselves have generative powers and sometimes they require the grace of gods for the sake of generation. Thus we know the magicoreligious significance of music.

Many sāmans are said to be identical with generation. Thus JB III.48 identifies Vairūpa-sāman with generation (*prajanana-*). Moreover, it helps to procreate heroic progeny. Bharadvāja obtained many sons and cattle by means of the Pṛśni-sāmaṇ. This sāman has also been identified with generation (JB III.75). The Apsarases named Svāśir were nothing but herbs. They desired to become many, to procreate. They saw the sāman which came to be known as Svāśirām arkaḥ. They sang with it and became many. This sāman also has been identified with generation (JB III.226). ŚB V.1.3.12, identifies the Vāmadevya-sāman and TMB VII.7.16 identifies the Rathantara-sāman with generation. Cyāvana-sāman is identical with procreation (*prajāti-*) and one who praises with it procreates (TMB XIII.5.12; cp. XIX.3.6f). Similar is the case of the Aiṣira-sāman (TMB XIV.11.21). The Vasiṣṭhasya janitre-sāmans are also described to be identical with generation because they are helpful to obtain progeny. Thus when Vasiṣṭha's sons were killed, he saw these sāmans and praised with them. Then he obtained progeny and cattle. Therefore these sāmans help in generation (JB I.150; cp. JB III.28; 83; TMB VIII.2.3; XIX.3.8).[5]

Many times creation of all the beings is ascribed to the generation-power of sāmans. Thus while proving that by praising with the Āśva-sāmans one gets progeny, JB III.14 says that Prajāpati having become a horse (*aśva*) created the beings with the help of Āśva-sāman and therefore it is identical with generation (cp. TMB XI.3.5). The beings created by Prajāpati were not able to give birth to progeny. Then Prajāpati saw the Sākamaśva-sāman. Having himself become a horse he sniffed at them. Then the beings could procreate themselves. "This sāman is indeed identical with generation" (TMB XX. 4.5f). Elsewhere we read about the Āmahīyava-sāman. "Prajāpati desired, "May I be more than many; may I generate". Then he was in somewhat languishing and unhappy (*āmahīyamānaḥ*) state of mind. He saw this Āmahīya-sāman and created these beings by means of it. The beings when born became happy (*amahīyanta*); because they were happy, therefore, it (the sāman) is the Āmahīyava" (TMB VII.5.1). According to TS VII.5.9.1 Prajāpati created beings by means of the Arkya-sāman and when this sāman is sung in a sacrificial session the performers generate offspring. On another occasion, Prajāpati desired to be without any lacuna (*acchidra*) in connection with the progeny and cattle. Then he saw the sāman which came to be known as Acchidra (without any lacuna) and praised with it. Then his desire was fulfilled (JB III.218). Similarly at another time Prajāpati desired to be complete (*samanta*) by means of progeny and cattle. Then he saw the Samanta-sāman and praised with it. Thereby his desire was fulfilled (JB I.186). JB III.98 ascribes the creation of human beings along with that of cattle to the Mānava-sāman. Thus Manu desired to be many by means of progeny and cattle; to create human progeny (*mānavīḥ prajāḥ*). Then he saw the sāman which afterwards came to be known as Mānava-sāman praised with it and got his desire fulfilled (cp. TMB XIII.3.15).

Like Prajāpati, some other mythological persons also obtained progeny by means of some sāmans. Thus Kakṣīvān Auśija obtained progeny and became many by means of the Kākṣīvat-sāman. One gets progeny, becomes many by praising with it (TMB XIV.11.17). Similarly, Udala Vaiśvāmitra got progeny and became many by praising with Audala-sāman (TMB XIV.11.34) and Kuḍmalabarhis obtained progeny by praising with the Kauḍmalabārhiṣa-sāman (TMB XV.3.21).

Sometimes the act of singing of the sāman is described as an act of "pouring seed" or as an act of generation. Thus the Abhīvarta-sāman is described as bull (*vṛṣā*) capable of pouring (seed) and as seed-placer. When one sings it, one places seed continuously into the pragātha-verses (TMB IV.3.8). The Gaurivīti-sāman is also described in a similar way - "This sāman is indeed, a bull (*vṛṣā*) and is powerful one; the bull is the seed-placer .... It is sung on the Anuṣṭubh-metre-verses. For the Anuṣṭubh is the womb of the metres; he thereby places the seed into his own womb, for the sake of generation" (TMB XI. 5.16f). On the ninth day of the Daśarātra of the Dvādaśāha-sacrifice, Kāśīta-sāman with hitherward directed *iḍā*[6] is to be sung. By means of the iḍās that are directed thither-wards one continually places the seed into the womb; but this Kāśīta-sāman with the iḍā hitherward directed, is applied for the sake of generation (for delivery of the young) (TMB XV.5.16). JB I.305, the whole process of generation is described as involved in the singing of various sāmans. Thus when the Rathantara-sāman is sung, the seed is poured. When the Vāmadevya-svāra-sāman is sung, the vital breath (*prāṇa*) is put in that seed; for *svara* is identical with vital breath. Further when Naudhasa-nidhana-sāman is sung that is the delivery and birth. Then, when Kāleya-aiḍa-sāman is sung, food is given to those beings that are born; for *iḍā* is identical with food and cattle (JB I. 305). Similarly another process of generation is as follows - When the Yajñāyajñīya-sāman is sung, the seed is poured; when the Sākamaśva-sāman is sung vital breath (*prāṇa*) is put in the seed; for the *svara* is vital breath. When the Saubhara-sāman is sung, delivery happens and when Nārmedha aiḍa-sāman is sung food is given to them who are born; for *iḷā* is food and cattle (JB I.306).

Some sāmans are to be sung with "repeated push (*anutunnam*)". This activity implies the repeated push of the penis in the vagina. Therefore this manner of singing is considered to be generative. Thus for example, in the Vairāja sāman repetition is made in the following manner - *mā-datu tvā-dtu-tva* while the basic text is *mandantu tvā* (SV I.398). This repeated push is made for the sake of impregnation. For, from the repeated push, the seed is implanted (TMB VIII.9.13. cp. XII.10.11; JB III.70). Similarly the Vātspra (JB III.81) and Ānūpa-sāman (JB III.97) are sung with repeated push; for from the repeated push progeny and cattle are born.

The Bṛhat and Rathantara-sāmans are described as a divine generative pair (*daivyam mithunaṁ prajananam*). Thus in the Virāj and Svarāj-sacrifices both the Bṛhat and the Rathantara sāmans are sung for the sake of generation. They are a divine generative pair (JB II.95). This pair is also used in the Manustoma-sacrifice (JB II.108), Citistoma-sacrifice (JB II.162), and in the Catūrātra-sacrifice (JB II.281) with the same intention. JB I.297 it is said that the Bṛhat and the Rathantara place embryos in the beings at the middle part (*bṛhadrathantare vai madhyataḥ prajāsu garbhaṁ dhattaḥ*).

The stomas are supposed to be generative. Thus it is said, "Prajāpati created the beings by means of the Trivṛt-stoma" (MS III.6.7; KS XXIII.4; KPKS XXXVI.1) The Apūrva-sacrifice is to be performed by one who wants to get progeny. In this sacrifice the Trivṛt-stoma is used. For the Trivṛt is "lacking (*nyūna*)"; Whatever is lacking, is generative". Here the expression "lacking" implies the female generation-organ. The Trivṛt-stoma consists of nine verses and one verse is "lacking" in it for being decimal (*virāj*). Therefore, the Trivṛt-stoma is generative (JB II.174; for the same in connection with the Vaiśvadeva-sacrifice see JB II.146). Vasiṣṭha desired that his progeny should be leading and topmost. Then he saw this Trivṛt-stoma. Now the Trivṛt-stoma is the leading and topmost of all the stomas. And by using it Vasiṣṭha got the desired progeny (JB II.217). In the Virāṭ-svarājau-sacrifices Trivṛt and Pañcadaśa-stomas are used. These are "lacking" and "exceeding" stomas respectively. Similarly the Saptadaśa (seventeen-versed) and Ekaviṁsa (twentyone-versed) stomas which also are "lacking" and "exceeding" respectively are used in those sacrifices. Now from the "lacking" (i.e. female organ) and "exceeding" (i.e. male organ) beings are born. Thus these are generative, productive "pairs" (JB II.95). The Triṇava-stoma consisting of twenty seven verses, is also considered as generative because it is regarded to be a trippled Trivṛta-stoma and because Trivṛt-stoma is generative, the Triṇava-stoma is also generative. Taking into consideration this way of thinking, some ritualists prescribe this stoma to be used in the Vaiśvadeva-sacrifice for the sake of generation (JB II.147). Atri desired to obtain many sons who would be "seers". He then saw this Triṇava-stoma and having used it got his desire fulfilled (JB II.279).

The Goṣṭoma and Āyuṣṭoma are supposed to be "exceeding" and "lacking" respectively. Thus the Goṣṭoma contains 241 verses. Here is a plus of one verse above the decimal number (*virāj*). The Āyuṣṭoma has 259 verses. Thus here it is a minus of one to the decimal number. Therefore, these stomas form a pair and are generative (TMB XVI.3.7). In the fourth forty-nine-day-sacrifice, there are the Goṣṭoma and Āyuṣṭoma-days. They are exceeding and lacking respectively and therefore form a productive pair. Thus they are helpful for generation (TMB XXIV.14.6). In the Gavāmayana-sacrifice (TMB

XXI.1.12) also this productive pair is used, because it helps in generation.

The stomas containing an even number of verses and the one containing an odd number of verses also form a productive pair and are generative. In the Citistoma-sacrifice both these kinds of stomas are used. They are described as a divine pair. One should use them for the sake of generation (JB II. 162). Similarly they are to be used in a four-day-sacrifice with the same intention (JB II.281). In the Aṅgirasāṁ Dvirātra-sacrifice also both kinds of stomas are used for the sake of generation (TMB XX.11.10; cp. XXI.9.5; XXII.6.5; 7.7).

The Saptadaśa (seventeen-versed) - stoma is generative because it has a mystical connection with Prajāpati who is supposed to be the seventeenth. Therefore in the Pañcaśāradīya-sacrifice, this stoma is used for the sake of getting progeny (JB II.175). Jamadagni desired to get progeny and cattle. He saw this stoma which is identical with Prajāpati. Then he obtained progeny and cattle (JB II.218). Similarly the Trayastriṁśa (thirty-three-versed) stoma is generative because it is identical with Prajāpati, the generation. Therefore it is to be used in the Vaiśvadeva-sacrifice in order to obtain progeny (JB II.147). Some other stomas are also described as being generative. Thus Agastya desired to go to the heavenly world after having produced progeny. Then he saw and sang with ṣoḍaśa (sixteen-versed) stoma and got his desire fulfilled (JB II.220). When one uses the Navadaśa (ninteen versed) stoma, in the Vighana-sacrifice, one obtains progeny (TMB XIX.18.3). Bharadvāja desired to get powerful progeny. He saw and sang with the Pañcadaśa (fifteen-versed) - stoma. Then his desire was fulfilled (JB II.217). Similarly Gautama desired to obtain progeny worthy of faith, and possessing brahman-lustre. He saw and sang with the Ekaviṁśa (twentyone-versed) - stoma. Then he got the desired kind of progeny (JB II.218). In the Marāya-sacrifice, Astācatvāriṁśa (fortyeight-versed) - stoma is used and Bṛhat-sāman is sung. The Aṣṭācatvāriṁśa-stoma is identical with the Brahman (priestly power) and the Bṛhat-sāman with the Kṣatra (royal power). One uses them with the intention, "May I produce progeny and cattle with the joint priestly and royal power". (JB II.164). For the generative nature of the Aṣṭācatvāriṁśa) - stoma see also TMB XV.6.7.

The hiṁkāra which is uttered at the beginning of a recital is supposed to be generative. Thus according to JUB I.1.4.1ff, "They utter this hiṁkāra as *him bhā* .... In that he, saying *bhā* approaches the secret parts of women, therefore, thence is born a brāhmaṇa, like a ṛṣi (seer), piercing a kingly hero" (JB I.1.4.1f). At the time of reciting the samidhenī (five-enkindling) verses, the hiṁkāra is to be uttered by the Hotṛ. Thereby the sacrificer produces offspring (TS II.5.7.1). ŚB I. 4.1.2, explains how the hiṁkāra uttered before the sāmidhenī-verses is generative. "The hiṁkāra is breath (*prāṇa* masc.), because it is indeed breath; he cannot therefore pronounce the hiṁkāra when he closes his nostrils. He recites a verse with speech (*vāc* fem.). Speech and breath are a productive pair. Thereby a productive union is formed at the outset". According to TMB VI.8.5, the hiṁkāra (masc.) is Prajāpati and the verses (ṛcs - fem.) of the out-of-doors chant are women. By holding, after the hiṁkāra has been made, the prastāva, one effectuates a copulation at the beginning of his (the sacrificer's) sacrifice, for the sake of generation. The Mahāvrata-day should begin, according to some ritualists, with the hiṁkāra. The hiṁkāra (masc.) is a bull (male) and the ṛc (fem. verse) is a female. Thus a productive pair is formed, for the sake of generation (AĀ I.3.1).

Some Pratipads (opening tristiches) help in generation. On the proceeding day (*prāyaṇīyam ahaḥ*) of the Gavāmayana-sacrifice, the tristich beginning with *pavasva vācaḥ* (SV II.125-127; ṚV IX.62. 25-27) should be made the opening tristich of the Bahiṣpavamāna-laud. TMB IV.2.18 gives the significance of this tristich as follows - "This utterance is indeed a productive pair. The word *pavasva* is a male and *vācaḥ* a female .... One thus puts a productive pair at the very beginning of the sacrifice" (cp. JB I.91). In the Agniṣṭoma-sacrifice, for the opening tristich of the Bahiṣpavamāna-laud, the verses beginning with *upoṣu jāta* ... (SV II.685-687; ṚV IX.61.13-15) should be used by one who is desirous of offspring. "The word *upa* (unto) is identical with offspring. He produces this offspring with the word *jātam* (born) (TMB VI.9.4; cp. I.90). If there are many sacrificers, the tristich beginning with *ete asṛgram* (SV II. 180-182; ṚV IX.62. 1-3) should be made the opening one. By the word *ete*, Prajāpati created the gods. By the words *asṛgram* he created men; by the word *indavaḥ* the fathers ... by the word *abhhisaubhagā* the other creatures (TMB VI.9.15; cp. JB I.94).

The first dhur-verse of the Bahiṣpavamāṇa-laud is called *retasyā*. This word means "conveying seed" and thus the retasyā-verse is closely connected with generation. When Prajāpati desired to create the beings, he sang this verse wrapped in a sāman. The Udgātṛ also has to sing it wrapped in a sāman. If mere verse is sung without a sāman, then there will be mere bone without flesh; if mere sāman is sung without verse, then there will be mere flesh without bone. Therefore both are to be sung (ṢaḍB II.1.1; cp. JB I.259). When one sings Retasyā-verse, one pours seed as it were (JB I.100; 267; 313). This verse is to be sung continuously; for the seed is continuous as it were. At the time of singing the Retasyā-verse, one should not make any hiṁkāra. For the hiṁkāra is identical with the thunderbolt, and one would in that case, divide the ejaculated seed (ṢaḍB II.1.4f; cf. JB I.101; 313). Some other verses are also said to be generative. Thus in the Aupaśada-sacrifice, which is to be performed by one who wants to get progeny, to each stotra of the normal Agniṣṭoma-sacrifice, a verse is added (literally: is engendered, is born). Then the schema is - 10, 16, 16, 16 / 16, 18, 18, 18, 18, / 18, 22. When one adds verses in this way, one causes progeny to be born to the sacrificer (TMB XIX.3.3). TMB XIX.3.9 gives further explanation - The total number of the verses (viz. 202) in this sacrifice exceeds Virāj (decimal number) by two. A women lacks two. Therefore generation can be brought about. In the Pṛtanājit sacrifice, the total number of verse is 288. Thus this number is "lacking" by two for being the number decimal. From "lacking" generation takes place. For two (limbs) are lacking there from which a woman procreates" (JB II.93). In the Viśvajit-sacrifice, at the time of out-of-doors-chant, one verse belonging to Sarasvat (ṚV VII.96.4; SV II.810) and one verse belonging to Sarasvatī (ṚV VI.61.10; SV II.811) are used. "Sarasvat and Sarasvatī are a pair. At the beginning of his sacrifice, he brings about a pairing for the sake of obtaining progeny" (TMB XVI.5.3f). In connection with the Mahānāmnī-verses, it is said, "Beings are born after the Mahānāmnī-verses are recited" (JB III.102). The Āhanasyā-verses (AV XX.136.1-10) also are connected with generation. The word *āhanasya* means the male organ. "From the *āhanasya* (seed) is poured; from seed offspring are born. Thus verily, he secures generation. Then he recites. The Virāj has ten syllables; the Virāj is food; from food is seed poured; from seed offsprings are born .... In them he inserts the sound *O*; the sound *O* is food; from food ..." (AB VI.36).

Inaudible recitation has a distinct significance from the point of view of generation. Thus in the Darśa-pūrṇamāsa-sacrifices, the Patnīsaṁyājas (offerings to the wives of gods) are offered. They are significant for generation. They are to be made with clarified butter. "The butter means seed; hence one thereby pours seed". Those offerings are to be made in an inaudible voice. "Secretly, doubtless, union takes place; and secretly is that what is inaudible" (ŚB I.9.2.7f; cp. KB III.9). An offering of ghee to Agni at the time of the third pressing of the Agniṣṭoma-sacrifice is also to be made inaudibly. "For ghee is pouring of seed; inaudibly is seed poured" (KB XVI.5). The procedure of drawing the Pātnīvata-cup is inaudible; "for Pātnīvata-cup is pouring of seed; inaudibly is seed poured" (KB XVI.6). The invitatory and offering verses, at the time of the Establishment of fires (Agnyādheya) are to be recited inaudibly. "The establishment of fires is pouring of seed; inaudibly is seed poured" (KB I.1). The Muttering of Hotṛ (hotṛjapa) is to be made inaudibly. "One thereby pours seed; for seed is poured inaudibly as it were (*upāṁśviva retasaḥ siktiḥ*" (AB II.38). Then a call is to be made and then the silent-praise (Tūṣṇīṁśaṁsa) is recited. The silent-praise is also helpful in the generation-process. When it is recited, the seed which is poured by means of Muttering of the Hotṛ, becomes "developed (*vikṛ-*)" (AB II.39).

Metres are also closely connected with generation. Thus TMB XX.11.9, Gāyatrī has been identified with generation (*prajananaṁ gāyatrī*). JB II.36 and 37 Jagatī is said to be identical with generation. In the Aupaśada-sacrifice, which is performed in order to get progeny, the verses in the Kakubh-metre are to be shifted to the forepart. "The Kakubh is indeed man. He (the man, i.e. the sacrificer) is placed (conceived) as a foetus in the middle. By applying the two-feeted verse [SV II. 717 (-719)] at the place of Kakubh, one causes the foetus that has been conceived, to be born" (TMB XIX.3.4f). The recitation in the Virāṭ and Svarāj-sacrifices amount to the Anuṣṭubh-metre. "Prajāpati, verily, is connected with Anuṣṭubh; Prajāpati is generation". "This is done so for the sake of generation" (JB II.95). The four-day-sacrifice named (Jāmadagnya) is performed with transposed metres. The metres are, in that sacrifice interwinned (*vyatiṣakta*). "From an interwinned pair, the beings, the animals, are born. This (interwinning) is done for the sake of generation". (JB II.287). The metre named Virāj is described, as accomplished, perfect and generative (*sampannam iva vā etac chandaḥ pūrṇam iva prajananam* JB II.95).

Thus we note that many elements of Vedic music are connected with generation. As in other fields, in the generation also music works magicoreligiously. Music is double-natured. It is connected with fertility as well as sterility.

REFERENCES

1. For the connection of music with the creation of all see Schneider, in Wellesz, *AOM*, p. 47f.
2. For the performance of music after the birth of Pārvatī cf. Skandapurāṇa, Māhe. Kedāra. XX.72; of Kumāra, XXVII. 89ff; of Tārakāsura Skandapu. Māhe. Kaumā. XV. 29
3. Referred to by Belvianes, *Sociologie de la musique*, p. 136.
4. Rf. Gonda, *Eye and Gaze*, p. 21.
5. Rf. Oertel, *JAOS*, XVIII. p. 47.
6. Its last words are *au' 23 ho*[4] *vā*[5,4] *ḍā*[5] whilst usually the aiḍa-sāmans end on *0*[1]*', 2345 i/ḍā* or *h o*[4]*' g*[3] *i / ḍā*, These last are called Pratīcīnceḍa (cf. Caland, *Pañcaviṁśabrāhmaṇa*, p. 404.)
7. Cf. Sāyaṇa's commentary on ṢaḍB II.1.1.

(G) MUSIC AND DEATH ETC.

Music has close connection with death, Yama (who is the God of Death), funeral ceremonies, and ancestors etc.[1] JB II 69f, a battle between Death and Prajāpati is described. They, were both sacrificing and there was a keen competition, which was nothing less than a battle. The sacrificial utensils were the weapons. The army of Prajāpati consisted of whatever was praised with the sāman, whatever was recited with the ṛcs and whatever was acted with the Yajus in the course of sacrifice. The army of Death, on the other hand, was whatever was sung, whatever was danced and whatever was done unnecessarily. Here the close association of Death and music is worth noticing. A sound can be so powerful that it may kill others. Thus AV XII.7.10, the cow of brahman (*brahmagavī*) when she makes the *hiṁ*-sound, is considered as identical with death. Goddess Pārvatī killed the demon called Vihuṇḍa by means of the sound *hum* (Padmapurāṇa II.121. 50f). A student of the Vedas was expected, according to the rules, not to be a singer or a dancer. "If he were to be a singer they will have to cleanse out weepings again and again. If he were to be a dancer, they will have to remove dead bodies again and again" (GB I.2.7). In the Vāyupurāṇa superstitious signs of the arrival of death are given. There it is said that when one finds oneself in the dream, going while singing, then one may know that one is about to die. Or if in the dream, a singing black woman wearing black garments leads a man towards southern direction then there is no hope that he will live (XIX.13f).[2] Again if in the dream a man goes to the southern direction with loose hair, laughing, singing and dancing, then his life is supposed to be over (Vāyupurāṇa XIX.25).[3]

In the old ballads of Sweden and of Scotland there is a story of skillful harp-player who prepares his instruments with the bones of a young maiden, drowned by a wicked woman. Her fingers form the pins which serve to accord the instrument and her golden hair its cords. The harpist plays and his music kills the murderer.[4] The witches among the Talalo, a hilltribe of Madagascar work at night naked except for a turban, visit graves and engage in dances which strengthen their power of causing deaths in the village[5]. In New Guinea, women may not look at certain flutes, else, they would die. The Malu music in Murray islands is so sacred that no woman or child may hear the tunes and live.[6] In Malaya some musical instruments are considered to be so sacred that none can handle or use them save one tribe of Malayas, and only at the proper time and season; Sounded at any other time or by any other person, they would cause instant death.[7] In Greek and Roman Mythology, Sirens are described as attracting the navigators by their sweet and lovely songs and thus leading them obviously to destruction of ships and death of the navigators.[8] Death itself as the result of the killing charm of music is recorded in the Arabian Nights.[9] It has the force of enchanting death.[10] Therefore music is used in some Abhicāra-rites (black-magical rites) for killing the enemy (details elsewhere).

The God of Death Yama is also closely connected with music. ṚV X.135.7, the house of this god is described. There his flute is said to be being blown. He himself is described as adorned by songs (*gir-*) (ṚV X.135.7). "Triṣṭubh, Gāyatrī (and) all (other) metres are deposited in Yama (*triṣṭubh gāyatri chandāṁsi sarvā tā yama āhitā* ṚV X.114.7). When Naciketas goes to Yama and asks for mystic knowledge, Yama tries to divert his interest and offers him various objects of enjoyment. Among them, he offers dance and vocal music to him (Kenopaniṣad I.26). ṚV X.14.4, it is hoped that the formulas (*mantra*) may bring Yama. Duḥsaha, a demon is said to be the son of Nirṛti (who represents disorder, rupture of the organic circuit)[11] and Yama, (rf. Mārkaṇḍeya-Purāṇa 47.38f). He is connected with everything that is evil, dirty etc. (in 52 he is addressed as *yakṣma*: disease). The food that is sneezed upon, upon which insect has fallen, seen by dogs, etc. belongs to this demon. In this list, the food that is accompanied by music (*nṛtyavādyasvanākulam*-46) is also mentioned. Thus it is implied that if one takes food while listening to music that will cause one's death.

A Gandharva and an Apsaras who have much connection with music are said to be the parents of Yama and Yamī (rf. ṚV X.10.4)[12]. The Gandharvas kill the foetuses[13] and newly born children (AV VIII.6.19). TS III.4.7.2f, a Gandharva is said to be identical with death.

The Buddhist Māra[14] is connected with death as well as with music. The word *māra* itself means a destroyer, killer etc. One of his manifestations is *Maccu-Māra* specially connected with death. He possesses numerous musical instruments. Once in a dream he saw his own death and destruction of musical instruments like *bherī, mṛdaṅga, paṭaha* etc. *(bherīśaṅkha-mṛdaṅgapaṭahatuṇavīṇāvallakītāḍasampādīṁśca vādyabhāṇām-śchinnavicchinnān bhūmau nipatitānapaśyat* Lalitavistara, p. 301 (Leufman's edition). Māra's army consisted of women whom he sent to the Buddha in order to disturb him. These women came near to the Buddha and began to sing and dance (Lalitavistara, p. 320). Thus the connection of Māra with death and music is obvious.

The Manes are closely connected with music.[15] They are described as those who shape the praisehymns (*stomataṣṭāsaḥ*) by means of the songs (*arka-*) (ṚV X.15.9). ṚV X.124.3, the poet-singer says, "I recite a friendly song for father Asura (*śaṁsāmi pitre asurāya śevam*)". In the Mahavrata-ceremony, if one stands near the Mārjālīya-fire-hearth, praising with the Yāma-sāman, one gets the worlds of fathers (TMB V.4.11). The Maruts who may be supposed to be like manes[16] are described to have sung songs (*ya ugrā arkamānṛcaḥ* ṚV I.19.4) The Sāmaveda, according to Manusmṛti IV.124, belongs to the manes (*sāmavedaḥ smṛta pitryaḥ*). There are some verses in the Sāmaveda which are called *pitryāṇāṁ saṁhitā* i.e. they belong to the Manes. Thus in the SVB I.4.20 it is said - "*yadvā u viśpatiḥ* (SV I.114), *sanādagne...* (SV I.80) *akṣannamīmadanta hi* (SV I.415), *abhi tripṛṣṭham* (SV I.528), *akrān samudraḥ* (SV I.529), *kanikranti* (SV I.530), these verses are called *pitryāṇāṁ saṁhitā*. By means of them one can please the ancestors. In Bṛhaspatismṛti, Śrāddhakāṇḍa 78, it is said that by means of a ṛc the father is satiated, by means of a yajus, the grandfather, and by means of a sāman the great-grand-father. The priest belonging to the Sāmaveda is, therefore, superior to the others.

In the Śrāddha-ceremony performed in honour of the ancestors, some particular priest only are described to be worthy. They are called *Paṅkti-pāvana* and they *deserve to be fed* in that ceremony. Among such priests, singers of the Jyeṣṭha-sāmans are mentioned (Manusmṛti III.185: *triṇāciketaḥ pañcāgnis trisuparṇaḥ ṣaḍaṅgavit / brahmadeyātmasantāno jyeṣṭhasāmaga eva ca //;* cp. Viṣṇusmṛti 83.4: *jyeṣṭhasāmagaḥ (paṅktipāvanaḥ)* Vasiṣṭhasmṛti III.22: *triṇāciketaḥ pañcāgnis trisuparṇavāṁścaturmedhā vājasaneyī ṣaḍaṅgavid brahmadeyānu-santānaś chandogo jyeṣṭhasāmago mantrabrāhmaṇavidyaḥ svadharmānadhīte yasya daśapuruṣaṁ mātṛpitṛvaṅśaḥ śrotriyo vijñāyate vidvāṁsaḥ snātakāścaite paṅktipāvanā bhavanti;* Śaṅkhasmṛti XIV, 5: *ṣaḍgṅgavit trisuparṇo bahvṛco jyesṭhasāmagaḥ / triṇāciketaḥ pañcāgnir brāhmaṇāḥ paṅktipāvanāḥ //* Baudhāyanasmṛti II.8.2: *trimadhus triṇāciketas trisuparṇaḥ pañcāgniḥ ṣaḍaṅgavicchīrṣako jyeṣṭhasāmaka iti paṅktipāvanāḥ /* Baudhāyanadharmasūtra II.14.2: *trimadhus triṇāciketas trisuparṇaḥ pañcāgniḥ ṣaḍaṅgavicchīrṣako jyeṣṭhasāmikaḥ snāta iti paṅktipāvanāḥ* /Gautamadharmasūtra II.6.29: *paṅktipāvanāḥ ṣaḍaṅgavijjyeṣṭha-sāmikas triṇāciketas trimadhus trisuparṇaḥ pañcāgniḥ snātako mantravid dharmajño brahmadeyānusantāna iti* /Mbh XIII.90.20: *triṇāciketaḥ pañcāgnis trisuparṇaḥ ṣaḍaṅgavit / brahmadeyānusantānaśchandogo jyeṣṭhabrāhmaṇaḥ // ;* Viṣṇupurāṇa III.15.If: *brāhmaṇān bhojayecchrāddhe yadguṇānstannibodha me / triṇāciketastrimadhustrisuparṇaḥ ṣaḍangavit* / / 1 / / *vedavicchrotriyo yogī tathā vai jyeṣthasāmagaḥ* // Vāyupurāṇa 82.54: *brahmadeyasutaścaiva chandogo jyeṣṭhasāmagaḥ / puṇyeṣu yeṣu tīrtheṣu abhiṣekakṛtavratāḥ* //.[17] The qualities of the Brāhmaṇas to be invited for the śrāddha-ceremony are enumerated by the Prajāpatismṛti 70ff in the following manner. The Brahmaṇas who are devoted to the activities of the Brāhmaṇas, quiet, worshippers of fire, observing their duties, practising penance, knowing the meaning of the Veda, belonging to the good family, devoted to the parents, getting the livelihood by means of the way prescribed for the Brahmaṇas, belonging to the Śrāddha-performer's own branch of the Veda. Among such brāhmaṇas, there should be one knowing the Sāmans (*brahmakarmaratāḥ śāntā apāpā agnisaṁśritāḥ / karmaniṣṭhāstaponiṣṭhā vedārthajñāḥ kulodbhavāḥ* // 70 // *mātṛpitṛparāścaiva brāhmavṛttyupajīvinaḥ / adhyāpakā brahmavido brāhmaṇāḥ śrāddhasaṁpadi* // 71 // *svakīyaśākhino mukhyāḥ śrāddhe vedavidāṁ vara / paṅktipāvanāḥ sarveṣāmeko vai sāmavid bhaved* // 72 // cp. Laghuśātāpasmṛti 99f. *yatnena bhojayecchrāddhe bahvṛcaṁ vedapāragam / śakhāntagamathādhvaryuṁ chandogaṁ vā samāptikam* // 99 // *chandogaṁ bhojayecchrāddhe vaiśvadeve tu bahvṛcam / śāntikarmaṇi cādhvaryuṁ kharakarmaṇyatharvaṇam* // 100 //).Thus in the Śrāddha ceremony there seems to be special importance of the Brāhmaṇas belonging to the Sāmaveda. While the Brāhmaṇas are eating, in the course of that ceremony, verses from the Ṛgveda, Yajurveda and Sāmaveda are to be recited (Baudhāyanadharmasūtra II.14.4f: *ṛco yajūṁṣi sāmānīti śrāddhasya mahimā / tasmādevaṁvidaṁ sapiṇḍamapyāśayet* / 4 / *rākṣoghnāni ca sāmāni svadhāvanti yajūṁṣi ca / madhvṛco'tha pavitrāṇi śrāvayedāśayan śanaiḥ* / 5 /; cp. Baudhāyanasmṛti II. 8.6: *rākṣoghnāni ca sāmāni svadhāvanti yajūṁṣi ca / madhvṛco'tha pavitrāṇi śrāvayedāśayan śanaiḥ*; cp. Padmapurāṇa V.9.165ff: *svādhyāyaṁ śrāvayet pitryaṁ purāṇānyakhilāni tu* // 165 // *brahmaviṣṇvarkarudrāṇāṁ stavāni vividhāni ca / indreśasomasūktāni pāvamānīśca sarvataḥ* // 166 // *bṛhadrathantaraṁ tadvajjyeṣṭhasāmasya gauravam / tathaiva śāntikādhyāyaṁ madhubrāhmaṇameva ca* // 167 //. According to Gobhilasmṛti I.40, Somasāman is to be murmured at that time. This murmuring is described as auspicious (*na cāśnatsu japedatra kadācit pitṛsaṁhitām / anya eva japaḥ kāryaḥ somasāmādikaḥ śubhaḥ*). Thus the close connection of the music and Manes is obvious. In some other parts of the world also this connection is observed. Thus among Australian tribes songs are believed to be obtained by bards from spirits of the dead in dreams or while awake.[18] In Malaya, the dance *Manora*, is supposed to be obtained by the original ancestors from gods. One begins the dance with a salute to the original dancer.[19] Similarly, all the dances of Sakaë which may be destined to provoke a good hunt, good finishing, or simply to make the members of the group happy, begin with an incantation. So that the ancestors may inspire the movements of feet.[20]

Music is amply used in some other rites connected with the dead. There are Yamagāthās (verses dealing with Yama) which are used in the performance of fire-building, at the time of putting the head of a man as a brick. Thereby the man is said to be redeemed from Yama (cp. TS V.1.8.2; KS XX.8; Kpks XXXI.10, Māśs VI.1.2.26 etc.). There is a sāman named Yāma. If during the performance of the sacrifice, anybody among the sacrificers dies, then this sāman is to be used. Thereby the deceased is led to the world of heaven (TB. III.9.20.1; TMB IX.8.4). "Three verses they chant; for in the third (world) are the fathers. They chant them right off (or "thitharward" i.e. without repeating); for the yonder world is situated thitherward from this (world). They chant the verse of Sārparājñī. By means of these verses the serpent Arbuda removed his dead skin: their dead skin they remove by these verses. Reciting these verses after the (laud) they walk around the Mārjālīya, beating their left thighs (TMB IX.8.5ff; cp. JB I.345f; Kātyāśs XXV.13.3; Satyāśs XV.5.34ff., Māśs III.8.4). Here we get clear indications of chant and dance[21] connected with the funeral. It is however in TMB IX.8.11, said that those who officiate for the deceased, go away from the path (cp. JB I.345). Thus there seems to be a fear of death to the performers of music for the dead. Further, however, expiations are prescribed to be performed so that the performers of music for dead may not die. Thus the priests who have officiated for the dead, have to take soma-draughts in such an order that the one destined for Indra and Vāyu comes first. "Thereby they return to the path" (TMB IX.8.11. JB I.346).

Vṛddhahārīta-smṛti prescribes that music should be made at the time of funeral procession (*vāditranṛtyagītādyair vrajeyaḥ kīrtayeddharim / hatāgnimagrataḥ kṛtvā gaccheyustasya bāndhavāḥ*

// IX. 98).Kātyāyanaśrautasūtra describing the procedure of the ritual of the dead mentions the use of music (XXI.3.7). Thus after the body is burnt, the bones put in a pot are to be brought near the village. The pot is then surrounded by new cloth. The *āyasa* (metal) wind instruments are played upon and the lute is struck. At that time the relatives of the dead go round the pot thrice fanning it by means of their upper garments[22] (*śarīrāṇi grāmasamīpamānīya kumbhena talpe kṛtyāhatapakṣeṇa paritatyāyaseṣu vādyamāneṣu vīṇāyāṁ coddhatāyāmamātyāḥ triḥ triḥ parikrāmanti uttarīyairupavā-janairupavājayantaḥ* Kātyāśs XXI.3.7). For the whole day there should be dance and instrumental music (Kātyāśs XXI.3.11). The Ṛgveda-verse which is believed to be connected with this rite contains a reference to dance. Thus ṚV X.18.3, we read. "We have gone towards dance and laughter, extending our life still longer (*prāñco agāma nṛtaye hasāya drāghīya āyuḥ prataraṁ dadhānāḥ*)". The sacrificial fires are to be mixed at the time of funeral. When they are mixed the Udgātṛ sings '*nāke suparṇam*'; when the smoke comes up, he sings "*tveṣaste ṛnvati* ..." and when there are flames he sings "*agne mṛḍa* ...." (Māśs VIII.19.21). If an initiated boy dies he is burnt and that time, the Yamagāthās are to be sung (Yājñavalkyasmṛti. III.2).

References can be given to the use of music at the time of performance of funeral rites. Thus when Pāṇḍu was dead, his body was kept in a palanquin which was decorated with various fragrant flowers. All kinds of sounds of musical instruments were then made (Mbh I.118.10). At the funeral of Droṇa, three sāmans are said to be sung (Mbh XI.23.38). When funerals were made for those who were dead in the great *Bhāratīya* war, Pitṛmedhas (oblations to manes) were performed and in them, sāmans were sung (Mbh XI.26.39 f). In the Pitṛmedha for Bhīṣma also sāmans were sung (*tato'sya vidhivaccakruḥ pitṛmedhaṁ mahātmanaḥ / yājakā juhuvuścāgniṁ jaguḥ sāmāni sāmagāḥ* // (Mbh XII.154.12). When Vasudeva's dead body was kept on pile and was inflamed, there came the sound of inflamed fire, of the sāman-singers and of the weaping men (Mbh XV.8.26) After the death of the Buddha, people honoured his body by means of dances, songs, sounds, of instrumental music, garlands and fragrances (*bhagavato sarīraṁ naccehi gītehi vāditehi mālehi gandhehi sakkaronta* (Dighanikāya II. Nalanda, 1958, p. 122).

In other parts of the world also music and funerals are associated. Thus among the Chinese music is said to accompany the funeral.[23] In Jou times a ceremony of exorcism performed by a wizard used to take place at the time of funeral in China. It used to consist of dances and songs executed by a troupe of performers marked as animals and led by a wizard. The aim of this ceremony was believed to drive away the ghost.[24] In Egypt at the time of funerary proceedings, there were not only gruesome lamentations of more primitive animistic times, but also the joyous sounds of singing, harping, fluting, and dancing.[25] Hermes was, according to the Egyptian tradition which was accepted by Greeks, the inventor of music and was supposed to guide the souls.[26] In the Bible we get some references to the use of music after a death among the Hebrew people.[27] Thus a dirge was sung by singing men and women when Josia was dead (2. Ch. 35.25). Flutes were used at the time of funerals (Mt. 9.23). In Greece, there were lamentation-songs, as for example we know from the Homer's description of dirges sung over Hector's body. The professional bards began the lamentation, then the chorus of women keened. Then Hector's widow, his mother, his sister in law lamented in turn with a keening of women after each.[28] In Rome, no funeral was complete without wailing pipes and trumpets. The phrase, "You may send trumpets (*ad tubicienes mittas*)" signifies "prepare for the funeral".[29] On christmas Eve, in the Isle of Man, all the servants find out a wren and kill it. They carry it in a procession chanting and singing. Then they bury it and afterwards form circle and dance to music.[30] In the funerals of American Indians, songs are prepared either in advance or on the spot and sung.[31]

Sometimes the music at the time of funerals has the aim of resurrection of the dead. That is kind of musical magic for provoking reveille of life.[32] The primitive men used or use to think that death is just a long sleep and the music can be useful in awakening the dead. Musicians like Orpheus can please even the God of Death. Thus it is told that he pleased the God of Death and asked for his dead wife Eurydice back and this request was granted by the god.[33] The seers named Vaikhānasas were dear to Indra. They were killed by Rahasyu Devamalimluc (the god-robber). Indra revived them by means of the Vaikhānasa-sāman (TMB XIV.4.6; JB III.190). Śukrācārya was in possession of Sañjīvanī lore (that which revives) and he could revive Kaca by means of it (Mbh I.71.30f). Some times the funeral music seems to have the purpose of banishing the soul as an evil spirit until it is released from this world and transformed by the sacrifice of banishment into a good spirit.[34] It has an apotropaeic as well as propitiatory significance. It sometimes aims at pleasing the god of death and thereby to avoid him for the surviving people so that they may live long.[35] When one of the sacrificers is dead during the performance, the others perform the funeral ritual for the dead (see above); But the remaining performers undergo a fear of their own death. In order to avoid it, they perform the rites in an expiatory manner. In those rites, the tristich beginning with *agna āyūṁṣi pavase* (O Agni thou purifiest the lives) is taken as the opening tristich. Thereby life is put in those who are living (TMB IX.8.12). Further, the pavamāna-lauds which are used in those rites should be threefold. For threefold are the vital airs. By taking the threefold stoma they come to the vital airs (TMB IX.8.15; JB I.346). In the ṚV X.18.3, the surviving people say "We have gone extending our lives still further" .... Thus the music performed after the death seems to have the purpose of avoiding immediate death for those who survive.

Music is often supposed to have some magical power of removing and avoiding death. It is often used with this intention. In a story told by AB III.14, it is said that Agni was the hotṛ-priest of the gods. For him death waited in the Bahiṣpavamāna-stotra. he began the Ājyaśastra with an Anuṣṭubh-verse. Then he could evade the death. Similarly death waited for him in the 'Ājyastotra'. He removed it by means of *prauga*. Then he removed it similarly from the Mādhyandina-pavamāna by means of Marutvatīya-śastra in Anuṣṭubh. Death could not wait for him in the Bṛhatī verses. For they are identical with the vital airs. It then waited in the third pavamāna. Agni removed it by means of Āgnimāruta-śastra in Anuṣṭubh. It then waited in the Yajñayajñīya-sāman. He removed it by means of Āgnimāruta-śastra with a triplet for Vaiśvānara. Thus Agni removed the death completely (AB III. 14; Cp. KB XV.5). The recitation of nine Bahiṣpavamānī-verses is useful for avoiding death. They are said to be equivalent to the six Bṛhatī-verses. Now there are six mouths of death viz. the six seasons. Bṛhatī alone and no other metre is capable to struggle with the mouths of the death. Each Bṛhatī closes one mouth and thus one conquers the death thereby (JB I. 247). Prajāpati created the gods. Death was born after them. Prajāpati asked the gods to create metres and to protect themselves with the help of them and thus they protected themselves from death by means of metres (JB I.283). According to MS III.4.7, the gods, after having killed the Asuras became afraid of death. Then they saw the metres, entered therein and covered themselves with whatever they liked. Then they could protect themselves from death. Prajāpati protected himself from death by means of a three-day-rite ending with the word *iḷā* (JB III.311). Some used to say, "He is the Udgātṛ who releases the fetters of death from the vital aims of the sacrificer (*sa vā udgātā yo yajamānasya prāṇebhyo'dhi mṛtyupāśānunmuñcati*)" (JUB IV.7.1.3; for various musical elements useful in freeing oneself from the death see JUB III. 2.4.10; 3.2.2f; 6.7.8; IV.7.1.5; 2.4).

We have given above some details showing the close connection of music and manes. But sometimes they are disassociated. Thus the musicians in general are said to be *apāṅkta* (not worthy to be fed in the śrāddha-ceremony) (Gautamadharmasutra II. 6.18: *kuṇḍāśisomavikrayyagāradāhigaradāvakīrṇigaṇapreṣyāgamyāgāmihiṁsraparivṛttiparivetṛpayāhitaparyādhātṛtyaktātmadurvālakunakhiśyāvadantaśvitripaunarbhuvakitavājaparājapreṣyapratirūpikaśūdrāpatinirākṛtikilā-*

sikusīdivaṇikśilpopajīvijyāvāditratālanṛtyagītaśīlān (na bhoyajet śrāddhe) cp. Mbh XIII.2.4.16: *gāyanā nartakāścaiva plavakā vādakāstathā kathakā yodhakāścaiva rājannārhanti ketanam*[36] /; XII.90.6: *kitavo bhrūṇahā yakṣmī paśupālo nirākṛtiḥ / grāmapreṣyo vārdhuṣiko gāyanaḥ sarvavikrayī // (apāṅktāḥ)*; cp. also XIII.9.40: *yathāgnau śānte ghṛtamājuhoti tannaiva devānna pitṛnupaiti / tathā dattaṁ nartane gāyane ca yāṁ cānṛce dakṣiṇāmāvṛṇoti //*. Money taken from musicians should not be used for the expenses of the śrāddha ceremony (Prajāpatismṛti 49: *dhanaṁ cikitsāsaṁbandhi grāmayāca(ja)kagāyinī (nām) / kathayatva (yā ca) samānītamagrāhyaṁ pitṛkarmaṇi //*).

At the time of singing during the course of the sacrifice one should take care that his singing does not get any mystic connection with the manes. Thus at the time of singing the Gāyatra-sāman one has to take care of not making the manes as its deity (JB I.112). While singing the Yajñāyajñīya-sāman, according to some ritualists, the singer should cover himself. Their reasoning is as follows: - This sāman is identical with fire. So there is fear that it will burn the singer. By covering himself he avoids the danger. But this view is to be rejected according to the JB I.174. For if the singer were to cover himself Manes will be the deity of the sāman and this is not good.

Thus we see that music and manes are sometimes disassociated. The relations of music and manes seem to be two-fold: association and disassociation. Music has a double nature it brings death; it removes it. It removes the dead; it attracts them[37]. It has twofold magicoreligious significance. It kills (as we have shown) it generates (details elsewhere). Thus for example in TMB XXI.2.1, Death and Prajāpati (who creates the being) are identified. It is said that by means of the Ājidoha-sāmans, the Death, Prajāpati kills the beings and creates them. Thus the same sāmans can kill as well as generate.

REFERENCES

1. Rf. R. Pischel, in *R.* Pischel, *K.F.* Geldner, *Vedische Studien,* I, Stuttgart, p. 242.

2. *gāyannatha vrajet svapne vidyān mṛtyurupasthitaḥ // 13 //*
 kṛṣnāmbaradhara śyāmā gāyantiī vātha cāṅganā /
 yaṁ nayeddakṣiṇāmāśāṁ svapne so' pi na jīvati // 14 //
 (Vāyup. XIX. 13f).
3. *muktakeśo hasaṁścaiva gāyannṛtyaṁśca yo naraḥ /*
 yāmyāśābhimukho gacchet tadantaṁ tasya jīvitam //
 (Vāyup. XIX. 25).
4. J. Combarieu, *La musique et la magie,* Paris, 1909, p. 261.
5. H. Webster, *Magic, a sociological study,* Standord, 1948, p. 404.
6. J. Hastings (ed.) *ERE* (= *Encyclopaedia of Religion and Ethics*), IX, New York, 1956, p. 26.
7. W.W. Skeat, *Malay magic,* New York, 1967 (reprint), p. 25 ff. 40.
8. E. Belvianes, *Sociologie de la musique,* Paris, 1951, p. 49.
9. H.G Farmer, in E. Wellesz, *AOM = Ancient and Oriental Music* London, 1966, (reprint), p. 437.
10. Belvianes, *Sociologie de la musique* p. 54.
11. Rf. L. Renou, "Vedic *Nirṛti*" *S.K. Chatterji Jubilee Vol.* Madras, 1955, p. 11 ff.
12. Rf. L.V. Schroeder, *Mysterium und Mimus in Rigveda,* Leipzig, 1908, p. 282, n. 2; according to V. Schroeder (p. 477) the Gandharvas are the spirit of dead, the manes. According to J.W. Hauer, *Der Vrātya,* Stuttgart, 1927, p. 350, the great priest-ancestors were considered as Gandharvas.
13. Rf. J. Gonda, *Die Religionen Indiens,* I, Stuttgart, 1960, p. 101.
14. Rf. G.P. Malalasekera, *Dictionary of Pāli proper names,* London, 1960 (reprint), under the word.
15. Contrast, M. Bloomfield, *WZKM,* 17 (1903), p. 163.
16. Rf. A. Hillebrandt, *Vedische Mythologie,* II., Hildersheim, 1965 (reprint), p. 285f.
17. Cp. Mānavaśrautasūtra, XI, 9.4.16 f; Viṣṇudharmottarapurāṇa I.143.13f; Garuḍapurāṇa I.99.3ff. It may be noted that Padmapurāṇa V. 0.79 in the similar context does not mention a singer of Sāman.
18. Hastings *ERE,* IX, p. 6 (b); cp. Schneider in Wellesz, *AOM,* p. 9.
19. Rf. J. Cuisinier, *La danse sacrée,* Paris, 1951, p. 19.
20. Rf. Cuisinier, *La danse sacrée,* p. 31.
21. For the custom of dancing at the time of funerals see Belvianes, *Sociologie de la musique,* p. 38.

22. Rf. further, W. Caland, *Die altindischen Todten- und Bestattungsbräuche,* Wiesbaden, 1967 (reprint), p. 138.
23. Hastings, *ERE,* IX, p.17(a); cp. M. Courant in A. Lavignac, *Encyclopedie de la musique,* I. Paris, 1913, p. 188.
24. L. Picken in Wellesz, *AOM,* p. 104.
25. H.G. Farmer in Wellesz, *AOM,* p. 261.
26. Belvianes, *Sociologie de la musique,* p. 108.
27. Hastings, *ERE,* IX, p. 39(b); see Belvianes, *Sociologie de la musique,* p. 107.
28. I. Henderson, in Wellesz, *AOM,* p. 378.
29. E. Scott in Wellesz, *AOM,* p. 413.
30. G.J. Frazer, *The Golden Bough* (abr. ed.) London 1963, p. 536f.
31. Hastings, *ERE,* IX, p. 11f.
32. Combarieu, *La musique et la magie,* p. 279; cp. p. 100, 101, Cp. also Seeman in H. Bächtold-Staubli, *Handwörterbuch des deutschen Aberglaubens,* Berlin-Leipzig, 1927-42, VI. 650; G. Van der Leeuw, *Religion in Essence and Manifestation,* London, 1928, p. 405; Belvianes, *Sociologie de la musique* p. 11.
33. H.S. Rose, *A handbook of Greek Mythology,* London, 1965 (reprint), p. 255.
34. Schenider in Wellesz, *AOM,* p. 51.
35. Music can hinder the death; rf. M. Abert, *Die Lehre von Ethos in der grieschischen Musik,* Wiesbaden, 1968, p. 52f.
36. Cp. Mbh. XIV, app. I. 4.2088 f; *gāyakā nartakāścaiva plavakā vādakās tathā / 2088 / kathakā yodhikāścaiva śrāddhe nārhanti satkṛtim / 2089 /.* Cp. Vāyupurāṇa 79. 69: *kārukādīnanācārān sarvavedabahiṣkṛtān / gāyanān devavṛttāṁsca sarvabhakṣān vivarjayet / /.* Cp. Vāyu p. 82.61. *kitavo madyapī yakṣmī paśupālo nirākṛtiḥ / grāmapreṣyo vārdhuṣiko gāyano vaṇijastathā / /*
37. Belvianes, *Sociologie de la musique,* p. 108, see p. 53: by means of music *Kwang-ti* made the union of the kings with the spirits of dead and gods possible.

(H) REMOVAL OF EVIL

We have already dealt with a few aspects of apotropic powers of music, in connection with the evil spirits. Sometimes music is used for removing the abstract evil (*pāpman-*) in general. Thus by singing the Traiśoka-sāman on the fourth day of the Daśarātra of the Dvādaśāha-sacrifice, one abolishes sin (TMB XII.10.23). When the stotriyā-verses in the Bhurij-Śakvarī-metre are sung, then also the evil is removed (TMB XIII.13.22 f). When Indra raised his thunderbolt against Vṛtra, Vṛtra encircled Indra with sixteen coils. Indra then saw the Padastobha-sāman and by means of it, unwinded them. "The evil (in the form of encircling) had indeed seized him (Indra); through the Padastobha-sāman he had repelled it. He who lauding, applies the Padastobha-sāman repels the evil" (TMB XIII.5.22 f; JB I.129 has a similar story in connection with Prajāpati who removed the evil by means of this sāman). In the course of singing the Kārtayaśa-sāman, one should use the word *hi* as its finale. Thereby one removes the evil (TMB XIV. 5.22 f). Other seers abused Vasiṣṭha, "You are a Vaiśya; a non-brahmin". He then desired to cross over this evil in the form of bad fame. Then he saw the Plava (ship) sāman and crossed over this evil (JB III.95).

When a stotra in praise of Indra is recited then all the evil of a sacrificer is "killed" (JB III.89). At the end of a sacrificial session, when the performers creep along right under the axle of the southern cart, they utter a verse (VS VIII.53; ṚV I.132.6) which is in the Aticchandas-metre. Since this metre is, according to the Brāhmaṇa texts, identical with all the metres, its use helps the performer to remove the evil and then the evil does not overtake the performers (ŚB IV.6.3.19). The knowledge of metres is also helpful in repelling any evil (AĀ II.1.6). By using the twenty-five-versed stoma, in the Sarvajit-sacrifice, Āṅgirasa crossed over all the evil (TMB XVI.7.7). The ascending (*āyatī*) type of viṣṭuti (mode of singing a stoma) of the Trivṛt-stoma is helpful for removing the evil (TMB II.1.4). Thus the various elements of Vedic music repel evil.

It is, however, important to note that sometimes music brings also evil. Thus the Kulāyinī-viṣṭuti of the Trivṛt-stoma brings evil to the sacrificer (TMB II.3.6). Thus music is double-natured; It is sometimes beneficent and sometimes maleficent.

(I) MUSIC AND EVIL BEINGS

Music is well known for its apotropic significance. It has power against evil-beings.[1] Various musical elements are used in order to kill the evil beings or to repel them. In the Vedic literature also formulas, verses, sāmans (melodies) and, many other details of Vedic music are directly said to be useful in killing or repelling evil beings such as Asuras and Rakṣases.

The poet-singers of the Ṛgveda seem to be aware of the anti-evil-being-power of the music. God Agni is supposed to be a killer of evil beings.[2] Music helps him by increasing his power in destroying the evil beings. Thus ṚV X.162.1 we read, "May Agni the killer of Rakṣases, united with the formula *(mantra-)* destroy the bad-named (demon of disease)". In Vedic literature, dove is considered to be a messenger of Nirṛti (disorder).[3] (ṚV X.165.1; AV VI.27.1; cp. 29.2) and also of Yama, the God of Death (ṚV X.165.4). The priests are therefore requested, "Remove the dove by means of a verse (*ṛc*)" (ṚV X.165.5; cp. Kauśikasūtra 46.7). ṚV VII.8.6, the poet-singer hopes, "May this speech (*vacas-*) be a killer of Rakṣas". The whole hymn ṚV VII.104 or at least its frame[4] is meant for burning and destroying the wicked demons. Even the sound of pressing stones has the power of killing the evil beings. Therefore, Vasiṣṭha says, "may the pressing stones kill the evil beings by means of their sounds (*grāvāṇo ghnantu rakṣasa upabdaiḥ* ṚV VII.104.17). A magician-singer says that by means of his powerful hymn (*brahman-*) he kills the evil Gandharva who haunts women. (AV IV.37.11).

In the Brāhmaṇa-texts, the sāmans are very often described as having the power of killing the demons etc. Thus in the course of Avabhṛtha-bath, the Adhvaryu asks the Prastotṛ to sing a sāman. The reason why he sings the sāman is that the evil spirits may not injure the body of the sacrificer outside the sacrifice. For the sāman kills away the evil spirits (*sāma hi nāṣṭrāṇāṁ rakṣasām apahantā*" ŚB IV.4.5.6; cp. *sāma vai rakṣohā* TS VI.6.3.1). Similarly in the course of Pravargya-ceremony, a sāman is to be sung by Prastotṛ and in connection with it also the rakṣas-killing power of the sāman is mentioned in the same words (ŚB XIV.3.1.10; cp. TĀ V.9.4: *sāma vai rakṣohā*). On both these occasions the sāman is to be sung based on the verses addressed to Agni. Agni is also mentioned there to be a killer of evil spirits. Thus the music does not work, according to some Vedic texts, without the agency of the gods. It works magicoreligiously. The Hārivarṇa sāman is to be used by one who is caught by rakṣases. When the Aṅgirases were going to the world of heaven, the rakṣases pursued them. Harivarṇa Āṅgirasa saw this sāman and killed the evil beings from these worlds (JB I.183; cp. TMB VIII.9.5). Similarly when the gods were going to the heaven, the rakṣases pursued them with the desire to kill them. The gods saw the Tairaśca-sāman and killed them. "One who knows this kills away the rakṣases" (JB III.56; cp. TMB XII.6.12 where Aṅgirases instead of gods are mentioned). In another story we are told that the rakṣases pursued Agastya. He saw the Kayāśubhīya-sāman and killed those evil beings. "Evil beings pursue, as it were, those who press soma simultaneously (*saṁsunvanti*: two soma-sacrificers not separated by a river or mountain perform a soma-sacrifice simultaneously)". Kayāśubhīya-sāman is therefore used for killing away the evil beings (JB I.344). Once, the third day in the Daśarātra of the Dvādaśāha collapsed. The rakṣases pursued it. The gods killed away them by means of the Paurumudga-sāman (TMB XII.3.13). Manu created the beings by means of the Mānava-saman which he had seen and sung. According to another story, the evil beings desired to kill the created beings. Manu then desired to kill these beings and then saw the Mānava-sāman. Having sung this sāman he killed away them (JB III.98). Thus we notice that music has a double-nature. One can create or one can destroy with it. The Vaiśvamanasa-sāman is also described to be a killer of enemies and a killer of rakṣases (JB III.267). Dīrghajihvī was a female rakṣas who used to lick and destroy the sacrificial performance. Saumitra and Indra killed her with the help of the Saumitra-sāman (cp. TMB XIII.9.6; cp. JB I.161 f).

Asuras form another category of the evil beings. Gods used to kill them by means of various sāmans. Thus gods killed the Asuras by means of the Gauṅgava-sāman (JB III.185). At the time of a contest the gods desired to kill the Asuras first. They saw the Pauruhanmana-sāman and having praised with it, they killed the Asuras first (*pūrve aghnan*). Therefore, the Pauruhanmana has got this name. One kills one's hateful enemy by means of knowing this (JB III.215). During another contest between the gods and Asuras, Indra desired to kill the Asuras, having surrounded them all. Then he saw the Sāṁvarta-sāman and killed the Asuras having surrounded them all (JB III.233).

The sāmans are supposed to be useful in securing a victory over the evil beings. Thus when once the Gods and Asuras were contesting in these worlds, the gods desired to conquer these worlds and achieve victory over the Asuras. Then they saw Saṁjaya-sāman and praised with it. "Because they conquered these worlds, that is why Saṁjaya has its name. One conquers these worlds, wins the contest and (defeats) the hateful enemy who knows thus" (JB III.132). The Gods conquered the Asuras quickly (*āśu*) by means of the sāman named Āśu (JB III.211). The Gods possessed righteousness by means of the Dharma (righteousness) - sāman. Then they defeated the Asuras by making them devoid of righteousness with the help of their own righteousness. The user of this sāman also defeats his enemy in the same way (JB III.231). At another time of contest, the gods desired to defeat the Asuras by means of Agni as their mouth (leader). Then they saw the Daivānīka-sāman and praised with it. Then they killed the Asuras. "This sāman is victory; one who knows this, becomes victorious and kills the enemy" (JB III.275).

Further, the possessions of the evil-beings also can be acquired by means of the power of sāmans. Thus by means of the Sabhasāman, the gods obtained the light, power, sense-power, valour, cattle and food of the Asuras (JB I.160). By means of the Gauṅgava-sāman, Gods won the cattle of Asuras. One wins the cattle of one's hateful enemy by using this sāman (JB III. 185). At the time of a contest between the gods and Asuras, the gods desired to rob the lustre (*haras-*) of the Asuras. The gods then saw the sāman named Hārāyaṇa and having praised with it, robbed (*aharan*) the lustre of the Asuras. Therefore Hārāyaṇa is the name of the sāman. One robs the lustre of one's hateful enemy who knows this (JB III.217). At another time the gods desired to win the possession (*vaśa-*) of Asuras. They saw and praised with Vaśa-sāman and got their desire fulfilled (JB III. 220). By means of the Vājajit-sāman, the Gods won the wealth, cattle and food of the Asuras. One obtains these things of one's hateful enemy by means of this sāman on the tenth day of the Daśarātra of the Dvādaśāha-sacrifice (JB III.299). At another contest between the Gods and Asuras, Indra desired to obtain the glory of the Asuras. He saw the sāman named Hariśrīnidhana and obtained the glory of the Asuras. "One who knows thus enjoys glory, obtains the glory of his hateful enemy" (JB III.249). According to the Brāhmaṇa-texts, even the sacrifice was, once in the possession of Asuras. The Gods obtained it by means of the magical power of the Yajñāyajñīya-sāman. "With the Asuras, once was the whole sacrifice. The gods saw the Yajñāyajñīya-sāman. By means of the words *yajñā yajñīya vo agnaye* (by sacrifice on sacrifice in honour of Agni) they took from them the Agnihotra; by (the words) *girā girā ca dakṣasā* (and by hymn on hymn in honour of the skillful), the New and Full-moon-sacrifice; by *pra pra vayamamrtaṁ jātavedasam* (continually we (will extol) the immortal Jātavedas), the seasonal sacrifices; by *priyaṁ mitraṁ na śamsiṣam* (as a dear friend I will extol), the sacrifice of soma .... " (TMB VIII.6.5f).

The apotropic power of the Vedic music is sometimes directly mentioned. Thus sāmans are expressedly said to have the power of removing the Asuras.[5] On the verses which accompany the night-rite, the Ūrdhvasadmana-sāman is used by way of modification. "The Asuras were in these worlds; by means of the Ūrdhvasadmana-sāman, the Gods drove them out of these worlds. Therefore, he who knows this, performs, after having driven his rival out of these worlds, a sacrificial session on his abode" (TMB IX. 2.10ff). The Vaikhānasas saw the Vaikhānasa-sāmans as a repetition and constant return of the sacrifice. By means of repetitions the gods removed the Asuras from the sacrifice (JB III.190). The same remarks are found in connection with the Vāmra-sāman also (JB III.99). Indra also took the help of Śyena-sāman in removing away the Asuras. Thus JB III.158 informs us that Indra, having become a falcon removed the Asuras. The Kāleya-sāman also has apotropic power. "The gods and Asuras contended for (the possession of) these worlds. The gods resorted to Prajāpati. He gave them this sāman (saying) "By means of this sāman ye will be able to drive them away". By it they drove them away from these worlds. Because they drive them away (*akālayanta*) therefore it is called Kāleya" (TMB VIII.3.1; cp. JB I.153).

Sometimes some other expressions are used in describing the anti-evil-being-power of the sāmans. Thus in connection with the Satrāsāhīya-sāman we read, "Whatever had been left not overcome of the Asuras, that was overcome (*asahanta*) by the gods by means of the Satrāsāhīya-sāman". Because they thought "We have overcome them finally (*satrā*). Therefore the Satrāsāhīya-sāman is called thus. He who praises with the Satrāsāhīya, overcomes finally his enemies" (TMB XII.9.21f; cp. JB I.182 where Indra, instead of gods in general is mentioned to have accomplished this activity). Similarly by means of the Sahas-sāman, the gods *overcame (asahanta)* the Asuras (JB II.103). At the time of a contest between the gods and Asuras, the gods, by means of Paurumadga-sāman, drowned the boroughs of the Asuras. Because they *drowned* their boroughs (*puro'majjayan*) therefore it is called Paurumadga. One drowns one's hateful enemy by this sāman (TMB XII.3.14; cp. JB III.43). In connection with the Rathantara-sāman, it is said,

"Gods, having *packed* up the Asuras with the Rathantara-sāman, *oppressed* them with the Bṛhat-sāman, with a net as it were. One who knows this does the same in the case of his enemy" (JB I.136). Another story mentions of an occasion when the gods *crossed over* the evil beings with the help of the Ṙathantara-sāman. Thus when the gods had gone to the heaven, the Asuras and Rakṣases, ninety nine in number covered these worlds. They (Asuras and Rakṣases) were called "Chariots (*rathāḥ*)". The gods having sung with the Rathantara-sāman i.e. having mounted upon the Rathantara as it were, came to the heavenly world. Then they said, "We have crossed over (*atāriṣma*) these Rathas". Therefore, the Rathantara is so called. One who knows thus crosses over the hateful enemy (JB I.135). The Gāyatra-sāman has served for *protection* from the Asuras. Prajāpati created the beings which were at that time without the vital airs. Now the Gāyatra-sāman is identical with the vital airs ..... While the beings were receiving vital airs, the Rakṣases pursued them. Then Prajāpati protected them from the Rakṣases with the help of the Gāyatrā-sāman. "Because he, while singing, protected (*gāyan atrāyata*) them, therefore, the Gāyatra is so called. It protects him, who knows thus, from all the evil" (JB I.111). The Gods, having *stopped* (*niṣṭabhya*) the Asuras, from these worlds, by means of the Vaiṣṭambha-sāman, performed a sacrificial session in their own place (JB III.50). Gods *scorched* the Asuras by means of the Raurava-sāman and one who knows this having been better scorches as it were one's hateful enemy (JB III.184). By means of the Abhīvarta-sāman, the gods at the time of a contest *turned themselves against* (*abhyavartayanta*) the Asuras. The Abhīvarata-sāman is a thunderbolt as it were. The performers turn themselves against their enemies and progress (JB III.294; cp. TMB VIII.2.8).

Vedic literature ascribes the anti-evil-beings-power to the metres also. Even gods have taken help of the magical power of metres in killing the demons. Thus JB I.342 says, "By means of metres, the gods overpowered the Asuras". Therefore offerings to metres are to be offered in case of two sacrificers performing a soma-sacrifice simultaneously. When these offerings are given, one subdues one's competitor (JB I.342). According to KS XXXII.5, the Gods, under the leadership of Viṣṇu, removed the Asuras by means of metres. According to JB I.99, the Gods excluded the Prāṇa of the Asuras by means of Gāyatrī; eye by means of Triṣṭubh, ear by means of Jagatī and speech by means of Anuṣṭubh. They removed the Asuras from this world by means of the Gāyatrī-metre; from the intermediate region by means of the Triṣṭubh-metre; from the heaven by means of the Jagatī-metre and from the cattle by means of Anuṣṭubh-metre. Then the gods became victorious and Asuras were defeated. "One who knows thus becomes victorious and his enemy is defeated".

The Triṣṭubh-metre possesses the power of killing away the evil rakṣases. Therefore in the course of the fire-altar-building-ceremony, the offering to be made upon the golden man is to be offered with verses in the Triṣṭubh-metre viz. *kṛṇuṣva pājam......* (VS XIII.9-13). Since the metre Triṣṭubh is identical with thunderbolt (*vajra*) one thus kills the evil beings with the help of thunderbolt (ŚB VII.4.1.34). Similarly on the Nirṛti-bricks in the same ceremony, one throws down a seat, a netting, a sling of the gold plate and two pads with the verses in the Triṣṭubh-metre (VS XII.65). In this connection also, the same reason is given (ŚB VII.2.1.15). The apotropic character of the Aticchandas-metre has been declared by ṢaḍB III.1.7, when it says: "The Aticchandas is a warding off (of the demons) (*vāraṇamiva vā etacchando yadaticchandāḥ*)". In the Paurvatitha-sāman, the verses beginning with *indra suteṣu someṣu* are to be used. They are in Uṣṇih-metre. By means of them one keeps away the Asuras (JB I.227). In connection with the Anuṣṭubh-metre it has been said that the Anuṣṭubh-metre is killing (*nighnat*) as it were. By means of Anuṣṭubh which is identical with speech, the Gods killed the Asuras (JB I.261).

The stomas are described to be helpful to the gods in removing the Asuras. Thus "The gods headed by the stomas (conquered MS I.6.4) removed the Asuras from these worlds

(KS VIII.5; KPKS VII1). Prajāpati also took the services of the Triṇava-stoma in removing the Asuras from these worlds (TB II.2.4.6). The Trivṛt-stoma was used by the Gods in removing the Asuras (JB II.104f).

In the vedic literature, the speech, voice or sound in general (*vāc*) also is attributed with the anti-evil-beings-power. Thus by means of speech (*vāc*) the Gods faced the Asuras (ŚB VII. 4.2.34). The Asuras according to another story, tried to kill the *vāc* which was continuously killing them. But their attempts were unsuccessful. Thus the story runs as follows: Manu was in possession of a bull. An Asura-killing, foe-killing voice (*vāc*) had entered into that bull and by his snorting and roaring, the Asuras were continuously being crushed. Kilāta and Ākuli were two priests of the Asuras. They went to Manu and requested him to sacrifice with that bull. When the bull was killed, the voice went to Mānavī (the wife of Manu). When the Asuras and Rakṣases heard her speak, they were continuously being crushed. The two priests of Asuras again requested Manu to sacrifice his wife. When she was killed, the voice entered into the sacrifice viz. into the sacrificial vessels. And the two Asuras were unable to expel it from the vessels. "This same Asura-killing, foe-killing voice sounds forth from the millstones when they are beaten with the wedge. And for whosoever that knows this they produce their discordant noise, his enemies are rendered very miserable". (ŚB I.1.4.14ff). For the magical power of the sound of pressing stones, see also ṚV VII.104.17. There the sound of soma-pressing-stones is described as killing the Asuras.

The recitation of verses also has an anti-evil-beings-powers. "The most sweet" were the animals among the gods and "the most pleasant" were the animals among the Asuras. But by reciting the words *svādiṣṭhayā madiṣṭhayā* (by the most sweet, by the most pleasant) the Gods took away the animals of Asuras. One who knows this takes away the cattle of his rival (TMB VIII.4.6f). At the time of soma-bringing, a guest-offering is performed. At that time fire is produced through rubbing the two pieces of woods. But if at that time fire is not produced or is produced late, then some verses (ṚV X. 118.1ff) are to be recited. These verses are in Gāyatrī-metre and are described as rakṣas-killing (AB I.16). On the tenth day of the Daśarātra of the Dvādaśāha verses beginning with *sūryasyeva raśmayo* (ṚV IX.69.6) which contain the word *sūrya* (sun) are to be recited for the sake of killing the rakṣases (JB III.298).

Some other aspects of Vedic music also are described to be powerful in destroying or removing the evil spirits. Thus the *udgītha* i.e. the second part which in principle is the most important one of a sāman (or the third, if one counts hiṁkāra as the first) and chanted by the Udgātṛ-priest[6] has this anti-evil-beings power. Thus, Gods killed the Asuras by means of *Udgītha* (ChāUp. I.2.1ff; cp. JUB I.18.4.1ff; BṛhUp. I.3.1ff). The Paryāyas are the "sounds" of a chant, consisting of a triad of verses separated from that which follows, by means of the sound *hum*. Three of the Paryāyas constitute a viṣṭuti.[7] Now these Paryāyas are supposed to possess apotropic power. Thus, the Gods, encircling the Asuras on all sides drove them away. Because they drove them away encircling (*paryāyam*), therefore they are called Paryāyas. By the first round they drove them away from the first part of night; by the second from the middle part and by the third from the last part (AB IV.5; cp. TMB IX.1.3; JB I.208). "In that in the first rounds, they repeat in the first quarters, verily thus they remove the Asuras from the first part of night; in that in the middle rounds they repeat in the middle quarters, verily thus they remove the Asuras from the middle part of night; in that in the last rounds they repeat in the last quarters, verily thus they remove the Asuras from the last part of night" (KB XVII.8; GB II.5.5; cp. JB I.208). A Pragātha is a complex of two strophies transformed into three. The Gods with the help of the Pragātha which has an Anuṣṭubh at the beginning, killed the Asuras in the night. One who uses this Pragātha also killed the enemy in the night (TMB IX.1.1f). Similar observation can be made in the case of stobhas which are unintelligible,[8] modificatory syllables inserted in the course of singing. Thus once the Asuras hemmed the Gods in. Then Agni saw two burning, all-divergent stobhas. Through them he scorched the Asuras (TMB VII.5.1). Similarly the nidhana (finale) has the anti-evil-beings-power. Thus the nidhana of the Yaudhājaya-sāman is *om.* "The nidhana of the Yaudhājaya-sāman is indeed a thunderbolt. The Gods killed the Asuras, the evil enemies by means of this nidhana. One also kills one's evil enemy by using this nidhana" (JB I. 323). The gods removed the Asuras from every house with the Vaitahavya-sāman which has the word *okas* (house) as its finale. One drives away one's wicked enemy by means of this sāman (JB I.214). The *dhur*-verses (belonging to the out-of-doors-chant) were also used by the gods to overthrow the Asuras. "And because they overthrew (*adhūrvan*) them with these verses, therefore they became the *dhurs (etābhis taddevā asurān adhūrvan yad adhūrvans tasmād dhuro'bhavan*" JB I.318; cp. I.99; ṢaḍB. II.3.1ff). The pratigara (response) serves for removing the evil beings. Thus if the hotṛ recites by half-verses, the Adhvaryu has to respond at each half-verse and if the Hotṛ recites by hemistichs the Adhvaryu has to respond at each hemistich. The reason is as follows: Whenever in reciting, the Hotṛ draws breath, there the Asuras and Rakṣases rush into the sacrifice. The Adhvaryu closes the sacrifice by means of Response and then no evil beings rush in (ŚB IV.3.2.6). By means of *hiṁkāra* also the Gods removed the Asuras from these worlds (KB III.2). The gods killed the Asuras with the help of the silent praise (Tūṣṇīṁśaṁsa) (AB II.31). According to the Vāyupurāṇa 50.165 the water which is consecrated by means of a verse in the Gāyatrī-metre and having the power of the sacred syllable *om* burns the evil beings. Mbh XII.315.21 describes the anti-evil-beings-power of the Vedic recitation in general. Thus Nārada requests Vyāsa, "While removing the darkness created by the feat of evil beings by means of the noise of the Veda-recital, you, along with your son, please recite the Vedas". In order to appease the evil, one has to perform an offering to Nirṛti. At that time a big noise of musical instruments along with a loud din is to be made (Viṣṇudharmottarap. II.132.36).

Thus music seems to be considered as possessing a magicoreligious power of killing or removing the evil spirits. This power has in general a bearing upon the anti-inimical practices. So the apotropic power of music constitutes also the black-magic power in general.

REFERENCES

1. For the anti-evil-beings-power of music see in general - Crook, *Popular Religion*, I. p. 168; Abert, *Musikanschauung*, p. 102; 157; v. Schröder, *Mysterium und Mimus*, p. 210; Combarieu, *La musique et la magie*, p. 114ff; Hauer, *Yogopraxis*, p. 55; the same *Der Vrātya*, p. 130f; Frazer, *Golden Bough*, p. 566. Keith, *RPV*, p. 384; Sachs, *Geist und Werde der Musikinstumente*, p. 17f; Gunkel, Zcharnack, *RGG*, IV. 296f; Seeman in *Handworterbuch der deutschen Aberglaubens*, VI. 650; 652; Belvianes, *Sociologie de la musique*, p. 105f; Gonda, *Kingship*, p. 56.
2. Rf. Meyer, *Trilogie*, II. 33.
3. Rf. Renou, "*Vedic Nirṛti*", *S.K. Chatterji Jubilee Vol.*, p. 11ff.
4. Geldner, *Der Rigveda*, II. 273.
5. Cf. Keith, *RPV*, p. 384.
6. Renou, *Vocabulaire*, p. 40.
7. Renou, *Vocabulaire*, p. 95; cp. Eggeling, *SBE* 26, 308, n.2.
8. For the significance of unintelligible words in magic spells see Webster, *Magic*, p. 94.

(J) MUSIC AND LIGHT

Both sound and light[1] are the basic principles of the world. In the ancient way of thinking sometimes each is considered to be the highest truth of the world. Thus in the philosophy of grammar "sound" is supposed to be the *brahman* - the highest principle. Thus in Bhartṛhari's Vākyapadīya I.1, the "sound (*śabda*) is described as the *brahman* and the process of the world is said to be originated from it (See also Pāṇinīyadarśana in the Sarvadarśanasaṁgraha,[2] p. 298ff). On the other hand, in the Brahma-sūtra for example I.1.24; *Jyotiścaraṇābhidhānāt* and I.3.40 *Jyotirdarśanāt,* the brahman is said to be luminous. (See also e.g. Śaṅkara's commentary on these sūtras; cp. also Rāmānuja on I.1.2). According to Kāvyādarśa I.4 the highest principle is of the nature of light and "sound" is its name. Without the "sound" however, the world will be dark (*idamandhātamaṁ kṛtsnaṁ jāyeta bhuvanatrayam / yadi śabdāhvayaṁ jyotirāsaṁsāraṁ na dīpyate //*). In Vedic literature the "light" is so important that L.v. Schroeder[3] rightly observes, "Was die Sänger der Rigveda-lieder pflegten und forderten das war eine Religion des Lichtes". I am inclined to add to this and say that the Vedic religion was a religion of "light" and "sound". According to the ancient Weltanschauung, "word" and "light" are very closely connected with each other even from the beginning of the world. Thus in the Bible (*John,* I.1 ff) where the process of the creation of the world is given we find how they are associated. "In the beginning was the word and the word was with God and the word was God (1). The same was in the beginning with God (2). All things were made by him and without him was not anything made that was made (3). In him was the life, and the life was the light of men (4). And the light shineth in darkness and the darkness comprehended it not (5) ..." According to TMB XX.14.2 in the beginning there was Prajāpati and Speech (*vāc*) was the only possession of him. From speech he created besides the earth and middle region, the heaven (*dyaus*) which is of luminous nature. "This has shone yonder (*adyutat*); hence the name heaven (*dyaus*)" (TMB XX.14.2). In Vedic literature we get numerous references where various aspects of words, sounds, recitations and broadly speaking, of Vedic music are associated with light.[4] Now let us see this association in detail and try to explain why such an association might have happened.

In Vedic literature music is often mentioned to be bright, shining, full of light etc.[5] Thus ṚV I.173.1, it is said, "Let us sing a bright (*svarvat*) sāman". ṚV II.9.4, the singer addresses Agni, "You are the knower of bright speech[6] (*tvaṁ śukrasya vacaso manotā*)". The same adjective is used in connection with *manīṣā* (a poem coming out of emotional excitment),[7] when the poet-singer says, "May this bright (*śukrā*)[8] *manīṣā*-goddess go like a powerful well-shaped chariot, unto the gods from us (*praśukraitu daivī manīṣā asmat sutaṣṭo ratho na vājī*" ṚV VII. 34.1). For *manīṣā* described as bright and shining see also ṚV X.177.2 where it is said that the poets guard the bright and shinning *manīṣā* at the place of *ṛta* (order).[9] The poet-singer of ṚV VIII.87.1, tells that the praise-hymn (*stoma-*) of Aśvins is full of light (*dyumnī*).[10] The warriors address Manyu (the God of Fury) who is of undivided lustre and say that they make a bright (*dyumantam*) noise for victory (AV IV.31.4). The son of Atharvan is requested "Sing at evening loudly; put it lightfully (*dyumat*); praise the god Savitṛ O son of Atharvan" (AV VI. 1.1). The war-drum (*dundubhi*) is similarly requested "Speak thou shining (*rocamānaḥ*) and speak lightfully (*dyumad vada*)" (AV V.20.6). Elsewhere the poet-singer expects from the war-drum that the brilliancy (*tviṣi-*) which is in it may come to him (AV VI.38.4). The poet-singer of AV VI.35.3, hopes that Vaiśvānara Agni may extend light (*dumnam*) and brightness (*svaḥ*) into the praise-hymns. Here Whitney[11] translates the word *svaḥ* as "heaven"; but that is out of context. The praise-hymn is mentioned as "of glowing drive (*dyuta-dyāman*)" in ṚV X.93.12. Bṛhaspati says to Devāpi that he will lay a speech full of light (*dyumatīṁ vācam*) in the mouth for the sake of him (Devāpi) (ṚV X.98.2). In ṚV X.98.3 Devāpi requests Bṛhaspati to do so: "Lay a speech full of light for us in the mouth O Bṛhaspati". ṚV X.177.2 also speech is described as shining (*dyotamānam*) and bright (*svaryam*). The poems (*mati-*) are described in ṚV X.43.1 as "finding the sun-light (*svarvidaḥ*)". Aśvins are solicited to anoint the singer with honey so that he may speak "brilliant (*bhargasvatīm*)" speech (AV VI.69.2). The poets are described in ṚV X.67.10 as "bearing light" in the mouth (*bibhrato jyotir āsā*)". Here "light" metaphorically means a song. Similarly Aśvins are requested, "Do light unto the eloquent poet (*jyotir viprāya kṛnuta vacasyave*)" (ṚV I.182.3) where the "light" can be nothing else than the inspiration for preparing songs.

Identification with light etc.

Many details of Vedic music are said to be identical with the light and help, if properly employed, to obtain light according to the Vedic texts. Thus the āprī - verses are identical with the light and brahman-splendour (*tejo vai brahmavarcasam āpriyaḥ*) (AB. II.4). The opening tristich of the sixth day in the Daśarātra of the Dvādaśāha-sacrifice means as follows: "The lustre (*jyotiḥ*) of the sacrifice is being purified, the sweet, the dear ...." (RV IX.86.10-12). By using this tristich one holds lustre and even the son of one's son becomes possessor of lustre (TMB XIII.7.2). In the Vājapeya-sacrifice the stotriyā-verses to be used at the morning-soma-pressing should contain the word "śukra (bright)" and *jyotis* (lustre)". By these verses one obtains light and the brahmansplendour (TMB XVIII.7.2).

Some stomas are often identified with light. Thus the trivṛt-stoma is identical with the light (*tejas-*) and brahman-splendour (*brahmavarcasa-*) (Cp. e.g. JB I.253; II. 332; TMB XVII. 6.3; XX.10.1; XXV.6.3). AB VIII.4 says that among the stomas the Trivṛt is the light (*tejo vai stomānāṁ trivṛt*). In the sacrifice named "Pakṣī (Bird)" there are the trivṛt-stomas on both sides and as the trivṛt - stoma is identical with light and brahman - splendour one thereby gets these. In the same manner, the Triṇava-stoma is also the light among the stomas (*tejo vai triṇava stomānām* JB II.219) and the Trayastriṁśa is lustre (*jyotiḥ*) among the stomas (*jyotiḥ trayastriṁśa stomānām* TMB XIII.7.2). Prajāpati held glow (*ruc-*) by means of the Ekaviṁśa-stoma and one who uses it also gets the same result (TB II. 2.4.6f). Another stoma, the Caturvisṁśa-stoma is also identical with light. Its identification with light is based on the identification of Gāyatrī metre with light (for Gāyatrī and light see further). The Caturviṁśa-stoma consists of twenty-four verses and the Gāyatrī-metre consists of twenty-four syllables. Thus they are equivalent. Now Gāyatrī is identical with light and therefore the Caturviṁśa-stoma also is identical with light. By using this stoma e.g. on the seventh day of the Daśarātra of the Dvādaśāha one becomes possessor of light and brahman-splendour (see JB III.176; cp. TMB XIV.1.14; see and cp. also TMB XV.7.8; 11.16).

The sāmans are also in close relationship with light. According to TB III.12.9.2 "all the light is always of the nature of sāman (*sarvaṁ tejaḥ sāmarūpayaṁ ha śaśvat*)". GB I.2.9 identifies the Brahman with the sacrifice. The body of this sacrifice is nothing but ṛcs; motion is yajus; *lustre is sāman*; and the power (*māyā*) is bhṛgvaṅgirases. Elsewhere some of the sāmans are identified with light and it is said that they help to obtain light. He who desires to get light and brahman-splendour should use the Gaurivīta sāman as the ṣoḍaśi-sāman. For the Gaurivīta is identical with light and brahman-splendour (AB IV.2). The Vārṣasāman is identical with the brilliance (*dīpti-*) and brahman-splendour. By means of this Vārśa-sāman Ikṣvākus obtained the glowing power of Agni (fire). He who employs this sāman, also will be possessor of light and brahman-splendour (JB III.96). The Hārāyaṇa sāman is also helpful for obtaining the glowing power (*haras-*). Thus at the time of a battle between the Gods and Asuras, the gods desired to obtain the glowing power of the Asuras. Then they saw this sāman and praised with it. Thereby they were able to rob the glowing power of the Asuras; the knowledge of this enables man to win the glowing power of his enemy (JB III.217).

According to TMB XIV.9.34 this Hārāyaṇa sāman was discovered by Indra who was desirous of obtaining light and glowing power. He got his desire fulfilled by means of this sāman. Another sāman named Yajñāyajñīya is also identical with light and by using it one puts light in the Mādhyandina as it were (JB III.290). The Udvaṁśīya sāman is light of all the Pṛṣṭhas[12]. For when the pṛṣṭhas were created, whatever light, whatever sap had overflown, that became the Udvaṁśīya sāman (TMB VIII.9.6 f). The names Bhāsa ("shining") (TMB XIV.11.2) and Bharga ("Lustrous") (TMB XV.3.2) of two other sāmans themselves indicate their luminous nature.

The metres do not lack luminousity. Thus Gāyatrī is very often identified with light and Brahman-splendour. One who is desirous of these should make the saṁyājyā-verses of the Sviṣṭakṛt offering of the dīkṣaṇīyeṣṭi in the course of the Agniṣṭoma in the Gāyatrī-metre (AB I.5). Similarly, in the same sacrifices at the time when Agni is being brought forward, the Hotṛ recites a verse in Gāyatrī-metre (viz. ṚV X. 176.2), if the sacrificer belongs to the Brāhmaṇa-class. For Gāyatrī is identical with light and brahmansplendour (*tejo vai brahmavarcaṁ gāyatrī*) and thus the Hotṛ makes the sacrificer prosper in light and brahman-splendour (AB I.28). Gāyatrī is sometimes identified with light alone without any reference to the brahman-splendour (see *tejo gāyatrī* - KS XXXIV.9; ŚB XIII. 2.6.4; *tejo vai gāyatrī* - JB II.346; 353; 361; GB II.5.3; etc; cp. *tejo vai gāyatrī chandasāṁ* - TMB XV.10.7; *jyotir vai gāyatrī* KB XVII.6). KPKS XXXVII.1, it is said that Gāyatrī is the most lustrous among the metres because she brought Soma from heaven. The metre named Śakvarī also possesses the power of light. It "heated" the sixth day of the Daśarātra in the Dvādaśāha-sacrifice by means of its light (JB III.143). The Virāj-metre is similarly said to be the brilliance (*jyotiḥ*) among the metres (*virāṭ chandasāṁ jyotiḥ* TS V.5.2.3; KS XX.11; KPKS XXXI.12; cp. MS III.2.9).

The importance of *svara* (note) is obvious in the music. It is said to be identical with the Sun (*ya ādityaḥ svara eva saḥ* JUB

III.6.5.1). According to GB I.5.14, it is Soma who having become the Sun shines (*svarati*) in "that" world. Because he shines (*svarati*) therefore *svara* is so called. The close verbal connection between the two words *svara* (note) and *svar* (light) cannot be easily overlooked.[13] In this respect we may refer to an Egyptian word *hoisiou* which is a plural of a word which signifies *fascination by the look* as well as *incatation* (in the etymological and Latin sense).[14] We may also quote J. Grim's opinion that there is etymological affinity between "peeping and "piping". The German word *svegel* means "pipe" and "light" (*Deutsche Mythologie* Göttingen, 1844, p. 706ff).[15] It may further be added that in ancient Mesopotemia, music was connected with brightness. The word *zahra* meant to shine brightly and hence that which produced "brightness", i.e. a tambourine, was called *mizahr.*[16] A Chinese emperor Fouhi got a musical instrument prepared out of the wood of a tree on which he saw five *stars* precipitating themselves.[17]

Music is sometimes shown to be closely connected with the sun which is the most prominent source of light. We have just mentioned the identification of *svara* and the sun. The origin of the Sāmaveda, according to the ŚB XI.5.8.3 is from the sun (*sūryāt sāmavedaḥ ajāyata*; cp. AB V.32; KB VI.10; JB I.357; ṢaḍB IV.1.2; GB I.1.6; ChāU IV.17.2). In the Ṛgveda the origin of two sāmans is said to be from Savitṛ (one of the forms of the sun) and other gods. Thus Vasiṣṭha fetched the Rathantara sāman from the glowing (*dyutānāt*) creator (Dhātṛ), Savitṛ and Viṣṇu (ṚV X.181.1). Further, Bhāradvāja is said to have fetched Bṛhat-sāman; similarly from the glowing creator, Savitṛ, and Agni (ṚV X.181.2). Thus at the origin of music there is the idea of light.[18]

Conversely the sun is mentioned as born out of sāman and ṛc (JUB I.17.2.8). According to ṚV I.164.25 and AV IX.10.3, the creator of the world, saw the sun, in the Rathantara-sāman (*rathantare sūryaṁ paryapaśyat*). ṚV VIII.89.1, the sun is indirectly said to be originated from the Bṛhatsāman. There, the Maruts are requested to sing the Bṛhatsāman - "Sing the

Bṛhatsāman, the most powerful killer of Vṛtra, O Maruts, for Indra, through which the increasers of *ṛta* (order) created the divine waking light for the god". Here the divine light is obviously the sun and that is said to be created through the Bṛhatsāman. JUB I.1.1.5 ascribes the origin of the sun to the sap of the Sāmaveda. Thus Prajāpati took the sap (*rasa*) of the Sāmaveda viz. *svar*; it became the sky. The sap of it which streamed forth became Āditya (sun).

The close relations of music and sun will be clear from GB I.1.29 where Āditya is said to be the deity of sāmans (*sāmnām ādityo daivatam*; cp. I.2.24; see also Padmapurāṇa V.24.74 according to which sun is the lord (*adhīśa*) of sāmans. Similarly ŚB IX.4.1.8 explains VS XVIII.39, Viśvasāma (possessor of all sāmans)[19] by saying that the sun is identical with the whole sāman (*eṣa hyeva sarvaṁ sāma*). ChāU I.6.1 also identifies the sun with sāman (*ādityaḥ sāma*). The Mahānārāyaṇa Upaniṣad XII.2 says: what in this disk there shines is the flame that are the sāmans (*ya etasmin maṇḍale'rchiḥ dīpyate tāni sāmāni*). JUB I.3.2.5 suggests the identification of sāman and the sun when it remarks, "This sun is the same (*sama*) as all the worlds. Therefore it is sāman". Earlier, in the same text it has been narrated how Prajāpati gave different parts of sāman to different creatures. Thus he gave *hiṁkāra* to cattle, prastāva to men; *ādi* to birds, *udgītha* to gods; *pratihāra* to the beasts of forests, *upadrava* to the Gandharvas and Apsarases and *nidhana* to the fathers (JUB I.3.1.1ff). Then it is said, "In that he gave this sāman, he gave this sun" (JUB I.3.2.3). Now follows a metaphorical description of the sun as sāman "When it (sun) is not yet risen, it is *hiṁhāra*; when half-risen, it is *prastāva*; at the time when the cows are driven together, it is *ādi*; noon is *udgītha*; afternoon is *pratihāra*; when it turns red towards the sunset it is *upadrava*; having gone to the setting, it is *nidhana* (JUB I.3.2.4). The following passage from ChU II.9.1ff, where one is advised to meditate on the sevenfold sāman in the sun, agrees very much with the JUB I.3.2.4. Thus we read: "It (sun) is the *sāman* because it is always the same. It is the same with everyone since people think, "It faces me", "It faces me" ... Before rising it is *hiṁkāra.* On this depend the animals .... When it is just after sun-rise, that is *prastāva*; on it men depend .... when it is the time of cow-gathering, it is *ādi* ; on it depend the birds ... when it is noon, that is *udgītha*; on it depend the gods ... when it is past midday and before afternoon that is *pratihāra*; on it depend the foetuses ... When it is past afternoon and before sunset, that is *upadrava*; on it depend the beasts of forests ... When it is just after sunset, that is *nidhana*; on it depend the fathers ..." Here we get a description in connection with the sāman in general. But similar description in connection with the Bṛhat sāman is to be found in ChU II. 14.1 - "The rising sun is *hiṁkāra*; the risen is *prastāva*; the noon is *udgītha*; the afternoon is *pratihāra*; when it is setting, it is *nidhana.* This is the Bṛhat (sāman) as woven in the Sun". Śaṅkhāyana Āraṇyaka also expressly says that the sun is connected with the Bṛhat (sāman) (*bārhato vā eṣa ya eṣa tapati.* II. 17). JB II.15 identifies the sāman named Rājana with the sun (*ādityo rājanam*).

In the Chāndogya-Upaniṣad the sacred syllable *om* is described to be *udgītha* (the main part of a melody) and one is advised to meditate on *udgītha* in various ways. "Him who glows yonder (the sun) one should meditate as *udgītha*; verily on rising, he sings aloud for creatures. On rising, he dispells darkness and fear" (I.3.7). Thus the sun is said to be a singer and his rise and music are closely connected with the removal of darkness and fear i.e. removal of evil spirits. Thus both light and music are of an apotropic nature. (This point will be dealt with in more details further down). For the identification of *udgītha* and sun one may also refer to ChU I.5.1 *asau vā āditya udgīthaḥ*: - this sun indeed is udgītha. While in the passage ChU I.3.1, cited above, the sun is said to be singing for creatures, elsewhere ChU describes the creatures singing for the sun. Uṣasti a moneyless philosopher of music says, "Verily, all beings here sing of the sun when he is up. This is the divinity connected with the *Udgītha*" (ChU I.11.7). ŚB X.5.1.4

identifies speech with the sun (*sā yā sā vāg asau sa ādityaḥ*). According to ṚV X.177.2 the Bird i.e., sun, holds the speech by means of mind (*pataṅgo vācaṁ manasā bibharti*). Caraṇa-vyuha IV. describing the Sāmaveda tells us that its colour is like that of the sun (*ādityavarṇo varṇena*).

The description of the sun as a Gandharva[20] (a semidivine genie with music as a speciality) can further point out the close connection of the sun and music and thereby of the light and music. Thus ṚV IX.85.12 describes sun-rise as the rise of a Gandharva :- "The Gandharva has risen to the sky exhibiting all his forms. His ray flashed in bright glow. He has enlightened both the worlds". In the *mantra* in which Savitṛ is requested to instigate sacrifice, he is described as the heavenly Gandharva and is requested to purify thoughts (*divyo gandharvaḥ ketapūḥ ketaṁ naḥ punātu* VS IX.1; TS I.7.7.1; IV. 1.1.2; MS I.11.1; KS XI.7; XXX.1; ŚB V.1.1.16; for the description of sun as the "divine Gandharva" see also AV II.2.1.; 2). ŚB VI.3.1.19 explaining this remark says clearly "This sun indeed is the divine Gandharva (*sūryo gandharvaḥ*; cp. TS III.4.7.1; MS II.12.2; KS XVIII.14; KPKS XXIX.3, ŚB VI.3.1.19). According to Lātyās's I.12.16, the Udgātṛ while muttering the prayer "Obeisance to Gandharva" looks at the sun. Sūryavarsas (having the light similar to that of the sun) is a very significant name of a Gandharva (AV VIII. 10.27). In the Buddhistic canon (Majjhimanikāya, Sapkapañhasutta) an Apsaras (divine damsel) named Suriyavaccasā is mentioned. This name has the same significance as the Sūryavarcas.

Music is often mentioned to be helpful to the sun. It helps the sun to rise up: "You O Sūrya, rise up before us (drawn) by the praise-hymns (*stoma*) (*sa sūrya prati puro na udgā ebhiḥ stomebhiḥ* ..." ṚV VII.62.2).[21] The sun shines when music is performed. Thus ṚV VIII.29.10, it is vaguely said, "Some made the sun shine by means of sāmans (*arcanta eke mahi sāma manvata tena suryamarocayan*)". Here according to Sāyaṇa Atris are meant by the word "some (*eke*)". Geldner[22] has accepted Sāyaṇa's suggestion. But Lüders[23] and Oldenberg[24] refer to Aṅgirases. It is indeed said in ṚV X.62.3 that the

Aṅgirases have elevated the sun into the heaven by means of the *ṛta* (order). But as far as "making the shining" of the sun by means of music is concerned, it is better to agree with Sāyaṇa in understanding Atris by the word "some". About the activity of Atris we shall speak afterwards. The stomas named Viśvajit and Abhijit are said to be identical with valour (*vīrya*) and are to be used for supporting the sun according to TMB IV.5.11. The sun likes music as can be conjectured on the basis of his description as *sāmapriya* (one who loves sāman) in the Skandapurāṇa (Māheśvarakhaṇḍa, Kaumāri, 43.30). Earlier, in the eleventh verse of the same Purāṇa, Nārada is mentioned informing that he has pleased the sun by means of sāmans (*sāmabhir vividhair devaṁ (= suryaṁ) paryatoṣayam īśvaram*).

The gods also use music in supporting and helping the sun. Thus AB IV.19 tells a story in which significance of Divākīrtya-sāmans is told. "The gods were afraid of this Āditya falling from the world of heaven. They fastened him up with five ropes; The Divākīrtya-sāmans are the ropes; the Pṛṣṭha is the Mahādivākīrtya, the sāman of the Brāhmaṇācchaṁsin is the Vikarṇa, the Agniṣṭoma-sāman is the Bhāsa, the Bṛhat and Rathantara are those of the Pavamānas; thus they fasten up Āditya with five ropes, for support and to avoid falling down (*tad ādityam pañcabhir udvayanti dhṛtyai anavapātāya*"; cp. KS XXIII.6; TB I.2.4.2; cp. VII.3.10.1). The same story is told in connection with the Saptadaśa-stomas in TMB IV.5.9- "The gods were afraid lest the sun should fall down from the world of heaven; they fastened him by means of these seventeen-versed stomas; there are stomas for the sake of supporting the sun (cp. KS XXIII. 6 where the Caturstriṁśa-stomas are said to have done the same work)". In TB I.2.4.2, the gods are said to be afraid of the going too high of the sun. Therefore they supported and fastened it by means of the metres. Earlier, in TB I.2.4.1, it is said that the gods elevated the sun by means of the Ekaviṁśa-stoma (cp. KS XXXIII.6). Then TB I.2.4.3 says that the gods conveyed the sun to the heaven by means of Para and Spara-sāmans. They delivered the sun (from darkness)[25] in the heaven (cp. KS XXXIII.6). In every season different groups of Gandharvas and Apsarases increase the light of the sun. Thus in spring Tumbaru and Nārada are the Gandharvas and Kṛtasthalā is the Apsaras who follow the sun and increase his light. In the summer Hahā and Hūhū are the G. and Menakā and Sahajanyā are the A. who do the same work. In the Rainy season Śucisena and Ugraratha are the G. and Pramlocantī and Vimlocantī are the A. in the Autumn Citrasena and Vasuruci are the G. and Viśvācī and Ghṛtācī are the A. In the winter Citrasena and Ūrṇāyu are the G. and Pūrvacitti and Urvaśī are the A. Finally in the cold season Dhṛtarāṣṭra and Sūryavarcas are the G. and Tilottamā and Rambhā are the A. These singing and dancing genii increase the light of the sun (Viṣṇudharmottarapurāṇa III.168.2ff, 26; cp. Garuḍapurāṇa I.58.20f). Music increases the power of the sun,[26] nay, the music itself is the power of the sun. Thus Ādityas are described by ṚV X.63.3 as *ukthaśuṣman-* (those, the praise-songs are power of whom).

Music has an important role in rescuing the sun from eclipse. Thus the gods delivered (*aspṛṇvan*) the sun when the demoniac Svarbhānu struck the sun with darkness. The gods delivered it by means of the Svarasāmans (TMB IV.5.2; cp. KB XXIV.3). According to TMB IV.6.13, perhaps at another time, gods removed the darkness and rescued the sun by means of the Divākīrtya-sāman (cp. JB II.390). It is, however, important to see that according to TMB VI.6.8 and XIV.11.14 it was Atri who removed the darkness by means of the Bhāsa-sāman. The name Bhāsa itself suggests the luminous nature of the sāman and accordingly TMB XIV.11.14 gives the derivation of the word Bhāsa as follows: The demoniac Svarbhānu struck the sun with darkness; so that it did not shine; by means of the Bhāsa ("light") Atri repelled the darkness, so that it again shone. Because it (the Sun) got this as its light, therefore, it (the sāman) is called "light (Bhāsa)". When we take into account such stories, then we can support Sāyaṇa when he interpreting ṚV X.62.3 ("Some made the sun shining by means of sāman") says that by the word "some" we have to understand Atris. The power of music of Atris used for the rescue of the sun from darkness (i.e. eclipse) has already been mentioned in the ṚV V.40. which "entzauberung der Verfinsterten Sonne durch Atri enthält" can be regarded as a family - hymn of the Atris.[27] In this hymn[28] verses 5 ff contain the eclipse-removing activity successfully accomplished by Atris. The sun was struck by the demoniac Svarbhānu (verse 5). When Indra destroyed the marvellous powers (*māyāḥ*)[29] of Svarbhānu, Atri discovered (or rather recovered) by the fourth powerful text (*brahman-*)[30] the sun hidden by the hostile darkness (verse 6). Atri placed the eye of the sun in the sky (verse 7). The Atris discovered the sun which Svarbhānu had struck with darkness; no others could (verse 8).[31] Thus it seems that Atri must have recited four prayers and after the fourth prayer darkness was removed. So in the Ṛgvedic references also the power of Atri's music in removing the darkness viz. the eclipse is mentioned. AV XIII.2.12 the sun is addressed, "Atri maintained thee in the sky, O Sun, to make month".

In the Mahābhārata, Kṛṣṇa tells Yudhiṣṭhira to use a praise-formula in Gāyatrī-metre addressed to Viṣṇu or Śiva at the time of Sun - or Moon-eclipse. The sound of conch-shells, and other musical-instruments, and of bells of bronze is also said to be made. By means of music, offerings, mutterings (*homajapyaiḥ*) and well-sounding noises, Rāhu becomes powerless and soma (= moon) becomes powerful.[32]

The use of the power of sound and of music in general, in order to remove the eclipse or its bad consequences is familiar to the other parts of the world[33] also. Livy refers to the custom of making noise during an eclipse of the moon, presumably to frighten away the beast that is supposed to be devouring it.[34] Tacitus has referred to the practice of driving away an eclipse, by means of beating drums and cymbals. The habitants of Turin long continued this practice.[35] The Chinese people suppose that a dog or a beast swallows the sun or moon at the time of eclipse. The Chinese then beat gongs to rescue the sun or moon[36] or make vacarmes[37] or set fire to crackers and clash pots and pans[38] to put in flight the dragon who will swallow the light at the time of eclipse. Cambella, a Dominician monk predicted that an eclipse would be fatal to him. In order to avoid the evil consequences, he burnt romantic herbs day by day and played sweet and harmonious music - a magical practice as mentioned by Picard.[39]

Metres and the sun are closely associated with each other. Thus the sun is said to be belonging sometimes to Bṛhatī-metre (*bārhataḥ sūryaḥ* KS VI.8; KPKS IV.7; cp. KB XV.4; GB II.5.7), sometimes to Triṣṭubh metre (*traiṣṭubho vā eṣa ya eṣa tapati* KB XXV.4) and sometimes Jagatī-metre (*jāgato vā eṣa ya eṣa tapati* - KB XXV.7). The seven metres viz. Gāyatrī, Uṣṇih, Anuṣṭubh, Bṛhatī, Paṅkti, Triṣṭubh and Jagatī are said to be seven horses of the chariot of sun (Viṣṇudharmottarapurāṇa III.67.12; cp. Agnipurāṇa 120.26). The seven metres mentioned above, and the Virāj as the eighth, are said to be "protecting" the sun (KB XXIII.4).

Music is connected with the run of the sun.[40] Thus the sun goes, in the morning, with the help of ṛcs, stands in the Yajurveda at noon; and becomes honoured by the Sāmaveda in the evening; thus the sun goes with all the vedas (TB III. 12.9.1).

Like the sun, Fire (Agni) is another source of light and music in the Veda is also connected with Fire. It is kindled by means of music.[41] Thus ṚV X.118.5, Agni is addressed, "you, being praise-sung are being kindled". The Urukṣayas kindled the fire by means of songs (*gir-*) (ṚV X.118.9).[42] Further, Bhṛgus inflamed (*virurucuḥ*) Agni by means of praise-hymns (*stomas*) in the house (ṚV X.122.5). Coming to the Brāhmaṇa-texts we find that TMB relates the following story of the use of Āgneya-sāman which is to be used on the fifth day of the Dvādaśāha-sacrifice. "Agni being created did not flame. With this sāman, Prajāpati blew on it and thereupon it did flame up. This sāman is indeed brilliancy (*dīpti*) and brahman-splendour. By means of this sāman one obtains brilliancy and brahman-splendour" (TMB XIII.3.22). According to JB III. 100 this sāman was perceived by Agni himself, desiring to be the eater of food and to be superior among his own. The connection of sāman with the flaming up of the fire is further narrated in JB III.101 by means of a dialogue between Sākamaśva and Kakṣīvat. Kakṣīvat asks, "Who is he who kindles but does not inflame?" The answer given by Sākmaśva was, "He who employes a ṛc-verse but no sāman, it is he who kindles but does not inflame". Thus the sāman is said here to have the power of inflaming the fire. By means of Vārśa-sāman the Ikṣvākus obtained back the glowing power (*haras*) of Agni (JB III.96). Agni was in the beginning as much as hot charcoals (*aṅgāra-*). He wanted to have flames. He saw the Śnauṣṭa-sāman and praised with it (JB III.165). Thus for getting flames, Agni had to take the help of music.

Metres and fire are closely associated. "With the metres Agni reached the Uttaravedi" (KPKS XXXI.7). With the metres Agni is carried towards the Uttaravedi (MS III.2.5). If the fire is extinguished before the Agnihotra is offered, then fire is rekindled with the verses *itaḥ prathamam* .... etc. Having prescribed this TS II.2.4.8 comments, "One produces it with the metres, from his own womb". KS XIX.10; XX.4; KPKS XXX.8; XXXI.6, metres are said to be the womb of Agni (*chandāṁsi vā agner yoniḥ*). TS V.7.9.3 identifies fires with metres (*agnayo vai chandāṁsi*). Metres are described to be the garments of Agni (*chandāṁsi vā agner vāsaḥ* MS III.1.5; KS XIX.5; KPKS XXX.3). Metres in general are the dear form of Agni (KS XX. 1). Sometimes however, Anuṣṭubh is said to be the dear form of Agni (KS XIX.5; KPKS XXX.3). Gāyatrī is the metre of Agni according to MS I.6.9. On the other hand Agni is said to be belonging to the Gāyatrī metre in TS III.5.4.4; MS I.9.5; KS IX.13; KPKS VII.6; KB I.1.

Agni is described to be a Gandharva in TS III.4.7.1; MS II. 12.2,3; KS XVIII.14.

Music and Lightning[43]

It is worthy to be noticed how lightning, another form of light is connected with music. Indra, it is said in ṚV X.99.2 desires sāman by means of lightning (*sa hi vidyutā veti sāma*).[44] JB I.128 two lightnings are mentioned. The horizontal lightning is supposed to be belonging to the Rathantara-sāman and the vertical lightning belongs to the Bṛhat-sāman (*yā vai tiraścī vidyut sā rāthantarī yordhvā sā bārhatī*). The sāman named Aniṣedha is identified with lightning by JUB I.9.3.4.

Dīpa-rāga

In connection with the Dīpa-rāga in classical music there is a tradition that whoever shall attempt to sing the Dīpa (or Dīpaka, "Lamp") rāga, he will be destroyed by fire, because it creates heat in the body of the singer. King Akbar asked Gopal Nayak inspite of the latter's reluctance, to sing the rāga. He sang the rāga placing himself in the Yamunā river upto the neck. As soon as he had performed a strain or two, the river became hot and afterwards began to boil. He requested the king to ask him to stop but in vain. He continued singing and was burnt though immersed in the waters and was consumed to ashes.[45]

The Dīpa-rāga is to be sung in the evening and according to traditional belief, when it is sung (of course correctly and powerfully enough), the lamps are automatically lighted by the mere power of the tunes of that melody. Thus in the Śanimāhātmya[46] we are told that when the king Vikrama who was well-versed in music, began to sing the Dīpa-rāga, lakhs of lamps were automatically lighted up in all over the city (*to dīparācā avasara / dhyānāta āṇirājeśvara / rāga āḷavitase madhura / susvara kaṇṭhe karonī // 227 // rāga-uddhāra karitā pratyakṣa / dīpa lāgale lakṣānulakṣa / jaiśī dīpāvaḷīca dekha / prakāśamāna nagarāta // 228 //*

A question will naturally arise why music should have such close connections with light. In answering this question we shall have to take into consideration that both sound and light are of apotropic nature. Both are used in removing the evil spirits. Music can kill evil spirits. Thus sāman is said to be killer of evil spirits (*sāma vai rakṣohā* TS VI.6.3.1; TĀ V.9.4).[47] The sacrificer possessed by evil-spirits (*rakṣogṛhītaḥ*) has to employ Hārivarṇa as the brahma-sāman in order to repel the rakṣas (JB I.183). The Asuras once robbed the sap of three pressings of the soma-sacrifice and entered into blind darkness. The gods defeated them by means of the Ukthas (JB I.179f). The evil spirits, demons, ghosts and the like are generally associated with darkness[48] and light is a means of removing or killing them.[49] Thus ŚB I.3.4.8 says, "The sun is the repeller of destructive evil (*sūryo vai nāṣṭrāṇāṁ rakṣasām apahantā*)". Similarly Agni is also a repeller of evil spirits. AV I.28.1 describes Agni as the killer of Rakṣas (*rakṣohā*, cp. AV IV.23.3; cp. VI. 34.2; TS VI.1.4.5 f; ṢaḍB III.1.9). AV VI.32.1, one prays Agni to burn demons (*ārād rākṣāṁsi pratidaha*). Sometimes both these apotropic powers are employed in ritual to remove or kill evil spirits. Thus on the tenth day in the Dvādaśāha-sacrifice verses containing the word "sun" (viz. *suryasyeva raśmayo drvāvayitnavaḥ* ṚV IX.69.6; SV II.720) are to be employed for the sake of killing evil spirits. Here both the powers namely the light-power of the sun and the musical power of the recitation of the verses work together. Similarly, during the Pravargya ceremony in the soma-sacrifice the sāman is to be sung in the verses relating to Agni. The sāman is sung with the purpose of killing the evil spirits (ŚB XIV.3.1.10 f). And as the sāman and Agni each are killers of the evil spirits here the power of both of them are jointly to be used in order to get the expected result more quickly and surely.

It is, however, interesting to note that sometimes music is connected with darkness, evil spirits, black colour etc. Thus sound is regarded as the substance of powers of darkness and a dwelling place of them.[50] The sāmans are connected with the *tamoguṇa* (quality of darkness) in Mārkaṇḍeyapurāṇa 99.7 (*ṛco rajoguṇāḥ sattvaṁ yajuṣāṁ ca guṇo mune / tamoguṇāni sāmāni tamaḥ sattvamatharvasu //*). In the black-antelope's skin there are two colours: White and black. The white colour represents the ṛcs and the black the sāmans according to TS VI.1.3.1 (cp. ŚB VI.7.1.7; contrast KS XXIII.3). JUB IV. 11.3.12, ChāU I.6.5 f and 7.4 f also the sāman is connected with the black colour.

Thus we find that music is double-natured. It is brilliant; it is also dark. It is supposed to be apotropic as well as a dwelling place of evil spirits.

From the above observations the following points can be obtained.

(1) Vedic literature along with other literatures show that the music and light are, according to the primitive Weltanschauung, closely connected. Thus (a) Music is described to be "bright", "shining" etc. (b) The repertoires of light like Sun, Fire, Lightning are found to be closely associated with music and are strengthened by music. (c) Music and light are at various places described as the origin of each other. (d) Music is used in magical rites against the eclipses, and thus for making light.

(2) The main reason of such close connections can be considered as concealed in the apotropic nature of both. They both remove or kill evil spirits.

(3) Music is also connected with darkness, black colour etc. Thus it is double-natured. It is supposed to remove evil beings and it is also a dwelling place of them.

REFERENCES

1. For the "light" in Veda and elsewhere rf. Gonda, *Vision of the vedic poets*, p. 266; see in general also Hastings (ed.) *ERE*, VIII, p. 47 ff.
2. Ed. Vasudevashastri Abhyankar, Poona, 1951.
3. *Mysterium und Mimus im Rigveda*, p. 54.
4. On music and light in general see Belvianes, *Sociologie de la musique*, p. 5 ff. The author has observed there the close connections of Apollo, Hermes, Minerva, Pan and Viṣṇu with light and music.

5. Pindar qualifies a hymn used in a festival of Jupiter with an objective meaning "eclatant" (Combarieu, *La musique et la magie*, p. 301). In the modern period Dostoevsky described La Marseillaise (song connected with the French Revolution and now the national anthem of France) as "shining" (rf. Belvianes, *Sociologie de la musique*, p. 188 f; on p. 187 we read that Michelet also described it as "cet eclair du ciel").
6. Rf. Renou, *EVP*, XII, p. 47.
7. For the word *manīṣā* see Grassmann, *Wörterbuch zum Rigveda*, 936 ("Andachtslied") Renou, *EVP*, I. p. 3 (inspiration poetique), Thieme, *Kleine Schriften*, p. 103 ("Erregheit").
8. Renou, *EVP*, *V*. p. 38 translates the word *śukrā* as "pure".
9. Gonda, *Vision of the Vedic poets*, p. 273.
10. Geldner, *Der Rigveda .... Übersetzt* II, p. 87. Sāyaṇa understands by the word *dyumnī*, *Dyumnīka*, proper name of a seer and he takes *stoma* to mean "one who praises". This is too artificial.
11. *Atharvaveda-Saṁhitā*, I, p. 307.
12. The pṛṣṭhas themselves are identical with light (*tejo vai pṛṣṭhāni* JB II.376) and brahman-splendour (*tejo vai brahmavarcasaṁ pṛṣṭhāni* TMB XVI.15.7).
13. Rf. Schneider in Wellesz, *AOM*, p. 49.
14. Combarieu, *La musique et la magie*, p. 140.
15. Refered to by Schneider, in Wellesz, *AOM*, p. 49.
16. Rf. Farmer in Wellesz, *AOM*, p. 423.
17. Referred to by Combarieu, *La musique et la magie*, p. 259.
18. Cf. Belvianes, *Sociologie de la musique*, p. 10.
19. Eggeling, *SBE*, XLIII, p. 231 translates the word sāman as "wealth" but that is out of the context.
20. Cp. Oldenberg, *Religion des Veda*, p. 245 f; For the connection of light and Gandharvas see also L.v. Schroeder, *Mysterium und Mimus*, p. 54.
21. Cf. Geldner, *Der Rigveda ..*, II. p. 238.
22. *Der Rigveda in Auswahl*, II. (Kommentar), p. 126.
23. Ludwig, *Commentar zur Rigveda-übersetzung*, I , p. 230 says: "Natürlich musz das Lied einen Aṅgirasa zum Verfasser haben. S. aber erklart die Atri; es ist disz wol auffallend; es erklärt sich zwar ausz V. 40. 5-8; enbert aber der warscheinlichkeit".

24. Oldenberg, *Rigveda ... Noten*, II, p. 101, agrees with Ludwig; he, however, adds, "doch ist Gedanke an Maruts nicht Weggelassen".
25. For music as removing darkness see Combarieu, *La musique et la magie*, p. 48.
26. For music as increasing the power of the sun, see Seeman, in *Handwörterbuch der deutschen Aberglaubens* VI. 649.
27. Geldner, *Der Rigveda* ..... II, p. 38.
28. For this hymn see V. G. Rahurkar, in *JGRI*, XXV, 1969 (*Umesh Mishra Commemoration Vol.*) p. 511 ff.
29. For *māyā* see Gonda, *Four studies*, p. 119 ff.
30. Cf. Gonda, *Notes on Brahman*, p. 14.
31. For the story of Atri, removing darkness from the Sun see also KS XXVII. 4 (for this text see also Weber, *IS*, III, 1855, p. 465); KPKS XLIV, 4; JB I. 80 (for this text see H. Oertel, "Contributions from the Jaiminīya-brāhmaṇa to the history of Brāhmaṇa-literature", *JAOS*, 26, 1905, p. 191); KB XXIV.4; GB I.2.17; II.3.19.
32. Mbh (Critical edn.) XIV. app. I.4.3105 ff:
    candrasūryagrahe vāpi mama vā śaṅkarasya vā / 3105 /
    gāyatrīṁ māmikāṁ vāpi japed yaḥ śaṅkarasya vā / 6 /
    śaṅkhatūryaninādaiśca kāṁsyaghaṇṭāsvanair api / 7 /
    kārayet tu dhvaniṁ bhaktyā tasya puṇyaphlaṁ śruṇu / 8 /
    gāndharvair homajapyaiśca śabdair utkṛṣṭanādibhiḥ / 9 /
    durbalo'pi bhavedrāhuḥ somaśca balavān bhavet / 10 /
33. See Combarieu, *La musique et la magie*, p. 48.
34. *ERE*, X. p. 368 (b)
35. *ERE*, X. p. 368 (b).
36. *ERE*, X. p. 369 (a), cp. Courant, in Lavignac, *EnM*, I. p. 185.
37. Belvianes, *Sociologie de la musique*, p. 46.
38. *ERE*, VIII, p. 51 (b)
39. Belvianes, *Sociologie de la musique*, p. 55.
40. Hillebrandt, *Ritualliteratur*, p. 106.
41. Cf. Hubert, Mauss, "Magie" *L'Annee Sociologique*, VII (1902-3), p. 98, see also Combarieu, *La musique et la magie*, p. 250.
42. Geldner, *Der Rigveda*, III, p. 344; Renou, *EVP*, XIV, p. 28
43. Cf. the description La Marseillaise by Michelet in n. 5.
44. Geldner, *Der Rigveda*, III. p. 311
45. Cf. W. Ousley, "Anecdotes of Indian Music" in S.M. Tagore (ed.) *Hindu Music*, p. 166.

46. A mediaeval Marathi poem describing the powers of the Planet Saturn.
47. For music as removing the wicked spirits see Gunkel, Zscharnack (ed.) *RGG*, IV, 296; cp. also II. 524.
48. Cf. e.g. *ERE*, VIII, p. 50 (a).
49. For apotropic nature of light see e.g. Meyer, *Trilogie* II. p. 102 ff.
50. Schneider, in Wellesz, *AOM*, p. 51.

(K) MUSIC AND WAR

Music is closely associated with war. Among the Hebrews it used to be performed at the time of war.[1] Plutarch gives some details of the use of music in the war.[2] There was military music in Rome.[3] Among some African tribes, when the husbands were at war the wives must dance until they (the wives) fall down.[4] Music is performed at the time of war for the sake of getting victory.[5]

In Vedic literature also we find that music is supposed to be helpful for being victorious in war.[6] It encourages the fighters, increases there enthusiasm and makes them accomplish the valourous activities successfully. ṚV I.152.7 a poet-singer expresses his hope, "May our powerful hymns (*brahman-*) be victorious in the battles". ṚV VIII.1.8 a poet-singer is addressed, "Sing loudly a song for him (Indra) by which Indra will come to sit upon the barhis of Kaṇva and will break the fortresses (of the enemies)". Similarly ṚV VI.34.5, we read, "For him (Indra) a praise-song (*āṅgūṣa-*) is sung, for him a praise-hymn (*stotra-*); for him a thoughtful poem (*mati-*), so that Indra may become a helper and supporter in the battle". The priests-singers celebrate Indra with praise-songs and strengthen him for killing the dragon (ṚV V.31.4). Indra growing powerful by means of praise-songs (*uktha-*) crushed down Vṛtra (ṚV II.11.2). According to ṚV IV.17.19, "Indra when praised, being alone, kills many opponents". ṚV IX. 11.3; it is hoped, "The praise-songs, the powers have gone to him; may they make Indra enthusiastic for victory".

At the time of battles, the priest-singers of both the sides sing the praises of gods and try to attract the gods towards their own side. Thus ṚV VII.83.7, it is said, "Both parties call you (O Indra and Varuṇa) at the time of battles for the sake of winning", cp. "We invoke you O bulls (Indra and Varuṇa) by means of our good songs (*suvṛkti-*) (ṚV VIII.83.8); cp. also the following request: "The cry is raised upto the heaven O Indra and Varuṇa .... Come here with favour, O hearers of calls" (ṚV VII.83.31). ṚV VII.33.5, the power of the songs of Vasiṣthas is expressed by saying: "Indra listened unto Vasiṣṭha when he was singing praises and made wide world for Tṛtsus". Similarly ṚV VII.83.4 we read, "You listened unto the hymns of these at the time of the emergency-call. The Purohitaship of the Tṛtsus proved to be successful". In the sacrifice of one who desires of fighting in a battle, the following opening tristich is prescribed to be used: *tayā pavasva dhārayā* (JB I.92). The weapons are stirred up by means of speech (*vacas-*) and the powers are sharpened by means of powerful formula (AV V.2.5). At the time of battle din is produced for the sake of victory (*dyumantaṁ ghoṣaṁ vijayāya kṛṇmasi* AV IV.51.4; cp. ṚV X.84.4).

Among the musical instruments, Dundubhi (m.) (drum) is the most important in the war. The power of this instrument was well recognised. ṚV VI.47. 29-31 (= AV V.126), AV V.20. and 21 are in praise of the drum. In these texts many magicoreligious significances of this instrument are expressed. He (the Drum) is loud-noised (*uccairghoṣa-*) (AV V.20.1) and shril-crying (AV V.20.4). He whets his sound (AV V.20.1). He is a speaker (*vāgvī*) (AV V.20.11). He thunders like a lion (AV V.20.1; 2). Sometimes he is compared to a roaring bull (AV V. 20.2; cp. 3). He is able to overpower his enemies (*śatruṣāṭ, abhimātiṣāha* AV V.20.11) and dominate them (*damayan sapatnān* AV V.20.1). He conquers the hosts (*mṛdho jetā* AV V. 20.12) but he himself can not be conquered (*ayodhya-*) (AV V. 20.12). He is virile (*vṛṣan*) while his rivals are impotent (*vadhri-* AV V.20.2). He is asked to pierce the heart of the adversaries with pain (AV V.20.3), remove them (ṚV VI.47. 29; AV VI. 126.1), smite them down and to bring the possessions of the enemies (AV V.20.4 cp. in general AV V.21.1 ff). In this way the drum is considered to be magically potent to help the warriors in destroying etc. the enemies. But it is said that God Indra is behind the powerful activities of the drum. Thus the drum is described to be the fist (*muṣṭi-*) of Indra (ṚV VI.47.30; AV VI. 126.2). The vehemence (*śuṣman-*) of the drum is said to be Indra-like (AV V.20.2). He (the Drum) is allied with Indra (*indrameḍhī* AV V.20.8; cp. ṚV VI.47.29), made safe by Indra (*indreṇa guptaḥ* AV V.20.12). Thus the drum is not merely magically powerful. It is powerful magicoreligiously.

Kauśikasūtra XVI.1 prescribes AV V.20 and VI.126 in a battle-rite. So also the Āśvalāyanagṛhyasūtra III.12.17 prescribes ṚV VI.47.29-31 in a battle for being victorious. Similarly in Agnipurāṇa 269.35-37 it is prescribed that one should address the war-drum as follows: "O drum, you shake the hearts of the enemies by your sound. Be victory-increasing for the armies of the king. As the elephants of good quality get enthusiasm when there is roaring of clouds, so let there be enthusiasm in us, O you bringer of enthusiasm. As the women are frightened by the cloud-roar, similarly let our enemies be frightened on account of your sound (*dundubhe tvaṁ sapatnānāṁ ghoṣād hṛdayakampanaḥ/bhava bhūmipasainyānāṁ yathā vijayavardhanaḥ // 35 // yathā jīmūtaghoṣeṇa hṛṣyanti varavāraṇāḥ/tathāstu tava śabdena harṣo'smākaṁ mudāvaha // 36 // yathā jīmūtaśabdena strīṇāṁ trāso'bhijāyate / tathā tu tava śabdena trasyantvasmaddviṣo raṇe // 37 //*". It was considered to be an ill-omen, at the time of battles if drums even when unbeaten make sound. Thus Vyāsa indicates this as an ill-omen to Dhṛtarāṣṭra (*anāhatā dundubhayaḥ praṇudanti viśāṁ pate* Mbh VI.2.27). Similarly Vyāsa points out another ill-omen viz. the other war-music-instruments like *bherī* and *paṭaha* are gushing burning coals (Mbh VI.3.39). Thus musical instruments are of double-nature. They can indicate victory or defeat. Therefore they are very much important in a war. In many descriptions of wars the musical instruments are very often mentioned (cf. e.g. (Skandap. Māhe. Kedāra. 3.59 ff.).

REFERENCES

1. Rf. Saalschutz, *Musik bei der Herbraern*, p. 12.
2. Abert, *Lehre von Ethos*, p. 56
3. J.E. Scott in Wellesz, *AOM*, p. 411 f.
4. Schröder, *Mysterium und Mimus*, p. 24; for war-dance cf. also Webster, *Magic*, p. 333.
5. Combarieu, *La musique et la magie*, p. 109, 289 etc; Belvianes, *Sociologie de la musique*, p. 177; 185.
6. Hauer, *Vrātya*, p. 55; 183.

(L) MUSIC AND VICTORY OVER THE WORLDS

Victory over all the worlds is possible by means of the various musical elements. In a contest between the Gods and Asuras the Gods desired to win these worlds (i.e. the earth, sky and the heaven). Then they saw the Saṁjaya-sāman and sang with it. Then they won all and all the world (JB III.132). The Gods obtained all these worlds by means of Sapha (sāman) (TMB XI.5.6; XV.11.5). Ayāsya Āṅgirasa sang the Gāyatra-sāman, holding his breath three times. Then he obtained all the worlds (JB III.281). The Kāvā-sāman is described as winner of worlds (*lokavit*) (JB I.166; TMB XI.5.25). By singing the Gāyatrapārśva-sāman, one becomes established in all the worlds (JB III.214).

In the Aśvamedha-sacrifice, on the third day which is of the Atirātra-type, all the stomas are to be used. For the stomas are identical with all that there is. Therefore this use of *all* the stomas is helpful for obtaining *all* the worlds (JB II.274). When, in the course of any process of singing, one modifies (*stobhati*) three syllables, one gets three worlds (JB I.131). Similarly by singing the Sārparājñī-verse also one obtains three worlds (JB III.305).

One can go to the world of Gandharvas by singing some sāmans. Thus Uśanā Kāvya desired to go to the world of Gandharvas. That world is qualified as the "immortal among the gods". Then he saw the Auśana-sāman and got the desired result. The user of this sāman also goes to the same world (JB I.127; III.232). Similarly Kavi Bhārgava desired the world of Gandharvas and won it by means of the Kāva-sāman (JB I.166).

Many sāmans are said to have been helpful to the gods etc. in obtaining the world of *heaven*. Thus by means of the Rathantara-sāman the gods went to the heaven (JB I.135). Similar use of the Āśva-sāman (JB III.258) or the Bṛhat-sāman (TMB XVIII.2.8) has been mentioned. The gods once desired to ascend the heavenly world quickly (*añjasā*) and then they saw the Añjaḥ (quick) - sāman and accomplished their desire successfully (JB III.209; cp. III.211: the case of Āśu-which also means quick-sāman). The Auśana and Kāva-sāmans are said to be the path leading quickly to the heaven (*eṣa vai svargasya lokasya panthā añjasāyano yadauśanakāve* JB II.421). Ghṛtaścut and Madhuścut accompanying the Āṅgirases who were going to the heaven, fell back. Then they desired to reach the heavenly world; they practised penance and saw the sāmans viz. Ghṛtaścut and Madhuścut". Ghee (*ghṛta-*) is the end (the best part) of the milks; the heaven is the end of the worlds; honey (*madhu-*) is the end of the saps, heaven is the end of the worlds; therefore, they, by means of these sāmans which belong to the end, reached heaven which is an end (JB I.224). Kruṅ Āṅgirasa reached the heaven by means of Krauñca - sāman (JB III.32), Śukti Āṅgirasa by means of the Śaukta-sāman (JB III.53; cp. TMB XII.5.16) and Saṁvarta Āṅgirasa by the Sāṁvarta-sāman (JB III.233). Some persons reached the heaven quickly by means of some other sāmans. Thus Ukṣorandhara Kāvya reached the heaven quickly by means of the Auṣṇorandhra-sāman (TMB XIII.9.19), Śnuṣṭi Āṅgirasa by means of the Snauṣṭa-sāman (TMB XIII.11.23), Puruhanmā Vaikhānasa by means of Paruhanmana-sāman (TMB XIV. 9.29); Babhru Kaumbhya by means of the Gatanidhana-sāman (TMB XV.3.23); and Śāmmad by means of the Śāmmada-sāman (TMB XV.5.11). Iḷan Kāvya obtained establishment (*pratiṣṭhā-*) in the heaven by means of the Aiḷata-sāman (JB III. 210). Many other sāmans are also helpful to obtain the heaven and therefore are called *svargya* e.g. the Antarikṣa (JB III.45); Vācaḥsāman (JB III.52); Caturnidhana Āṅgirasa (JB III.69); Udvat (JB III. 164); Śārkara (JB III.194); Śyāvāśva (JB III.196); Devasthāna and Arkapuṣpa (JB III.256); Aurṇāyava (TMB XIII.11.10 ff) etc. sāmans. In connection of many other sāmans it is metaphorically said that they "carried" those who sang them, to heaven. Thus the gods desirous of the heavenly world practised penance. Then they saw the Sākamaśva-sāman and sang with it. Then this sāman, having taken the form of a horse "carried (*avahat*) them to the heaven (JB I.182). Similarly the Śyena-sāman, having become a falcon (*śyena*) carried the gods to heaven (JB III.158). On another occasion the gods, desirous of the heavenly world practised penance, saw the Bṛhat-sāman and praised with it. Then the Bṛhat-sāman, having become great (*bṛhat*) carried the gods to the heaven (JB III.78; cp. also the story about the Viśāla (big) - sāman - JB III.219). The Gāyatra-sāman carried the gods to heaven having become *Gāyatra* (JB III.214). The Bṛhat and Rathantara-sāmans are said to be like bulls (*anaḍuhau*) going to the gods (i.e. to heaven). These sāmans when yoked (i.e. sung) are useful for obtaining the heavenly world (TMB XII.4.14).

Metres have some power to lead the sacrificer to the heaven. Thus ŚB VI.5.4.7 it is said, "They verily go to the heaven by means of the metres (*chandobhirhi svargaṁ gaccanti*)". The gods are said to have reached heaven by means of the Bṛhatī-metre (TMB XVI.12.7). The heaven-leading capacity of the Bṛhatī metre is so great that AB VI.21 remarks, "That metre (viz. Triṣṭubh) does not fail until it has made them (the performers) go to heaven; for it is the strongest (*na ha vā etachhando'gamayitvā svargamupāvartate vīryavattamaṁ hi*)". One who is desirous of going to heaven is advised to use the verses in the Anuṣṭubh-metre as the invitatory and offering-verses of the Sviṣṭakṛt offering in the Dīkṣaṇīyā offering (AB I.5).

Some other elements of Vedic music are also helpful in obtaining the world of heaven. Thus the Bahiṣ-pavamāna-stotra is said to be like a ship carrying the sacrificer to heaven (ŚB IV.2.5.10). Gaurivīti Śāktya won heaven by means of a hymn beginning with *janiṣṭhā ugraḥ* ... (ṚV X.73). The sacrificer also gets the same result when this hymn is recited in the sacrifice (AB III.19). The stomas like Trivṛt (TMB XVII.12.3), Pañcadaśa and Saptadaśa (TMB V.1.10), Caturviṁśa (TMB XIX.11.6) etc. and the Pṛṣṭhas (TMB VII.7.17; JB II.297) are also helpful for obtaining the world of heaven when used in various sacrifices. The gods once desired to go to heaven having become pure. Then they saw the verse beginning with *punānas soma dhārayā* (ṚV IX.107.4) purified themselves with them and reached heaven (JB I.121). In the Mahāvrata-ceremony which is a part of a sacrificial session dance is performed by maidens. That is also helpful for obtaining the heavenlyworld (TMB V.6.15).

(M) MUSIC IN THE ABHICĀRA- (SORCERY-) RITES

Introduction

Music is often used in the abhicāra- (sorcery-) rites. The Sāmaveda is specifically connected with the Abhicāra-rites by the Mārkaṇḍeyapurāṇa. Thus it is said there that the threefold lustre of the Atharvaveda was kept separately in the three Vedas. The pacificatory (*śāntika*) lustre dissolved in the Ṛgveda; the propitiatory (*pauṣṭika*) in the Yajurveda; and the sorcery-like in the Sāmaveda (*śāntikaṁ pauṣṭikaṁ caiva tathā caivābhicārikam / ṛgādiṣu layaṁ brahmanstritayaṁ triṣvathāgamat //* 99.11). Further it is said that this threefold lustre was kept in the Sun who represents the Vedas in the morning, in the noon and in the evening respectively (16). All the parts of Vedic literature beginning from Ṛgveda and ending with the sūtra-literature (not excluding the philosophical upaniṣads) show ample traces of abhicāra-rites and music has a prominant role in them. Music is used in order to defeat, overpower or destroy the enemy.

Use of music in the abhicāra-rites in ṚV and AV

In the hymns of the ṚV and AV we get some references to the use of music in sorcery. Thus ṚV VI.73.3, it is said about Bṛhaspati that he kills the enemy by means of his songs (*bṛhaspatir hantyamitram arkaiḥ*). Those who are in possession of the musical power can easily practise sorcery and can overpower those who do not possess that power. Thus in ṚV X. 105.8 we read, "We shall conquer the verseless (*anṛcaḥ*) by means of verse (*ṛc*)". The Bṛhat-Sāman is described to be the most powerful killer of Vṛtra—the enemy of Indra. The Maruts are, therefore, requested "Sing (*gāyata*) the Bṛhat-sāman, destroyer of Vṛtra (*vṛtrahantamam*) for Indra, O Maruts" (ṚV VIII.89.1). In the AV, a performer of sorcery says, "Seven breaths, eight marrows, them I hew (off) for them with a powerful formula (*brahman*) (II. 12.7).

Sāmans

There are many sāmans with which one can kill the enemy. Thus Indra wanted to kill Vṛtra. He requested Viśvāmitra to teach him a sāman. Then Viśvāmitra "saw (*apaśyat*)" a sāman and sang with it. Thereafter Indra killed Vṛtra. The power of sāman made Indra wonder-struck. Then Indra expressed his wonder in the following words, "It is indeed great (*mahad*) of Viśvāmitra". Therefore that sāman got the name Mahāvaiśvāmitra. This sāman is further described as "a killer of the enemy (*bhrātṛvyahā*) (JB III.134). Elsewhere it is told that Indra, desirous of killing Vṛtra, went to sage Kaṇva and asked for a sāman. He saw a sāman and praised with it. Then Indra could kill Vṛtra. This sāman is called Abhinidhana-Kāṇva-sāman and is described as a "killer of the enemy (*bhrātṛvyahā*)" (JB III.189). The gods killed the Asuras, according to a story to by JB III.185, by means of the Gauṅgava-sāman. This sāman is also described as "a killer of the enemy". At another time when gods and Asuras were contesting, the Gods desired to kill the Asuras quickly. Then they saw the Pauruhanman-sāman, praised with it, and then killed the Asuras quickly. Similarly one who knows this kills his hateful enemy quickly (JB III.215). There are many other sāmans which can be helpful in killing enemies and therefore are described as *bhrātṛvyahā*. Thus e.g. Jamadagneḥ saptaham (JB I.152), Traita (JB I.184), Sujñāna (JB III.30), Śaiśava (JB III. 102), Śyena (JB III.158), Saumitra (JB III.210), Āśubhārgava (JB III.211), Vaiyaśva (JB III.221), Vaiśvamanasa (JB III.267), *Devānīka* (JB III.275), etc. are useful in destroying the enemy and the adjective *bhrātṛvyahā* is used in their description.

Some other sāmans also can be used in various kinds of sorceries practised against one's enemy. Thus in the Marutstoma-sacrifice the following sāmans which are of the form of sorcery are to be sung: -Jamadagneḥ saptaha, Vidratha and Cakṣūṁṣi (JB II.169f). At the mid-day-pressing of the Agniṣṭoma-sacrifice which is being performed by a sacrificer who has an enemy, the Abhīvarta-sāman should be used as the chant of the Brahman. By means of this sāman, the Gods turned themselves against the Asuras; by using this sāman, one turns oneself against the enemy (TMB VIII.2.17 f). At the time of a contest between the Gods and Asuras, the Gods made sink boroughs of the Asuras with the help of Paurumudga-sāman. Similarly anyone who praises with this sāman, makes his enemy sink down (TMB XII.3.14; cp. JB III.43). Indra took help of the Pramaṁhiṣṭhīya-sāman while hurling his thunder-bolt against Vṛtra and then he could cast him down. One who has any rival can make use of this sāman in order to destroy him by introducing the Uktha (lauds) with this sāman, in the evening - pressing on the third day of the Daśarātra of the Dvādaśāha-sacrifice. Then he casts down his enemy and fares better (TMB XII.6.6). Gods crossed over these worlds by means of Rathantara-sāman. One who knows this also crosses over one's enemy (JB I.135). In the Iṣusacrifice one has to use Jamadagneḥ saptaha-sāman. Then one's rival becomes supportless, upto his seventh descendant (ṢaḍB III.9.6). By means of the Satrāsāhīya-sāman, the Gods conquered whatever had been left unconquered of the possession of the Asuras. Similarly, by singing this sāman, one conquers finally, one's rival (TMB XII.9.21 f).

Pratipads

A Pratipad (opening tristich) is also useful for anti-enemy purpose. For him who desires that alien cows may fall to his lot, the tristich beginning with *tayā pavasva dhārayā* (SV II.786-788; ṚV IX.49.2-4) should be used as the opening one in the Bahiṣpavamānalaud (TMB VI.10.19). According to JB I.93, the tristich beginning with *agna āyūṁṣi pavase* should be used instead of *tayā pavasva dhārayā* .... as the opening verse for one who wants to practise sorcery. "For, Agni is the Brahman - priest of the gods. One thus slays him whom one hates, by means of Agni, the Brahman-priest of the Gods".

Stomas

The stomas also can be used with the intention of doing harm to the enemy. Thus when in the Vighana-sacrifice, one uses the twenty-seven-versed stoma, one hurls the thunderbolt towards the enemy thereby (TMB XIX. 18.3). The knowledge of the Trivṛtstoma being identical with the thunderbolt enables a sacrificer to protect himself from the sorcery of another sacrificer. Moreover, the other sorcers themselves then become exercised (JB I.248).

Verses

Recitation of verses is helpful in practising sorcery against the enemy. Thus Indra killed Dīrghajihvī, a female demon, with the thunderbolt in the form of the verse *purojitī vo andhasaḥ* (ṚV IX.101.1). The verses beginning with these words are called "killers of the enemies (*bhrātṛvyaghnyaḥ*)" and reciting them, one can kill the enemy (JB I.163). The verses beginning with *paryū ṣu pra dhanam* (ṚV IX.110.1 ff) should be used on the tenth day of the Daśaratra of the Dvādaśāha - sacrifice by one who wants to practise sorcery (JB III.297).

Stobhas

The Stobhas (modificatory utterances) also serve to harm the enemy. Thus when one modifies nine syllables, one appropriates the nine vital organs (prāṇa) of the enemy; for a man has nine vital organs (JB I.132). Similarly, when one modifies sixteen syllables, one lays down the enemy in his every digit (*kalā*); for a man consists of sixteen digits (JB I.132). The black-magical significance of uttering sixteen modifications is also told in another way. Thus the fifteen syllables out of those sixteen are identical with the thunderbolt and the sixteenth is Indra. The Udgātṛ priest makes the sacrificer Indra; and by means of the thunderbolt in the form of fifteen syllables he destroys the enemy (JB I.331).

Viṣṭuti

Viṣṭuti[1] is a mode of getting the number of verses required for a laud out of a group of three verses by means of repetition. The Viṣṭuti also has black-magic power. Thus the Daśasaptā Viṣṭuti also has a black-magic power. Thus the Daśasaptā Viṣṭuti consists of the following schema - *hum*, 1, 1, 1, 2, 3; *hum*, 1, 2, 2, 2, 2; *hum*, 1, 2, 2, 2, 3, 3, 3; and thus in all we get seventeen (*daśa-sapta*) verses. By means of this schema the gods overcame the Asuras. He who practises this schema at the time of chanting, overcomes his wicked enemy (TMB II.7.3). Another Viṣṭuti called Saptāsthitā consists of the following schema of chanting - *hum*, 1, 1, 1, 2, 2, 2, 3; *hum*, 1, 2, 3; *hum*, 1, 2, 2, 3, 3, 3. He who has a rival should practise this schema. "Just as one harrows with a harrow reposing on seven sharppointed (pins), so he breaks to pieces his wicked rival (TMB II.9.2). Another kind of the same Viṣṭuti (viz. *hum*, 1, 1, 1, 2, 3, 3, 3; *hum*, 1, 2, 3; *hum*, 1, 1, 1, 2, 3, 3, 3) can be used as a protective means against the sorcery practised by one's enemy (TMB II.10.5).

Nidhana

The finales (*nidhana-*) of a melody also work effectively against the enemy. While singing the Aurdhvasadman-sāman, by means of the finale *suvṛktibhiḥ* the Gods appropriated the cattle of the Asuras; by *nṛmādanaṁ*, they killed the Asuras and by *bhareṣvā* they reached the heaven. The singer of this sāman does the same thing using the same finales in connection with his enemies and wins the heavenly world (JB I.218). Similarly by the sāman named Abhinidhana, i.e. which has the word *abhi* as its finale, Indra hurled the thunderbolt at Vṛtra and killed him. One kills one's enemy by means of this sāman (TMB XIV.4.5). In the Gāyatra-sāman which is to be sung at the time of the bahiṣpavamāna-recital, the word *haṁsi* (thou slayest) is to be made the finale for the sacrificer who is practising exorcism (TMB VII.1.11).

Hymns

Some hymns are used with the abhicāric purpose. Thus the Vihavya-hymn (ṚV X.10.16 ff) (TMB IX.4.13; TS III.1.7.3). Sajanīya-hymn (ṚV II.2.1 ff); and the Kayāśubhīya (ṚV I.23.1 ff) are recited when there are two soma-sacrifices being performed simultaneously. By means of the recital of these hymns, the sacrificer can practise sorcery against the other performers (TMB IX.4.17 f; JB I.344). On the third day of the Daśarātra of the Dvādaśāha, a hymn beginning with *hatho vṛtrāṇi* is to be recited. It is called "Killer of Vṛtra (*Vārtraghna-*). When this hymn is used as an ājyā-laud, one kills the enemy (JB III.39).

Number of the verses

In the recitation of the verses their number is significant. Khaṇḍika Audbhāri and Keśī Dārbhya were contesting. Keśī Dārbhya defeated Khaṇḍika Audbhāri and removed him from the "year" by means of the performance of Parikrī-sacrifice in which he had used a particular number of verses in each of the rites included in it. Thus its Bahiṣpavamāna consisted of three verses, Ājya-lauds of four verses, midday-pavamāna-laud of five verses, pṛṣṭhas of four verses, ārbhava-pavamāna-laud of seven verses and Agniṣṭoma-sāman of one verse. These in all become twenty-four verses to be sung (*stotriyā-*). Now a year consists of twenty-four half months. Thus Keśī Dārbhya removed Khaṇḍika Audbhārī from the year (JB II.124). In the Darśapūrṇamāsa-sacrifice, there are eleven kindling (sāmidhenī-) verses. But by reciting the first and the eleventh verses thrice each, the number of the verses becomes fifteen. Now the number fifteen mystically signifies the thunder-bolt according to the Brāhmaṇa-texts. If one has an enemy, one should crush him by means of his great toes (i.e. he should press the earth) at the time of reciting these verses by saying, "I crush so and so". One thus, indeed crushes the enemy with that thunderbolt (ŚB I.3.5.7).

Metres

Metres also have anti-rival powers. Thus at the time of the three Viṣṇu-steps, in the course of Darśapūrṇamāsa-sacrifices, the sacrificer utters the following words, "On the earth, Viṣṇu strode with the Gāyatri metre;excluded therefrom (i.e. from the earth) is he who hates us, and whom we hate" (VS XI.25). Thus one removes the enemy from the earth as it were. Here alluding to Viṣṇu's striding with the help of the Gāyatrī-metre, one uses the mystic power of that metre. One thus removes the enemy from the earth with the help of that power. Similarly the sacrificer, further alludes to the Viṣṇu's strides in the air and in the sky with the help of Triṣṭubh and Jagatī respectively. He thus removes his enemy from those worlds also. The same formulas are used in the reverse order while stepping back for three times (ŚB I.9.3.10; 12). Here one uses the mystic power of the metres for the sake of removing the enemies from all the three worlds. The gods killed the hateful, evil enemy by means of praising thrice with the Triṣṭubh metre and similarly one can also kill one's hateful enemy in the same manner (JB I.324). By means of the metres named Uṣṇih and Kakubh, Indra struck upon Vṛtra with his thunderbolt. "One who knows this can slay one's enemy" (JB III.295). The gods went to the heaven but they wished that others should not come to that world. Therefore they put the metres in the reverse order. Similarly by putting the metres in the reverse order the sacrificer can prevent the enemy from getting the heavenly world (MS IV.7.5).

Miscellaneous

Some other elements of Vedic music also have been prescribed to be used in black magic. Pratigara is the response given by the Adhvaryu to the recital made by the Hotṛ. When the Adhvaryu utters the response, he thereby destroys the world (i.e. the heavenly world) of his enemy (ŚB IV.3.2.6). One who wants to perform sorcery against one's enemy, should offer with the Daśa (ten) hotṛ-formulas. "For there are nine vital organs and the navel is the tenth. One thus practises black magic against him (the enemy) along with his vital organs". In this offering, instead of the Vaṣaṭ-call the words which are described as "cruelty of speech" are to be used. They are the following ones and mean "cut", "kill" etc. : - *Khaṭ, phaṭ, jahi, chindhi, bhindhi, handhi* and *kaṭ*. Any of these words is to be uttered and then the offering is to be made (TB II.2.1.7). Musical instruments like drum (*dundubhi*) also appear to be efficient in sorcery-rites. Thus ṚV VI.47.29, at the time of battle, the drum is asked to fill up the earth and heaven by means of its noise and remove (*apa sedha*) the enemies by means of its noise (cp. 30 and 31).

Music is used in some special sacrifices of the abhicāra-nature. Significantly enough, they are detailed in the ṢaḍB which belongs to the Sāmaveda. This fact alone will show the connection of music and sorcery.

Śyena

Among the Abhicāra-sacrifices Śyena is the foremost. He who wants to perform sorcery should perform this sacrifice. The falcon (*śyena*) is the swiftest of the birds. Just as the falcon catches the other birds, in just the same manner, the sacrificer catches his rivals by this rite. In this sacrifice, each of the three pavamāna-lauds is threefold; for the threefold stoma is the swiftest of all the stomas. This helps for defeating the enemy. Similarly, all the other details of the Śyena-sacrifice are of such a nature that they would be helpful for defeating the enemy. The havirdhāna-vehicles are two-wheeled chariots; thereby the sacrificer throws a thunderbolt in the form of two-wheeled chariots, at his rival. The Vajra-sāman is sung in this sacrifice. It is also a thunderbolt (*vajra*). If the sacrificer desires, "May the rival be defeated, " he should take the Bṛhat for the Pṛṣṭha-laud and the Rathantara for the Brahma-sāman. The Bṛhat is the ruling power and the Rathantara is the cattle. With ruling power he kills the cattle of his rival and then the rival gets defeated. If the sacrificer desires, "May the rival go astray, may he have no firm support", then he should apply the Rathantara-sāman in the midday-pavamāna-laud, make the Bṛhat the first Pṛṣṭha-laud and apply plava for the Bṛhat-sāman. By both the Bṛhat and the Rathantara, he removes the rival from both of these worlds viz. heaven and earth and by the Plava, he causes him to float away. The rival thus goes astray and has no support. In this Śyena sacrifice, the sacrificial post is to be made of the Bādhaka or Tailvaka wood and it must have a point like a sword. The planks for pressing out the Soma-juice are made from the central planks of the wheels. The sacrificial animals dedicated to Agni should be red. The sacrificial grass consists of reeds (*śara-*) for the sake of hurting (*śīrtyai*) the rival. The fuel consists of Vibhītaka-wood, for cleaving the rival. The priests discharge their sacred functions wearing red turbans, red clothes and having their brahmanic threads round their necks, for the sake of destroying the rival. In each group of cows (which according to the commentators are nine one-eyed, nine lame, nine paralysed and nine with defective horns etc.) there are nine cows. These cows are to be given to the priests as sacrificial gifts (ṢaḍB III.8.1 ff).

Iṣu

The sacrifice named Iṣu (Arrow) is similar one. By means of this sacrifice, the sacrificer can hurt his enemy. In this sacrifice, the Viṣṭuti named Iṣu is used. "Death strikes the rival prematurely by an arrow when the Iṣu Viṣṭuti is used". There is the Vaṣaṭkāṛa-ṇidhana-sāman to be sung. Then the Saptaha-sāman is also sung. The word Saptaha means that which kills seven. When this sāman is sung, there remains no support for him against whom sorcery is made by means of this sacrifice. The remaining details are the same as those of the Śyena-sacrifice (ṢaḍB III.9.1 ff).

Saṁdaṁśa

The next sacrifice is named is Saṁdaṁśa (Tongs) with the similar purpose against the enemy. "As with a pair of tongs a blacksmith takes hold of a thing, which is difficult to take hold of, so also the sacrificer takes hold of the enemy". This sacrifice is similar to a pair of tongs, because there are two chants each time. The group of stomas amounts to the Trivṛtstoma. The number of the stotra-verses amounts to the bṛhatī-metre. The Trivṛt-stoma is thunderbolt; the Bṛhatī-metre is cattle. "With the thunderbolt he strikes his rival's cattle". There is the Vaiyaśva-sāman to be sung. By this sāman one makes the rival horseless. The finale is pariṣṭubdheḍa by means of which the rival is cut. There are the two Vātsāhara-sāmans, the Kāśīta and Apagava-sāmans and Nānada-sāman at the beginning of the midday and Ārbhavapavamāna-lauds. The Udgātṛs compose injurious sāmans for destroying the rival. The sacrifice is performed without the Saptadaśa-stoma. The remaining details are the same as those of the Śyena-sacrifice (ṢaḍB III.10.1 ff).

Vajra

Next comes the Vajra (Thunderbolt) sacrifice. There are fifteen lauds in this sacrifice. Fifteen is the thunderbolt and by it, the rival is destroyed. The Vajra-sacrifice is an Ukthya (which has fifteen lauds) combined with a Ṣoḍaśin. The Ukthyas are cattle; the Ṣoḍaśin the thunderbolt. With the thunderbolt, a thunderbolt is hurled at the rival and he is then destroyed. This sacrifice has the Mahānāmni-verses and sixteen sāmans. The Mahānāmnī verses and the ṣoḍaśin are identical with the thunderbolt and that is hurled at the enemy. The remaining details are the same as those in the Saṁdaṁśa-sacrifice (ṢaḍB. III.11.1 ff).

In this way the above sacrifices of the nature of abhicāra are described in the ṢaḍB which belongs to the Sāmaveda. In these sacrifices various kinds of recitations and sāmans have a distinct role in the desired result of destruction of enemy.

Music in other abhicāra-sacrifices

There are some abhicāra sacrifices which are also treated in the Brāhmaṇas belonging to the Sāmaveda and based on a particular kind of arrangement of recitations. Thus for example the twin-sacrifices Abhibhū and Vinutti are of the nature of sorcery. The gods are told to have been superior to the Asuras with the help of Abhibhūsacrifice. The performer of this sacrifice can also be superior to his hateful enemy by performing this sacrifice. "There are Trivṛt-stomas on both the sides. Trivṛt-stoma is identical with the brahman (power). The gods became superior to the Asuras with the help of this power". One can, therefore, be superior to the enemy by means of the brahman-power in the form of Trivṛt stoma used in this sacrifice. Similarly gods drove away the Asuras by means of the Vinutti-sacrifice in which the Trivṛt stomas are used in the middle. Thus as the gods removed the Asuras with the help of the Brahman power in the form of the Trivṛt stoma, similarly one removes one's hateful enemy with that power (JB II.104). If the Manuṣtoma-sacrifice is to be performed by one who is practising sorcery against the enemy, the following sāmans are sung: Jamadagni's Saptaha, Vidratha and Cakṣūṁṣi. These sāmans are described as "dreadful (*ghora*)" (JB II.169 f). According to TMB XIX.18.2, Indra killed his enemy by means of this sacrifice. "Because there is the Triṇava-stoma in this sacrifice, he (the sacrificer) hurls thunderbolt to his enemy" (TMB XIX.18.3). The Gods conquered the Asuras by means of the Abhijit sacrifice and one who performs this sacrifice also conquers the enemy (JB II.178). The first Sādyaskra-sacrifice is to be performed by one who has enemy and wants to perform sorcery (JB II.117. cp, TMB XVI.12.2).

Similarly, sacrifices like Anukrī (JB II.120), Parikrī (JB II. 122), Antarvasu (JB II.279), Saṁsagyau (JB II.310), etc. are of the nature of abhicāra. It is noteworthy that all of these sacrifices are treated by the brāhmaṇas of the Sāmaveda. The later Śrautasūtras belonging to other Vedas also have incorporated these sacrifices. But it will hardly be a mistake to surmise that these abhicāra-sacrifices must have originated in the circle of the Sāmaveda. The special features of these sacrifices are moreover connected with the particular ways of singing. This again supports our surmise.

Saṁsava

In the Soma-sacrifice, there happens sometimes a situation which is called *saṁsava* (confusion of soma-pressings). When two soma-sacrificers are performing soma-sacrifices at the same time and at places which are not separated from one another, either by a river or by a mountain, then the *saṁsava* occurs; and it is regarded as a great sin.[2] According to two lost brāhmaṇas[3] viz. Kāṅkatī-Brāhmaṇa and Chāgala-brāhmaṇa, there is no defect of *saṁsava*, if the performers are not inimical and do not hate each other. But otherwise it is a defect. It is to be avoided as far as possible; for, the sacrificer, the sacrifice of whom is stronger, robs the sacrifice of the other (GB I.3.19). Thus there is some scope for abhicāra, for making one's sacrifice stronger, than that of the other. Thus those who perform soma-sacrifices at the same time are enemies of each other, according to JB I.343 (*sapatnāyantīvaite ye saṁsunanti*).

Then naturally one may try to make the sacrifice of the other performer unsuccessful and to defeat him. In this abhicāra, music has an important function.

Thus when two sacrificers are being performed simultaneously, the Adhvaryu-priest should, at the dead of night make the summons for the morning-litany. Then he becomes the first to appropriate the speech, the metres and the deities. He should take the opening tristich of the Bahiṣpavamāna-laud, the one that contains the word "bull (*vṛṣan*)". "Indra, verily is a bull; he thus takes away Indra from the morning pressing of the other sacrificer" (TMB IX.4.1 ff; cp. JB I.342; TS VII.5.5.1 Māśs III.7.4). Then there are some offerings to be offered in the fire for the sake of conquest of the metres. They are to be performed with the words, "For lying down; for sitting down; for the conquest of the Gāyatrī-metre svāhā; For lying down ... Triṣṭubh-metre svāhā; For lying down .... Jagatī-metre svāhā;" (TMB IX.4.6; cp. JB I.342; TS III.1.7.1; TB I.4.6.4; Baudhāśs XIV.4; Kātyāśs XXV.14.16). Both the Bṛhat and Rathantara-sāmans are to be sung. They are identical with the bay steeds of Indra and by means of these the sacrificer "wins the race". (JB I.343). There are two Tauraśravasa-sāmans and by means of them, the sacrificer appropriates the oblation-material of the other performers (TMB IX.4.9 f). The ājyalaud belonging to Agni and beginning with the verse *pra vo vājā abhidyavaḥ* is to be sung. That verse contains the word *pra* which results in defeating the other sacrificer (JB I.344). There are Ābhīka, Abhinidhana, Abhīvarta and Ābhīṣava-sāmans to be sung. They also help for defeating the others (JB I.344). The Vihavya-hymn (ṬV X.10.16 ff) is to be recited by the Hotṛ. Jamadagni and other seers, once, performed soma-sacrifices simultaneously. At that time Jamadagni saw this hymn and attracted Indra towards him. Similarly the sacrificer, when this hymn is recited can take away Indra from the sacrifice of others (TMB IX.4.13; cp. TS III.1.7.3, according to which Viśvāmitra and Jamadagni contested against Vasiṣṭha and Jamadagni appropriated the valour and sense-power of Vasiṣṭha with this hymn). Similarly Sajanīya (ṚV II.12), and Kayāśubhīya (ṚV I.23) hymns are also to be recited (TMB IX.4.17 f; JB I. 344). If the sacrifice of the other performers is Agniṣṭoma, then one should perform the Ukthya-sacrifice; if Ukthya, then Ṣoḍaśī; if Ṣoḍaśī then Atirātra; If Atirātra, then a two-day sacrifice; if two-day sacrifice, then he should perform three day sacrifice. In this way, one should perform a sacrifice which contains a greater number of recitations (*śastra*) and songs (*stotra*). Thereby one can attract more deities towards one's sacrifice and defeat the other performers (JB I.344; TMB IX.4.15; TS III.1.7.4; TB I.4.6.3 f). There is, however, another opinion according to which one should perform a sacrifice consisting of less number of recitations. Then one can reach the end of the sacrifice more quickly and "win the race" and get the desired result etc. (See JB I.344).

Priestly abhicāra-rites

Upto now we discussed the abhicāra-rites which are to be performed by a sacrificer or for a sacrificer in order to destroy the sacrificer's enemy. Now there are some abhicāra-rites which are performed by the priests against the sacrificer in the sacrifice being performed under his auspices only. The reason why the priests perform such rites against the sacrificer may be something like internal dispute, dissatisfaction etc. In such abhicāra-rites also the elements of Vedic music are very much significant.

Thus if the Hotṛ-priest desires to make the sacrificer supportless (*anāyatanavān*) he should not recite the Tūṣṇīṁśamsa, which is the "root" of the sacrifice. Then the sacrificer comes to ruin along with the sacrifice which being without a root, falls to ruin (AB II.32). The Hotṛ can perform sorcery against the sacrificer in the recitation of the Nivid also. Thus if he desires to deprive the sacrificer of the lordly power (*Kṣatra*) he should recite the hymn in the middle of the Nivid. If he desires to deprive him of the people, he should recite a Nivid in the middle of the hymn. But if he desires of a sacrificer, "May all be in due and proper order and correct, for him, he should first call, then insert the Nivid and then recite the hymn". Thus the priests can create both the good and bad results according to their desire[4] and according to the way of recital. A similar observation can be made in connection with the recitation of Prauga-litany which is described as a litany of "vital airs, organs". If the Hotṛ desires to deprive the sacrificer of the expiration (*Prāṇa*) then he should recite the triplet to Vāyu in confusion i.e. he should pass over a verse or line. If he desires to deprive the sacrificer of his expiration and inspiration, then he should recite the triplet to Indra and Vāyu in confusion. Similarly if he desires to deprive the sacrificer of his eye, ear, strength, limbs, and speech, he should recite the triplets to Mitra and Varuṇa, Aśvins, Indra, All-gods and Sarasvatī respectively, in confusion. But if he desires that the sacrificer should prosper with all his members, with all his self, then he should recite them in the proper order (AB III.3). The Hotṛ can execute his twofold power in pronouncing the Vaṣaṭcall also. Thus if he wants to make the sacrificer worse, he should, having recited the ṛc in a more raised tone, say the Vaṣaṭ-call in a more depressed tone. If he desires to make the sacrificer better, he should, having recited the ṛc in a depressed tone, utter the Vaṣaṭ in a more raised tone (AB III.7; GB II.3.3). The Hotṛ can perform sorcery also in reciting the final verse of the morning litany. Thus if he wants to make the sacrificer worse, he should recite it before the sunrise. If he wants to make him neither better nor worse, he should recite it at day-break. And if he wants to make him better, he should recite it after the sun-rise (JB I.213).

The priest Adhvaryu also can do good or bad to the sacrificer according to his desire by means of a particular way of calling for the Śrauṣaṭ. When he wants to make the sacrificer worse, he should begin in a high tone and conclude in a low tone. If he wants to make him neither better nor worse, he should conclude in the same tone in which he has begun. If he wants to make him better, he should begin in a low tone and conclude in a high tone. If he wants to make him feeble and submissive to his (sacrificer's) spiteful enemy, he should call for the Śrauṣaṭ in a thin, long-drawn, toneless way (ŚB XI.4.2.5 ff).

The chief of the priests belonging to the Sāmaveda, viz. Udgātṛ can equally exercise his good or bad power while performing his activities. Thus if he hates the sacrificer, wants to make his sacrifice destined to the Asuras, and wants to possess his power of speech, he should, while pushing the Droṇa kalaśa forward, touch the axel with his arms. If, however, the sacrificer is dear to him, he should push the Droṇakalaśa forward without touching the axel. "The Droṇakalaśa is the breath; thus he brings the breathings in good order" (TMB VI.5.15). Similarly, if the Udgātṛ is hating the sacrificer, he should put down the pressing stones with their faces averted and then shove (the Droṇakalaśa) away with the words, "Here I shove (i.e. I separate) from the clan so and so, from the food so and so, the member of the family so and so, the son of the mother so and so. "He thereby shoves him (the sacrificer) asunder (separates him) from his clan and food. But if the sacrificer is dear to him, he should put down the soma-pressing stones with their faces towards each other and then shove the Droṇakalaśa on them with the words: "Here I put on the clan so and so ..." He thereby puts him over the clan and in food" (TMB VI.6.2 ff cp. JB I.79).

Thus the priests have a double working power which they can execute with the help of musical elements for or against the sacrificer.

Concentration of attention

At the time of performing the music in the abhicāra-rites, one is advised sometimes to concentrate one's attention (*dhyai*)[5]. Thus at the time of uttering the Vaṣaṭ-call, one should concentrate one's attention upon him whom one hates. Since the Vaṣaṭ-call is identical with the thunderbolt, one thus puts thunderbolt in him (AB III.6). On the contrary, when about to recite the Vaiśvadeva-litany one should concentrate one's attention on all the directions except the direction in which there is the rival. He thereby puts sap in all the directions and appropriates the strength of the enemy (AB III.31; ĀŚS V.18)

Knowledge of music

We saw above how various elements of the vedic music are employed in the sorcery rites. It is further interesting to note that not only the performance of music has an effective role in the sorcery rites, even the mere knowledge of the music and its whereabouts also works effectively against the enemy. Thus one who knows that the gods drove away the Asuras with the help of Kāleya-sāman, drives away one's hateful enemy (JB I. 153). The Bhurij-Śakvarī-metre is regarded as Viṣṇu's metre. Indra killed Vṛtra by means of verse in this metre and obtained wealth. "He kills his evil enemy and obtains wealth who knows this" (JB I.205). The knowledge of the origin of *dhur*-verses and of the etymology of the word *dhur*, is sufficient for overthrowing one's enemies. Thus, at the time of the battle between the gods and Asuraṣ, the gods resorted to Prajāpati who gave them dhurs in the form of Prāṇas viz. mind, prāṇa, eye, ear and speech. With these five, the gods made man and cattle. With that man they overdrew (*adhūrvan*) the Asuras. In that they overdrew (*adhūrvan*), that is the *dhur*-ship of the dhurs (i.e. therefore they are called dhurs). "He overthrows his evil enemy who knows thus" (ṢaḍB II.3.1 ff). Further, another explanation of the dhur-verses is given and the knowledge of it also is said to lead one to be richer than one's enemy. Thus "The dhurship of dhurs is that in spite of their different power, form, metre, and deity they have a common hiṁkāra. He who knows thus overthrows his evil enemy" (ṢaḍB II.3.5).

Protection from sorcery

Music can be offensive and defensive. We have seen above how music is used in the rites against enemies. Now let us see what role the music plays in defending the performer. AV II.12 is a hymn to be sung in destroying the enemies. In the fourth verse of this hymn, the speaker prays for his own protection, while managing for the destruction of others. There, he prays for being protected by means of the sacrificial performances and the good deeds, done by his forefathers. In this protection, he expects the help of the "Singers of sāmans

(Sāmaga-)", along with that of others like the three times, eighty verses, Ādityas, Vasus, and Aṅgirases (AV II.12.4). For the person against whom sorcery is being performed, the verses beginning with *apaghnan pavate mṛdhaḥ* (ṚV IX.61.25) should be used as the pratipad. "For indeed evil foes (*mṛdhaḥ*) attack upon him against whom incantation is being performed (*abhiśasyamānaḥ*)". And by using the above pratipad, one kills the evil foes (JB I.96). Similarly a person against whom sorcery is being performed (*abhicaryamāṇaḥ*), should use the verses beginning with *agna āyūṁṣi pavase* (ṚV IX.66.19) as the pratipad. In this pratipad there is a prayer to Agni to destroy Ducchuna, an evil spirit. "He is a Ducchuna who practises sorcery, is antagonistic, desires to do evil". And by using this pratipad one destroys that enemy (JB I.93). JB II.322, prescribes the performance of Daśarātra-sacrifice for him against whom sorcery is being done.

On the basis of the above given details one can say that Vedic literature provides us with ample references to the use of Vedic musical elements in the sorcery rites[6]. Music was supposed to have destructive powers. Therefore one believed that with the help of music one could defeat or destroy one's enemy. It is however note-worthy that music has a double nature. It can be harmful; it can be helpful. So one can use it according to one's desire. The sacrificer can practise black magic against the enemy or can protect himself from the black magic of others. Thus the music is for both offensive and defensive purposes. Moreover, the priests can do good or bad of the sacrificer according to their desire with the help of musical elements. This again indicates the power of music and its double nature.

REFERENCES

1. Rf. Caland, *Pañcaviṁśa-Brāhmaṇa*, p. 19.
2. Rf. Haug, *The Aitareya-Brāhmana*, II, p. 9, n. 19, see in general-Hillebrandt, *Vedische Mythologie*, I. p. 260; Gonda, *Change and Continuity*, p. 376 f; see for details TMB IX.4.1 ff; JB I.342 ff;

TS VII.5.5.1 ff; III.1.7.1 ff; MS III.7.5; KS XXXIV.4; TB I.4.6.1-4; Śāṅkhāśs XIII.5.4 ff; Baudhāśs XIV.4; Āpśs XIV.19.1 ff; Kātyāśs XXV.14.1 ff; Lāṭyāśs I.11.10 ff; Drāhyāśs III.3.1.8 ff.

3. Ed. by B.K. Ghosh, *Collection from the Lost Brāhmaṇas*, p. 103 and 105.
4. R f. Lévi, *La doctrine du sacrifice*, p. 128.
5. For this rf. Gonda, *Vision of the Vedic poets*, p. 293. For the magical power of thinking see Webster, *Magic*, p. 79.
6. For the use of power in Sorcery in general see Combarieu, *La musique et la magie*, p. 92; Max Weber, *The Sociology of Religion*, p. 242.

(N) MUSIC AND SLEEP

Music is supposed to have a soporific significance[1] also. Thus ṚV VII.55 is traditionally regarded as a hymn[2] which has a magical force of making others sleep. Sarvānukramaṇī[3] describes the ṛcs of this hymn as *prasvāpinyupaniṣat* (soporific mystery; cp. Bṛhaddevatā VI.2). According to Bṛhaddevatā VI. 11-13, Vasiṣṭha, in his dream goes to the house of Varuṇa. Vasiṣṭha addresses a dog and pronounces a spell so that it may sleep (ṚV VII.55.2 ff). He then continues his spell in order to lull as it were, all the persons in the house to sleep (ṚV VII.55.5 ff). Ṣaḍguruśiṣya's commentary on Sarvānukramaṇī (p. 133) gives a slightly different story. "Once upon a time Vasiṣṭha was thirsty and hankering after food, having had to starve for three nights. On the fourth night he came to the house of Varuṇa to steal. In order to lull the sentry and the hounds to sleep, while he entered the house, Vasiṣṭha saw these seven verses (of the ṚV VII.55), commencing with *yad arjuna* etc.". Ṛgvidhāna II. 26.5, prescribes this hymn to be used for putting to sleep evil beings.

The Tvāṣṭrī-sāman is also connected with sleep. Thus "When Indra was suffering from a disease of the eyes, the (other) beings could not cause him to sleep (but) the daughter of Tvaṣṭṛ by means of this melody (viz. the Tvāṣṭrī-sāman) brought sleep to him ...." (TMB XII.5.19).

A Gandharva (a genus connected with music) named Priyaṁvada taught Aja a missile named *sammohana*. The result of the use of this missile is that the enemies of the user enter into deep sleep and thus one gets 'victory without violence' (cp. Raghuvaṁśa V.57). Later on Aja is said to have used this missile and made his enemies sleepy (Raghuvaṁśa VII.61 f). This missile coming from a Gandharva must have some connection with music. In other parts of the world also the soporiferous significance is attached to music. In Hupa of northern California, the people who largely resorted to magic in warfare as well as in other activities, had certain songs which put the enemy into a sound slumber when a night-attack was to be made[4]. Among the Greeks there was an expression *katabukalesis* which means "action of making (somebody) sleep by means of a charm"[5]. Ovide mentions the magical formulas employed by Medee for making the dragon sleep[6]. Swooning as a result of the "killing charm" of music is well-known in Arabian stories[7].

On the other hand, music can be useful in making somebody awaken. ṚV V.14.1, a poet-singer is asked, "Awaken (*bodhaya*) Agni with a praise-hymn (*stoma-*)". ṚV VII.80.1, Vasiṣṭhas are said to have awakened Uṣas with the praise-hymns. Indra swooned when he was troubled by Vṛtra, his enemy. Then the seer Vasiṣṭha awakened him by means of the Rathantara-sāman (Mbh XII.272.21: *tasya vṛtrārditasyātha moha āsīcchatakratoḥ/rathantareṇa taṁ tatra vasiṣṭhaḥ samabodhayat//* The protestant reformer, Martir Luther was brought to a state of wakefulness with the help of music[8].

Thus music is double-natured. It brings sleep and it awakens.

REFERENCES

1. Rf. Combarieu, *La musique et la magie*, p. 314.
2. Cp. AV IV. 5; see also Th. Aufrecht, "Der leibende besucht die beliebte" *IS*, IV, 1858, p. 341; Pischel in Pischel, Geldner, *Vedische Studien*, II. p. 55.
3. Ed. A. A. Macdonell, Oxford, 1886, p. 26.
4. Webster, *Magic*, p. 334.
5. Combarieu, *La musique et la magie*, p. 313.
6. Combarieu, *La musique et la magie*, p. 314.
7. Farmer in Wellesz, *AOM*, p. 433.
8. J. Race, *Luther, Student, Monk, Reformer*, London, 1884, p. 46.

(O) MUSIC AND FULFILMENT OF DESIRES

We saw above how music can be a sure means for obtaining various kinds of results. But that is not all. Really speaking, Vedic texts maintain that music is omnipotent. It can give us any result that we are seeking for. Many elements of Vedic music are henoistically said to be useful for obtaining all the desired objects.

Thus many sāmans are described as "fulfilling the desire (*kāmasani*)" It is further added in their description that by means of such sāmans one gets fulfilled any desire. Such remarks are found in connection with e.g. Saubhara (JB I. 166), Apāla (JB I.221) Okonidhana Vaitahavya (JB I.214), Durṇāyava (JB III.76), Saindhukṣita (JB III.82), Vārṣa (JB III.95; TMB XIII.3.12), Rohitakūlīya (JB III.183), Śārkara (JB III.193; TMB XIV.5.15), Yauktāśva (TMB XI.8.8), Tvāṣṭrī-(TMB XII.5.20), Saumitra (TMB XIII.6.9), etc. sāmans. In connection with the Mahānāmnī-verses, it is remarked that there are all the objects of desire in them (*sarve vai kāmā mahānāmnīṣu* ŚB XIII.5.1.10). Even by studying the sāmans one can fulfil all the desires (ŚB XI.5.7.7).

The Ghṛtaścunnidhana and the Madhścunnidhana-sāmans are described as the breasts of the sacrifice "Indra "milked" by means of these two sāmans all the objects of desires. One who knows this also milks all the objects of desire by means of these sāmans" (JB I.225; cp. TMB XIII.11.19). Similarly the Saubhara-sāman (TMB VII.8.20), Nidhanakāma-sāman (TMB XII.9.20), and Vājajit-sāman (TMB XIII.9.20) are helpful for getting all the desires fulfilled. In the course of the Agnicayana (fire-building-ceremony) Satya (Effective) sāman is to be sung. By means of this sāman, gods got all their desires realised. Similarly by means of this sāman the performer gets all his desires realised (ŚB VII.4.1.3 ff). With whatever desire one sings the Ākūpāra-sāman, that desire is fulfilled (TMB IX.2.14). In the sacrifice named Ādityānāṁ madhye pṛṣṭhyam ayanam, the nine-versed and fifteen-versed stomas are used. In the context of these stomas, TMB XXV.1.6 makes the following remark:

"The nine-verses and fifteen-versed-stomas are two wheels revolving together. What wish they hope to see fulfilled, that they obtain by this (sacrifice). For wherever one wishes to go by means of a (car) with wheels, that one reaches."

CHAPTER IX

Doctrine of Music in the Veda

(A) NATURE OF MUSIC COMPARISONS AND IDENTIFICATIONS

Although there are a few references to the instrumental music and dance in the Vedas, Vedic music is mainly vocal. Mostly, it consists of singing sāmans, recitations etc. Thus during the course of the Avabhṛtha-bath, the Adhvaryu has to ask the Prastotṛ to sing a sāman. In this context ŚB IV.4.5.6, we read, "He then says, 'Sing the sāman' or 'speak the sāman'. But let him rather say 'sing'; for they do *sing* the sāman (*athāha sāma gāyeti vā brūhīti vā / gāyeti tveva brūyād gāyanti hi sāma*" ŚB IV.4.5.6). The same words occur in the context of the Pravargya-rite also (ŚB XIV.4.5.6). From this it will be clearly seen that the chief nature of Vedic music is that it is sung. It is mainly vocal music. But occasionally, in Vedic texts, we get numerous metaphorical descriptions of the musical details. These descriptions contain many comparisons and identifications. These metaphorical descriptions are very much interesting and instructive from the point of view of the magico-religious significances attributed to music by the Vedic texts. Thus for example, JB II.421, the Auśana and Kāva-sāmans are said to be the quickly-leading paths[1] to the heavenly world. Here it is implied that these sāmans are helpful to reach the heavenly world. Similarly many such comparisons and identifications throw good light upon the magico-religious significances of Vedic music.

Some musical elements are considered to be like ships. Thus ṚV X.116.9 the poet-singer says - "I set in motion my good speech (*suvacasyā*). By means of songs (*arka-*) I drive it forwards like a ship in ocean". At the time of the great deluge, when a great flood was wiping out all the worlds, Manu desired to get out of it, to find some way out, and to obtain firm foundation. Then he saw two sāmans which came to be known as Mānava-sāmans. Then he praise-sang with it. Consequently the two sāmans became golden ships and remained floating. They sailed him across the water safely (JB III.99). The Śaṅku and Sujñāna-sāmans are said to be identical with ships useful in reaching to the heavenly world (TMB XI.10.15). The sacrificial performance is sometimes compared to a voyage and the sāmans are used in it like ships. Thus the Bṛhat and Rathantara-sāmans are said to be like ships which facilitate the performers to cross over the sacrifice (AB IV.13). Similarly TMB XIV.5.17, we read, "A sea they cross—they say—who enter upon the twelve-day-rite. He, verily, who without a boat crosses the sea, does not come out of it. There is the Plava-sāman, and it is for reaching the world of heaven". The performance of the Ārbhava-pavamāna is like floating upon sea. The Tvāṣṭrī-sāman with the finale in the middle, serves for getting a firm foundation (JB III.19). Agni could sail the oblations from the ninth day to the tenth day in the Dvādaśāha-sacrifice by means of the Yadvāhiṣṭhīya-sāman as a ship (JB III.269). The out-of-doors-chant is described as a ship leading to the heaven. "The priests are its spars and oars, - the means of reaching the heavenly world. If there be a blameworthy one, even that one (priest) would make it sink ..." (ŚB IV.2.5.10).

Some of the musical elements are considered to be chariots. Thus ṚV I.94.1, the stoma is considered to be a chariot - "We have prepared this stoma by means of thought like a chariot for Agni who deserves it". ṚV VII.34.1, the bright thoughtful poem- (*manīṣā*) goddess is expected to go unto the gods like a powerful, wellshaped chariot. Elsewhere also reference is made to the shaping out of the chariots in the form of hymns etc. Thus we read, "May these strengthening hymns (*brahman-*) which we have shaped out like chariots be pleasant unto Aśvins" (ṚV V.73.10). Cp. ṚV X.39.4 - "We have made this praise-hymn (*stoma-*) for you O Aśvins; we have shaped it out as the Bhṛgus a chariot". Similarly ṚV V.2.11, the poet-singer says, "I have shaped out this *stoma* as a knowing artizan does a chariot". (cp. V.29.15). The songs (*gir-*) and praise-hymn (*stoma*) jump up like chariots (ṚV VIII.3.15). The Rathantara-sāman has been identified with the divine chariot by TMB VII. 7.13 f. The singer is ṚV I.113.17, conceived as charioteer - "The praising singer drives the shinning morning-goddess like a charioteer (driver : *vahni*) with the ropes of speech". Elsewhere the songs (*gir-*) themselves are described as charioteers (ṚV VIII.95.1).

Sometimes the comparison to a chariot is indirectly implied. Thus ṚV VIII.26.15, a poet-singer says to Aśvins, "You have *carried* the sacrifice by means of a song (*gir-*)".

ṚV X.114.6, the ṛc and sāman are implied to be wheels of the chariot in the form of the sacrifice.[2] "The wise men, having measured out the sacrifice thoughtfully make the chariot go by means of ṛc and sāman".

Many times musical elements are described to be animals. Thus ṚV X.13.1, the hymn is described as being yoked to the sacrificial wagons. The praise-hymn (*stoma*) roars for Indra like a bull (ṚV VII.20.9). Metres are supposed to be draught animals and ṚV X.110.9 it is asked, "Who knows the yoking of the metres?". Elsewhere metres are said to be identical with the draught animals. (*paśavo vai chandāṁsi* ŚB VII.5.2.42). The metres "carry" the three soma-pressings (ŚB IV.2.5.20 ff). One satiates the stomas as one satiates the bulls etc., after they have worked for a long time (TMB II.16.3). At the end of the six-day-rite, the verse (*ṛc*) and melody (*sāman*) are "unyoked" (TMB XIII.12.13). Then one should neither speak much nor ask another nor answer another. "For at that time when the sixth day is completed, the speech (*vāc*—considered here as a draught animal) has fulfilled its task of "carrying" (the sacrifice to the gods) (so it must take rest) .... He (the sacrificer) shall feed (the officiating priests) with honey or melted butter. This is as if he besmeared the shoulders of (the animal) that conveyed (its burden) to its destination" (TMB XII.12.14 f).

ṚV VII.24.5, about the praise-hymn (*stoma*), it is said that it is being put forth like a horse running for winning the race, at the yoke (*dhur-*). The praise-hymns in the form of horses carry the Sun - "You O Sūrya rise up before us drawn by the praise-hymns i.e. by the quick Etaśa (horses)". (ṚV VII.62.2). The hiṁkāra which is uttered in the process of singing a *stoma* is said to symbolise the yoking of the stomas (TMB VI.8.6). TMB VI.3.8, the sacrifice is compared to a chariot and stomas are supposed to be its horses. Similarly JB I.129, sacrifice is said to be the divine chariot and the Bṛhat- and Rathantara-sāmans are said to be its horses. The Sākamaśva-sāman "carried" the gods to the heaven, having become a horse (JB I.181). Elsewhere verse (*ṛc*) and melody (*sāman*) are said to be the bay horses (*harī*) of Indra (AB II.22, ŚB IV.4.3.6). JB I.343, the Bṛhat- and Rathantara-sāmans are said to be the bay horses of Indra (cp. TMB IX.4.8).

Music is sometimes described as a messenger sent by the human performers to the gods for inviting the gods and conveying the desires of the performers to them. Thus ṚV V. 43.8, it is said "May the great, big, the most agreeable song (*gir-*) go like a messenger to the Aśvins, in order to invite them"; similarly ṚV VIII.26.10, We read, "May the most powerful bringer among all the calls, this praise-hymn (*stoma*) call you O Aśvins like a messenger". ṚV X.47.7, the poet singer says, "My praise-hymns, asking for favour go to Indra like messengers".

Many times the songs etc. are compared to cows and the gods to calves. ṚV IX.61.14, the poet-singer hopes, "May our songs (*gir-*) strengthen him (*Soma*) as the cows with the suckings their calves". Indra (or Agni[3] ?) in the form of Laba says, "The poem (*mati-*) has come to me like the belowing cow to the calf" (RV X.119.4). ṚV VIII.41.5, one addresses Indra, "Our poems (*mati-*) lick you as cow licks the calf" (cp. ṚV I. 186.7). ṚV IX.86.46, the poem-cow comparison is implied by making reference to the licking - "The poems (*mati-*) lick the stalk (*aṁśu-*) of Soma". The songs (*gir-*) cry out for Indra as cow for the calves (ṚV VIII.95.1). ṚV X.123.1, praise-singers themselves are said to be licking Vena by means of their poems (*mati-*) as (the cow does to) the calves. On the other hand ṚV

VIII.92.12, the god Indra is considered to be a cow - "We shall make you happy in the praise-song (*uktha-*) like the cows in the willows". Similarly "In order to milk the cow in the form of Indra, Vasiṣṭha releases hymn (*brahman-*) (like a calf)" (ṚV VII. 18.4).

A poem like a cow "milks" various kinds of good results (cp. ṚV II.2.9). ṚV IV.41.5, a poet-singer hopes - "may (the poem) milk all the objects of desire for us as a milk-cow which gives milk in thousand jets".

Sometimes poems are said to be the cows and gods the bulls. There is a mutual attraction between a poem and a god. Thus Soma is ṚV IX.86.19, said to be a bull (*vṛṣan*) of the poems which are implied to be cows. ṚV IV.41.5, Indrā-Varuṇā are exhorted, "Be lovers of this visionic poem O Indra and Varuṇa as bulls of a cow".

Many times sāmans etc. are considered as birds. Thus the Yajñāyajñīya-sāman is said to be a bird. Now, according to some ritualists, if the Udgātṛ desires that the sacrificer should reach the heaven, he should, in this sāman, make the words *vayo yajñā vo agnaye* the prelude. Then the sāman, having become a bird (*vayas*) carries him to the heaven (JB I.175). The Vilambasauparṇa-sāman, applied on the eighth day of the Daśarātra of the Dvādaśāha-sacrifice is identical with the trunk of a bird and the Sauparṇa-sāman used on the seventh and ninth day of the same sacrifice are the wings at the side of the trunk. "The trunk soars (*vilambate*) as it were between the two wings". Therefore the Vilambasauparṇa-sāman is so called (TMB XIV.9.20). Elsewhere also the Sauparṇa-sāman is said to be a bird and when it is used in the sacrifice named Bird (Pakṣī), the sacrificer, having become winged and luminous goes to the pure worlds (TMB XIX.11.8). The metre named Gāyatrī, having become a bird brought Soma from the heaven (ŚB III.9.4.10; cp. ŚB III.6.2.8; XI.7.3.8). AB IV.23, Gāyatrī is said to be a luminous female bird with the help of which the performer can go to the heaven (cp. ŚB XI.4.1.8; 16).

The fourth Sāhasra-sacrifice has been identified with the Mahāvrata-rite and then described as a bird by TMB XVI.

11.11. Numerous sāmans are said to be the limbs of this bird. Thus the Gāyatra-sāman is its head; Rathantara and Bṛhat are its wings; Vāmadevya is its trunk and the Yajñāyajñīya-sāman is its tail (TMB XI.11.11). Similarly other rites like the Jāmadagnya-sacrifice (TMB XXII.7.8), the built up Fire-altar (ŚB VI.7.2.6; Māśs VI.2.4.9), Agniṣṭoma-Jyotiṣṭoma-sacrifice (ŚB X.1.2.7) etc. are considered to be birds and various musical elements are described as being their limbs.

Sometimes the musical elements are useful to the sacrificer as wings for flying to the heavenly world. Thus the fifteen-versed and the seventeen-versed stomas are used on the Mahāvrata-day of a sacrificial session. The sacrificer, having become a bird flies upto heaven with these wings (TMB V.1.10). Similarly on the seventh day of the Daśarātra of the Dvādaśāha-sacrifice the nine-versed and fifteen-versed-stomas are used. The performers of this sacrifice then go to the heaven with these stomas as their wings (TMB XIV.1.13).

Sometimes music is regarded as the food or drink of gods. Thus ṚV VII.36.2, the poet-singer says, "this newer song, I prepare for you O Mitrāvaruṇas like food (*iṣam*)". ṚV VIII. 19.22, a poet-singer is addressed, "Sing for Agni a feast (*prayas-*)". The praise-hymns (*stoma-*) approach Agni like the vessels of honey (ṚV VIII.103.6). While ṚV VIII.24.20 a poet-singer is asked to sing for Indra a speech sweeter than ghee and honey, ṚV VIII.3.15, the songs (*gir-*) and praise-hymns and ṚV VIII.8.11, the speech are described to be sweetest (*madhumattama-*).

JB I.71 says that Sāman (melody) is the food and uduṁbara is the power of gods (*sāma devānām annam ūrg udumbaraḥ*) "Therefore when the Udgātṛ-priest sits upon the seat of uduṁbara-wood he puts food and power in the sāman. Wherever, priesthood is accomplished by means of sāmans, there the gods eat a lot" (JB I.71; cp. TMB VI.4.13). In the Agniṣṭoma-sacrifice at the time of recital of the midday pavamāna laud, Auśanasa-sāman is to be sung. This sāman should end with a *svarita*-toned syllable. "By means of the tone (*svara-*) food is offered to the gods towards the end; (the singer) thereby offers, by means of the tone, food to the gods at the end" (TMB VII.3.26). When Prajāpati asked Agni to choose any part of the sāman Agni chose the soft (*mandra-*) part of it which is identical with food. Therefore whosoever will sing it, will be a food-eater (JUB I.6.2.5 f). ŚB IX.3.3.14, we read that by means of the vaṣaṭ-call, food is given to the gods. The out-of-doors chant is described as a meal (*bhakṣa-*) of both the gods and men (AB II.22).

Many times musical elements are compared to rivers, flowing water etc. Thus ṚV VI.36.3, we read, "Into him (Indra) enter the songs (*gir-*) strengthened by praise-songs (*uktha-*) as the rivers (*sindhavaḥ*) into the sea". ṚV VIII.44.25, Agni is addressed, "To you go the songs (*gir-*) making noise as rivers (*sindhavaḥ*) into sea". ṚV V.44.9, the poem and river comparison is implied - "Their first poem (*mati-*) has come to the sea". ṚV X.89.4, the songs are compared to the waters going to the sea - "I impel songs (*gir*) like the waters which flow in large gushes from the depths of the sea". Sometimes the speeches are supposed to be waves. Thus Soma is said to have startled the speeches as the river the waves (*ūrmi-*) (ṚV IX.96.7). On the other hand, poems are described to be like waves of waters which, hastening themselves, instigate soma (ṚV IX.95.3). ṚV VIII.17.5, Indra is requested to enjoy the praise-hymn (*stoma-*) which swells like the sea. Thus here, the praise-hymn is compared to the sea. In ṚV VI.34.4, invocations are compared to waters- "Him (Indra) have the invocations along with the sacrifices strengthened as the waters strengthen a man in a barren land when they meet him".

Many times the relation of gods and musical elements is like that of a husband and wife also. Thus ṚV X.91.13, a poet-singer says, "This newer good-praise (*suṣṭuti-*) I sing for him who desires for it; ..... May it touch his heart from near as the desirous good-clothed wife the husband". The poems (*mati-*) embrace Indra as wives their husbands (ṚV X.43.1). ṚV I. 186.7, it is said, "Our speeches embrace him (Indra), the most fragrant one, as the wives the husband".

Sometimes music is supposed to be a man. Thus TMB XII. 10.7, Prastāva (prelude) is said to be the mouth of sāman and thereby sāman is implied to be a man. According to JUB I. 3.3.5, Prajāpati transferred the sāman to a man - "He made the mind the *hiṁkāra*; speech the *prastāva*; breath the *udgītha*; sight the *pratihāra*; hearing the *nidhana*; seed and off-spring he made the sixth and seventh (part of the sāman)". According to JUB III.1.4.4f, the *uktha* is identical with man.

Sometimes however, the sacrifice is described as a man[4] and various musical elements are described as the limbs of man in the form of the sacrifice. "The nine-versed stoma, is its head; the fifteen-versed its neck; the seventeen-versed (-they say-) corresponds to its chest; they make the twenty-one-versed its belly and the twenty-nine-versed corresponds to the two sides as well as to the ribs ..." (ŚB XII. 3.1.6 ff). Similarly according to JB I.251, the out-of-doors-chant is the feet of the sacrifice-man; the four ājyas his thighs and bones; the three-metred mādhyandina-recitations his that part which is below the navel; the pṛṣṭhas are his back .... (JB I.257).

There are many other miscellaneous metaphorical descriptions of Vedic musical elements. ṚV V.29.15, the hymns are described as cloths. In the primordial sacrifice, which is conceived as a cloth, the sāmans are supposed to be its cross-threads (*otu-*) (ṚV X.130.2). Sometimes music is compared to salary. Thus ṚV VIII.66.11 the poet-singers say, "We bring unto you (O Indra) new hymns like salary (*bhṛti-*)". ṚV IX.103.1, a poet-singer is requested, "Bring for Soma a speech like salary". Sometimes the songs are compared to oblations. Thus ṚV II. 27.1, the poet-singer says, "I offer (*juhomi*) these songs (*gir-*) to Ādityas with the spoon (in the form of tongue)". Similarly, ṚV VII.13.1, we read, "I bring for Vaiśvānara (a poem) like an oblation (*haviṣ-*)". Sometimes music is compared to rain. ṚV IX.10.3 a poet-singer is requested, "Release a poem as a cloud the rain". ṚV VIII.87.4, the song of praise is considered as a water-trough when Aśvins are exhorted, "Come (O Aśvins) unto the good-praise (*suṣṭuti*) from the heaven as the bulls to a water-trough". ṚV VI.69.3 the poem (*mati-*) is considered to be like some liquid - "May the praise-hymns (*stoma-*) which are being recited along with the praise-songs (*uktha-*) anoint you with the ointment of poems". ṚV I. 116.1, stomas are compared to clouds - "I push the stomas as wind the clouds". ṚV VIII.89.7, sāman is compared to the milk-pot in the Pravargya-rite - "Like the milk-pot (*gharma-*) make the Bṛhat-sāman glow with good-hymns (*suvṛkti-*)". ṚV VIII. 102.3, the songs (*gir-*) are considered to be the sisters (*jāmi-*) of each other.

The comparisons and identifications detailed above can throw a good light upon the nature of vedic music and thereby on its magico-religious power to work out its results. Thus the comparisons of music with ship, chariots etc. is significant from this point of view. It is implied by these and such comparisons that music is a sure means to reach to the desired objects. The comparison of husband and wife with gods and music as well as of food with music will show the close relations of gods and music. They will also suggests intensity with which gods like music and the usefulness of music in making gods favourable to fulfil the desires of the worshippers. Thus the comparisons and identifications are very much helpful for understanding the magico-religious significance of music.

REFERENCES

1. On the significances of path see J. Gonda, "*Adhvan* and *Adhvaryu*, *VIJ*, III. 21 (Sep. 1965), p. 165 etc.
2. For sacrifice-chariot comparison rf. my *Sacrifice in the Brāhmaṇa-texts*, p. 284 f.
3. For this opinion rf. Hauschild, *Weller Felicitation vol.* p. 247.
4. For details rf. my *Sacrifice in the Brāhmaṇa-texts*, p. 290 ff.

(B) WAYS OF PERFORMING MUSIC

In the process of Vedic sacrifices music is amply used. There are numerous mannerisms and innumerable ways of performing a particular musical element. These mannerisms and ways have their own magicoreligious significances. Now I propose to study these mannerisms and ways of Vedic music.

There are some external mannerisms at the time of singing. Thus in the Agniṣṭoma-sacrifice, at the time of the third pressing, the Yajñāyajñīya-sāman is to be sung. At that time the Udgātṛ covers himself completely with his garment in order to prevent himself from being burnt by Agni (For, while singing this sāman the Udgatṛ is mystically going near to Vaiśvānara-Agni) (TMB VIII.7.6). TMB VIII.7.7 however, says that if one would cover oneself completely, the Manes will not be able to know him. Therefore he should cover only upto the ears. So he is covered as well as uncovered. Then the Manes will be able to know him and Agni will not burn him. The rule given by the JB I.174 is, however, totally different. According to it, the Udgātṛ should sing the above mentioned sāman without any cover at all. "For if he were to cover himself, he should belong to the manes". (Probably because at a sacrifice for manes, the performer covers himself) - and this must be avoided. If one were to chant having covered oneself upto the ears, one would be deprived of his eyesight and hearing. Therefore, one should not cover oneself at all at the time of singing the Yajñāyajñīya-sāman (JB I.174). A ritualist named Nāka has said:- "At the time of uttering the response viz. *hum bhā ovā*, one should turn about unto something greater; then one becomes the owner of a great village, the owner of a great resting place". (JUB III.3.3.5). In the course of singing of the stotras of the Vaiśvānara overnight-rite, one should not sleep; lest one's vital airs would be depleted (JB III.8).

At the time of singing of the Rathantara-sāman, the Udgātṛ should make full cheeks. For this sāman is identical with glory (*śrī*). One thus puts glory in oneself. Thus this sāman is helpful for good results. But it can be harmful also. Therefore one has to take care in singing it. At the time when the *prastāva* (prelude) of this sāman is being chanted, the Udgātṛ should shut his eyes. "The Rathantara, verily is liable to destroy the eye-sight of the Udgātṛ; whilst its *prastāva* is being chanted, he should shut his eyes and upon them at (the word) "*svardṛśam* (seeing the light)"; then he is not deprived of his eyesight" (TMB VII.7.15).[1] Music is a power like electricity and as such its contact is dangerous. So one has to prevent oneself from any undue contact. This same remark appertains to the rule given by JB I.330, according to which the Rathantara-sāman should be sung "swiftly", for it is identical with fire. Therefore one should get oneself relieved of it *swiftly*.

At the time of singing the Vāmadevya-sāman, the Udgātṛ should sit without making any movements. Then the domestic animals turn to him (TMB VII.9.7; JB I.138). Further, TMB VII.9.9, it is said, "The Vāmadevya is the intermediate region; He must sing it without shaking his limbs; for unshaken is the intermediate region. The Vāmadevya is cattle; he sings it without hurting in order not to hurt the cattle". The manner of singing "without hurting" is further described with the help of two similes. "(He should sing the Vāmadevya) in the same manner as a she-cat takes her young one between her teeth without hurting or biting, (or) in the same manner as the wind blows gently over the water" (TMB VII.9.10). But at the time of singing the Rathantara-sāman, however, the Udgātṛ should sing it shaking himself. Then the plants and trees grow swiftly; one also swiftly gets progeny and cattle (JB I.330).

On the fifth day of the Daśarātra of the Dvādaśāha-sacrifice, at the time of recital of the Śakvarīverses, water is to be kept nearby. By this one separates the good and bad (TMB XIII.4.8; cp. Lāṭyāśs III.5.13. ff; Drāhyāśs IX.1.14 ff).

While singing the Padastobha-sāman, the Udgātṛ makes a gesture of one who winds himself loose from encircling evil. The reason given by TMB XIII.5.22 while explaining this is as follows : "Indra raised his thunderbolt against Vṛtra, but he (Vṛtra) encircled him with sixteen coils. He (Indra) saw the

Padastobha-sāman and by means of it winded (them = coils) off. He the (Udgātṛ) should chant the udgītha (part of this sāman) unwinding as it were in order to repel the evil" (cp. JB III.129).

There are some particular ways of pronunciation and they have some magical significances. Thus the syllable *om* must be uttered in a nasalized way (=*oṁ*). "Some sing it as *om*. Let one not sing it thus. He is then liable to hide it by the sap. So also (in the way of pronunciation of some), there come to be two as it were viz. *o-m*. Some sing *O*. Let him not sing it thus either. Let him sing *oṁ*. Thus he combines it with the sap". (JUB I.7.2.3).

While chanting the prelude of the Rathantara-sāman the Prastotṛ hurls thunderbolt as it were against the Udgātṛ. Then the udgītha-part of that sāman is to be sung by the Udgātṛ strongly. Thereby the Udgātṛ throws back the hurled thunderbolt" (TMB VII.7.10). Moreover, the Udgātṛ should sing his part *stammeringly (balbalākurvatā)* and *confoundingly (abhilobhayatā)*. Thereby he confounds the thunderbolt. Music can be at times dangerous. So one has to take care of protecting oneself from likely danger.

In some recitations *nyūṅkha*[2] is used. *Nyūṅkha* should be made in reciting the morning litany at the second syllable of each half-verse and in the Ājya-recitation in the third foot (at the second syllable) except the last verse (cf. Āśs VII.11). The *nyūṅkha* consists in altering the vowel of the above mentioned syllables to *o* and lengthening it. The *nyūṅkha* is said to be identical with food. "When the farmers run about shouting, thus does food come into existence". On the fourth day of the Dvādaśāha-sacrifice the *nyūṅkha* is made; then food will be obtained (AB V.3; cp. KB XXII.8)

On the sixth day of the Dvādaśāha *ninarda*[3] is to be made. The *ninarda* affects the second vowel of the third foot which is the normal place of *nyūṅkha*. It is a special kind of accent described in the Āśs VIII.3.9 ff. Thus the first vowel is pronounced as *anudātta*, the second and the next as *ekaśruti*.

The *ninarda* is to be made at the time of reciting the Vṛṣākapi-hymn, Raibhī-verses, Parikṣit-verses (AB VI.32).

In reciting hymns or verses, one has sometimes to recite quarter by quarter or half-verse by half-verse. Thus on the Mahāvrata-day, the hymn beginning with *ya eka iddhavyaś carṣaṇīnāṁ* (ṚV VI.22.1) is to be recited quarter by quarter (SāṅĀ II.4). In a soma-sacrifice, the pāvamāni-verses must be recited by half-verses. This helps to obtain support (AB VI.2). At the time of the initiation-ceremony, the teacher while teaching the Sāvitrī-verse to the student, recites it first by quarters. "The breaths are three: the out-breath, the upbreath and thorough-breath: it is these that he (the teacher) lays into him (the student)". Then the teacher recites it by half-verses. "There are two principal breaths: the outbreath and the up-breath. It is the out-breath and the up-breath that he thus lays into him". Then the teacher recites the whole verse. "There is only one breath in man. He thus lays the whole vital air into the whole of him". (ŚB XI.5.4.15). Thus every kind of recitation has its own significance.

Significance is attached to the *tone* of the utterances of recitations. Thus there are six kinds of the *āśrāvita* (= the Adhvaryu's call *"om śrāvaya"*) viz. the descending, the level, the ascending, the feeble, the outward-tending and the inward-tending: (1) The descending: When one begins in a high tone and concludes in a low tone, it is the descending. This kind makes the sacrificer poor. (2) The level: When one concludes in the same tone in which one has begun, it is level. This makes the sacrificer neither poor nor prosperous. (3) The ascending: When one begins in a low tone and concludes in a high tone it is ascending. This makes the sacrificer prosperous. (4) The feeble: When the call is made in a very thin, long-drawn, toneless way, it is feeble. This makes the sacrificer feeble and submissive to his spiteful enemy. (5) The outward-tending: When one opens the lips wide and utters his call at a high toneless pitch, it is outward-tending. "The tone is prosperity; the prosperity is thus put outside oneself and the sacrificer remains hungry". (6) The inwardtending: When one closes the lips and utters the call in a loud, toneful pitch, it is inward-tending. "The tone is prosperity and thus prosperity is put inside oneself. The sacrificer then becomes the eater of food" (ŚB XI.4.2.5 ff).

Similarly there are three kinds of vaṣaṭ-call having different significances - (1) Thunderbolt - when one pronounces the vaṣaṭ loudly and forcibly it is thunderbolt. One hurls it as a missile at the rival. (2) One who hides one's abode - the vaṣaṭ-call which is even, continuous and without loss of (any part of) the verse, it is one who hides one's abode; offspring and cattle depend on it. (3) Empty - The *vaṣaṭ* in which the *ṣaṭ*-part fails is empty. This vaṣaṭ makes the priest as well as the sacrificer empty (AB III.7).

There are various rules about the tone of the recitation of strophe, antistrophe etc. and the particular tone in a particular recitation has its own signification. Thus at the time of recitation, one should recite the strophe with a middle tone; for the strophe is the self. Thereby one makes the self perfect. The antistrophe is identical with offspring. One should recite it in a louder tone. Thereby one makes one's offsprings better than oneself. The inserted verse is identical with one's wife. One should recite it with a lower tone. When one knowing this recites the inserted verse in a lower tone, one's wife will not answer back. The Pragātha is identical with the cattle. It is to be recited in a sonorous voice. Then it serves to win cattle (AB III.24).

Sometimes one should stretch the tone. While reciting the Gāyatra-sāman during the course of out-of-doors-chant, the Udgātṛ should stretch (*avanardayet*) the tone twice and at the third time make the hiṁkāra (TMB VII.1.2).

Some particular ways of intoning are called *āgā-s*. They refer to the strength of tone or to the pitch of tone in chanting.[4] In TMB XIII.10.8 following incident is mentioned. The Vāmadevya-sāman showed itself in human form to Keśī Dālbhya and complained, "Unskilled chanters chant me. Let them not chant me" and then requested, "I must be intoned. Let them chant me intoning as it were; for the sake of obtaining firm support" (TMB XIII.10.8). JUB I.12.3.1 ff, three kinds of *āgās* are given. They belong respectively to Agni, Indra, and the Viśvedevas. "That which is low belongs to Agni; with it the *udgītha* of the morning-pressing is to be chanted. Verily, the morning pressing belongs to Agni. This world belongs to Agni. He sings the *udgītha* of the morning-pressing with his (Agni's) own *āgā*; then he enjoys this world". Similarly the loud and noisy intonation belongs to Indra. It is to be used at the midday-pressing. Thereby one enjoys the yonder world (JUB I.12.3.3). The *āgā* which is sung shakingly, spreadingly as it were belongs to Viśvedevas and is to be used at the third pressing. Thereby one enjoys the intermediate world (JUB I.12.3.4). According to some ritualists, however, the *udgītha* should be chanted with one *āgā* only viz. with that which is in the middle voice (JUB I.12.3.5). The *āgā* which is plover-like, belongs to God Bṛhaspati. He who is desirous of brahman-splendour should sing the *udgītha* with it (JUB I.12.3.6). A ritualist named Caikitāneya is referred to be singing only one *āgā* viz. that of the Gāyatra-sāman (JUB I.12.3.7).

Sometimes one has to sing with the "repeated push (*anutunnam*)". Thus the *Vairāja*-sāman is to be recited with the repeated push i.e. with repetitions. The Vairāja-sāman is to be sung on verses which contain the words - *madantu tvā* (SV I. 398). At the time of singing, these words take the following form - $\overset{1}{\textit{mā}}$ *datu* $\overset{2}{\textit{tvā}}$ 3 - $\overset{1}{\textit{dā}}$*tu* $\overset{2}{\textit{tvā}}$ (TMB VIII.9.13; cp. XII. 10.11). Similarly, the Ābhīśava-sāman is to be sung with the repeated push (TMB XII.9.17). This way of singing the sāmans is supposed to have a bearing upon the generation - ideology. Thus TMB XII.10.11, it is said, "The seed is implanted from the repeated push". Ātharvaṇa- (JB III.66), Vātsapra- (JB III.81), Ānūpa- (JB III.97) sāmans are to be sung with the repeated push. In connection with these sāmans also it is said this way of singing is based on the generation-ideology.

In reciting verses, one has sometimes to intermingle them. Thus while reciting the Ājya-lauds on the eighth day of the

Daśarātra of the Dvādaśāha-sacrifice, one has to intermingle the verses. One has to take a Rathantara-tristich as the first and third Ājya-laud and the Bṛhat-tristich as the second and fourth Ājya-laud (TMB XIV.8.4; cp. 9). "The chandoma-days (i.e. 7th, 8th, and 9th day of the Daśarātra of the Dvādaśāha) are like a ford difficult to cross over. Just as in the daily life, people enter into a stream which is difficult to cross over, hanging themselves close to one another so he intermingles the two characteristic features closely together in order that the chandomas may not oscillate (TMB XIV.8.4;9; cp. XV.2.6;9).

The intermingling of verses is also sometimes connected with the generation-ideology. Thus in the Vighana-sacrifice one has to praise-sing with the verses having inter-mingled them. "For from an intermingled pair, beings and cattle are generated; that (intermingling) is for the sake of generation" (JB II.143). Similarly in a four-day-sacrifice named Jāmadagnya, intermingling is done and that is for the sake of generation (JB II.287).

Sometimes, one is advised to sing swiftly. Thus in the Agniṣṭoma-sacrifice, at the time of midday-pressing, the Rathantara-sāman is to be sung swiftly (*kṣipram*) for the sake of (swiftly) obtaining the heavenly world (TMB VII.7.12). JB I. 329 gives the same prescription with a different explication - "Mind (thought) comes first; then the speech. The Bṛhat is the mind; the Rathantara is the speech. When Bṛhat and Rathantara ran their race, the Bṛhat won the race and the Rathantara was left behind. By chanting the Rathantara swiftly, he makes the mind (thought) and speech equal (i.e. associated with each other). Then the Rathantara thinks, "He who has made me equal (to the Bṛhat), come, let the bad lot (of him) leave him swiftly". He leaves his bad lot swiftly who knowing thus sings the Rathantara-sāman swiftly" (JB I.329). Thus by singing the Rathantara-sāman swiftly, one can remove one's bad lot swiftly. In the overnight-rite (*atirātra-*) the Āśvina śastra is to be recited before the sun-rise". It should be recited swiftly; for they (the performers) run a race as it were. Before sun-rise he (the Hotṛ-priest) should recite it, for they (the gods) had made the sun the goal (in the race they had run (TMB IX.1.38).

Sometimes it is necessary to sing without exhaling i.e. having held one's breath. Thus in the Agniṣṭoma-sacrifice, the Vāmadevya-sāman is to be sung without exhaling upto the Response (*pratihāra-*). "For the Vāmadevya is breath; lest I should discontinue the breath" (JB I.333). Similarly in the same sacrifice the verses in the Uṣṇih and Kakubh-metre are to be recited without exhaling upto the Response (*pratihāra-*) (JB I.336). Once the gods and Asuras were struggling; they said, "Whosoever of us will sing the Gāyatra-sāman for three times, without exhaling, will win these worlds and inbreathing, outbreathing and thorough-breathing". Ayāsya Āṅgirasa sang the sāman accordingly and obtained the result. When, in the Dvādaśāha-sacrifice, the Gāyatra-sāman is sung in this manner, then also the above-mentioned result is obtained (JB III.281). According to JUB III.1.3.1, one should not exhale during the stotra of the Gāyatra-sāman thinking, "May I not be cut off from fortune". TMB VII.1.9, also it is said, "The Gāyatra-sāman is identical with breath; one should not exhale during the singing of it, for the sake of not discontinuing the breath. If one exhales, one will die (before time); if one does not, one will live the full life". The finale of the Ātīṣādīya-sāman is to be chanted until the breath fails (*ātamitoḥ*)". Thereby the performers get a long life (TMB XII.11.17; JB III.79).

At the time of singing, sometimes one has to sing expressedly and sometimes unexpressedly (*niruktam* and *aniruktam*).[5] Thus the Nābhāhediṣṭhīya-hymn is to be recited in an unexpressed manner i.e. no mention of the deity is to be made in that recitation. For this hymn is identical with seed and seed is poured unexpressedly, secretly (AB VI.27). In the Vājapeya-sacrifice, the morning-service is unexpressed. The sacrificer thereby reaches Prajāpati because Prajāpati is also unexpressed (TMB XVIII.6.8). On the Mahāvrataday, the Rājana-pṛṣṭha-sāman is to be sung on the unexpressed verses. For Prajāpati is unexpressed i.e. mysterious. Therefore, to recite anything unexpressedly is a form of Prajāpati (ŚāṅĀ II.1). Thus the unexpressed way of recitation is helpful for generation or for obtainment of Prajāpati.

Sometimes there is some positive danger if one recites expressedly; and therefore it is essential to sing unexpressedly. Thus at the time of out-of-doors-chant, the Gāyatra-sāman is to be sung unexpressedly. "For whatever is expressed that is the "cruel" part of the Gāyatra-sāman; when one recites unexpressedly, one avoids the cruel part of it" (TMB VII.1.8). At the time of the midday pressing of the Agniṣṭoma-sacrifice, the Vāmadevya-sāman is to be sung unexpressedly. If one were to sing it expressedly one would deliver the cattle to Rudra and Rudra would kill the cattle in the same year (TMB VII.9.17 f).

Sometimes neither the unexpressed way alone nor the expressed way alone is advisable. Therefore both ways are partially prescribed. Thus while reciting the Retasyā-verses in the Anuṣṭubh metre, some quarters should be uttered expressedly and some unexpressedly. If one were to recite all the quarters expressedly, the off-springs would go on speaking incessantly and will never keep quiet. If on the other hand, one were to recite all the quarters unexpressedly, the offsprings would be dumb. So, in order to avoid both these extremes, one should recite some words expressedly and some unexpressedly (JB I.102). The ājya-recitations of the tenth day of the Dvādaśāha-sacrifice are to be recited in an unexpressed manner. The last quarter, however, should be recited expressedly i.e. with a reference to Indra and Agni as the deities of it. Thereby the sacrifice becomes "declared" (JB III.282).

Some recitations are made in an inaudible manner (*upāṁśu*).[6] Especially, whatever is recited or connected with the deity named Prajāpati should always be inaudible. ŚB I. 4.5.8 ff gives a story explaining this rule. Once there was a quarrel about the superiority between Mind and Speech. They both came to Prajāpati for decision. Prajāpati declared the Mind to be superior. The decision, naturally made Speech angry. She declared that she would not accompany any rite connected with Prajāpati. In some other cases also inaudible manner is prescribed. Thus before reciting the enkindling verses, one has to pronounce the *hiṁkāra* (the sound *hum*); but it must be pronounced inaudibly (ŚB I.4.1.3). In the course of Darśapūrṇamāsa-offerings there is an inaudible offering (*upāṁśuyāga*). The significance of this offering is as follows: Gods went near the Asuras by means of this offering and killed them with the *vaṣaṭ*-call which is identical with the thunderbolt. The sacrificer does the same in connection with his enemy (ŚB I.6.3.28). Thus the inaudible way is at times very effective and is helpful in destroying the enemy.

The inaudible performance is sometimes attributed with a bearing upon the "generation" - ideology. Thus the melted-butter-offerings (*ājyahavīṁṣi*) which form a part of the New and Full-moon-offerings, are to be performed inaudibly. "For the melted butter is identical with seed; they put seed as it were ..... Inaudibly do they perform this rite. Secretly, indeed, union takes place; and secretly also takes place what is spoken inaudible; that is why they perform inaudibly" (ŚB I.9.2.7). In the Agniṣṭoma-sacrifice, silent-praise (*tūṣṇīṁśaṁsa*) is recited. This recitation is said to be a "development of seed" as it were (AB II.39). The priest Agnīdh inaudibly utters the offering-verse for the cup for (Tvaṣṭṛ) with the wives. The cup for Tvaṣṭṛ with the wives is identical with seed; seed is poured thereby (AB VI.3).

An expression quite similar to the above one is "to sing coveredly (*channam*)", which also means to sing in a low voice. Thus the part after the prastāva (prelude) of a sāman should be sung in the "covered" manner. That part then serves to the sāman as a support in the ṛc. The singer then gets himself supported (JB I.326). According to JB I.274, the Pavamānas are to be sung in the "covered" manner. For they are identical with gods. "For gods are covered, beyond the sight and unexpressed as it were". It is further said that the Pṛṣṭhas and Ukthas are identical with men. Men are uncovered; they can be seen and they are expressed as it were. Therefore the

Pṛṣṭhas and Ukthas are to be sung in an uncovered, open, expressed manner i.e. audibly (JB I.274).

Excess of "covered" singing is dangerous. JB I.337 gives a rule according to which not all the recitations at the time of the third pressing in a soma-sacrifice should be recited in a "covered" manner. Otherwise, the Udgātṛ would burn himself and the sacrificer. It will thus seem that music is double natured. It can be useful; it can be harmful.

Sometimes one sings mentally[7] only. Thus on the tenth day of the Daśarātra of the Dvādaśāha-sacrifice one sings the Gāyatra-sāman mentally. This sāman is identical with mind. Therefore by singing it mentally one makes it successful. This sāman marks the end of the Daśarātra. In this connection it is said, "Whatever the gods could not complete (of the sacrifice) they completed it with the mind". Similarly here, mental singing is helpful for completing whatever is incompleted (JB III.305; AB V.23).

There are some miscellaneous ways of singing which also have some magico-religious significances. Thus while singing the Yajñāyajñīya-sāman some changes should be made in the original text on the basis of which this sāman is to be sung. Thus originally there are the words *girā girā* (song by song). Instead of these words one should utter *irā irā*. For the words *girā girā* can also mean "swallow swallow" and in order to avoid the evil implied by those words this change is to be made (TMB VII.6.9 f). According to some ritualists no two sāmans having the *svarita* tone in their finales, or having some other word than *iḍā* as the finale or the two sāmans based on the same verses should be sung together. For such singing is dangerous. But JB supports the opposite view according which such sāmans may be sung together and this manner of singing can be profitable (JB I.301 f). While singing sāmans, the following order should be followed - (1) the sāman with the word *iḷā* as its finale; (2) the svāra-sāman i.e. a saman with the *svarita* tone in its finale; (3) the sāman with any other word as its finale. The finale is identical with body; the *svara* is identical with the vital breath and *iḷā* is identical with cattle. Since the *svara*-sāman is sung in between the other two sāmans, therefore the body and cattle of the sacrificer get continuously held by the vital air. For the vital air covers the creatures and cattle in the middle (JB I.307).

The Paurumudga-sāman is to be sung with an "upbeat (*abhyāghātyam*)". This manner of singing consists of certain way of repetition. Thus the syllables of the verse (SV I.273 b) (*bhir a*) *driguḥ* become in the chant *dhrā*^{2} 1 *igū2ḥ*- *dhra*^{1} - *igū2ḥ* (TMB XIV.9.30).

The ṛc (verse) and sāman (melody) must be intimately connected. "If one were to sing the ṛc without sāman, only bone will be born and no flesh; if only the sāman without ṛc, then only flesh (will be born) and no bone. One sings the ṛc covered with sāman. Therefore a man is covered with hair, skin, and flesh". Thus equal importance is given to the text and music.[8]

In singing one does not totally neglect the aesthetic sense. But this aesthetics is also magicoreligious. Thus ṚV X.91.4, the poet-singer says, "I create a beautiful (*cāru*-) poem from my heart (for Agni)". ṚV IV.36.7, the *stoma* is regarded as an ornament - "The most beautiful (*śreṣtha*-) worth-seeing ornament (*peśas*) has been put before you: a praise-hymn (*stoma*-) - enjoy it O Vājas; Ṛbhus :" ṚV VII.32.13, the poet singers are told, "Make for the sacrifice-deserving Indra a meditational formula (*mantra*-) which is not too short, which is well constructed and ornamental". The Atris "beautify" Indra by their songs (ṚV V.39.5). The *stobhas* are described as the embellishments (*alaṁkārāḥ*)[9] of the mahānāmnī-verses. One should recite these verses embelishing and adorning as it were (*tā alaṁ kurvanniva śobhayanniva gāyet*). "To him who knows this accrue unbought forms" (JB III.113). It seems that a beautiful song etc. is supposed to be more efficatious magicoreligiously.

It can be now clearly seen how significant are the particular ways of singing. Music is supposed to be a power-substance and naturally the ways of handling it have their own significances.

Music is double-natured and therefore can be at times useful and at times harmful. So one has to know exactly what way of singing is to be followed at a particular moment. Although at times, the aesthetic sense is also revealed the main emphasis is on magicoreligious significances.

REFERENCES

1. Rf. Caland, Henry, *L'Agniṣṭoma*, p. 307.
2. For *nyūṅkha* see Keith, *RBT*, p. 226.
3. For *ninarda* see Keith, *RBT*, p. 283.
4. Rf. Caland, *Pañcaviṁśabrāhmaṇa*, p. 340.
5. For these terms see Renou, Silburn, "*Nirukta* and *anirukta* in vedic" *Sarūpabhāratī*, p. 68 ff.
6. For this term see Renou, "La valeur du silence dans le culte védique", *JAOS*, 69 (1949), p. 11, the same, "Two vedic words *upāṁśu* and - *Tuṣṇīm*" *PAIOC*, 15, (1951), p. 165 ff.
7. In the mediaeval Christian thought more importance was given to the mental singing than to the loud chanting. "Non voce sed corde canere" was the central doctrine of that music. The Church-Fathers of that period used to say "We must sing by heart and not by voice" (Abert, *Musikanschauung*, p. 90). According to Porphyrius, "We cannot approach god by means of prayers audible to the sense-organs but with pure silence and pure thoughts" (Abert, *Musikanschauung*, p. 53).
8. Contrast with this the opinion of the mediaeval Church-Fathers for whom the text-word was more important and music was only a means to the end. Aurelianus Reomnesis says that the meaning of the text is more important than the melody and according to Johannes Cottonius the singer should direct his song in such a way that the meaning of the words will be expressed (Abert, *Musikanschauung*, p. 147).
9. For this term see Gonda, "The meaning of the word *alaṁkāra*", *New Indian Antiquary* 1939 (*Festschrift-Thomas*) p. 97-114. According to Johanes Tinctoris, music adorns the praise of gods (Abert, *Musikanschauung*, p. 145).

(C) DIRECTIVES OF THE MUSICAL PERFORMANCE

We have seen how different ways of singing are magicoreligiously significant. As has been said in this book often music is regarded as a power-substance and as such it is double-natured. In order to get good results and avoid bad ones it is essential to follow some directives in the performance of Vedic music. These directives are also said to be significant in many respects. Let us study them.

Antiquity and novelty of the songs have their own significances. Arbitrarily importance is given sometimes to the ancient songs and sometimes to both the ancient as well as new songs and other times, only to the new songs.

ṚV III.10.5, the poet-singers are being requested, "Prepare for the Agni the ancient (*pūrvyam*) great speech (*vacaḥ-*)". ṚV V.72.7, the poet-singers say that they are imitating the old fashion of the founder of Atri-family in their sacrifice accompanied by songs :- "We sacrifice like Atri for Mitra and Varuṇa by means of songs". Addressing the sacrificial wagons, one says, "I yoke the ancient (*pūrvya-*) powerful hymn (*brahman-*) by means of obeisances" (ṚV X.13.1). In the case of Soma, it is said, "They (The singers) praised him with ancient (*purāṇyā*) song-verse (*gāthā-*)" (ṚV IX.99.4).

The old songs are supposed to be power-increasing. Thus Agni was made grow powerful (*vāvṛdhe*) by means of old (*pratna-*) poem by a poet-singer (ṚV VIII.44.12).

There seems to be some special importance attached to the new songs.[1] For the poet-singers refer to the newness of their songs more frequently than to their antiquity. Thus ṚV II. 24.1, Bṛhaspati is addressed, "We worship you with this new song (*girā*)". ṚV II.62.7 Pūṣan is informed, "This is, O Pūṣan, a new good praise (*suṣṭuti-*) being sung by us for you". In many hymns addressed to Indra we find the following expression - "We have prepared a new powerful hymn (*brahman-*)" (ṚV IV. 16.21; 17.21; 19.11; 20.11; 21.11; 22.11; 23.11; 24.11). ṚV V. 42.13, it is not definitely known what deity is being addressed. While according to Sāyaṇa it is either Indra or Parjanya,

Geldner[2] perceives Tvaṣṭṛ as being addressed. In that verse the poet-singer says, "For that great god who gives good refuge, I carry the song (*gir-*) which is being newerly born". In ṚV VIII. 36.2, the poet-singer is preparing a new song (*suvṛkti-*) like food for Mitra and Varuṇa. Elsewhere, another poet-singer says to the same gods, "In order to praise you, I carry these new poems (*manmāni*)" (ṚV VII.61.6).

Sometimes the poet-singers claim that they are preparing or have prepared a newer poem-song. ṚV I.109.2 a poet-singer says, "I prepare (*pra-bhare*) a more powerful and newer (*navīyasīm*) poem (preceded by "vision") (*dhīti-*) for Agni". ṚV VIII.14.7 also, Agni is addressed, "This newer, thoughtful poem (*mati*) is dedicated by us to you O Agni !" Another poet-singer says, "This, O Agni, is the newer (*navyasī*) inspired poem for you" (ṚV X.4.6). ṚV X.91.13 contrast is maintained between the deity and the poem. While Agni is there described as old (*pratna-*), the poem consisting of good praise (*suṣṭuti*) is described to be newer (*navīyasīm*). Similarly ṚV VI.62.5, the poet-singer says, "I worship the ancient Aśvins with the newer speech".

The poet-singers are, on the other hand, sometimes requested to sing the new songs. Thus ṚV VI.50.6, a poet-singer is requested, "Praise (*abhi-archa*) Indra, who loves songs (*girvaṇas-*), O singer (*jaritaḥ*), by means of a new powerful hymn (*brahman-*)". Similarly ṚV VIII.16.1, we read, "Sing (*pra-stota*) praises newly for Indra the emperor of people, with songs (*gir-*)". ṚV X.89.3, a poet-singer is requested to sing newer songs". "Sing for Indra a collective newer (*navyam*) powerful hymn which does not deviate from the right path and which has no equal on the earth and heaven" ṚV VIII.51.3 also a poet-singer is requested to praise Indra by means of newer (*navyasā*) powerful poem (*mati-*). A poet-singer named Saubhari is asked in ṚV VIII.20.19 to sing the newest song for Maruts. "Sing (*abhi-gāya*) for the younglings (i.e. Maruts) finely O Saubhari, with the newest (*naviṣṭhayā*) song (*girā*)".

The newness of a poem is considered to be some kind of power of it. Therefore, a newer (*navīyasī*) poem is in ṚV

I.143.1 described as more powerful (*tavyasī*). The new song is not only powerful in itself, but it also extends the power of gods and thereby makes them do valorous activities. Thus Indra is described to have become the most powerful (*śaviṣṭha-*) by means of the newer (*navyasā*) visionic poem (*dhiyā*) (ṚV VI. 22.7). Agni is requested to listen unto the new praise-hymn (*stoma-*) and then to burn out the Rakṣases, the posessors of the magical power, by means of his glow (ṚV VIII.23.14).

Efficacy of a new song is suggested when it is compared to food. Thus ṚV VII.36.2, a poet-singer compares his new song to food. One likes fresh food. One obtains strength out of it. Similarly the gods like new songs. They are nourished and strengthened by them (details of music as the food of the gods elsewhere). ṚV VIII.66.11, the new hymn is compared to salary. As one requires salary to be obtained, the gods also like the new songs to come. Thus there is some efficacy in the newness of songs.

The new songs are so powerful that they can attract the gods, they can command them. Thus ṚV VI.17.13, one says, "May this newer (*navya-*) powerful hymn (*brahman-*) turn (*āvavṛtyāt-*) you (O Indra) herewards for doing favour". Similarly, ṚV VI.49.1, it is hoped, "I praise the (divine) people and Mitrāvaruṇa by means of the newer (*navyasībhiḥ*) songs (*gīrbhḥ*). May they come and listen". The commanding power of the new songs can be seen in ṚV III.53.2, where one says to a poet-singer, "make the two first-born parents (viz. Dvāvāpṛthivī), sit upon the two seats of order (*ṛta-*) by means of your newer songs (*navyasībhiḥ gīrbhiḥ*)".

The new speech or song has an inciting power within it. Thus ṚV VI.48.11, the poet-singers are requested, "O friends, drive (*ajadhvam*) the divine cow with the newer speech (*navyasā vacaḥ = vacassā*)". Incitation is implied in ṚV VII.20.19. There, a poet-singer is asked to praise the Maruts with the newest songs in the manner of a cultivator who incites the bulls.

The gods like the new songs and desire for them. Thus ṚV X.71.13, Agni is addressed, "This newer (*navīyasīm*) good-praise (*suṣṭutim*) I shall sing for him who is desirous of it (*uśate*), may he listen". Similarly, one says to Indra, "You desire (*haryasi*) a newer pleasing poem" (ṚV X.96.11). The poet-singer of ṚV VII.26.1, feels sure that Indra will enjoy the new praise-song: "For him (Indra) make a heroic, newer praise-song (*uktha*) which he will enjoy (*jujoṣat*) and will hear". Assuming that the gods like new songs, a poet-singer requests Indra, "Listen unto the new hymn-singer (*brahmaṇyataḥ*)" (ṚV VI.21.8). ṚV V.29.15 also Indra is requested, "Enjoy O Indra, those powerful hymns (*brahman-*) which we have newly prepared". Likewise, ṚV VII.35.14, it is said, "May Ādityas, Rudras, Vasus, enjoy this newer powerful hymn being prepared". ṚV V.12.3, a poet-singer anxiously asks, "How will you (O Agni) be a knower of new praise-song (*ucatha-*)"?

The special soft corner in the hearts of the gods for the new songs can be inferred from the request made to Indra for making the poet-singer create a new praise-song (*uktha*) (ṚV VI.18.15). Aśvins are described to have strengthened (*upa-bhūṣ-*)[3] the thoughtful poems (*manman-*) of a newer singer (*navyaso jaramāṇasya*). In a prayer to Varuṇa, the poet-singer hopes, "May a new, righteous (song) come out" (ṚV I.105.15).

The poet-singers believe that the gods will be pleased by means of the new songs and will give wealth, food and progeny in return. Thus ṚV I.12.11, a poet-singer says to Agni, "Being praised by a newer song, give us wealth and food accompanied by a heroic son".

In the Ṛgveda we also observe attempts to show simultaneously the importance of old as well as new songs. Thus ṚV IX.92.5, it is implied that a newer song is to be prepared in the "old" fashion; and the help of the god Soma is solicited in this attempt. "Prepare as ago (*pratnavat*) O Soma, the paths for the newer good hymn (*sūkta*)". Tiraści prepared newly a song out of his own old vision (*dhī-*) (ṚV VIII.95.5). Similarly a poet-singer says, "Like Kaṇva, I adorn my songs with the old thoughtful poem (*pratnena manmanā*)" (ṚV VIII.6.11). In the same verse Indra is told to have been powerful through it. ṚV VI.44.13 also he is said to have been strengthened by means of the old and new songs of the praising seers. Maruts are requested to enjoy both the old and new songs - "Be knowers, O Maruts, of old (*pūrvya-*) or new (*nūtana-*) whatever is being spoken or sung" (ṚV V.55.8).

It thus seems that in the ṚV magicoreligious significance was attached to both the old and new songs. They were supposed to contain some special powers. The poet-singers sometimes believed that the old songs would strengthen the gods and sometimes that the new songs would strengthen them. The gods although favouring both types of songs are supposed to have some special desire for the new songs. Therefore it was an unmentioned directive viz. one should praise-sing the god, with new songs or with the old songs according to the occasion.

In the Ṛgveda some emphasis is laid on the loud singing and it seems that there was a directive about loud singing. Thus a poet-singer says that he will sing a loud-toned (*bṛhat*) speech in praise of the river Sarasvatī (ṚV VII.96.1). ṚV VIII.46.14, a poet singer is asked, "Sing about Indra a loud (*mahā*) song". The loudness of singing is sometimes denoted by the prefix *pra*. Thus ṚV VIII.92.1 we read, "Sing loudly (*pra-gāyata*) for Indra" ṚV VIII.10.5 the same is said about Mitra and Aryaman, and ṚV IX.13.2 about god Soma (for similar expressions see also ṚV IX.97.4; 104.1; IX.113.9). ṚV IX.60.1; a poet singer is requested to sing loudly by means of a Gāyatra-sāman. It seems that to sing loudly was supposed to be efficacious in bringing the gods favourably to the singer.[4] Therefore one is required to follow the directive of singing loudly. In a sacrifice ṛcs or sāmans are sung loudly (KPKS 45.3).

A poem-song is often described to have come out from the bottom of the heart of the poet-singer. We often meet with the expressions like "shaped out by the heart" which qualify the songs etc. Thus ṚV I.67.4, the meditationful formulas (*mantra-*) are said to be shaped out by the heart (*hṛdā taṣṭān*). ṚV II.35.2, the poet-singers say, "May we sing well for him (viz. Apāṁ napāt) a meditationful formula well-created and come out of heart". Elsewhere Maruts are addressed in the following way, "This praise-hymn (*stoma-*) prepared by heart and mind is formed for you, O Maruts : "(ṚV I.17.2). Similarly, ṚV X.91.4 the poet-singer says, "I create a beautiful poem from my heart for Agni". It is the god Varuṇa according to ṚV I.105.15, who discloses a thoughtful poem through the heart (of the poet-singer). Compare in this respect, the exclamation of Indra in the form of Laba, "I rotate around the poem by means of heart as a carpenter the seat in the chariot". ṚV X.119.5). Thus it seems that for Vedic poet-singers there must have been a directive of singing a song from the very bottom of the heart. Moreover, it is the gods who inspire songs in the heart of a poet-singer.

According to another directive, the songs etc. are expected to be "pure". The poet-singers often claim that they offer pure songs or they have purified them. Thus ṚV VII.93.1, it is said, "Enjoy O Indrāgnī this pure (*śuci*) praise-hymn". ṚV VIII. 12.4, Indra is implored to enjoy the praise-hymn which has been purified (*pūta-*) like ghee. ṚV X.39.4, the poet-singers claim to have cleansed (*nyamṛṣāma*) the praise-hymn. ṚV IX. 2.7, Soma is told, "The songs (*gir-*) are being cleansed (*marmṛjyante*) by means of your power".

The songs must be amiable and pleasant to the gods. The gods desire such songs. In order to win their favour, such songs must be offered to them. ṚV X.96.11, it is said, "You, O Indra, desire a newer amiable (*priya*) poem (*manman-*)". ṚV X.54.6 mention is made of an amiable poem sung for Indra. Elsewhere, a poet-singer is asked to sing an amiable poem, for Varuna (ṚV VI.69.9). ṚV VIII.101.5, the poet-singers are requested to sing a pleasant (*chandyam*) praise hymn (*stotra-*) for Varuṇa. Even the soma-pressing stones are requested in ṚV VIII.101.5, to make sound that will please the gods (*devya-*).

Coming now to the context of sacrifice proper we find that in the course of sacrificial music-performance one has to follow certain directives which have magico-religious significances.

In the process of singing, sameness (*jāmitā-*) should be avoided. All the Ājya-lauds in the Agniṣṭoma end with the *svarita* accent. This rather creates some sort of monotony, sameness etc. This monotony can be mystically avoided by using verses which belong to *different* deities (TMB VII.2.5). In the Atirātra-sacrifice, both the Pṛṣṭha-laud and the twilight (*sandhi*) are based on the Rathantara-melody. Then there is a fear of the defect of sameness (*jāmi*). By chanting, however, the Saubhara-sāman in between the two, the defect of the sameness can be mystically avoided (TMB VIII.8.10). Both the sixth and seventh days of the Daśarātra of the Dvādaśāha belong to the Bṛhat-sāman. Thus there is the defect of sameness. In order to avoid it, the Kaṇva-Rathantara-sāman is to be sung on the seventh day (TMB XIV.3.17).

The directive of avoiding the montony has a distinct bearing on the generation-ideology. Thus JB I.300, it is said that two males or two females cannot produce an offspring since difference in sex is required. Similarly in singing also sameness is not productive. There must be some difference. This, thought has been expressed by a ritualist named Śāṭyāyani without using the terms *jāmi* and *ajāmi*. Thus he dislikes the way of uttering *stobha* with the syllables like *bhā bhā*. For this is a monoformal (*ekarūpa-*) *stobha* and is therefore sterile. One should rather make *stobha* by uttering *abhubhābhibhabhebha* this being multiformal, is fertile (JB I.330).

JB I.133 also, the avoidance of sameness is implied indirectly; but no connection with generation-ideology is maintained therein. Thus one should make Bṛhat and Rathantara-sāmans different from each other. In the Bṛhat-sāman, one should sing *ho vā ha* and in the Rathantara *o vā ha*. "Thereby one separates oneself from the evil".

At the time of singing, continuity is important. In the sacrifice also continuity plays an important role[5] and singing helps to keep that continuity intact. In the Dvādaśāha-sacrifice, on the Prāyaṇīya (introductory) day, five groups of three ṛcs are to be sung continuously. "For they (the performers) who separate the tercets from the Prāyaṇīya-days, verily, lose their vital breaths". When the verses are recited *continuously*, the vital breaths also remain *continuous* (JB III.21). On the third day of the Daśarātra of the same sacrifice, at the time of singing the Ariṣṭa-sāman, the word *iḍā* is to be uttered thrice. The last utterance is however, to be made in a very swift ('running') way. This helps to *connect* the third day with the fourth and to preserve continuity (TMB XII.5.25). On the fifth day in the same rite, the Yaṇva sāman is to be sung continuously, for the sake of continuity of the sacrifice (TMB XIII.3.7). In singing this sāman, one leaves the *Prastāva* (prelude) out of the second and third verse, on which this sāman is based and thereby makes it continuous. In the Agniṣṭoma-sacrifice the Aponatrīya-hymn should be recited continuously so that Parjanya rains continuously for one's offspring (AB II.19). In the Darśapūrṇamāsa-sacrifices, the sāmidhenī (enkindling) verses which are recited at the time of enkindling the fire, are to be recited continuously, without any break. As a result of this, the days and nights of the year are made continuous (ŚB I.3.5.16).

While singing, one must pay attention to the equilibrium. In the Dvādaśāha-sacrifice, on the seventh day of the Daśarātra, two groups of twelve verses are to be recited. For, "The year is equal to twelve months. One thus counterbalances the year to the preceding six-day-period (which is, mystically, nothing but the year: for a year has six seasons and the six-day-period has the six pṛṣṭha-sāmans); for the sake of equilibrium (*savīvadhatvāya*)" (TMB XIV.1.9 f). In the sacrifice named Jamadagneḥ saptarātraḥ, the seventh day is supposed to be like a bird. Its head is nine-versed; its trunk is seventeen-versed. "Its wings fifteen-versed (each). That is for the sake of equilibrium (*savīvadhatvāya*)" (TMB XXII.7.8).

One should take care of not to "fall down" in the course of musical performance. This falling down is of course mystical and musical too. The third day of the Daśarātra of the Dvādaśāha-sacrifice, belongs technically to the Jagatī-metre which is forty-eight-syllabled. The fourth i.e. the next day belongs to the Anuṣṭubh-metre which is thirty-two-syllabled. It is falling down, as it were since first a larger metre is used and then a smaller one. Therefore, in order that one should not fall, following device is to be made. In the Brahman's pṛṣṭha-stotriya-tercet, a verse in the Atijagatī-metre (i.e. a Jagatī-verse with one or more verse-quarters of thirteen syllables instead of twelve) is to be applied. Then one "ascends" (as it were) and does not fall (TMB XII.10.2 f). In a fortynine-day-sacrifice, the sandhistotra is chanted on verses the number of syllables of which increases by four: 24, 28, 32, 36, 40, 44 and 48. This is for the sake of avoiding the falling down (TMB XXIV.1.8). One should take proper care of observing this directive. Carelessness is dangerous. This we find in the following example. In the fourth Vrātyastoma-sacrifice[6], the schema of the stomas to be applied is as follows - 9, 9, 15, 17, 21/24, 44, 48, 27, 33/32, 32. Thus the order is increasing, ascending one. "From the top they ascend to the top. The stomas go upwards (increase in number of verses): in order that they may not fall" (TMB XVII. 4.2). It will however, be seen that although in the beginning the order is increasing one, it has not remained so towards the end. Therefore, when this kind of sacrifice was being performed by some Vrātyas under the leadership of Kuṣītaka Sāmaśravasa, Luśākapi Khārgaleya cursed them, "They are fallen off". In consequence of this curse, none of the descendants of Kuṣītaka amounted to much; for they fell off from the sacrifice (TMB XVII.4.3).

A further directive of the vedic music is that the recitation must be firm (*dṛḍha*). The Narāśaṁsa-hymn is supposed to be soft and slipping. Therefore the Acchāvāka, who recites last, does not recite the Nārāśaṁsī-verses. So that all the recitations remain founded firmly (AB VI.16). While singing, one tries to give "support (*āyatana-*)[7]" to what one sings. According to JB I.326, one who sings the verses and melodies which are with support (*āyatanavadbhyām*), gets himself supported.

In the sacrificial music there must be freshness, unexhaustedness (*ayātayāmatva-*). Anything that has been pale, exhausted etc. is to be avoided. When something is used, it becomes useless, sapless, exhausted. It should not be used unless made "freshened" up. On the Viṣuvat-day, which is in the middle of the year-long sacrificial session, all the performers should restrain the speech. "Milked out, as it were, are now the metres, used up and gone to the end; there they thereby invigorate with juice" (TMB IV.9.16 f). In the Dvādaśāha-sacrifice, on the sixth day of the Daśarātra, the Pṛṣṭha-laud is based on the Gāyatrī-metre. For, upto this day, other metres are used for the sake of the first Pṛṣṭha-lauds; but Gāyatrī has not been used for that purpose upto now. Therefore it is fresh and is to be used for the first pṛṣṭh-laud on the sixth day (TMB XIII. 10.1). On the seventh day in the same rite verses containing the word *hari* are to be recited. For upto that day, all the metres and stomas are used. So there is a fear of exhaustion. The verses containing the word *hari* are said to be giving energy (TMB XII.13.7). Therefore on this day the verses with the word *hari* are to be recited for the sake of freshness (TMB XIV.1.8).

Closely connected with the directive of "freshness" is the directive of putting sap (*rasa-*) in the music. According to Vedic texts, the music must be sapful. Attempts are therefore made, during the performance of the sacrifice to put sap in the music and thereby in the sacrifice. Thus the Subrahmaṇya-priest recites the Subrahmaṇya-formulas in which he utters *om*. For the Subrahmaṇya-priest is identical with the speech (*vāc*) and *om* is identical with sap. Therefore the utterance of *om* gratifies the speech with sap (JB II.78). During the Āmahiyava-sāman also the utterance of *om* has the same function. "As one would mix parched grains with honey, similarly one puts sap in this sāman by means of this syllable and thrives it (JB I.322; cp. the same remark in connection with the Kāleya-sāman :- JB I.336). The hiṁkāra is considered to be the sap of the sāmans. Therefore when one, having uttered hiṁkāra recites the *prastava* (prelude), one begins the chant after moistening the verses of the out-of-doors-chant with the sap (TMB VI.8.7). At the time of the third-pressing, verses in the Triṣṭubh-metre are recited even though this pressing, generally speaking, is connected with the Jagatī-metre. The reason, is "The third-pressing has the sap sucked out; the Triṣṭubh-metre is one with the sap not sucked out, but full of pure juice. Therefore (it serves) to make it (the third pressing) full of sap" (AB VI.12).

Care should also be taken lest the sap would flow out. Thus on the sixth day of the Daśarātra of the Dvādaśāha-sacrifice, at the time of the out-of-doors-chant, there are two dekastiches to be recited. In the recitation of the second dekastich, there are the following words at the closing of each verse - *athā no vayasas kṛdhi.* "This is in order that valour, strength (and) sap may not flow out (*anatikṣārāya*) (TMB XIII.7.9; for this expression see also XIII. 8.1;4; 5).

The song must be correctly sung. "When the praise-singer dedicates the songs correctly (*ṛtuthā*) then he is called clear, pure, and wonderful (ṚV VIII.13.19). ṚV VIII.95.5, a poem overflowing with correctness (*ṛtasya pipyuṣī-*) is mentioned. A powerful hymn (*brahman-*) is expected to come out of the orderliness (*ṛta-*). ṚV I.147.1, it is asked "In what way do the gods take delight in the right sāman?". Devāpi tells Bṛhaspati, "For us put a shining speech (*vāc-*) which is diseaseless (i.e. correct)" (ṚV X.98.3). ṚV X.89.3 a poet-singer is requested to sing for Indra a hymn which has not deviated (from the right path) (*anapāvṛt-*). In all these texts, the directive of correctness is implied.

At the time of singing or reciting in the course of sacrifice, it is necessary to follow the correct way and nothing essential should be omitted. Thus in the performance of the over-night (*atirātra-*) sacrifice, one should not deviate from the Nārmedha-sāman. If one were to go away from this sāman one would go away from night and day (JB I.188). On the fourth day of the Daśarātra of the Dvādaśāha-sacrifice, the verses in the Gāyatrī-metre are used when actually Triṣṭubh verses should have been used. But the verses here used contain the word *Vṛṣan.*

Now whatever is with *vṛṣan* is mystically a form of the Triṣṭubh-metre. Therefore no deviation from the correct way occurs (JB III.69). On the seventh day of the same rite, a nine-versed hymn is recited. Thereby the performers do not deviate from the Trivṛt (nine-versed) stoma (JB II.176). On the Prāyaṇīya-day of a sacrificial session, the Jarābodhīya-sāman is to be taken as the Agniṣṭoma-sāman according to some ritualists. But their view is refuted in the following words, "The Yajñāyajñīya-sāman only is to be taken (as the Agniṣṭoma-sāman). The Yajñāyajñīya-sāman is the way; in this manner (i.e. by using that sāman alone) they do not deviate from the way (TMB IV.2.21)".

Nothing should be omitted in the course of recitation. Thus the hymns viz. the Mābhānediṣṭha (ṚV X.61, 62), the Vālakhilya (ṚV VII.49-59), the Vṛṣākapi (ṚV X.86) and the Evayāmarut (ṚV V.87) are designated as accompaniments (*sahacarāṇi*). They must be recited together. If any of these is omitted, the sacrificer will suffer. Thus if the Nābhānediṣṭhīya were to be omitted, then the sacrificer would be devoid of seed; if the Vṛṣākapi, then of his body; and if the Evayāmarut, then of his divine and human foundation (AB V.15). In this way the sacrificer is likely to suffer from some harm if any part of the recitation is omitted. Therefore nothing should be omitted.

One should pay attention, during the sacrificial singing to the *rūpasamṛddhi* (mystic appropriateness of form). Thus there is a directive not to deviate from the normal form (*rūpān na yanti*). As for example in a two-day (dvirātra) sacrifice the Dvaigata-sāman is to be sung. This sāman is to be sung with *two* hiṁkāras. Thereby one does not deviate from the form of the two-day-sacrifice (JB II.237). The first day of this sacrifice belongs to the Gāyatrī-metre, while the second to the Triṣṭubh; but none belongs to the Jagatī-metre. Therefore JB II.237, an attempt is made to show that *mystically* this sacrifice *has* some connection with the Jagatī-metre. Thus the verse *uccā te jātamandhasā* containing the word *andhas* is the form of Jagatī. Therefore when this verse is recited, the danger of likely deviation from the form of Jagatī is avoided. Similarly, the Vaikhānasa-sāman, which belongs to the Jagatī-metre is sung in this sacrifice. This is also for the sake of avoiding the deviation from the Jagatī-form (JB II.237). On the introductory day of the Dvādaśāha-sacrifice, at the time of the midday-pressing, the verses *marutvate ca matsaraḥ* .... which contain the word *marut* are to be recited. The general, normal form of the midday-pressing is accompanied by *marut*. So by reciting these verses they do not deviate from the form of the midday-pressing (JB III.23; cp. for similar remarks JB III.40; 66; 143; 283).

In music, there should be congruence (*salomatā*). Thus in the year-long sacrificial session, in the first half the sāman (melody) is the same but the Pragātha-verses (on the basis of which it is sung) are different. But in the second half, the Pragātha-verses are the same but the sāman is different. (In the first half) one milks the Pragāthas by means of the sāman and in the second half one milks the sāman by means of the Pragātha, for the sake of congruence (TMB IV.3.9). In the Atirātra-sacrifice, there are recitations during night also. But there is "congruence" between the recitations during the day and those during the night. Thus at the time of midday, one sings the Yaudhājaya-sāman which has triple finale. Similarly at midnight, the Aurdhvasadmana-sāman which also has a triple finale, is to be sung. This is so for the same of congruence (TMB IX.1.15). In a soma-sacrifice, if the soma-juice is left over from the morning-service, that is to be used at the midday-service. But this use is to be made in a congruent manner. Thus at the midday-time, they praise Maruts who are the special deity of the midday-service but they praise in verses which are in Gāyatrī-metre which is closely connected with the morning-pressing. The same stoma (viz. Trivṛt) after which the soma is left over from the morning-pressing, is to be used at the midday-service also. This is for the sake of congruence. Similarly if the soma is left over from the midday-service, it is to be used in the third service but again, for the sake of congruence, the Saptadaśa-stoma (after which it has been left over from the midday-service) is to be used in the third pressing also (TMB IX.7.3; cp. 8).

The singing or recitation should be mystically similar (*salakṣma-*) to the sacrificial rite of which it is a part. Thus on the Mahāvrata-day, the Āngirasa-sāman with twenty-five syllabled finale is to be sung. "For Prajāpati is twentyfifth; and the Mahāvrata belongs to Prajāpati. Thus "Similar (*salakṣma*)" recitation is done" (JB II.14). In the Indrastoma-sacrifice, fifteen-versed stoma is to be used. For this stoma is identical with the thunderbolt. Indra is also identical with thunderbolt. This sacrifice belongs to Indra. Thus the Stoma is made similar to the sacrifice (JB II.140).

At the time of singing or reciting one has to take care of another directive viz. of *samṛddhi*[8]; which signifies appropriateness, efficiency, success, prosperity etc. On a particular occasion, such a sāman is sung or recitation is made which is mystically connected with occasion; is appropriate. Thus if in a soma-sacrifice one of the stones for pressing the soma, is broken, the sāman of Dyutāna of Maruts is to be sung. For the stones of pressing belong to the Maruts. Thus there is an appropriateness of form (*rūpasamṛddhi-*). And the stones are made successful thereby (TMB IX.9.13 f). In the Rājasūya-sacrifice, the Yajñāyajñīya-sāman is to be sung on the verses in Anuṣṭubh-metre. Now Yajñāyajñīya-sāman is identical with speech (*vāc-*) and the Anuṣṭubh-metre is also identical with speech. So this sāman is made prosperous by the appropriate verses (JB II.212). In a three-day-sacrifice, on the third day which belongs to the Jagatī-metre, the song of Dīrghatamas is to be recited. This song is also based on Jagatī-verses. Then the day itself is made successful by this appropriateness (JB II. 255). In a seven-day sacrifice, on every day a different stoma is used. "It is, verily, prosperity (*samṛddhi*) of the days that they are carried by different stomas" (JB II.302). On the seventh day of the Daśarātra of the Dvādaśāha-sacrifice, Raurava-sāman is sung. This sāman is in praise of Agni. This day which belongs to the Gāyatrī-metre, belongs also to Agni. For the Gāyatrī-metre is, mystically, nothing but Agni. So there is appropriateness in using the Raurava-sāman on this day, and the day is made successful, thereby (JB III.184; cp. For similar argument in connection with the sāman named Agnerarkam- JB III.191).

Sometimes the appropriateness is not directly mentioned, but only implied. Thus on the midday-pavamānalaud of the third day of the Daśarātra of the Dvādaśāha-sacrifice, verses containing the word *viśvā* (viz. *enā viśvānyarya ā* ...) are to be recited. For this day belongs to the Viśvedevas (JB III.40). Here there is a mystical magical relation between the word *viśvā* and the deity Viśvedevas. Thus here the mystical appropriateness is implied without any direct statement of it. Similarly, on the same day, the Triṣṭubh-verses *tisro vāca irayati* ... which contain the word *tisraḥ* (three) are used. They are a form of the third day (JB III.46). Thus here also one gets an example of implied appropriateness. The song (*stotra-*) and recitation (*śastra*) are expected to be equivalent. In the Agniṣṭoma-sacrifice, the sāman-singer sings the verses in which Agni is praised and the Hotṛ-priest recites the verses in which Vāyu is praised. Now a question arises whether this is correct or not. In the answer, it is told that Agni is identical with all the deities (and of course with Vāyu). So the two kinds of verses are ultimately equivalent. Thus where even though, there is apparent inappropriateness, appropriateness is implied to be there (AB III.4).

Whatever is inappropriate, unsuccessful etc. (*vyṛddha-*) in the music, that must be avoided. In the case of the soma-cup belonging to Indra and Vāyu, some ritualists use Anuṣṭubh-verses (8 X 4 = 32 syllabled) as the invitatory-verses and Gāyatrī-verses (8 X 3 = 24 syllabled) as the offering-verses. But AB II.26 remarks that this is inappropriate viz. to make invitatory verses larger than the offering verses. When the offering-verses are larger than the invitatory ones or both of them are equal, then only it is appropriate, successful etc. (*samṛddha-*). Therefore, the way suggested by the other ritualists is inappropriate etc. and must therefore to be rejected (AB II.26).

Further there is the directive of singing independently. Thus at the time of singing a sāman one should not imitate the manner of another sāman. One should not "follow the path of another one (*no hānyasyānuvartma geyam*)". If one were to follow the path of another sāman while singing a sāman, one would be dependent on somebody else for the sake of one's livelihood. Therefore, e.g. one should sing the Vāmadevya-sāman independently (JB. I.194; 333; cp. TMB VII.9.12 ff).

One should not sing too much, "in excess". According to JB I.356, "Whatever is sung too much, is badly sung". After the Pavamāna-laud, at the time of the third soma-pressing of the Agniṣṭoma-sacrifice Ṛksāma is to be sung. The Ṛksāma, most probably, is a hymn-tune involving little or no modification of the text chanted to it.[9] "Thereby (by singing the Ṛksāma), one does not make the ṛc exceed the sāman, nor the sāman the ṛc" (JB I.166). In the course of the Manustoma-sacrifice, if one chants verses more than those which are proportionate to ten (= Virāj), it means that one sings in excess. One has to sing therefore, the verses in a number which is in proportion of ten (JB II.170). Singing too much of the praise-hymns etc. destroys the good results of singing. By singing in excess, the woven beeds are made unwoven as it were (JB II.190). At the time of singing the Gāyatra-sāman only for *two* times the tone is to be stretched and then the hiṁkāra (the sound *hum*) is to be made. "If one stretches thrice, one makes the Gāyatra-sāman excessive". (TMB VII.1.2 f). The first day of the Pṛṣṭhya-ṣaḍaha (six-day-rite), in the Dvādaśāha-sacrifice, technically belongs to the Rathantara-sāman. On this day when the Aśva-sāman is sung, the finale of it should be one -syllabled :- "So as not to exceed the Rathantara-sāman (which also has one-syllabled finale) in speaking (*anativādāya*)" (TMB XI.3.6).

TMB IX.3.7, however, takes the "spirit" and not the "letter" of the ritual into consideration and says, "Whatever is too much sung is well sung".

According to the directives of singing in the ritual however, one should sing neither too short nor too much. JB I.356 we read, "What is sung, too short, that is not sung; what is sung too much that is badly sung and what is sung exactly, that is sung.

If they sing too short (i.e. if the number of verses or syllables is too little) they should sing (in the next singing extra) as many stotra-verses have been omitted or they should increase the next stotra by as many syllables (as have been omitted). In what is lacking they must put something exceeding for the sake of pairing, generation. If they sing too many they should (in the next stotra) leave out as many (stotra-verses) as have been sung too many or they should shorten (the next stotra) by as many syllables (as many have been sung excessively)" (cp. TMB IX.3.7 ff; Kṣudrasūkta I.7).

Of similar purport is the further directive of vedic music namely "to keep the measurement". Thus while singing one must pay attention to the due measurements and keep them intact. These measurements also are significant in many ways and are connected with good results.

If one of the sacrificers dies during the performance of the sacrifice, after the undertaken sacrifice is finished a sacrifice is to be performed for the bones of the deceased. The bones here represent the sacrificer. In that sacrifice, the pavamāna-lauds should be threefold (i.e. nine-versed). For the vital airs are threefold. And when the pavamāna-lauds are made threefold, the performers become possessors of vital airs (TMB IX. 8.15) i.e. they live long. On the tenth day of the Daśarātra of the Dvādaśāha-sacrifice, Hariśrīnidhana-sāman is to be sung. This sāman should have three finales. For the worlds are three; thereby one holds these three worlds. (JB III.249). The Ātharvaṇa-sāman has four finales and by singing this sāman, one gets firm foundation (JB III.66).

The number of verses is sometimes mystically connected with the year. Thus in the Parikrī-sacrifice, the out-of-doors-laud consists of three verses; the Ājyas of four verses; the midday-pavamāna-laud of five verses; the pṛṣṭhas of four verses; the Ārbhava-pavamāna-laud of seven verses; and Agniṣṭoma-sāman of one verse. Thus in all the number comes to be twenty-four. In a year, there are twenty-four half-months. Thus when a sacrificer performs this sacrifice, he drives his enemy away from the whole year (JB II.124).

The metre named Virāj is ten-syllabled one. So Virāj often represents the number ten. Virāj is also often mentioned as a measurement. Thus in the Manustoma-sacrifice, one praise-sings with verses the number of which is proportionate to ten. Thus one does not praise-sing exceeding the measurement of Virāj. Since Virāj is identical with food, one gets food thereby (JB II.170; cp. similar remarks in connection with some other sacrifices - JB II.336; 390 etc.). JB I.233 gives two directives in this respect - "One should perform a sacrifice congruent to Virāj" ; and "one should not exceed Virāj".

The number of songs has its own efficacy. A greater number of songs and recitations in a sacrifice make it more effective than a sacrifice with less number of songs and recitations. When two rivalling sacrificers perform soma-sacrifices at the same time and if one of them wants to defeat the other by making one's own sacrifice more effective, then one has to use a greater number of songs (*stotra-*) and recitations (*śastra-*) and has to surrender to a greater number of deities. Then one can defeat the other (JB I.344).

Sometimes an incalculated, arbitrary number is said to be significant. Thus if any one of sacrificers dies, then after the undertaken sacrifice is finished, another sacrifice is performed in which the laud is based on incalculated number of verses - i.e. one is free to use any number of them as one likes. "For the yonder world is illimited (beyond any calculation)" (TMB IX. 8.14). Therefore, for the sake of obtainment of that world, such an indefinite number is helpful. AB I.17, prescribes different numbers of verses of the morning-recital in the Agniṣṭoma-sacrifice to be used for the sake of getting various results. But if one uses an indefinite, arbitrary number, then one gets all the objects of desire. For Prajāpati is unnumbered; and the morning -recital belongs to Prajāpati. Thus when one recites indefinite number of verses, that helps for obtainment of all the desires (AB I.17).

In the sacrificial performance sometimes it is necessary to use the verses of the same metre. Thus in the Upasad-rite which is a part of the Agniṣṭoma-sacrifice, one should use verses of the same metre. "If one were to make them of different metres, one would cause swelling on the neck; one would produce boils" (AB I.25). At the time of the sviṣṭakṛt-offering in the New-and full-moon-offerings, both the invitatory and offering-verses should be of one and the same metre either both Triṣṭubh or both Anuṣṭubh. If Triṣṭubh-verses are used, one puts power in that offering; if Anuṣṭubh-verses are used, one obtains prosperity. But a ritualist named Bhāllaveya used an Anuṣṭubh-verse as the invitatory-verse and a Triṣṭubh as the offering-verse with the hope, "I thus obtain (the benefits of) both". But this was a mistake and as a consequence of it, he fell from the cart and his arm was broken (ŚB I.7.3.17 ff; cp. ŚB XI.4.1.13). On the Mahāvrata-day of a year-long-sacrificial session, the Ilānda-sāman based on the Aticchandas-metre is to be sung. "The Aticchandas-metre, verily supersedes the other metres. The performers of the year-long sacrificial session also supersede the others. They thus become established in their own metre" (JB II.412).

Many times we get the directive of "reciting according to the metres (*yathāchandasam*)". Thus the morning-litany is said to be recited according to the metres i.e. the verses of the same metres should be recited together, without any mixture of the verses in any different metres (AB II.18). The Kuntāpa-hymn should also be recited according to the metres (KB XXX.5).

Some metres have some special connection with a particular deity. So it is necessary that one should use the metre of a deity in a rite addressed to it. At the time of enkindling the fire (Agni) verses addressed to Agni are recited. They should be in Gāyatrī-metre. "For verily Gāyatrī is Agni's own metre". (ŚB I. 3.5.4). Similarly while paying homage to Fires in the course of Agnihotra-offering, one does it by means of verses in the Gāyatrī-metre for the same reason (ŚB II.3.4.32). The Triṣṭubh-metre is believed to be belonging to Indra. Therefore, when one recites the Prauga-recitation in the course of the Mahāvrata-ceremony on the verses in Triṣṭubh, one makes Indra prosper with his own metre (SāṅĀ I.2; cp. II.16).

There are miscellaneous directives of the vedic music. ṚV X. 89.3, a poet-singer is requested to sing for Indra, a hymn which has no equal (*asama-*) and is unique. One is expected to sing nicely (*su*) (cf. e.g. ṚV VIII 20.19; 41.1). According to another directive, the songs should be simple. Thus ṚV VIII.90.3, Indra is addressed, "These powerful hymns are being prepared for you, O Indra, desirous of songs, which are not very wonderful (*anatidbhutā*)". Similarly ṚV VII.61.5, the songs are described to be without any wonderful and mysterious element. In Buddhist literature (e.g. Vin. I.5.6; D. II.36, 38 etc. the gāthās (sung verses) are also described as "not wonderful (*anacchariyā*)"[10].

In a sāman, the most important part is "tone (*svara*)". The tone is called the "own property (*sva*)" of sāman. Every priest should desire to have tone in his speech and should perform the priestly duties with toneful speech. In a sacrifice, therefore, the toneful priest is sought after (BṛhUp. I.1.27; cp. JB I.112). One has also to take care at the time of reciting not to let his singing, even mystically belong to the Manes. Thus if one sings while breathing with difficulty or being fatigued as it were, then the manes become the deity of that process of singing. Therefore one should rather breathe in between while singing instead of singing in a fatigued manner. (JB I.112). Similarly according to some ritualists the Udgātṛ should sing the Yajñāyajñīya-sāman having covered himself. But JB I.174 rejects this view saying that one would, thereby have the Manes as one's deity at that time.

In all the directives of music, it will be seen that the main emphasis is on the efficaciousness of the music. Thus songs are expected to be new, for they are believed to be liked by gods and thereby powerful enough to make gods grant the desired results. Similarly they are expected to be sung loudly, to come out of one's own heart, to be pure, pleasant, balanced, continuous, firm, fresh, full of sap, correct, appropriate, congruent, proportionate, well measured, of some definite metres etc. because they are then supposed to be magicoreligiously significant. Even when the songs are sometimes expected to be old, proportionless, numberless or simple ones, then also with a different logic they do contain magicoreligious power. But the whole of this study of the directives of Vedic music allows us to understand Vedic music as a very rigorously faultless, well-measured, firmly founded, proportionate vocal activity which owes its magicoreligious significances to such directives.

REFERENCES

1. For the new song see, Combarieu, *La musique et la magie,* p. 332, Abert, *Musikanschauung,* p. 114, J. Gonda, "Ein neues Lied", in *WZKM,* 48, p. 275 ff.
2. Geldner, *Der Rigveda,* II. p. 44.
3. Rf. Gonda, *Four studies,* p. 84.
4. Contrast with this the mediaeval Christian conception of music. Thus according to Philo, music should not be used loudly in the worship of Gods - Abert, *Musikanschauung,* p. 42.
5. See my thesis *Sacrifice in the Brāhmaṇa-texts,* p. 269 f.
6. Rf. Hauer, *Der Vrātya,* p. 81.
7. For the word *āyatana* see Gonda, *"Āyatana" A L B,* 33, 1969, p. 1 ff.
8. Rf. Silburn, *Instant et cause,* p. 6; See also my thesis *Sacrifice in the Brāhmaṇa-texts,* p. 277 f.
9. Rf. Eggeling, *SBE,* XLIII, p. 8.
10. Rf. my paper "Vedic *anatidbhutā* Pāli *anacchriyā*" *JUPHS,* 35, 1971, p. 31 ff.

(D) COSMIC MUSIC

Music is many times considered to be of cosmic nature. The Egyptian people attributed cosmic significance to it.[1] Among the Chinese people also there were similar beliefs. Thus Mencius thinks that music is an echo of the harmony between the heaven and the earth.[2] The Greek thinkers supposed that the world is music. The whole cosmos is according to them a sublime lyre.[3] Similar notions are prevalent in Judaism.[4] In Islam music is held as a part of macrocosmic system.[5] In the Vedic literature[6] also there are numerous references to the cosmic significance of music.

In the Chāndogya-upaniṣad II.2.1, one is advised to worship the five parts of the sāman in the worlds. The earth is said to be identical with the *hiṁ*-sound. The fire is the *Prastāva*; the sky is the *Udgītha*; the sun is the *pratihāta* and the heaven is the *nidhana*. This is the ascending order of worship. In the reverse order, the heaven is the *hiṁ*-sound; the sun is the *prastāva*: the sky is the *udgītha*; the fire is the *pratihāra* and the earth is the *nidhana*. TB III.12.9.1 various directions are ascribed to the various Vedas. Thus the eastern direction is ascribed to the Ṛgveda; the southern to the Yajurveda; the western to the Atharvāngirasaḥ and the northern to the Sāmaveda. Elsewhere, the Mahānāmnī verses are said to be identical with the waters (JB III.119). The wind, according to ŚB VII.7.3.12 belongs to the Triṣṭubh-metre. The earth and the heaven are held up, TS V.4.6.4, by the Virāj-metre. At the time when the naturally perforated bricks are put down in the course of the Fire-building ceremony, sāmans are sung. Thereby, it is said, the sap or the means of subsistence is put into these worlds;[7] for the naturally perforated bricks are identical with these worlds (ŚB VIII.7.4.4). Many times we meet with the remark, "All this is identical with the stomas only (*sarvaṁ hīdaṁ stomā eva*: JB II.236; 239; 274; 295; 314; 325; 326 etc.).

Many of the musical elements are said to be identical with the worlds. Thus the sāmans like Gāyatrapārśva-sāman (JB III. 214) and Ājidoha-sāman (JB II.255) are identical with the three worlds. Similarly the Mahānāmnī-verses (JB III.114), speech (JB II.253, 264), the twenty-seven-versed-stoma (TS VII.4.3.5; TMB VI.2.3), a tṛca (group of three verses) (JB I.312), the sacred utterances (vyāhṛtis viz. *bhūḥ, bhuvaḥ, svaḥ*) (TB II.2.4.1 ff) are also identical with the three worlds. According to TS VII.5.1.6 the sāman (melody) is identical with the world of gods and the ṛcs (verses) with that of men (cp. JB III.146; TMB IV.3.5). The metres are also identical with the worlds (TMB VII.3.4). Sometimes Gāyatrī is said to be identical with the earth, Triṣṭubh with the sky and Jagatī with the heaven (KS XIX.1). Because Gāyatrī is identical with the earth, it is also described to be the "foundation (*pratiṣṭhā*)"[8] of all the things (ŚB IV.3.4.9). A similar remark is made in connection with the Jagatī-metre also (ŚB I.8.2.11; VI.2.2.32).

For the Vedic texts these identifications of the musical elements with the worlds are significant in explaining the results of the sacrificial ritual that are connected with the worlds. Thus the Rathantara-sāman is said to be identical with this world; Vāmadevya with the sky and the Bṛhat with the heaven. Therefore, when one sings all these on the one and the same day of the fourth Sāhasra-sacrifice, one joins these worlds as it were (TMB XVI.11.4). Similarly JB I.129 says, "These sāmans (Rathantara, Vāmadevya and Bṛhat) are identical with these worlds. The Rathantara is identical with this world; the Vāmadevya with the sky and the Bṛhat with the heaven. When these sāmans are sung (respectively) on the first, second and the third beginning tristiches (*pratipad-*) one ascends on all these worlds" (JB I.229). In the Abhijit-sacrifice, the Rathantara is to be used as the Pṛṣṭha, the Vāmadevya as the sāman of the Maitrāvaruṇa-priest, and the Bṛhat is to be used as the ārbhava-pavamāna-laud. Since these sāmans are identical with the three worlds, one wins all these worlds without any disconnection, if one uses those sāmans in the prescribed way (JB II.179). At the time of the fire-establishment-rite these sāmans are to be sung. Then the fires become established in the three worlds as it were (TB I.8.1.1). JB I.173

the Yajñāyajñīya-sāman is said to be identical with the earth; JB I.146, the Naudhasa-sāman has been identified with the heaven, the Śyeta with the earth and the Vāmadevya with the sky and thus sometimes there is some difference in the identifications of sāmans and the worlds.

Sometimes the Gāyatra-sāman alone is said to be identical with the three worlds (*ime vai lokā gāyatram*- TMB VII.1.1). The chant (*udgītha*-) of this sāman is to be sung in three sections. Thus the chant of SV II.1 in the ārcika is as follows - *pavamānāyendave/abhi devāṁ iyakṣase.* This is to be divided in the following manner - (1) *pā 2 vā 2 mānāyendavā 2;* (2) *abhi devānāṁ iyā 1212* (3) *kṣāto.* "The worlds are three and by chanting the Gāyatra-sāman in these three sections, the singer makes the sacrificer equal to these worlds". (TMB VII.1.1).

Many musical elements are said to be at the origin of the worldly things.[9] From the Virāj-metre many worldly things were created with the help of the sāmans. Thus the gods considered Virāj as a milch-cow. They brought her near "Indra who was then the young calf (*vatsa*); Gāyatrī the halter and cloud the udder. Both the Bṛhat-and Rathantara-sāmans were two teats; both the Yajñāyajñīya- and Vāmadevya-sāmans (were the other) two (teats). Gods milked herbs (from her) by the Rathantara; expansion by the Bṛhat; waters by the Vāmadevya; sacrifice by the Yajñāyajñīya .... " (AV VIII.10.8 ff). In the Fire-building-ceremony, after the Viṣṇu-strides, there is an adoration to Agni with the verses ascribed to the poet Vatsaprī Bhālandana. This rite is called Vātsapra[10] and both these rites viz. Viṣṇustrides and Vātsapra are connected with the cosmic creation. "By the Viṣṇustrides Prajāpati created this world and by the Vātsapra the fire; by the Viṣṇustrides Prajāpati created the sky and by the Vātsapra the sun; by the Viṣṇustrides Prajāpati created the regions and by the Vātsapra the moon; ...... created that which has been and ...... created that which shall be ..... possession and .... hope; .... the day ...... the night; ...... the bright fortnights and ...... after - (= dark-) fort-nights; .... seasons and .... the year. Thus the reason why these two rites are to be performed, is that thereby he (the sacrificer) even now creates everything" (ŚB VI.7.4.7). The Vyāhṛtis or sacred utterances are significant in the creation of worlds. Thus Prajāpati uttered *bhūḥ* and created the earth; uttered *bhuvaḥ* and created the sky; uttered *svaḥ* and created the heaven (KS VI.7; cp. ŚB II.1.4.11). Similarly with these utterances he created the three castes viz. Brāhmaṇa, Kṣatriya and Vaiśya. He created also the self, the beings, and the cattle with these utterances (ŚB II.1.4.12 f). According to JB III.341, in the beginning there was only one divinity named Prajāpati. He thought of creation. He created the gods Vasus by means of the Trivṛt-stoma. The gods joined the worlds by means of the Kāleya-sāman (JB I. 155). The creator, by means of the Jagat-sāman made the sea firm in the heavenly world; by means of the Rathantara-sāman he discovered the sun (ṚV I.164.25). ṚV II.11.15 it is said that Indra expands the sky by great songs (*arka-*).

Some musical elements are said to be existing "in the beginning". Thus according to AB IV.28, in the beginning there were only the Bṛhat and Rathantara-sāman. These were respectively identical with Speech and Mind. Elsewhere, it is said that in the beginning there was merely one syllable viz. Vāc (Speech) (JB III.326).

Music helps the sun to sustain and to be free from eclipses. It increases the sun-light (see under "Music and light" elsewhere).

Music is cosmic from the spatial point of view as we saw it. But it is cosmic from the temporal point of view also. The Rathantara-sāman is said to be "today" while the Bṛhat "tomorrow". Further the Rathantara is said to be the "past" and the Bṛhat to be the "future" (TS III.1.7.2 f). Many musical elements are connected with the year-ideology. "Thus some say: The sāman is in the year. Of it, spring is the *hiṁkara*. Therefore, animals come together in the spring continually uttering the *hiṁ*-sound. The summer is the *prastāva*; the *prastāva* is indistinct; the summer is, among all the seasons, indistinct. The rainy season is *udgītha*; the rainy season sings as it were. The autumn is the *pratihāra*; verily in autumn most of the herbs ripen. The winter is the *nidhana*; in the winter, the creatures are put to an end (*nidhanakṛta*) as it were ...." (JUB I.12.1.1 ff). Elsewhere, the Gāyatra-sāman with twenty-four-syllables is shown to be identical with the year (JUB III.7.1.9: "The *prastāva* has eight syllables. The song (*gīta*) has sixteen syllables. Thus twenty-four are obtained; the year has twenty-four half-months; the year is sāman". The Bṛhat-sāman has twelve-syllabled prastāva. "Verily, the sāman is this (*prastāva*) much (*tāvaddhi sāma*). There are twelve months in a year; the year is sāman" (JB I.137). The sāman which is sung at the time of avabhṛtha-bath is to be sung thrice. That sāman is based on verses with seven verse-quarters. Thus when the sāman is sung thrice, the number of verse-quarters becomes twenty-one. Now we have to add three to these twenty-one for the sāman is sung thrice. Then the number twenty-four is obtained. "Twenty-four half-months make a year. The sāman is the year: the *hiṁkāra* is identical with day and night; the *prastāva* with the half months; the first part with the months; the *udgītha* with the seasons; the *pratihāra* with the days of the full moon; the *upadrava* with the eighth day after the full moon; the finale with the days of the new moon. Of this sāman being identical with the year, the *hiṁkāra* is identical with spring; the *prastāva* with summer; the *udgītha* with rainy season; the *pratihāra* with autumn; the *nidhana* with winter" (ṢaḍB III.1.20 ff). ŚB VIII. 4.1.11 ff, many stomas are said to be year-like. The metre Gāyatrī is identical with the year (*saṁvatsaro vai gāyatrī* TS II.4.3.2). Similarly the Virāj-metre is identical with the year (*saṁvatsaro virāṭ* TS V.6.7.1 ff). On the Prāyaṇīya-day of the sacrificial session called Gavāmayana there are fifteen stotras. "There are fifteen nights in a fortnight. Thus one obtains the year fortnightwise". Similarly on the same day there are thirty stutaśastras. "There are thirty nights in a month; thus one obtains the year monthwise" (JB III.377; cp. AB IV 12) The enkindling verses (*sāmidhenī-*) are to be recited in a continuous, uninterrupted manner. Thereby the days and nights are made continuous (ŚB I.3.5.16).

Music, as has been illustrated above to some extent, is connected with the seasons[11] also. TS IV.3.2.1 ff, various metres and various seasons are associated with each other. Thus Gāyatrī belongs to the spring. Triṣṭubh to the summer; Jagatī to the rainy season. Anuṣṭubh to the autumn and Paṅkti to the winter. The Vaṣaṭ-call also is connected with the seasons. For when one utters it one pronounces '*ṣaṭ* (- six)'. Now the number of seasons is also six and therefore one thereby puts the seasons in order (AB III.6). In the Aśvamedha-sacrifice, after the horse has been let loose, for a year, every day two singers, accompanied on lutes sing verses. The significance of this rite has been told by TB III.9.14.4 in the following way - "His seasons are not adapted - they say - he who performs the Aśvamedha. One (singer) sings three verses; another one three; they become six; six verily are the seasons; they verily adapt the seasons for him".

In the Vedic texts sacrifice is conceived as a microcosm.[12] The microcosm and macrocosm depend upon each other and are replicas of each other; the difference between them is of quantity and not of quality. According to whatever is done in the microcosm everything happens in the macrocosm. In the sacrifice, i.e. in the microcosm music is amply used and naturally it is supposed to exercise numerous effects in the macrocosm. Music, even, governs the activities of beings.[13]

Thus for example many features of the generation process are said to be the results of musical elements sung or recited in a particular way. While reciting the Anuṣṭubh-verses in the Ājya-śastra, the Hotṛ-priest separates the two first quarters (*pada-*) "Therefore a woman separates her thighs (at the time of coitus)". He joins the two last quarters. "Therefore a man joins his thighs" (AB II.35). One and the same sāman can be sung on different verses. The seed is poured as it were in this way. "Therefore one and same male lays his seed in many females (*tasmāt samāno bahvīṣu reṭo dadhāti*)" (JB II.80). Similarly with the same verses, many sāmans can be sung. This is like giving birth to many children out of the seed that is poured. "Therefore, one and the same female gives birth to many children (*tasmād samānā bahūn sūte*" JB II.80). Both the ṛc (text) and the sāman (tune) must be properly mixed together and sung. If one were to sing mere ṛc devoid of sāman a child with mere bones, devoid of flesh would be born. If on the other hand one were to sing mere sāman without ṛc, a child would be born with mere flesh and without bones. One sings the ṛc "covered (*abhilipta-*)" with sāman; therefore, a man is born covered by hair, skin and flesh" (JB I.259). The Dhurya-stotras are to be chanted in the manner in which repetition of verses is important. In this respect ŚB IV.2.5.8 comments: "Repeating they chant the Dhuryas; these creatures are directed towards these. Therefore, the creatures are produced repeatedly".

Some of the human peculiarities are explained on the basis of the musical practices. The Vāravantīya-sāman is sung on the verses which are in various metres. On this the following comment is made - "Therefore *one* man thrives in *many* ways" (TMB XIX.5.10). In the Darśapūṇamāsa-sacrifices, after uttering the invitatory-formula, one offers with the offering-formula; Therefore, the lower teeth grow first; then the upper ones. Similarly inasmuch as after uttering Gāyatrī-verse as an invitatory-formula, one offers with a Triṣṭubh-verse (which is bigger than the Gāyatrī-verse) therefore the lower teeth are smaller and the upper ones broader .... and inasmuch as the two saṁyājyā-verses are in the same metre. Therefore the melars are of equal size" (ŚB XI.4.1.13). In an overnight rite the beginning is made by the Vaitahavya-sāman. In this sāman the word *okas* (house) is used as the finale. "Into the darkness, as it were do they enter who undertake the night (-rite). That the word 'house' is the finale at the commencement of the night-rite, is for finding the way. When a man comes to his own house then he recognises all; all is for him as clear as by day" (TMB IX.1.10 f).

Elsewhere, the characteristics of the world of the animals, and birds are explained on the basis of music used in the sacrifice. Thus in the Aśvatrirātra sacrifice on the first day, at the time of recitation of the out-of-doors-chant, the three Anuṣṭubh-verses (8 X 4 X 3) are to be turned into four Gāyatrī-verses (8 X 3 X 4). "Therefore the horse is, whilst standing still, firmly established on three feet; but whilst running swiftly, puts down all four" (TMB XXI.4.6; cp. TS V.4.12.1; ŚB XIII.3.3.1). After the fire has been produced through the process of churning, the Udgātṛ makes the *hiṁkāra.* "Therefore, when a young (a calf) has been born, the cattle makes the *hiṁ*-sound (sniffs at it)" (TMB XII.10.13 f).

In the Pakṣī (winged) sacrifice, the schema of the stomas is as follows - 9, 15, 17, 21, 27, 33, 33, 27, 31, 17, 15, 9. This means that the stomas increase and decrease and in the middle, there are the stomas with the largest number of verses. This is a form analogous to the wings of the bird. Further, the winged (bird) sāman viz. the Suparṇa (eagle) sāman is used in the midday-pavamāna-laud of this sacrifice. "In that the winged one is deposited in the winged one, therefore, the winged ones (the birds) fly with their wings". (TMB XIX.10.3).

The social order and arrangement of various castes depend upon the musical details in the sacrifice. In a soma-sacrifice being performed by a person belonging to Kṣatriya-caste, the beginning tristich (*pratipad-*) should be *indrāyendo marutvate* .... in which the word *indra* comes first and then the word *marut.* The Kṣatriya-caste belongs to Indra while the Vaiśya-caste belongs to Maruts. By using this tristich, one makes the Vaiśya-caste inferior to the Kṣatriya-caste (JB I.95). During the performance of the Gāyatra-sacrifice, the morning-pressing is in nine-versed stoma and the recital of the Acchāvāka is in the fifteen-versed stoma. The Trivṛt-stoma is mystically identical with the Brahman's power and the fifteen-versed with the Kṣatra-power. Thus the Brahman is put before the Kṣatra; Therefore, in the world, a Brahmaṇa is the *Purohita* (literally "kept before, in front (like a shield)" of a Kṣatriya (JB II.171).

Many of the worldly phenomena are explained on the basis of the musical phenomena in the sacrificial performances.

Thus because in the course of Agniṣṭoma-sacrifice innumerable recitations (*śastras*) are recited, therefore there are innumerable beings in the world (*atha yasmādamitāni śastrāṇi tasmādvamitāḥ prajāḥ* JB I.279). In the Viśvajit-sacrifice, beginning tristiches (*pratipad-*) of *various* types are used. Therefore the cosmos consists of *various* forms (*tadyadetā nānārūpāḥ pratipado bhavanti tasmādu hedaṁ viśvaṁ bhūtaṁ nānārūpaṁ* JB II.184). In the twelve-day-sacrifice, the morning service of the first three days is in the Gāyatrī-metre; of the next three days the midday-service is in the Gāyatrī-metre (at least in the beginning and the end of it); of the next three days, the midday-service is in the Gāyatrī-metre (at least in the beginning and the end of it); of the next three days, the afternoon-service is in the Gāyatrī-metre (at least in the beginning and the end). In this connection TMB X.5.2 comments, "Because the first three-days-period has the Gāyatrī in the beginning, therefore, the fire flames upwards; because the second has it in middle therefore the wind blows horizontally; because the third has it at the end, therefore the sun sends his rays downwards" (cp. also JB III.6; 281; 310).

REFERENCES

1. Cf. A.G. Farmer, in Wellesz, *AOM*, p. 276.
2. J. Legge, *The Sacred Books of China, the texts of Confucianism, SBE*, XXVIII, Delhi 1966, (reprint), p. 100; cf. also Hastings, *ERE*, IX, p. 17(a).
3. Combarieu, *La musique et la magie*, p. 120 ff; cp. p. 190.
4. E. Werner, in Wellesz, *AOM*, p. 333.
5. H.G. Farmer, in Wellesz, *AOM*, p. 433.
6. For the cosmic significance of the music in the veda cf. A. Bake, in Wellesz, *AOM*, p. 199.
7. Cf. Schneider, in Wellesz, *AOM*, p. 48 - "Music not only creates the world, it also cultivates and preserves it".
8. For this term cf. Gonda, in *Saṁjñavyakaraṇa*, I. 1957.
9. For the connection of sounds, singing, drumming etc. with the creation of all see Schneider, in Wellesz, *AOM*, p. 47 f.

10. Cf. for this rite Renou, *Vocabulaire du rituel védique,* p. 136.
11. For seasons and music see Belvianes, *Sociologie de la musique,* p. 52.
12. Cf. My thesis, *Sacrifice in the Brāhmaṇa-texts,* p. 293 ff.
13. Cp. Belvianes, *Sociologie de la musique,* p. 5

(E) MUSIC AND KNOWLEDGE

In the Vedic doctrine of music equal importance is always given to the knowledge of music[1] and of the mysticism connected with it as to the actual performance of the music. All the divinities are said to be existing in him who knows, "I am the sāman; in me are all the divinities" (JUB I.3.4.2). The whole of the ṚV X.71 is, generally speaking, devoted to the praise of *knowing* the Veda rather than merely reciting it without any knowledge of its meaning (cf. especially the following verses: 2, 4, 5, 7, 8 and 9). The Udgātṛ-priest who knows sāman and then sings it, causes the sacrificer to go to the world of divinities (*tadyasya vai kila sāma vidvān sāmnodgāyati devatānāmeva salokatāṁ gamayati*" JUB III.6.2.2). The Udgātṛ possessing good knowledge of all the elements of a sāman releases the fetters of death from the breaths of the sacrificer and rescues him along with his limbs and his body from every death (JUB IV.7.1.8 f). The Udgātṛ who knows the delivery (*pratti*) of a sāman becomes superior to others (JUB III.2.1.5).

Many other results are also obtained by knowing the mysticism and use of various musical elements. Thus the Retasyā-verse is said to be identical with mind. One who sings the Retasyā-verse while knowing this gets a son who is of great mind and mindful one (JB I.261). One who knows that all the metres are mystically included in the Gāyatrī-metre, to him all his relatives recognise as the best of them (JB I.290). He who knows that, mystically, it is the Gāyatrī-metre alone which "carries" all the three soma-pressings (morning, midday and third), from him fame does not depart upto the old age (JB I. 289). In the Yajñāyajñīya-sāman which is the last to be sung in the Agniṣṭoma-sacrifice the word *vāc* (speech) is to be used as the finale. Thereby all the sacrifice becomes well-performed and deposited in the speech. One who knows this, his sacrificial and generous activities do not perish (JB I.309).

Importance is given to the knowledge of the origin of a sāman which is to be sung. Good results are said to be accruing when one knows the origin of a sāman. Thus Veṇu Vaiśvāmitra was desirous of being the chief, prominent and possessor of brahman-splendour. Then he saw the sāman which came to be known as Vaiṇava. Then he praised with that sāman and got his desire fulfilled. "One who knows this, becomes chief, prominent and possessor of the brahman-splendour" (JB I. 220). Similarly knowledge of the origin of the Abhinidhana Kāṇva Sāman is advantageous. Thus Indra wanted to kill Vṛtra. Then he asked Kaṇva to help him. Then Kaṇva saw the Abhinidhana Kaṇva-sāman and praised Indra with it. There-after Indra could kill Vṛtra. "One who knows this, kills one's hateful enemy" (JB III.189).

Thus the knowledge of music is important and useful. To sing, on the other hand, with ignorance is very dangerous. If one sings without any proper and complete knowledge of what one sings, one invites evil effects as it were. "Him who sacrifices not knowing the "milking" of the praise-songs and recitations, the sacrifice milks and he, after sacrificing becomes worse (*pāpīyān*)". (TS III.2.7.3). Similarly if in a sacrificial performance the *udgītha* is sung by one who does not know its mysticism the sacrificer becomes unable to go to the world of the gods. The sacrificer, moreover, cannot then thrive through food-eating (JUB III.3.4.10). Uṣasti a poor man, once went to a sacrificial performance and said to the Prastotṛ-priest there, "O Prastotṛ-priest, if you shall sing the *prastāva* (introductory part of a melody) without knowing the divinity which is connected with it, your head will fall off". Similarly he said to the Udgātṛ-priest, "Udgātṛ, if you shall chant the *Udgītha* (main part of a melody) without knowing the divinity .... fall off". Further he also said to the Pratihartṛ, "O Pratihartar, if you shall utter the *pratihāra* (response) without knowing the divinity .... fall off" (ChāUp. I.10.8 ff). In this way he pointed out the danger of singing without knowledge. Then he himself explained the various divinities connected with the various parts of a sāman (I.11.5 ff).

Music is sometimes supposed to be a means of for obtaining knowledge. Thus ṚV II.2.10, a poet-singer requests Agni, "May we be able, O Agni, to mark out our people (from others) by means of this powerful hymn (*brahman-*)" (ṚV II.2.10). When the gods were going to the heaven, they became afraid of ignorance. Then they discovered the Sujñāna- (literally "good knowledge") sāman and sang with it. Then they obtained knowledge (JB III.31; cp. TMB V.7.11).

Music is considered to be a step in progressing, towards the highest spiritual knowledge,[2] immortality etc. Those "who know the sāman by means of sāman" they know the unborn (*aja*) (AV X.8.41; the hymn AV X.8 deals with the mysticism of the "highest brahman"). According to the ṚV I.164.23, "They alone reach to the immortality who know the Gāyatra-foot is based on the Gāyatra-sāman; Triṣṭubha-foot is created out of the Traiṣṭubha-sāman and Jagatī is placed on Jagat-sāman". ŚaṅĀ II.1 the hiṁkāra as well as Sūdadohas is said to be identical with immortality. The singing of sāmans as well as of music in general are said to be useful for reaching to the highest brahman and obtaining salvation according to Yājñavalkyasmṛti III.112 ff: "If one chants verses from the Sāmaveda in conformity to the rules and attentively, one would attain by means of this practice, the high brahman. Aparāntaka, Ullopya, Madraka, Prakarī, Auveṇaka, Sarobindu, Uttara, Ṛggāthā, Paṇikā, Dakṣavihitā, Brahmagītikā, these songs are called *mokṣas* (salvations) because their repetition is a means of salvation. "He who is well-versed in the principles of playing on a lyre, who thoroughly understands the Śrutis and Jātis in music, or is expert in tālas, he will easily obtain the road of salvation".

REFERENCES

1. In China, Se ma-ts' ien has attached importance to the knowledge of notes: Combarieu, *La Musique et la magie*, p. 201.
2. Rf. Abert *Musikanschauung*, p. 72.

CHAPTER X
Conclusion

We started our investigation with a problem regarding the double social position of the music and musicians as reflected in the Vedic and allied literature. Thus they sometimes enjoy a very high position and receive importance. Sometimes they are looked down and avoided. Music is sometimes considered to be helpful and other times harmful to social order. Sometimes it is considered to be auspicious and promoting harmony, and it is also inauspicious, promoting quarrels. Therefore it is sometimes prescribed and sometimes proscribed. Thus music is treated in two ways because it is considered to be double-natured. This consideration of its being double-natured is based on another consideration that it is a power-substance. Now any power is by itself indifferent like electricity. It can be helpful or harmful according to the circumstances and the way in which it is used. The Vedic texts many times maintain the power-fulness of music. By means of music some supernatural activities also are believed to be done. One can control fire or water by means of music. But the results of music are not believed always to be produced merely magically; but rather magicoreligiously. For although sometimes music is held to be superior to the gods sometimes the gods are held to be superior to music. Thus music is supposed to have an attractive power. It carries, drags the gods unto the singers. The music strengthens the gods, enables them to do some heroic activities. Whenever gods are in need, they discover some melodies, sing them and get their desired objects and cross over the difficulties with the help of music. But music is also supposed to be a means of propitiating or pleasing the gods. So one makes gods favourable with the help of music. Then being pleased the gods fulfill the desires of men. Thus music works magicoreligiously.

Music is an important and essential constituent part of the Vedic sacrifice. It is meritfully used in the course of sacrifice.

It is necessary that the music is used correctly and in the prescribed manner only. Otherwise it is harmful. If used properly it helps the sacrifice in many ways. Thus it makes it continuous, well-established, well-supported, complete, and defectless. Music is, however, double-natured. So sometimes an antipatly of music towards the sacrifice is observed.

In the Vedic literature words are supposed to be powerful. By using a word or words mentioning the desired thing directly or indirectly one can obtain it. The utterances like vaṣaṭ, (*him / hum)* are also supposed to be power-substances. They are often used in the sacrificial performance. They can be magicoreligiously useful to obtain food, progeny, etc. They can be however sometimes dangerous also. The musical instruments also are power-substances and are useful in many ways. Vedic metres are an essential part of the Vedic music. They also have many magicoreligious significances and are useful in obtaining numerous results. They are helpful to the sacrificial performance, they "carry" sacrifice to the gods and propitiate them. But they are also supposed to be double-natured and sometimes there is non-cooperation between them and the sacrifice. The Gandharvas and Apsarases are the divine musicians who are also double-natured. They sometimes render some help to sacrifice and other times are antagonistic to it. They are specifically mentioned to be very sensual. The Gandharvas haunt women. They disturb pregnant women. They preside over both the fertility and sterility.

Music is supposed to give many results magicoreligiously. So it can be used for obtaining rain, food, diseaselessness, long life, progeny, even all the objects of desire. Thus it has some constructive significances. But it can be destructive also. Thus music and death are closely connected with each other. Music is amply prescribed to be used in the black-magic sorcery rites in order to destroy one's enemy or get his possessions etc. It is also used at the time of war for the sake of getting victory over enemies and destroying them. The Vedic texts ascribe an apotropic power to music. It can accordingly remove or kill the evil beings. Music is closely connected with light. It is brilliant by itself and helps to destroy darkness at the time of eclipses etc. by chasing away the evil spirits which create darkness. The close association of music and light seems to be based on the apotropic nature common to both.

In order to express the way in which the music can work, it is often described metaphorically. Thus it is many times described as a ship, chariot, draught-animal, bird etc. These descriptions show how music leads the performer to the desired result. Sometimes it is described to be food of the gods. Sometimes the gods are said to be like bulls and the music like a cow. They are elsewhere said to be like husbands and the musical elements then become their wives. Thus the way in which music works is magicoreligious. Sometimes it gives the desired result by itself; sometimes it pleases the gods to favour to grant the desired results. The ways in which music is performed, are also magico-religiously significant. There are some external mannerisms at the time of singing. Thus one sings sometimes having covered oneself, other times with full cheeks, sometimes having shut the eyes, sometimes having kept water nearby. All these mannerisms are significant. Similarly one sings in a nazalised way, loudly, silently, with repetitions, interminglingly, swiftly, without exhaling, expressing the deity (connected with the song) or not, or even mentally. These ways of singing have some positive or negative significances like obtainment of progeny, or avoiding evil etc.

Music becomes useful or harmful according to the way in which it is performed. So for the sake of obtaining good results one must perform it in the correct, prescribed way. Thus there are numerous directives of how music should be performed and if those directives are conformed to, music can be advantageous. Thus gods sometimes like new songs and sometimes old songs. So one must sing both kinds of songs accordingly. The song must come out of the bottom of one's heart, must be pure, pleasant etc. While singing one should avoid monotony. One should bring in one's singing continuity, equilibrium, firmness, freshness, sapfulness, correctness, congruence, appropriateness, proportion, etc. Music has a cosmic nature. The whole world is music. In the musical performance knowledge of what one sings is important. One can get the result of singing a Sāman by merely knowing it also. Music can itself help to obtain knowledge, even the highest spiritual knowledge and one can thereby get salvation.

Bibliography

Abert, H. *Die Musikanschauung des Mittelalters und ihre grundlagen*, Halle, 1905.

Abert, H. *Die Lehre von Ethos in der Griechischen Musik*, Wiesbaden, 1968 (reprint).

Abhyankar, V. (ed.) *Sarvadarśanasaṁgraha*, Poona, 1951.

Aiyangar, K.V.R. *Bṛhaspatismṛti*, Baroda, 1941.

Aufrecht, Th. "Der libende besucht die beliebte", *IS*, IV, 1858, p. 337 ff.

Bächold-Stäubli, H. *Handwörterbuch des deutschen Aberglaubens*, Berlin-Leipzig, 1927 ff.

Bapat, P.V. "Vedic sources of some Buddhist beliefs", *Journal of the Asian Research Society*, XIV, 1960.

Behn, E. *Musikleben in Altertum und Frühen Mitteralter*, Stuttgart, 1954.

Belaiev, V. "The Folk-Music of Georgia", *The Musical Quarterly*, XIX, 1933.

Belvianes, M. *Sociologie de la musique*, Paris, 1951.

Bergaigne A. *La religion védique d'après les hymnes du rigveda*, Paris, 1878 ff.

Bloomfield, M. "Contributions to the interpretation of the Veda", *JAOS*, XVI, 1896, p. 1 ff.

Bloomfield, M. *The Atharvaveda and Gopatha-brāhmaṇa*, Strassburg, 1899.

Bloomfield, M. "The God Indra and the Sāmaveda", *WZKM*, 17, 1903, p. 156 ff.

Caland, W. *Das Jaiminīya-brāhmaṇa in Auswahl*, Amsterdam, 1919.

Caland, W. *Pañcaviṁśa-brāhmaṇa*, Calcutta, 1931.

Caland, W. *Die altindischen Todten-und Bestattungsbräuche*, Wiesbaden, 1967 (reprint).

Caland, W. *Altindische Zauberei, Darstellung der altindischen Wunschopfer*, Wiesbaden, 1968 (reprint).

Caland, W. Henry V. *L'Agniṣṭoma*, Paris, 1906-7.

Combarieu, J. *La musique et la magie*, Paris, 1909.

Crook W. *The Popular Religion and Folkore of Northern India,* Delhi, 1968 (reprint).
Cuisinier, J. *La danse sacrée,* 1951.
Eggeling, J. *SBE = Sacred Books of the East* (*The Śatapatha-brāhmaṇa*), Delhi, 1966 (reprint).
Frazer, G.J. *The Golden Bough,* London, 1963 (reprint).
Geldner, K.F. *Der Rigveda in Auswahl,* Stuttgart, 1907-9.
Geldner, K.F. "Zur Erklärung des Rigveda", *ZDMG,* 71, 1917, p. 315 ff.
Geldner, K.F. *Der Rigveda,* Cambridge (Mass), 1951.
Ghosh, B.K. *Collection of the lost Brāhmaṇas,* Calcutta, 1947.
Gonda, J. "Ursprung und Wesen des indischen dramas", *AO,* 19 (1943), p. 346 ff.
Gonda, J. "The meaning of the word *alaṅkāra*", *New Indian Antiquary, (Festschrift Thomas)*, 1939, p. 97 ff.
Gonda, J. "The socalled secular, humorous and satyrial hymns of the Ṛgveda", *Orientalia Neerlandica,* 1948, p. 312 ff.
Gonda, J. *Notes on Brahman,* Utrecht, 1950.
Gonda, J. *The Ṛgvidhāna,* Utrecht, 1951.
Gonda, J. *Ancient Indian* Ojas, ...; Utrecht, 1952.
Gonda, J. "Pratiṣṭhā" *Saṁjñāvyākavaṇa (Studia Indologica Internationalia)* 1954, p. 1 ff.
Gonda, J. *Aspects of early Viṣṇuism,* Utrecht, 1954.
Gonda, J. *Four studies in the language of the veda's,* Gravenhag, 1959.
Gonda, J. *Stylistic repetition in the Veda,* Amsterdam, 1959.
Gonda, J. *Die Religionen Indiens,* I, Stuttgart, 1960.
Gonda, J. *Vision of the vedic poets,* The Hague, 1963.
Gonda, J. "Indian *Mantra*", *Oriens,* 16, 1963, p. 124 ff.
Gonda, J. "*Adhvan* and *Adhvaryu*", *VIJ,* III, 1965, p. 163 ff.
Gonda, J. *Ancient Indian kingship from the religious point of view,* Leiden, 1966.
Gonda, J. *Loka, world and heaven in the veda,* Amsterdam, 1966.
Gonda, J. *Eye and Gaze in the veda,* Amsterdam, 1969.
Gonda, J. "*Āyatana*", *ALB,* 33, 1969, p. 1 ff.
Grassmann, H. *Wörterbuch zum Rigveda,* Wiesbaden, 1964.

Gunkel, H. Zsarnack L. (ed.) *Die Religion in Geschichte und Gegenwart,* Tubingen, 1930.

Guthrie, W.K.L. *Orpheus and Greek Religion,* London, 1952.

Hastings, J. *ERE = Encyclopaedia of Religion and Ethics,* New York, 1965 (reprint).

Hauer, J.W. *Die Anfänge der Yogapraxis im alten indien,* Stuttgart, 1922.

Hauer, J.W. *Der Vrātya,* Stuttgart, 1927.

Hauer, J.W. *Der Yoga,* Stuttgart, 1958.

Hauschild, R. "Das Selbstlob (*ātmastuti*) des somaberauchten Gottes Agni", *Asiatica (Festschrift Weller),* Leipzig, 1954, p. 247 ff.

Hillebrandt, A. "Die Sonnwendfeste", *Festschrift K. Hofman* Erlangen, 1889.

Hillebrandt, A. *Ritualitteratur Vedische Opfer und Zauber,* Strassburg, 1897.

Hillebrandt, A. *Vedische Mythologie,* Hildesheim, 1956 (reprint).

Holztmann, H. "Die Apsarases nach dem Mahābhārata", *Zauber* 33, 1879, p. 631 ff.

Hubert, H. Mauss, M. "Esquisses d'une théorie generale de la magie", *L'Année Sociologique,* VII. 1902 f, p. 1 ff.

James, E.O. *The nature and function of priesthood,* London, 1955.

Keith, A.B. *RBT = Rigveda-Brāhmanas translated,* Cambridge (Mass.) 1920.

Keith, A.B. *RPV = The Religion and Philosophy of the Veda and Upanishads,* Cambridge (Mass.), 1925.

Konnow, S. *Das Sāmavidhāna-brāhmaṇa,* Halle, 1893.

Kuhn, A. "Gandharven and Kentauern", *ZVS,* I. 1852, p. 513 ff.

Lavignac, A. *EnM = Encyclopedie de la musique,* I. Paris, 1913.

Van der Leeuw, G. "Die do-des Formel in der Opfertheorie", *Archiv Fur Religionswissenschaft,* XX, 3/4, 1920, p. 241 ff.

Legge, J. *The Sacred Books of Confucianism,* Delhi, 1966 (reprint).

Lévi, S. *Le Theatre indien,* Paris, 1890.

Levi, S. *La doctrine du sacrifice dans les Brāhmaṇas,* Paris, 1898.

Ludwig, A. *Der Rigveda*, Prag, 1876 ff.

Macdonell, A. *Vedic Mythology*, Delhi, 1963 (reprint).

Malalasekera, G.P. *Dictionary of Pali proper names*, London, 1960 (reprint).

Mauss, M. "Anna-Virāj", *Melanges d'indianisme .... (Festschrift S. Levi)*, Paris, 1911; p. 333 ff.

Mayrhofer, M. *Kurzgefasstes etymologisches Wörterbuch des Alntindischen*, Heidelberg, 1956 ff.

Meyer, J.J. *Trilogie altindischer Mächte und Feste der Vegetation*, Zürich-Leipzig, 1937.

Mowinkel, S. *Religion und Kultus*, Göttingen, 1953.

Oertel, H. "Contributions from the Jaiminīya-Brāhmaṇa to the history of the Brāhmaṇa-literature", *JAOS*, XVIII, 1895, p. 15 ff; XXVI, 1905, 176 ff.

Oertel, H. "The Jaiminiya-upaniṣad-brāhmaṇa", *JAOS*, XVI, 1896, p. 79 ff.

Oldenberg, H. "Das altindsche Ākhyāna mit besonderer Rucksicht auf der Supavṇākhyānā", *ZDMG*, 37, 1883, p. 54 ff.

Oldenberg, H. *Die Religion des Veda*, Berlin, 1894.

Oldenberg, H. *Die Weltanschauung der Brāhmaṇa-texte*, Göttinge, 1919.

Oldenberg, H. *Vedic Hymns* II. *SBE*, XLVI, Delhi, 1966. (reprint).

Osterley, W.O.F. *Sacrifices in ancient Israel*, New York, 1937.

Patrids, C.A. *Milton and the Christian tradition*, Oxford, 1966.

Pischel, R. and Geldner, K.F. *Vedische Studien*, Stuttgart, 1889, 1892.

Plato, *The dialogues of Plato*, Trans. B. Jowett, New York, 1937.

Race, J. *Luther:Student, monk, reformer*, London, 1884.

Rahurkar, V.G. "Was soma a spirituous liquor?", *OT*, II, 1956, p. 131 ff.

Rahurkar, V.G. "Apropos the Ṛgveda V. 40", *JGRI*, XXV, 1969, p. 511 ff.

Renou, L. "Sur certains emplois d'a(n) priv. en sanskrit, et notamment dans le Ṛgveda", *BSOAS*, X, 1940-42, p. 1 ff

Renou, L. "Two vedic words - *Upāṁśu* and *Tūṣṇīm*", *PAIOC*, 15, Bombay, 1951, p. 265 f.

Renou, L. "Etudes védiques", *JA*, 240, 1952, p. 405 ff.

Renou, L. *Vocabulaire du rituel védique*, Paris, 1954.

Renou, L. "Vedique *Nirṛti*", *S.K. Chatterji Jubilee Vol.* Madras, 1955, p. 11 ff.

Renou, L. *EVP* = *Etudes védiques et pāṇineenes*, Paris, 1955.

Renou, L, Silburn, L. "*Nirukta* and *anirukta* in vedic", *Sarūpabhāratī*, Hoshiarpur, 1954, p. 68 ff.

Rhode, E. *Pscyche*, London, 1925.

Rose, H.S. *A handbook of greek mythology*, London, 1965 (reprint).

Saalschutz, J.L. *Musik bei der Hebreaern*, Wiesbaden, 1970 (reprint).

Sachs, C. *Die Masikinstrumente indiens und idonesiens*, Berlin, 1915.

Schmidt, W.P. "Die kuh auf der Weide", *IF*, 64, 1959, p. 1 ff.

Schröder, L. *Mysterium und Mimus im Rigveda*, Leipzig, 1908.

Silburn, L. *Instant et cause*, Paris, 1955.

Singer, I (ed.) *Jewish Encyclopaedia.*

Skeat, W.W. *Malay Magic*, London, 1900.

Tagor, S.M. (ed.) *Hindu music*, Varanasi, 1965 (reprint).

Thieme, P. *Kleine Schriften*, Wiesbaden, 1971.

Thite, G.U. "A propos of the Vājapeya", *JUPHS*, 29, 1968, p. 31 ff.

Thite, G.U. "Cāturmāsya-sacrifices researched", *JUPHS*, 31, 1969, p. 57 ff.

Thite, G.U. "Utsannayajña", *JOIB*, XVIII, 3, 1969, p. 179 ff.

Thite, G.U. "Henoritualism of the Brāhmaṇa-texts", *JUPHS* 33, 1970, p. 23 ff.

Thite, G.U. "Pankta yajña", *Ṛṣikalpanyāsya (Rejeshvarshastri Dravid Felicitation Vol.)*, Prayag, 1971.

Thite, G.U. "Vedic *anatidbhutā*, Pali *anacchariya*", *JUPHS*, 35, 1971, p. 31 ff.

Thite, G.U. *Sacrifice in the Brāhmana-texts*, Poona, 1975.

Thite, G.U. "Yajñaphala aṇi deva", *Ānandavana*, I.2 (April, 1993), p. 57 ff.

Wackernagel, J. Debrunner, A. *Altindische Grammatik*, Göttingen, 1957 ff.
Weber Max, *The Sociology of Religion* (trans. Talcott Parsons), London, 1965.
Weber, A. "Über die Literatur des Sāmaveda", *IS*, I, 1850, p. 25 ff
Weber, A. "Uber die Metrik der Inder", *IS*, VIII,1863, p. 1 ff.
Weber, A. "Zweiter buch der Atharvaveda-Saṁhitā", *IS*, XIII, 1873, p. 129 ff.
Webster, H. *Magic: a sociological study*, Stanford (California), 1948.
Wellesz, E. *AOM = Ancient and Oriental Music*, London, 1960.
Winternitz, M. *Geschichte der Indischen Literatur*, Stuttgart, 1968 (reprint).
Whitney, W. *Atharvavedasaṁhitā*, Delhi(1962) (reprint).
Wogihara, U. Stccherbatsky, Th. (ed.) *Abhidharma Kośavyākhyā*, Leningrad, 1931.

Index